Andrea Bolter has always been fascinated by matters of the heart. In fact she's the one her girlfriends turn to for advice with their love-lives. A city mouse, she lives in Los Angeles with her husband and daughter. She loves travel, rock 'n' roll, sitting in cafés and watching romantic comedies she's already seen a hundred times. Say hi at andreabolter.com.

Victoria Pade is a *USA TODAY* bestselling author of numerous romance novels. She has two beautiful and talented daughters—Cori and Erin—and is a native of Colorado, where she lives and writes. A devoted chocolate lover, she's in search of the perfect chocolate-chip-cookie recipe.

For information about her latest and upcoming releases, visit Victoria Pade on Facebook—she would love to hear from you.

Also by Andrea Bolter

Her New York Billionaire
Her Las Vegas Wedding

Also by Victoria Pade

The Marine Makes His Match
AWOL Bride
A Camden's Baby Secret
Abby, Get Your Groom
A Sweetheart for the Single Dad
Her Baby and Her Beau
To Catch a Camden
A Camden Family Wedding
It's a Boy

THE ITALIAN'S RUNAWAY PRINCESS

ANDREA BOLTER

SPECIAL FORCES FATHER

VICTORIA PADE

MILLS & BOON

First Published in Great Britain 2018
by Mills & Boon, an imprint of HarperCollinsPublishers,
1 London Bridge Street, London, SE1 9GF

The Italian's Runaway Princess © 2018 Andrea Bolter
Special Forces Father © 2018 Victoria Pade

ISBN: 978-0-263-26527-9

0918

MIX
Paper from
responsible sources
FSC™ C007454

This book is produced from independently certified FSC™
paper to ensure responsible forest management.

For more information visit: www.harpercollins.co.uk/green

Printed and bound in Spain
by CPI, Barcelona

THE ITALIAN'S RUNAWAY PRINCESS

ANDREA BOLTER

For Ellen

CHAPTER ONE

HER ROYAL HIGHNESS Princess Luciana de la Isla de Izerote finally inhaled the warm air of Florence, Italy. The secret journey from her home, an island near the coast of Spain, had been difficult. At last she was under the Tuscan sun, the yellow glow much different from the seascape she was used to. But the liberation she expected to feel as she took her first breath of freedom was hardly as she'd hoped.

As a matter of fact, Luciana was starting to feel afraid being alone. She was short of breath from walking too fast away from the encounter at the jewelry store, where she had been unsuccessful in converting a palace ruby into a typical tourist's spending money. Worse still, three teenage boys seemed to be following her. Swiveling her head enough to take a look at them behind her, she saw they were scruffy and wore shabby T-shirts and track pants. These unexpected companions made her entire escape plan seem not only reckless, but like it was about to become dangerous.

"*Bambolina*, let us see your necklace," one of the boys called out as they closed the distance between themselves and the princess. "We'll buy your jewel."

Luciana hastened her pace. She'd arrived in Florence

to have an adventure before she lived the rest of her life in royal duty. The escapade didn't include being chased by thugs who might be trying to steal the jewelry she'd brought with her to sell as a way to finance her trip, given that she had no actual money of her own. The princess quickened to almost a run as her hand clutched the ruby pendant that hung from a heavy chain. Her sense of direction turned all around, she didn't even know where she was headed.

The boys behind her may or may not have seen that she had other pieces of jewelry in the purse that hung from a long leather strap on one of her shoulders, crossing her body and slapping against her at the opposite hip as she rushed away from them. She might have been able to run faster had she not also been toting a wheeled suitcase that contained her belongings for her three weeks as a Florentine tourist. After which time, she'd return to Izerote. And to her obligations, including her arranged marriage to King Agustin de la Isla de Menocita, the widower thirty years her senior from a neighboring island.

Princess Luciana had thought about this getaway for a long time, plotting exactly how she'd make her way to Florence and how she'd finance the travels. What she hadn't counted on was how problematic it would be to sell jewelry. Having had no experience, she didn't know that the shops would require paperwork and authentication.

After she'd made it from the island to her first stop in Barcelona, she'd needed the first installment of cash for the train tickets to Florence and to buy some food. One jeweler had directed her to another of less repute, and he to another still, until she'd sold an amethyst cocktail ring for far less than its worth.

She knew little about city streets, having spent most

of her life behind the palace walls of Izerote. Leaving only to attend official engagements and social functions accompanied by palace security, she was always safely sequestered in private cars, boats and planes. That was exactly why she'd come to Florence, the place she'd fallen in love with through art, books and movies. To experience being a simple tourist, to wander here and there without an itinerary or bodyguards, was to be a once-in-a-lifetime dream.

Having trouble selling the jewelry and now being followed just after she'd arrived was turning it into a nightmare.

"Bella." One of the boys hurried even closer to her, his use of the endearment for *beautiful* sounding like a snake's hiss that terrified her.

"Signorina. *Carina. Tesoro...*" Another bounced around to the other side of her, trying every name he could think of to get her to stop and address him directly.

With a yank on her suitcase, she began to run faster, heart racing. She thought about calling out for help to the first person she saw, but she didn't want to attract attention to herself. Her tiny island country was not well-known to most the world, but nonetheless, if questioned, she was a princess and it would appear odd that she was alone on the streets of central Florence. No one knew she was here, and she wanted to keep it that way.

Turning a corner, the boys chased after her and one pulled on the strap of her purse.

"Stop. Leave me alone," Luciana cried out and broke free.

A part of her fully expected her father King Mario's security team to have outwitted her already, to know exactly where she was and to direct unseen bodyguards to arrive at any moment to whisk her back to Izerote without letting her have the grand escapade she'd planned. With these boys harassing her, she almost wished they would.

Thinking quickly, she worked in front of her stomach to block the boys' view as she removed the rest of the jewels from her purse and held them tightly in her free hand. If they managed to steal her purse, at least they would find it empty.

"You give us that purse, right now," one of the boys jeered in a threatening tone.

"Get away from me," Luciana shouted. She looked to see if anyone else was behind her, her suitcase wobbling. As she turned back around, she tripped over something on the ground and crashed right into…

The broad shoulders and chest of a man. Specifically, her face slammed directly into the center of the man's muscular chest. As she approximated where her nose hit into him, she estimated just how tall a man he was. Six foot three, at least. Her head involuntarily turned a bit sideways so that her cheek could replace her nose as she pressed against him. Because that exact spot was solid, warm, smelled like clean laundry, and she quite liked it. Although she knew she needed to bend her neck back in order to see the face of the man she'd crushed into, something in her resisted the idea and she simply wanted to nuzzle her face into his rock-hard chest for the foreseeable future.

"Hello," a voice from somewhere inside the man's body crawled into her. "Do you need help?" His very deep timbre completely enveloped her in muscles and sounds. He could be yet another foe, but it didn't feel that way.

One thing she knew for sure was that it was not the

chest of King Agustin de la Isla de Menocita, the man she was to marry in three weeks. Not only was King Agustin much smaller in stature than the man she pressed into, her fiancé spoke in a voice high and clipped. Nothing like the smooth-as-cappuccino voice of the man her cheek was touching.

"These boys are trying to steal my purse." Princess Luciana spoke into the good-smelling man's chest, knowing that he'd be able to hear her even though her mouth was far lower than his ear. She clutched her jewels so tightly that her fingernails cut into her palms.

His response was to do what every fiber in her being had actually hoped he would since she bumped into him. He placed both of his long arms around her and pulled her into a tight hold, encircling her in the most complete way. *"Mia amata—"* he used the words of a lover "—you're so late. I was running to the train station to find you."

Realizing that he was pretending to be with her as a way to shake off these would-be criminals, Luciana knew enough to play along. "I stopped at the jewelry store."

"Can I do something for you gentlemen?" The pretend lover turned his attention to the thugs. The boys seemed to be taking stock of the situation now that the good-smelling man had arrived on the scene. Without answering, they lingered awhile longer. "I repeat, can I do something for you?" the man with the gigantic strong arms around the princess shouted in a voice menacing enough to scare them.

Luciana craned her neck so that she could look up to see the man's face. As if the mere feel of his chest and tone of his voice wasn't enough, she now stared at one of the most handsome men she had ever seen.

Pale skin served to draw extra attention to the sparkling light blue eyes. He had high cheekbones, a full red mouth and a head full of beautiful golden curls, like a subject in a painting from the Renaissance, an era when Florence was abuzz with intellectual, scientific and creative discovery. A time in history that was one of the reasons Luciana had wanted to explore this important city.

"Oh, no, signore," said one of the boys behind her.

"We were taking a walk on this lovely day," another singsonged.

Only after they scattered away did the man with the lavish blond curls let go of Luciana. They looked directly into each other's eyes for the first time. She thought she might have been struck by a bolt of lightning, but the sunny skies rendered that unlikely.

The blue-eyed man then began to disentangle the long purse strap that had become twisted around Luciana's arm after the boys tried to pull it away from her. The strap was so mangled it became a puzzle to unravel it, and he gave his full attention to the task. Finally, he gingerly placed the strap back on her shoulder and the purse fell naturally across her opposite hip as intended.

The care this total stranger was extending to her was surprising. And also a first for Princess Luciana. Commoners were not permitted to touch her, except on occasions of handshakes during official processionals through the streets or when meeting military heroes, and under close supervision. But certainly nothing involving a gorgeous man with enormous hands putting his arms around her or arranging a purse onto her body.

Only then did Luciana remember what she held in her still tightly closed fist. "Oh, my gosh, I'd forgotten that I'd been holding my jewels all of this time. I thought surely those boys were going to tear my purse off me, so I grabbed the contents."

"Why are you carrying such valuables in a flimsy purse on a city street?"

"It's a long story."

The princess opened her purse and placed her jewels in a zipped pocket inside. As the man with the gigantic hands said, it was absurd that she'd let the few palace jewels, which she had chosen as sacrificial lambs to buy her this voyage of freedom, be tossed around in a thin pouch of leather not properly protected. That was only one of the possibly crazy decisions she had made.

There was no turning back now.

"Thank you." She bowed her head to the Renaissance painting of a man on the street. "You saved me from danger and harm."

"That's me. A regular Prince Charming."

Her Royal Highness Princess Luciana de la Isla de Izerote had never wished harder that words were true.

"May I show you to your destination?" asked the handsome savior after the thugs were long gone from view.

"All right," Luciana answered although she didn't know what her destination was. Which, as she was zooming to Italy through Spain and France on high-speed trains, felt like a marvelous relief. To be able to go wherever she wanted, whenever she wanted. Not to be bound by a schedule or accompanied by an entourage. Now, the unfamiliarity of all that liberty had her frightened.

"By the way, I'm Gio. Giovanni Grassi. And you are…?" He took hold of Luciana's suitcase handle and gave it a tug.

"Luci…" She left it at that, the nickname her mother

used to call her when she was a small child. A name she hadn't heard in years. It was fitting that she thought of her mother now, who had died without ever fulfilling her own quest for the bit of autonomy that Luciana hoped to have.

"It's a pleasure to meet you, Luci."

She wasn't sure that she should be letting this man she didn't know pull her suitcase. What if he ran away with it? Or what if he was luring her into some kind of trap so that he could steal her jewels for himself?

Princess Luciana sensed that he meant well. After all, no one had forced him to come to her aid as he did. And she couldn't just continue standing on the street now that those threatening boys had been chased off. She'd lost all sense of direction, not that she knew where she was going in the first place. Had she been able to sell the ruby, she would have returned to the train station to look for a tourist bureau that could help her find accommodations. That could still be her plan. But now she wasn't comfortable walking alone with the jewels.

So they began forward, Gio's grip on her suitcase keeping its wheels cooperating under his control. Princess Luciana caught a reflection of herself in the glass of a shop window. In the commotion of her arrival, her failure at the jewelry store near the train station and the threat from those boys, she'd completely forgotten that she wore a wig in disguise. While Izerote was not a famous island and her monarchy had not made her a recognizable face throughout the world, she knew there was a good chance that her father would send someone looking for her. Even though she had left him a note promising to return in three weeks to marry King Agustin as planned. If the cloak she donned could help throw any operatives of King Mario's off her track, it was well worthwhile. Plus, she liked the idea of having a new appearance.

Gone were the long girlish locks of hair that spent many evenings as a showplace for the family tiaras. Now the thick brown strands that fell halfway down her back were bound and tucked under a blond wig she'd bought in Barcelona. The wig was cut into a lob, a term the princess knew from idly flipping through fashion magazines was the hip description for a long bob.

The surprisingly realistic-looking hairstyle fell in sleek sheets to the tops of her shoulders where it curled under just a bit. Every move she made caused the lob to give a slight swish that Luciana found chic. The hair made her feel like a woman on the go. Which was quite unlike the fussy preplanned existence she had always known. Although her *let's see what happens* attitude, so out of character, had almost led her into hazard.

"Where to, signorina?"

The scare of those boys had been an immediate awakening to the perils she needed to look out for, and she didn't know what she should tell Gio Grassi. Yes, his beautiful crystal-blue eyes seemed trustworthy, but outward appearances told her nothing.

Nonetheless, she had to start somewhere.

"I don't know, Gio. I find myself arriving in Florence with less money than I had planned. Would you know of a reasonably priced hotel?"

"No, actually, I'm sorry I don't. I grew up here in Florence but I've spent many years traveling for business. I no longer know the city."

Disappointment rung through her. Barcelona had been quite an eye-opener once she discovered that the jeweler to whom she had intended to sell the first of her lot was unwilling to buy what Luciana referred to as her *estate pieces* without proof of ownership and certifications. She'd made up a story about the jewels belonging to her recently deceased grandmother.

At her begging, that jeweler put her in touch with another jeweler who refused her and sent her to yet another, this one located in a downtrodden part of town. He gave her far less than she had estimated for the first piece. She knew now that this trip would have to be on more of a budget than she'd originally envisioned.

That didn't matter. At least she was here.

"I'll need to sell more of my jewels."

"More of them? Does that mean you have already sold some?"

Yes, but she didn't need to tell that to Gio.

"I had tried at a shop near the train station. That's where those boys began following me."

"Florence is a big city with people both opulent and poor, honest and not. You should watch out at every turn."

Luciana was already learning that the hard way. But as they turned a corner into a piazza, a public square, her troubles receded and the widest of smiles swept across her face. Here it was. The Florence she'd seen in movies and travel websites, and read about in books. Firenze, the central city of Tuscany, with its centuries of trade and finance, art and medicine, religion and politics.

People moved across the piazza in every different direction. Fashionable girls giggled as they snapped selfies of themselves. A tour group of older travelers dutifully stopped so that their guide could point out landmarks. Four men stood in front of a shop arguing, their loud voices and hand gestures marking them as uniquely Italian. A flock of children chased pigeons, their overjoyed faces bursting with surprise every time one of the birds made an unexpected escape. Two lovers sat close on a bench while they shared a fresh orange, the woman holding the peel in her hand.

Every which way, people wove in between each other to get to where they were going. It was everything the princess had imagined it would be, alive and magnificent under the autumn of the Tuscan sky. She placed her hand over her mouth as she took it all in.

This was what Luciana came to see. To be a part of this city that had always held her fascination, if only for a stolen moment of her lifetime. She drew in a slow breath. The air wasn't as thick and pure as it was in pristine Izerote. Florence had a particular fragrance, one she suspected it had for centuries.

It smelled like free will.

Which she had never inhaled before.

As if the panorama of all these people and their doings and their businesses and their architecture and their dogs wasn't enough, Luciana stood witnessing it in the company of a chivalrous, and she had to acknowledge gorgeous, Italian man.

For the first time she took notice of what Giovanni Grassi was wearing. A tweed blazer with a pink button-down shirt and tan tie, jeans with a brown belt and brown oxford shoes. All of impeccable quality. He looked perhaps like a young professor, the type schoolgirls would giggle around but loved to gape at as he explained the important trigonometry equation on a chalkboard behind him. Reluctant hottie. That was the moniker the celebrity websites used for his type.

Hottie, for sure. Reluctant, she didn't know yet.

"Ah yes, Firenze," Gio chimed in. "There's nowhere

like it in the world. Some things change, others remain the same as they have for centuries."

Nothing ever changed in Izerote, Luciana reflected. It lagged far behind the rest of the world in technology and culture and commerce. Her father, King Mario, and his father before him were not forward-thinking rulers like some royal families were. The price they'd paid for the lack of progress was steep, as many residents or their adult children were leaving the island.

However, Princess Luciana was not in Florence to solve the issues of her island, although she didn't doubt that in this great city of thought and industry many dilemmas of the world had been debated.

"Here's my situation, Gio," Luciana started, not knowing what to do about her predicament. One way or another, this trip would come to an end. Either she'd have her three weeks here before she returned to Izerote to marry King Agustin and produce his heirs. Or her father would send someone to hunt after her and her visit would be cut short. Either way, now was all there was, so she had better make every second count. "I have no money. That's why I need to sell some of my jewels, in order to pay for a hotel room."

"Sell your jewels. That sounds so positively archaic. You may have noticed this is *modern day* where people pay for goods and services with credit cards or through apps on their phone," he said with a cute chuckle that sent a tingle down her spine. What a strange reaction she was having to this total stranger.

She couldn't explain to him that while she did carry credit cards, she couldn't use them because they were traceable. That's why she needed to obtain cash for the trip. "I know, it does sound rather medieval."

"Have you traveled forward in time? What era are you from?"

"You have no idea how right you are."

"Are you running from something?"

"You could say that."

"A mystery woman."

"You could say that, too."

"All right, Signorina Luci, if that's really your name. For how long do you need a hotel room?"

"Three weeks," she answered with ease. Because it was exactly three weeks and one day until she was to marry. Three weeks. That's how long she hoped to stay in Florence. If she had her druthers, she'd stay until the last possible minute and arrive back in Izerote just in time to be pinned into her wedding gown. The gown that had already been chosen for her, a chaste lacy puffball with a high neck and long sleeves that was as tight and confining as her impending marriage. Nothing like what she'd wear if the choice was up to her. If, for example, she was to be getting married of her own volition to a tall attractive man with sparkling blue eyes and golden curly hair.

"Three weeks," he repeated. "And how much do you expect to garner from the sale of those jewels?"

Nowhere near what she thought she might, Luciana mused. So, realistically, considering the price she'd fetched in Barcelona, she quoted Gio a figure. Still unsure if she should be confiding her financial woes to him.

"Twenty-one nights…"

"Twenty-one," she confirmed knowing that she wouldn't need a hotel room in Florence on the twenty-second, after her wedding. She winced at the thought of her wedding night and what would be expected of her from King Agustin, a widower who presumably had more experience in the matrimonial bed than she did. Hopefully he'd be patient and compassionate toward her when the time came.

"Then here is how much you'd have to spend each day." Gio performed a mental calculation and gave her a number that was far less than the rate of the hotels she had been looking at online.

"Do you think I could get a hotel room for that price? It doesn't need to be fancy, only clean."

"Luci, for that money I don't think you could find anything suitable, clean or safe."

He glanced at his watch.

It wasn't right to detain this man any longer, despite the fear that was returning in her.

"I'll figure something out. Thank you again for your assistance."

"You're quite welcome. Enjoy Florence," Gio said and then turned to walk away.

Prompted by his departure, a couple of tears smarted Luciana's eyes as she blinked them back. Which was ridiculous. She'd come to experience Florence alone. Gio had simply lent a hand to a damsel in distress. He was a stranger, now on his merry way as was appropriate.

After a few steps, he stopped and pivoted back.

"What are you planning to do?"

"I don't know. If you could point me in the direction of the train station, I'll go back there."

"I can try to find you a hotel. Let's get off the street. Come with me."

"Oh. No. I'll be fine."

He furrowed his brow. "Very well, then. Goodbye, Luci."

"Goodbye."

But when he walked away again, anxiety gripped Luciana's chest. Those boys had really scared her. And not having the cash she needed was a huge problem. She hadn't pictured herself alone and lost on the street.

"Gio," she blurted out, quickly catching up with him. "Thank you. I would appreciate your help."

Gio stopped in front of a large building with double doors made of oak, each bearing a brass doorknob. Although the structure was hundreds of years old, the fob entry system was proof it had been updated. When the tiny red light on the mechanism turned to green, Gio opened the door and held it wide for Luci to enter. Pulling her suitcase in with him, he then closed the door behind him. He led her through the stone tunnel passageway that kept the inner property well secluded from the busy streets of Florence.

The tunnel was a short distance, allowing Gio to see the sunshine that met it at the other end. He and his brother, Dante, used to play all sorts of games in this tunnel when they were kids.

"Where are we?" Luci asked with understandable trepidation.

"My home," Gio said as they came into the light of the central courtyard.

"Your home?" Luci began to take in the surroundings.

"My family's home. No one is here right now, but yes, this is where I grew up."

Up until a few days ago, Gio hadn't been home in many months. As the president of research, development and project management for his family's company, Grasstech, the world's largest manufacturer of computer components, Gio spent his life traveling among the company's operations centers all over the world. He touched down in Florence for crucial in-person meetings or for family occasions, but was then soon boarding a plane to his next destination.

"This is so beautiful," Luci exclaimed as she did a slow 360-degree turnaround in the inner courtyard of the villa compound.

"It's been in our family for six generations."

Indeed, Villa Grassi was a special place. It wasn't a showy high-tech complex befitting the Grassi family's standing in the computer science world. Instead the property retained its old-world charms, thanks to Gio's mother, although with plenty of modern conveniences. The villa comprised several stone buildings, all painted in a mustardy yellow color accented by the red terra-cotta roofs and wood trim.

"You live here?" Luci asked, still taking in the details of the central garden.

Mamma mia, but this young woman was pretty. Not just pretty, really, although Gio struggled for the right word to describe her. *Soulful*, maybe. There was depth in her light brown eyes. They were eyes with questions, eyes that longed. The dark, thick eyebrows that crowned those lovely pools served to set off their radiance even more. The sleek blond hair read as stylish, not that Gio knew much about fashion. Her petite frame was dressed with polish in her black skirt and gray blazer.

Why did this upscale-looking young woman have only jewels and no money? Something was quite off here, which Gio found suspicious. He would forever keep up his guard after the disastrous mistake he'd made in Hong Kong by trusting the wrong person. People weren't always who they said they were.

It seemed all but impossible that this woman in front of him could have somehow staged the incident with the boys on the street so that she could bump into him. That she had known where he was coming from and where he was headed. However, he'd learned the hard way that some people would say or do anything to get what they were after. Danger came in all shapes and sizes.

"I didn't understand what you said. Do you live here?"

"Not since childhood," he answered, still sizing her up. "But now I am home, so it seems."

The two-story main house anchored the buildings. Five steps led to the front door, constructed of the same oak as the door to the street. He looked up to the second-floor window that was his boyhood bedroom. Like all the windows, the sill was adorned with boxes holding plants in bright reds, oranges and yellows befitting the fall season. Beside it was the window in his brother Dante's bedroom. Late at night they'd tie up sheets to hold on to and swing into each other's bedrooms like Tarzan. Gio smiled at the antics of his daredevil brother, who hadn't changed a bit even as an adult.

In the courtyard, a cast-stone fountain gurgled with water, surrounded by the benches where his grandparents used to spend their afternoons. His grandfather would good-naturedly yell at Gio and Dante to slow down as they played their racing games in the tunnel. Their grandmother, content to sit for hours with her needlework, would ply the boys with blood orange juice from their fruit trees to drink, the color of which was still Gio's favorite hue in the world.

"We use the cottages now." Gio pointed to the two outbuildings beside the house, both of which had entrances that faced the courtyard.

"You said *we*. Who is we?"

"My brother, Dante, and I. And other relatives who come to stay. My parents still live in the big house when they're here, but we have a vineyard and winery in the countryside where they spend most of their time now that they've retired." His father had built Grasstech from a small purveyor of computer central processing units, known as CPU chips, into the multibillion-dollar conglomerate it was today. "Dante is working with our affiliates in India, now that…"

Gio was glad he stopped himself. Luci didn't need to know that Dante had failed at helming the company, which was why Gio had returned to Florence to do just that. Oversharing information had gotten him into trouble in the past, some of which he still needed to find a way to clean up.

In the silence of stopping himself, he focused on Luci's attentive face. There was something utterly enchanting about her, with that long stately neck and those curious eyes. She was much shorter than he had noticed at first. Of course, with him so tall, almost everyone was petite to him. Her bowed pink lips complemented her porcelain skin. Her posture was so straight and that throat so graceful she could pass for a noblewoman or a young duchess. Yet she had an inner spunk that made the thought of her as a stuffy royal thoroughly implausible.

Good heavens! Women should be the last thing on Gio's mind now that he'd returned home with a to-do list a mile long. And it was a woman who had got the company into trouble in the first place. He would be staying far away from them.

"That's the Duomo!" Luci pointed to the top of the dome visible in the distance past the villa walls. Florence's cathedral was one of the most identifiable sights in the city.

"Have you been inside?"

Her enthusiasm was contagious.

"No. I'm looking forward to seeing it. This is my first time in Florence. You rescued me just as I arrived."

A little wiggle traveled between his shoulder blades when she said the word *rescued*.

Now that he had, in fact, rescued her, what was he going to do with her? He'd find her a hotel. But some of Grasstech's investors were in town for dinner and he needed to get dressed, so it had to be quick. He wasn't looking forward to all their chitchat that bored him to tears. Nothing of substance was ever discussed at these things. Plus they'd all be bringing their stodgy spouses. The wives would ask why a nice young man like him didn't have a wife or a girlfriend.

With enough on his mind already, Luci's problems couldn't become his. Yet she'd been so shaken by those nasty boys following her, she finally accepted his offer of help.

She readjusted her purse on her shoulder, the one that contained her jewels. "May I ask you, Gio, would there be *any* hotel at *any* price that you could recommend for the night? I'll have to reevaluate my budget, but I do need somewhere for tonight."

He could give it a try. Pulling his phone out of his jacket pocket, he punched in a hotel search, hoping he'd recognize the names of some that were reputable.

"Yes," he spoke after calling one. "Do you have any rooms available for tonight? I see. *Grazie.*"

He phoned another. "Have you a room tonight? No? *Grazie.*" After three more, his patience was up.

"That's all right, Gio," Luci said, although the quaver in her voice belied her words. "I'll find somewhere."

With her obvious lack of street savvy? What if some other criminals tried to take advantage of her like the boys did with the jewelry? He might not know this vulnerable young woman, but a gentleman was a gentleman and he could not send her away alone.

"Why don't you stay here tonight?" Gio voiced the thought that had been bubbling up, despite raising caution. "I'm staying in this one." He pointed to one of the side-by-side cottages. "Why don't you sleep in the other?" He hoped that suggestion wouldn't prove to be a mistake, but he couldn't think of what else to do. He'd station her here, and the staff at his office could help get her situated tomorrow.

"Oh, no, I couldn't." Luci quickly shook her head with a side-to-side motion. "It wouldn't be right."

He put his hand over his heart in mock insult. "What do you take me for? I assure you I offer only to fulfill my quota of rescuing beautiful maidens from the mean streets of Florence."

Was he *flirting* with her?

"How are you doing so far?"

"I'm desperately behind. You'd be helping me out."

She looked at him with a bite to her lip. He knew she was deciding on his merits versus his potential risks.

"I'll only consent if you let me repay you in some way."

The idea quickly fell from his lips. "I have a very dull dinner with some investors to attend tonight. They will have no doubt chosen the poshest restaurant in Florence with a continental menu that manages to avoid anything authentically Italian. They'll pick an impressive bottle of wine chosen for its price and torture the sommelier as they swirl it around in their glasses pretending to know something about the vintage. They'll discuss the weather and the latest political scandal in Italy, and it will make watching paint dry sound compelling. Would you like to join me?"

"With an invitation like that, how could I possibly refuse?" Luci answered with a huge smile that shot straight into Gio's heart. He returned the grin.

Once he'd extended the invitation to dinner, it suddenly sounded like a marvelous idea. She was far more interesting than the blah-blah-blah he'd have to exchange with the investors. Rightly, they'd save any substantial conversation for boardroom conferences.

Why shouldn't he have a pleasant evening with an attractive woman? He knew he'd never take it any further than that. It was just dinner. And bringing her with him was better than leaving her alone on his property tonight. He'd get her out of the villa in the morning.

"It's set then? Pick you up right here?" He gestured to the fountain.

"I have a cocktail-length dress. Will that be sufficient?"

"And obviously you can accessorize." He pointed to the purse with all of the jewels. "You'll be the toast of the town."

"I hope not." Luci's eyes opened in alarm.

"I was only joking. See you at eight."

CHAPTER TWO

"THANK YOU, VIGGO." Gio acknowledged his driver as he parked the car in front of the villa. Viggo quickly got out of his seat and dashed around to the passenger side to open the door for Luciana and Gio. After Gio helped her out of the car, she straightened the skirt of the pale blue dress she'd worn to dinner with him and his investors.

It was her little secret that she'd chosen the dress to complement the color of her handsome companion's eyes. Of course, the color of Her Royal Highness Princess Luciana's dress for the evening was the least of her secrets. Nonetheless, with her cool blond wig, silver shoes and diamond earrings, she felt like a woman who had been on a real date with a real man, as opposed to a shielded virgin locked in a stone tower. Gio had quickly become part of her grand adventure.

"Do we have to go in?" Luciana touched Gio's jacket sleeve as he reached in his pocket for his fob entry to the wooden exterior door.

"Would you like to walk?"

"I'd love to."

Driving from the restaurant after the dinner, Luciana was agog as they drove past landmarks she wanted to visit while she was here. The incredible piazzas, historic churches, marketplaces, museums and neighborhoods she'd seen only as an armchair traveler in the solitude of her palace sitting room. While she'd traveled to many places in the world for ceremonies and royal engagements, she'd never seen them as a tourist, able to meander and linger, and appreciate anything that caught her fancy. She could hardly wait to get started.

"Let's walk this way." Gio gently placed his hand on the small of her back to direct her away from the villa door. Her awareness arched to meet his touch.

"Thank you for accompanying me to dinner. As I mentioned, I generally leave the finessing of investors to my brother, Dante, now that our father has retired."

"And Dante was unable to attend tonight?"

"Dante is spending some time at our offices in Mumbai. We have restructured the company and I will now serve as CEO."

"What did you do before?"

"Product development. Which is where my heart is. You'd find me happier trying to make an AGP bus that can carry graphics faster than anything else on the market than you would seeing me in a conference room."

"AGP?"

"Accelerated graphics port."

"Of course," she joked. "How would I not know that?"

"But now I'll do what needs to be done for the company. Actually, I welcome the opportunity to do things my way. To get them right."

"Are things not right?"

"Look at those two." Gio pointed to two dogs on leashes across the street that barked at and sniffed each other with great interest.

Ah, Luci noted, she had asked too snoopy a question

about Gio's work and he'd changed the subject. Her inner Princess Luciana should have known better than to pry, in spite of her curiosity to know more about him.

She hoped to recover with, "Your investors were a lovely group of people. I saw photos on many a smartphone of grandchildren performing in school plays and rosebushes that had yielded prizewinners."

The princess was only too used to smiling and taking interest in the lives of total strangers. In fairness, she was always quite honored that people she met wanted to share details about their lives with her. Meeting people was one of the things she did like about royal life. But not as much as she liked this, walking in the open air with Gio, and not a handler or schedule in sight.

"Enough about me," he said as they continued after watching the dogs perform mating rituals. "What do you do for a living?"

"I'm a teacher," Luciana fibbed. That was what she would be if she could. Royal duties combined with her father's outdated ways kept her ambition from coming to fruition. "I spend most of my days talking to fouryear-olds."

"A teacher? I never would have figured you for that."

"Why not?"

"You're very—" he searched for the right word "—elegant. The way you handled yourself at dinner was distinguished. Well, there we go when we stereotype or pigeonhole anyone. My apologies."

If he only knew. How badly she didn't want to always have to be elegant. How her father raised her in a very old-fashioned monarchy she didn't question, where Luciana had been groomed her whole life to make appearances. To never share anything of herself, her hopes, her likes. To be only in the service of the crown. While she led a life of luxury and privilege for which she was grateful, her heart ached for more.

Perhaps she'd be content if the man she was to marry wasn't so much older and who, in the handful of meetings she'd had with him, hadn't talked to her as if she were already his possession. Maybe her life would be sublime if she was to wed a bold and good-humored man like say, just for example, Gio.

She blushed at her own thought as she noted the shadows the night sky cast onto Gio's defined cheekbones.

"*Bellissima*, what is a teacher doing traveling alone with only a bag full of jewels to pay her way?"

As she had learned in her years of training, restraint was always the best policy, so rather than answer him, she occupied herself taking in the light of the moon and how it played against not only Gio's face but also the architecture of this great ancient city.

"Where are you from, Luci?" Gio pressed.

"Spain," she simplified.

She had a flush of concern that she was out late at night in a foreign country with a man she'd only just met. Half of her considered the potential danger, but the other half wanted to throw caution to the wind and grab as many experiences as she could out of this trip to Florence. Including this unexpected interlude with a beguiling man.

"Your Italian is flawless."

"I studied for many years."

Indeed, Princess Luciana had always been fascinated with Italian history, art and literature, especially the Renaissance period when Florence was the center of Europe. It was a thrill to finally use the language she had practiced so diligently. While she had been to Rome for royal occasions and adored it, the City of Lilies had always held her interest.

About a year ago, her father, King Mario, had informed her that she would be marrying widower King Agustin of the neighboring island Menocita. She didn't protest, always wanting to please her father after her mother had died.

Izerote was racked with problems. Because theirs was a tiny country with limited development, unemployment had become a crisis. As the current generation had grown, many households sent their offspring away for higher education or to seek jobs in Spain or the rest of the world. Without careers on the island for future generations, the population would continue to shrink.

On Menocita, King Agustin's father had brought tourism to their shores. Exclusive resorts along with family-friendly water sports and vacation rentals had turned the island into a year-round paradise that created thousands of jobs for the inhabitants. After King Agustin's wife died, he'd decided to find another island to merge with to create the same tourism and bring larger prosperity to his family name. When the proposal of marriage to his daughter came to King Mario, he could not refuse. In turn, Princess Luciana could not let her father or her subjects down, so she had no option but to agree to it.

Yes, a future she wouldn't have chosen for herself was looming. But at least she'd always have this. Florence. This journey of self-discovery and of making a single dream come true.

Luciana did feel badly that she had left her father a note saying only that she would return to Izerote to marry King Agustin, but that she was going to do this one thing before she did. She had previously begged him to let her, just once, leave the island without attendants, limousines and security details. It was a liberty she needed to know, if even for a short time. It was something she longed for, a wanderlust she wasn't able to silence. King Mario, an overly protective man especially after her mother was killed in a car accident in Madrid, denied her. And not wanting to cause him anymore grief, she acquiesced—until she could no longer.

She thought back to the trip to Paris King Mario did plan for Luciana and a cousin her age. When they were there, clothing stores were closed to the public so that they could shop alone, never paying for anything. When the girls walked down the boulevards, bodyguards trailed only a few paces behind. An entire hotel floor was rented despite their needing only two rooms. They visited a museum after midnight, fully staffed for just the two of them. While Luciana did appreciate her father's efforts, it was hardly what she'd had in mind.

With the wedding imminent, Princess Luciana's heart, her soul, the very essence of her being, insisted that she break away from the protocol that had been drilled into her. And drove her to do something completely for herself, as reckless as it was. So, she escaped the palace walls and her role as the perfect daughter and princess, leaving no hint of where she was going. She bought no tickets for her transportation, brought along no phone where her location could be traced. As drastic a step as it was to take palace jewels to sell, she hadn't been able to think of another way.

Three weeks that belonged only to her wasn't so very much to ask for.

After her walk with Gio and their return to his villa,

Luciana was tired. She'd face the issues of the jewels and finding a suitable place to stay tomorrow. For tonight, she was eternally grateful for his generosity.

They lingered at the halfway point between her guest cottage and his.

"I can't thank you enough for this."

"My pleasure, Luci. Thank you for accompanying me to the dinner." He crossed an arm over his waist and bowed forward to her in an exaggerated posture of formality that might have been funny if she was a different person.

"Did you sleep well?" Gio called up to Luci as she stepped out onto the small Juliet balcony of the guest cottage, wrapping her hands around the wrought iron railing. Properly known as a *balconet*, it wasn't large enough for a chair or table. It was meant for enjoying the view of the courtyard below and to peer out beyond the villa's walls. When Shakespeare included the architectural feature in his romantic tragedy, the nickname stuck.

It took considerable effort for Gio to pretend not to notice how the transparent fabric of the flowing white nightgown Luci wore hid nothing of her lovely curves underneath. But the sudden twitch in his core told the truth.

He placed the pot of coffee he was holding onto the small glass table near the fountain. "Would you like to join me for breakfast?"

"How magical to wake up and smell all of these flowers," Luci said with a sweeping arm surveying the courtyard's garden. "The lavender is so sweet."

The same view was available from Gio's bedroom, as the two cottages were identical. He had risen early and let himself into the main house to find some breakfast.

He glanced up to Luci again. It was actually nothing short of surreal that a beautiful woman stood on the balcony of his guesthouse in Florence, albeit that her status there was temporary. Surreal even that he was back home, as most of his adult life thus far had been spent living away. The idea of staying in one place might take some getting used to. "Come down and have some coffee."

Luci accepted the bid with, "Just give me a few minutes to get dressed."

An unfamiliar voice inside Gio wanted to beg her to come down as she was, so fetching did she look in her cotton gauze. But decorum won out.

Always buried in work, he had not been alone with a woman in quite a while. In spite of the fact that this unexpected maiden with the blond hair and the big brown eyes had landed in his lap yesterday, this was a very important morning. Which was why he'd chosen to wake at dawn, go for a run, shower and dress, all the while leaving himself enough time to have a relaxed breakfast.

Today was his first official day as CEO of Grasstech. He stepped into his cottage to gather a laptop and some briefings he had been looking over and brought them out to the courtyard so he was ready to leave after breakfast. The two cottages were small but sufficient with a sitting room on the first floor, and a bedroom and bathroom upstairs. They were decorated in yellow, black and gold with expensive, but simple, furnishings. Gio's mother had told him that she'd recently redone the guest quarters and looked forward to his seeing them. Later, he'd ring her at the vineyard to offer his compliments.

Such coziness was unfamiliar to him. President of research, development and project management, Gio Grassi was accustomed to traversing the world, and preferred the anonymity of hotels. Sleek, modern hotel rooms looked no different to him whether he was in Cape Town or Seoul or Dallas. Hotels perfectly suited the life he had been leading. Everything at his disposal and on his own time clock.

When he was lost in concentration on a new project it could be hours, sometimes even days, that would pass while he was surrounded by computer parts and algorithms. He lived immersed in a technological world most people had no understanding of. Where he laid his head to rest was of little concern to him. Until now, when his entire lifestyle was about to change.

Gio hopped up the five steps from the courtyard to the main house to fetch the rolls and fruit the housekeeper had left for him. When he brought them to the outdoor table, Luci was coming out her front door, suitcase and purse in tow. In the morning sun, her eyes caught glints of light.

"Is something wrong?" she asked in reaction to his expression.

"Please, sit." He pulled out a chair for her to take her place at the table.

After coffee was poured and rolls were bitten into, Luci asked, "You're going to the Grasstech office today?"

"Yes. I've got to go be the boss man now," Gio said with a titter belying his mixed feelings on the transition. On one hand he was relieved to be taking full control of Grasstech and knew he would fine-tune operations and move the company even further forward. Yet the other side of him rather dreaded becoming the face of the empire. He'd made a mistake that had cost the company dearly and he had a lot of mopping up to do. In trusting his ex-girlfriend, Francesca, there were now leaked company secrets to contend with and a press ready to bring that information public.

"Thank you so much for your hospitality. I'll leave right after breakfast, so don't let me add to your troubles."

"Have we settled where you are going?" he asked with a quick glance at his watch. As strangely intriguing as this domestic scene was, he had a million other things on his mind. He wouldn't be finding out who this lovely Luci in front of him truly was. Not only didn't he have time for a woman in his life, he couldn't buy the story that she was a teacher. There was more going on with her than met the eye, and that was something he hadn't any business getting involved in.

"That's kind of you to consider my lodging something *we* are concerned about, but I'll figure it out on my own."

"Of course." But he couldn't leave it at that. Her mysterious identity notwithstanding, Gio's mother had taught him to be chivalrous, and after hearing yesterday about Luci's budget issues he wasn't going to have her traipsing alone around Florence looking for a cheap hotel that might not be safe.

"I'll have someone at my office look into hotels for you." The sooner he squared her safely away, the less he'd fret about it later.

"I couldn't impose like that."

"It's no imposition."

"Thank you but…it wouldn't be…"

If he let her go, he'd be distracted all day worrying if she was okay. And he needed his concentration today. "Why don't you go out and see some sights? We'll meet later and I can complain to you about my workday."

A giggle escaped from her, which brought a lovable little blush to her cheeks.

She had been an utterly flawless dinner date last night, charming his investors by laughing at their unfunny jokes and asking questions about their families to get them talking about themselves. Gio despised making small talk. Luci, who had appeared poised and almost regal in her blue silk dress, knew exactly how to field the evening, which took the pressure off him. He could return the favor. After that, she'd be out of his life and on with her holiday.

"It's settled, then. Why don't you leave your luggage here?" Gio stood and gathered up his things, having been alerted on his phone that his driver was here. "Where can my driver drop you?"

"I'll just wander out on my own."

He escorted her to the street. "See you here at six."

Gio's driver, Viggo, delivered him to the street-level glass doors of the Grasstech headquarters. The family kept a much larger campus of offices outside the city, but this central Florence location was where the company's important decisions were still made. Gio passed through to the main reception area where a few employees were congregating.

"Hello, Mr. Grassi," one greeted.

"Good morning, sir," another followed.

"Welcome, Mr. Grassi."

While he generally interacted with everyone he met on a first-name basis, he quite approved of the employees here addressing him formally at first. It was important to establish sole authority immediately.

That had been part of the problem with his brother in the top seat. While he admired Dante as being more of a people person than he was—his brother had become a sort of brand ambassador for their company—

Gio doubted he elicited much respect among the staff. Because, unfortunately, Dante spent more time being photographed with a different woman on his arm each evening at social functions than he did overseeing the company's operations. Whereas Gio understood the ins and outs of Grasstech's stronghold in the tech world and had specific plans on how to increase their dominance against the competition.

While Dante had been happy to use the press to his advantage, the media were actually Gio's first challenge of the day.

As he made his way down the corridor to the corner office that was originally his father's, Gio was aware of a pretty assistant in step beside him. Although she was an attractive young woman, Gio found his mind immediately flashed back to Luci's gracious smile as she engaged the older ladies last night with a discussion of favorite holiday memories. Something about Luci had gotten under his skin. Which he needed to put a stop to right away. The last thing he wanted to be embroiled with was a woman, especially now that deceitful Francesca was the cause of his most pressing problem.

"What can I get you, Mr. Grassi?" the assistant asked as she escorted him into his office.

"A large bottle of cold water. And send in Samuele, thank you."

"Yes, sir."

"Mio amico." Samuele di Nofri greeted Gio with a bear hug and affirmation of their lifelong friendship. The older man was Grasstech's director of operations and had been working with the company since the day Gio's father conceived of it. "Finally, we have you back in Firenze."

"Sit." Gio gestured to one of the leather chairs that faced his sleek steel desk.

"It was like yesterday that you were a boy, sitting at one of those desktop computers we used to keep here." Samuele pointed to a wall where a row of clunky old computers used to be lined up. Before everyone had laptops that weighed less than a cup of coffee. "Six years old and you would sit for hours writing code."

"Technology has come a long way since then."

"Grazie al cielo." Samuele kissed two fingers and lifted them to the sky.

"Although then, we didn't worry as much about security and hacking. Now look what I caused the company to have to deal with."

"It happens."

Yes, Gio's early proclivity for computers had led him to eventually receive multiple degrees from Stanford University in California's Silicon Valley. Then after years of apprenticeship in Tokyo, he emerged as one of the world's most respected component designers.

What Gio's education and experience hadn't taught him was how to look out for Francesca and her kind. With her eight-foot-long legs and her crimson red lips, she was a skilled and practiced seductress. She had set her sights on the workaholic techie Grassi brother and had not relented until she'd got what she wanted. Which was not his heart.

No, what Francesca wanted were secrets about Grasstech's new memory modules that were destined to take drop-in compatibility wider than the industry had seen before. So while Gio was conceiving, designing, testing and troubleshooting, Francesca had done what she did best.

Francesca Nefando, who had been hired to run analytic reports, was actually a world-class hacker. In a tight skirt and high heels.

"Fine, Samuele, you say it happens." Gio grimaced at the memory of the day he found out his proprietary DIMMs, dual inline memory modules, were being developed by a rival company with information only an insider could know. Samuele's kindly eyes tried to offer some comfort. "But now that the industry press has found out, Grasstech could look weak in the field."

"That's why the board of directors tell me that they want you to issue a statement to the media. Because you are taking over as the CEO, they see this as an opportunity to solidify your name as the trailblazer of the company. That alone will help deflect the breach."

"Me? We have public relations people for this."

"Yes. But put it in your own words, Gio. It will sound authentic and announce your personal style of leadership."

He watched Samuele's mouth form words, but Gio was having a hard time actually listening. Because his blood was boiling thinking back to the strategy Francesca had designed to seduce him. Once he'd begun to trust her, she'd started to ask questions that required long nights of huddling together over a laptop in bed, her auburn hair almost sickly sweet from the gardenia-scented shampoo she used.

Francesca had taught him a lesson he would never forget. He would never let anyone get that close to him again. But, weirdly, his thoughts meandered back to Luci this morning, so seemingly harmless as she stood on the balcony in her nightgown.

"What should I say in the press release? That I let a woman get the best of me?"

"No, Gio. Mull it over. You'll come up with something."

"Samuele, before you go. Can you look for a room at a decent hotel for about three weeks?"

Samuele regarded him quizzically.

"One of our investors isn't happy with where he's staying."

Gio took a deep breath. He had a full schedule and a multibillion-dollar company to run. So why was he already looking forward to seeing Luci again tonight?

"Drop us here," Gio instructed Viggo as the car approached the Piazza della Signoria. It had been ages since the piazza had been his destination. If he'd seen it at all during the past few years, it had been because he was merely crossing through to get to a meeting at an office or restaurant. Viggo let him and Luci out of the back seat.

Gio had decided to take her out. They'd have dinner in one of the *osterias* whose piazza-facing patios would still be warm enough in the autumn evening.

"Oh, my gosh." Luci brought her hand over her mouth in genuine reverence as she took in the piazza. He could appreciate her sentiment, as it was one of Florence's most dramatic sights. In fact, historically, it had been the meeting place for all of Tuscany.

"There's the Fontana di Neptuno!" The marble-and-bronze Fountain of Neptune. "I've seen it in pictures so many times, I can't believe I'm finally here."

Luci's enthusiasm lightened Gio's mood after a long hard day of putting out administrative fire after fire in the remains of mistakes that Dante had made while he was at the helm. Mostly, though, he was still strategizing about the Francesca fiasco and its aftermath.

Still, he reiterated to himself that one of his goals when returning to Florence was to slow his pace a little and to enjoy relaxing pursuits. He worked too much; even his father thought so. A night out on the town with pretty Luci was just what the doctor ordered. Even though he had sworn never to get close to a woman again, it was only one evening. Okay, there was last night, too, but it was not as if he was going to devote his life to her.

Although when he presented a bent elbow for her to slip her arm through, he felt an unfamiliar lump at the bottom of his throat when she did so.

"Here is one of the fake *David*s." She pointed to the replica of Michelangelo's masterpiece. "The original used to stand in this place but was moved to the Galleria dell'Accademia to protect it."

"You'll want to visit there."

"There's another replica of *David* in the Piazzale Michelangelo. The views of the city are supposed to be astounding from there."

"They are."

"And this is the Loggia dei Lanzi." The outdoor gallery of sculptures in the piazza.

"You've certainly studied up on the city. That way is the Uffizi Gallery—" he pointed a finger "—which, of course, you'll want to explore." One of the world's finest museums.

"Oh, yes." Her squeeze on his arm sent pricks of energy through his muscles.

"I can find a professional guide for you if you'd like."

"No. Thanks. I spend too much time already with guides and companions as it is."

"I take it you mean the children you teach? That's a cute way of describing them."

"Right." Luci's voice rose. "It does seem like they are the ones leading the way most of the time."

At the restaurant he'd chosen, Gio asked the hostess to seat them outside facing the piazza. It was about as fine a night as could be with the dusk and the statues, Luci's face aglow with the breadth of it all.

"We'll have the prosciutto with melon, the mushroom risotto and the grilled *branzino*," he instructed the waiter. Gio was hungry so he ordered for them without consulting the menu.

"Is that all right?" He turned to Luci.

"Yes. Thank you for asking."

"And we'll have a bottle of the Pallovana Frascati," Gio finished the order.

After the waiter returned with the Frascati, Luci asked, "You haven't told me anything about your first day yet. How did everything go?"

As they sipped their wine and took advantage of the superlative people-watching their vantage point on the piazza offered, he filled her in on reacquainting himself with staff and about some restructuring he was intending.

"My biggest problem is how to handle the information about a hack we experienced recently when the design for a product was obtained and sold to a competitor." The information about the hack was to soon be public knowledge, so he wasn't disclosing any secrets by talking to Luci about it.

"Has it been in the news?"

"Not officially. I know there's talk in the industry."

"Will you speak to the press about it?" That was exactly what Samuele had been urging this morning.

"I suppose I ought to before trade gossips do."

"So, should you issue a press statement?"

The waiter delivered plates with paper-thin slices of pink prosciutto draped across wedges of ripe orange melon.

"Grazie." Gio acknowledged the arrival and returned his attention to Luci.

"It was my own personal security that was weak in order for the hack to have happened. I gave clearance to someone I shouldn't have." Gio didn't want to tell Luci about Francesca specifically, so he kept it general.

"You don't want the company to appear compromised in the press," Luci said with her fork dangling in the air.

"Exactly. I'd like to think it was a grave mistake on my part but that, in general, our safeguards are very good. Nothing like that had ever happened before and hopefully never will again."

"Do you have any new products that are about to launch?"

"Why do you ask?" The question came out sharply. But here it was. This young lady who called herself a teacher from Spain could be, right under his nose, trying to get proprietary information from him under the guise of dinner conversation. That was how these charmers worked, wasn't it?

"I'm sorry, did I offend you?"

"Are you interested in computer science?" he baited, paying attention to every word.

"Not especially." She took a sip of her wine. "I was going to make a suggestion about your press release. Pardon me if I was being intrusive."

"Go on." He rubbed his chin as he continued to study her.

"What if you wrote a statement that wasn't strictly about the hack but was a *state of the company* address now that you've taken over? Then you can mention the leak and what security measures you're putting in place. But sandwich it in between news about the company's latest accomplishments."

"That's a great suggestion," Gio exclaimed. He thought immediately of the achievements he would like to announce, and that in the context of a report on the company they wouldn't come across as showboating. Indeed, his new peripheral component interconnect, PCI, was revolutionary.

Gio toasted Luci. As they clinked their wineglasses together it was as if they touched each other, a powerful sensation that traveled from his fingertips all the way up his arm to his heart.

They made it through the next two courses of their meal talking a mile a minute. Luci asked so many interesting questions about computers and listened patiently to techie mumbo jumbo that she surely didn't understand. Gio didn't reveal anything about his designs, and by the time dinner was over, his spy theory had lost steam. Luci was wonderful company.

The conversation continued as they stood in the courtyard of the villa under the night sky. "The random access memory, or RAM, is temporary," he finished the explanation he was giving her in the car.

"Your work is interesting."

The scent of the flowers in bloom permeated the garden.

Silence fell upon them.

The air between them stilled.

Her mood changed.

She'd spent dinner asking him about work and had avoided talking about herself. He looked into her eyes to coax her on but she said nothing. She definitely harbored a secret, although he was now convinced it had nothing to do with him.

"Something is wrong?"

"Thank you again for your generosity."

It was as if the entire city was quietly holding its breath.

"You didn't tell me about your day. What sights did you see?"

With her head slightly bowed, she peered up at him through her eyelashes. "I'm embarrassed to tell you that I got completely lost. I was planning to visit the Piazza della Repubblica, but I ended up just sort of circling in a big loop. It was all beautiful, but I didn't see anything I had intended to."

Florence wasn't the easiest city to maneuver if you didn't know it, with streets jutting out from its many piazzas. Still, in this day and age, with all of the online resources and apps, a person should be able to find their way.

"You didn't use maps or tourist sites on your phone?"

She waited a beat before admitting, "I don't have a phone. I didn't bring one on the trip."

"*Bellissima*, is that even safe?"

"I wanted to unplug," she quickly responded, "to truly be a wanderer without any trappings of real life. Besides…"

"Yes?" he prompted. Unplugging wasn't something he'd ever experienced, as his life revolved around being so very plugged in. Although it was something he needed to learn to do a little of.

"I'm not sure I should have come to Florence at all."

Gio stood firm and pierced his eyes into hers. "I can

tell that you've come to Florence to lose yourself. That you're hiding something. Or hiding from something."

Luci scrunched her forehead. As if she was making a decision.

Then she reached to her head to run her fingers through her blond hair. Her hand moved farther and farther back until, with a tug, she lifted the blond hair completely off her head.

It was a wig! And from under the wig an avalanche of long brown waves cascaded down far past her shoulders.

"First of all, my name is not Luci. It's Luciana. I am Her Royal Highness Princess Luciana de la Isla de Izerote."

CHAPTER THREE

"*Brava.*" Gio used two fingers to mime tipping an imaginary hat toward Luci, or rather Princess Luciana. "That's quite a coup, a princess in disguise."

"You wouldn't believe it."

"Try me," he clipped. Luciana knew he would be upset to learn that she had pretended to be someone she wasn't, the deception made so much worse by the burn of the company hack he'd spoken of. He was quite sensitive during dinner when she'd asked about his upcoming products, as if he was suspicious of her and had been all along.

Now his jaw pulsed as he stood drilling into her with his big blue eyes, demanding an explanation.

"You've been so kind to me, Gio," she began constructing an apology. "I didn't expect to have a problem with selling my jewels. Then those boys were harassing me on the street and you came to my aid. And now you've given me this beautiful evening."

"You have an interesting way of showing your appreciation," he continued in a voice so low and tight she wasn't sure how the sounds were even escaping his throat.

Luciana fingered through the wig she held in her hand. The strands felt so fake despite how much she had liked wearing it. How silly it all seemed now, that she had tried to convince Gio she was a schoolteacher on a holiday. She supposed she had been trying that out on herself, a description of a woman and a life she could only imagine about.

"I'm so sorry. When I was sharing what I've learned about handling the media, you knew a schoolteacher wouldn't have any experience with that. I wanted to tell you the truth right then. I just didn't know how. I was trying to keep my identity hidden so that I could have just one anonymous adventure. I've never been on my own."

"I see."

"It's like what you're going through right now, having to transition from being a private to a public person. I've been in the palace my entire life. Although Izerote is not known to the rest of the world, on my own island I am under constant scrutiny."

Gio's expression slowly remolded from accusatory to something else, like he was truly listening to her.

"I'll just pack up my things and be out of your way." She turned from him to return to the cottage he'd been generous enough to let her stay in. She'd gather up as quickly as she could.

Over her shoulder she added, "Even though I have no right to, may I ask you one more favor? Could you not tell anyone about this? I would be eternally grateful if you forgot you ever met me."

As she swerved away, his big hand grabbed her arm.

"I didn't say you had to leave." Gio's voice kept its deep baritone but he didn't sound as angry anymore. "Please, Princess Luciana de la Isla de Izerote. Let me make us a cup of tea. I have to admit I'm intrigued. I've never hosted a real-life princess before. Let alone a runaway."

"I'm not made of fairy dust. Despite popular folklore."

If this had been a fairy tale, Gio Grassi could be her handsome prince. His armor would glisten as he swept her off her feet and hoisted her onto his proud white horse. Where they'd gallop away into the sunset to their kingdoms where marriages were conjured from love, not strategy.

"I'm dreading my entry into public life," Gio said. "So I do understand your desire for anonymity."

"That means a lot to me."

"You look quite different with your long and natural hair."

Luciana supposed she did. With her hair the same as she'd worn it her entire life she felt younger, like she was still a schoolgirl. How her father saw her.

"I actually love the wig," she confessed. "It's fashionable instead of how I usually look, stuck in time, born and bred to wear a tiara. What do you think?"

"Obviously, you should wear your hair however you want to."

His words stunned her. When was the last time anyone told her she should look however she wanted? Never.

"Shall we have tea?"

"Okay."

"I'll be right back."

As Gio went up to the main house, Luciana sighed with enormous relief. She couldn't have kept her identity a secret from him for a second longer. At first she thought he was so angry he was going to throw her out on the spot. Thank goodness his reaction changed. What a persuasive man he was. Her eyelids fluttered when he said she should do whatever she wanted with her hair.

Why couldn't she be marrying a compelling and progressive man like him? Why must she wed someone with a closed mind who had already told her that becoming pregnant was the first and only job he expected her to devote herself to? She did want children, but in all honesty, she dreaded the thought of giving her virginity to a man she would never love. That seemed a service past what was a reasonable expectation of any person.

"All right, Princess," Gio announced when he brought out two cups of tea and invited her to sit at the glass table in the courtyard where they'd had breakfast early that morning. "I want to hear all about this. How and why did you get yourself off your tiny island and all the way to Tuscany?"

Luciana took a sip from the steaming cup and then began to tell the story of what she'd been planning for months.

How she held no money, having no cause to ever pay for anything herself. That she did have credit cards but if she used them her whereabouts could be located. So she'd decided she would use a few precious stones to finance this expedition she was compelled to take. About how she carefully spread out on her bed all the palace jewels that had been worn by her mother, her grandmother, her great-grandmother and her lineage even before them.

Many were one-of-a-kind pieces crafted by the finest jewelry makers in the world and gifted to the royal family. Most of them were ornate and overdone, not at all pieces she would have chosen for herself. Yet she understood their legacy and importance. They would be passed down to her own children someday, either to a daughter or a daughter-in-law.

Returning those to the palace vaults, Luciana kept only a few plainer pieces whose stones would bring her enough money. They were everyday pieces that would never be missed.

The princess had also been keeping a careful watch on the schedule of supply boats that arrived regularly to bring goods onto the island. After reviewing her chart, she confirmed that one arrived at four o'clock every morning. Formulating her scheme, she'd creep outside the palace walls, avoiding security cameras and passing undetected through the pitch-dark of the wee hours to the shore. Finding a covering from which to spy, she'd timed the boatmen unloading their cargo and wheeling it through the service entrance of the palace. For at least ten minutes during the unloading process, the boat was unattended.

Gio put his elbows on the table between them, engrossed in her tale.

On the chosen night, Princess Luciana donned her darkest clothes, slid out the prepacked suitcase from under her bed and placed the jewels into a purse. She left a note on her desk for her father, climbed over the terrace off her sitting room and scurried her way to the dock in the darkness. Once on the boat, she'd covered herself in tarps and sailcloth. Shuddering with fear as she heard the crew return to the boat, she'd all but held her breath as they pulled away from the shores of Izerote.

When the boat touched land in Barcelona, she'd waited for the crew to disembark and then, having no idea what would greet her once she was on deck, was able to dash away from the dock unnoticed. Although she didn't get the money she expected for the sale of the first jewel, she'd had enough to board a train, and transferred from one train to another to another through France until she'd reached Florence.

"I'm astonished," Gio said as he leaned back in his chair.

Replaying the getaway in her mind, Luciana was just as shocked as Gio that she had pulled it off. Not just the actual escape, which was something out of a spy story. But that she'd had the will and the courage to do it. To take something for herself that every cell in her body was starving for. That she would have spent a lifetime regretting it if she hadn't.

Maybe a little piece of this was also a tribute to her mother, who Luciana knew was never happy under the confines of her tiara. Her mother's eyes had died long before the car accident took her life.

"One question," Gio mused. "Why did you come to Florence for specifically three weeks? Do you turn into a pumpkin after that?"

"Worse. I'm getting married."

"You're set to marry a man you don't love?"

"I must wed King Agustin of Menocita, an island near ours. It's my duty to my subjects. Izerote is a land of unspoiled green hills and clear blue waters. But our population has been shrinking over the last couple of generations. With globalization, the people of Izerote want more in their lives than what our island has to offer. Families send their children off to the great universities of Europe and the United States where technology is up-to-date and there are job opportunities."

Gio raked a hand through his curls as he listened attentively. They nursed the cups of tea he had prepared. He'd met a couple of royals in his life at social functions but never with any intimacy other than a handshake. He did remember that he got a standoffish vibe from them, as if they were separate from the rest of the world. Princess Luciana, Luci, was not like that at all, and from her he sensed a benevolence he almost never felt with anyone. If he hadn't known, he might indeed believe that she spent her days as a teacher among the needs and simple concerns of toddlers.

"How is it that marrying King Agustin will be good for your subjects?"

"Menocita was heading toward the same fate as Izerote until about thirty years ago when Agustin's father decided the island would become a tourist destination in order to create jobs and attract visitors. And it worked well. They built lavish beach resorts and all the ensuing industries, which have brought prosperity to the island. Although now their waters are polluted and they have to ship garbage out by the boatloads."

"King Agustin and your father want to do the same in Izerote."

"Yes." Luciana took a demure sip from her cup of tea. Those sensual bow-shaped lips had held him captive as she told him her story. He loved her upright posture as she sat on the chair opposite him while they talked. The moon glow, plus a couple of garden lights, cast perfect shadows of light and dark across her stunning face. She'd worn a simple dark green dress to dinner tonight, very modest with its high neckline and below-the-knee length. Last night for the dinner with his investors, it was a stiff-fabric light blue dress, quite formal. He wondered if princesses were ever allowed to dress in casual clothes.

Really, though, it was the sight of her in that sheer nightgown on the Juliet balcony this morning that he couldn't get off his mind. It made him want to run barefoot through a forest with her, crown or not.

"Agustin's wife died when they were quite young. He must remarry and bear children."

"You're being traded for a couple of hotels on the beach?"

Luciana laughed out loud, the dulcet tones carrying into the foggy air of the late night. "Yes." She continued to giggle so sincerely, it made Gio smile. "I love the way you phrased that."

"It's true."

"And what's sadder," Luciana added with a snicker, "is that I dislike Agustin, what little I know of him. He's stern and humorless."

Princess Luciana was not like any of the women he'd known before. First of all, with Grasstech's position as the world leader in its field, Giovanni Grassi and Dante Grassi were two eligible bachelors of accomplishment and wealth. With that, they attracted women who tried to glam onto them for a taste of the luxury life. That's exactly what Her Royal Highness Princess Luciana was running away from.

Many a woman like Francesca had crossed Gio's path. Dante's, too. The women who gravitated toward the Grassi brothers were nothing like their mother, the down-to-earth woman who was grateful for all of the blessings she and their family had. Noemi Grassi didn't have a phony bone in her body, and raised her sons to be the same.

Yet Gio and Dante were magnets for women who pretended they were one thing but were really another. Francesca being the state-of-the-art, and most costly, example. After her deception, Gio made a firm decision never to trust a woman ever again. It was ironic that now he was sitting across from a woman most definitely out to deceive, yet her reasoning was understandable. And he appreciated that she had come clean to him. In a strange way, now he thought of himself as her confidant. Partner in crime.

"I do have to marry him. The wedding is set. Invitations were sent long ago. The dinner menu has been selected. An ugly dress has been created. In fact, it was that horrible dress that pushed me into this trip. Once I saw myself all bound up in that lace like it was ropes of bondage, I decided it was now or never to claim something for myself."

"What if you didn't go back after the three weeks?"

"I have to. I owe it to my father. I'll be surprised if I even get the three weeks. I don't doubt that he has already contacted palace security and blueprints are being drawn up as to how to find me."

Gio winced when he thought of how that must be for her. Essentially a prisoner of her crown. Not permitted to be the schoolteacher she said she wanted to be. Not able to choose who, and if, she wanted for her husband. Bound by obligation to put the throne first, and herself second.

"How would anyone find you after that careful escape you executed?"

"You have no idea the lengths my father would go to." Luciana licked her top lip. "But in my letter to him I promised that I would stay safe and return, and remain in service to our people all the days of my life."

Gio would be in service to his family for the rest of his life, too. Although not unwillingly. However, he would have preferred to stay in the vocation that he loved. To create new products, to get lost in the mathematics, in the scientific discovery of hypothesis and proof. Now he would stand as the voice and face of the Grasstech empire. Analyze operations. Maintain a dedicated and productive staff. Make decisions about expansions and new territories. He would do it, with authority and justice, even if he had a tad of reluctance. Whatever his family needed, he would deliver.

While Luciana had an arranged union that she was loathe to undertake but must, Gio would trudge his road alone. In his parents, he witnessed the kind of love and partnership that dreams were made of. His parents were romantic, with genuine well-wishes and support for each other every day of their lives. Most important, they were friends who trusted each other completely. Gio never expected to see any of that in his lifetime.

Yet for reasons he didn't quite grasp, it bothered Gio that Luciana belonged to another. No one should be forced to live out their days with someone they didn't love. It was wrong.

Gio's phone buzzed in his pocket. He read Samuele's text out loud. "Not a decent hotel room to be had, with several large business conventions in town."

Luciana's face fell.

"Why don't you stay here while you are in Florence? You see I have room." What else could he do but take her in? If this was to be her one big hurrah before a life devoted to what others wanted for her, the least he could do was watch over her and try to keep her safe. Yes, because she was a princess. Yes, because she was a sheltered young woman who might not know how to avoid the menaces that anyone faced when traveling alone. And yes, because there was something special about her that had touched his heart.

Of course it didn't make sense, his urge to take her into his arms and kiss away any past and future. To bear her burdens. To take away everything other than this courtyard and the moon and the moment.

"And I can show you around a bit." Getting off the computer and out among the human race would be good for him. And would make him a better leader, too. He needed to take the long view of his well-being now that he was the company's CEO.

Gio didn't know what was prompting him to get so involved in this young woman's trip to Florence. Maybe it was only that he spent so much time alone, it was a breath of fresh air to talk and walk with Luciana. And he sensed that she needed him. Which felt strangely good. But after learning the hard way from Francesca that he couldn't trust anyone, it was essential not to get close. There was something so virtuous and sweet-natured about Luciana, it would be easy to forget that vow. Fortunately, she'd be in his life for only a short time.

"Hello, Viggo." Gio's driver met Luciana in front of the villa. After he'd secured her into the car and pulled away she asked, "Where are we going?"

"Signor Gio asked me to leave it as a surprise."

When Luciana had woken up this morning and stepped out onto the Juliet balcony of her room, Gio was nowhere to be seen. Which she had to admit was more than a little disappointing. The day before, she'd relished such a lovely breakfast with her handsome host. She was hoping for a repeat.

From the balcony, she had looked down on the courtyard and eyed a tray set with a coffee thermos and what looked like a plate of food under a cloth napkin. After a shower, she dressed and made her way downstairs.

Upon closer inspection of the tray, Luciana found that

it also held a single pink rose in a vase. Which made her heart skip a beat. She'd been given hundreds of elaborate flower arrangements and bouquets, whether at ceremonial processionals or formal introductions or sent to the palace. Yet she couldn't think of a flower she'd seen in her life that was as charming as that one rose on her breakfast tray. Because she knew it had come from Gio, and the mere fact that he had thought to include it brought a swell to her chest.

It wasn't merely out of respect for her title that he'd had the thought. Was it simply the gesture of a man who was innately hospitable? Or a man who appreciated the beauty of nature and thought to adorn the tray with a stem picked from the villa's garden? Or was it something else entirely? A time-honored gentlemanly practice of a man giving a flower to a woman as an act of romance?

Surprising herself with that thought, Luciana swallowed hard as she touched the velvety petals of the rose. Gio wasn't wooing her. And romance was never in the picture for Princess Luciana de la Isla de Izerote. Her parents and grandparents, and all the royal couples throughout Izerote's history, were beholden to the monarchy. Each and every one of the marriages had been carefully considered during meetings around a table between the male elders.

Some of the women in her lineage got lucky. Stories were passed down about her great-grandmother meeting her great-grandfather. At first, they clashed. He was a traditional man who concerned himself with laws and war. Whereas her great-grandmother was a nurturer, wanting to improve the lives of the poorest citizens of the island and a great lover of animals. It seemed they'd have nothing in common, and her great-grandmother grew quite sad.

Within a few years, three children were born. Luciana's great-grandfather fell in love with his children and their carefree pursuits of play and pleasure. Through those children, he and her great-grandmother fell in love with each other, some six years after they walked down the aisle at their wedding to each other as complete strangers.

It was important for Luciana to hope for the best. Maybe she'd find a camaraderie with Agustin. Or she'd uncover a good side of him. They might even become friends. She doubted she'd fall in love like her great-grandmother had in her arranged marriage. But romantic love wasn't necessary. The merger between the two islands was what mattered.

Luciana pulled back the napkin on the tray to see the same breakfast of rolls and fruit that she and Gio had lingered over the day before.

She thought of her grandmother and mother. They hadn't fared as well as her great-grandmother in their marriages to domineering men who did not allow their wives any independence or private pursuits. She remembered her mother's blank stare, that of a woman who was only going through the motions of her day. Although she knew her mother had loved her for the eleven years they'd shared together, even as a young girl Luciana could sense that something was wrong. Her mother fulfilled her obligations, but the deep corrosive peeling in her gut was too high a price to pay.

Harsh King Agustin had already informed Luciana that he expected her to begin producing heirs immediately and, in as many words, told her that a condition of his agreement with her father was the promise of her complete obedience. The thought of reporting to him as a servant was repulsive. Hopefully, in time, he'd come to see her more as a partner.

He would never set her heart on fire. Agustin would never on a whim present his wife with a single pink rose. Still, they'd find a coexistence she would come to terms with.

Luciana lifted the rose out of the vase and brought it to her nose to fully immerse herself in its lovely scent, the sweetness of the gesture and, most important, the man who had presented it to her. How they had sat here last night drinking herbal tea until the wee hours. She'd shared the story of her journey after assuming that she'd never tell it, that it would be a secret she'd take to her grave. Gio was so easy to talk to and listened attentively to everything she said rather than simply waiting for her to go silent so that he could resume talking like all of the other men she knew. They talked and talked and talked until they could barely keep their heads up.

After revealing her true identity to him, she assumed he would want her to leave his villa. Instead, after the shock, he seemed to understand her predicament. The backward ways of Izerote infuriated him. He was willing in his own small way to aid her on her voyage of discovery by offering her a safe haven.

Frankly overwhelmed by the incidents with the jewelry and the boys chasing after her and the lack of available hotel rooms, his kindly invitation was a relief she gratefully agreed to.

There was one other matter, too. The idea of spending time in Florence with a handsome, intelligent and free-thinking man was simply too exciting to pass up. What a thrilling ride this had already become!

As she sat down to eat her breakfast, she wondered what time Gio had left this morning, as it was still early. He'd left a note.

Viggo will pick you up at five o'clock to meet me for more of your sightseeing tour. Casual dress. Until then, Gio.

Now as Luciana was being driven through the streets of Florence to meet him, she kept replaying that *until then* salutation on the note. There was something incredibly alluring about those words.

She spent the entire ride trying to talk herself out of those thoughts. Certainly there would never be anything amorous between her and Gio. It was just an isolated girl's fantasies starting to spin out of control. She was about to be married, she was in Florence for three weeks and Gio was going through a transition, as well. He'd already declared that he was single and planned on staying that way. She felt guilty and wrong even having those thoughts about him.

But Gio had no idea what he'd done. Last night, she had satisfied a years-old yearning to visit the Piazza della Signoria, to sit in that storied square in the evening air. A scene she never could have imagined she'd be sharing with a man. One like him, no less. With his imposing six-foot-three-inch height and slim muscular build. The most bewitching eyes, blue as the midday sky. And that fascinating tousle of blond curls that she could convince herself wanted to have her fingers thread through them.

Something she knew wasn't the case and wouldn't be in a million years.

Although it was nothing she could have planned, the evening was infinitesimally better in his company. Unfortunately, it was an evening so perfect it made her wish. And there was no place for wishes in the life of Her Royal Highness Princess Luciana de la Isla de Izerote.

Viggo pulled the car over to the curb and Gio appeared to open her door and hold out an arm for her to take hold of. *"Buonasera."*

"Where are we going?" Luciana eagerly inquired, not used to surprises. That was another part of life as a princess. There was no spontaneity. Ever. A royal's life was plotted and protected from any intrusion that might throw off the organization. Plans were very important. People had to be notified, schedules had to be coordinated, itineraries had to be created. This rigidity was, of course, necessary to keep the palace running smoothly. "Your driver wouldn't tell me."

"Tonight, I'll show you one of my favorite pleasures from my adolescence. After dinner, we'll walk along the Arno River."

Luciana looked down at her dress shoes. They were made for appearances at children's charities, not for treading the streets of an ancient city.

Observing her hesitation, he said, "In my note, I suggested that you dress casual."

"This is as casual as I get." In fact, when the princess assessed the few outfits she had brought in search of the least formal, the best she'd come up with was a skirt that hit her midcalf paired with a lightweight jacket.

After nicking a suitcase for the trip from the palace storage room, she'd filled it with the only clothes she had. Dresses that were suitable for diplomatic luncheons and others for garden brunches. A few cocktail dresses for dinner. Luciana did not even own one pair of slacks. A princess worth her salt would never be caught wearing them.

"I see," Gio said as his mind shuffled through a thought.

"I'm curious about you." She gestured at his outfit. "This is the second time I've seen you in a jacket and tie with jeans. That's acceptable in your business?"

"I own fine bespoke suits. But yes, I work in jeans."

Obviously, she couldn't mention just how good he looked in said ensemble. This was a man who had a personal style and didn't care what anyone thought of it. He was unlike anyone she'd ever met before.

"I think we ought to buy you some jeans right now."

"Oh, no, I couldn't."

"So you'd stow away on a boat in the middle of the night, sell your family's jewels, sleep on trains to get to Italy, but you won't wear a pair of jeans?"

They both laughed. For Luciana, it was laugh or cry, and she'd done her fair share of the latter.

"You're an interesting study in contradictions," Gio pressed on. "Come on, I know of a shop near here."

He was going to take her shopping for casual clothes? Appearances were a big deal to royalty. They weren't supposed to look like commoners. The strict manner of dress garnered respect. She was again wearing the blond wig disguise, half assuming that operatives of her father were searching for her. The hair was enough of a change.

Yet she wasn't representing Izerote here in Florence. No one knew who she was other than Gio. Her heart began to beat double time. Walking the streets of Florence, both of them in jeans like a typical couple on a holiday? Simple denim was taking on a larger meaning. Maybe she really was pulling off the one thing she thought she'd never be entitled to. To know, just for a short moment in time.

Freedom.

Gio crooked his arm like he had last night, encouraging her to follow where he led. Silvery flashes almost dizzied her as she slipped her arm into his, opening her palm flat against the taut muscles of his biceps.

"Let's go, Princess."

CHAPTER FOUR

"I'VE NEVER BEEN in a shop like this," Luciana gushed when she and Gio stepped in off the street. Pinching herself, because she was surely living out a fantasy, in a busy boutique that sold everyday clothes to Florentine women, not tourists. It was as if she had inhabited someone else's body.

"You've never been to a clothing shop?"

"Not like this. Clothes are generally sent to the palace. Occasionally, we go to Paris or Milan to visit a designer's atelier. The building is cleared out and, of course, I'm accompanied by style associates, palace dressers and at least three bodyguards. I don't think I've ever in my life trolled through a rack of clothes on a sales floor."

"Have at it, Princess."

"Can I ask you a favor?" she whispered.

"Certainly."

"Will you call me Luci, like you did when I first introduced myself to you? I'm sure it's not anything anyone else would understand, but I love the idea of just having a regular first name without all of the pomp."

Gio's eyes smiled into hers, producing a hot whoosh that flowed right through her. It wasn't a sensation she was familiar with and, frankly, it was terrifying. Of all things, what she most wanted to do was kiss him. Right on that gorgeous mouth of his. She'd never kissed a man on the lips. Nor was she going to now, but apparently when in Florence in the company of the most unexpected of tour guides, a girl could imagine almost anything.

"Shop, Luci." Had he somehow read her thoughts, because he redirected her to their purpose in the store? He knew as well as she did that they could never kiss. Ever since she'd met him a mere two days ago, she'd already had to mentally repeat to herself a hundred times that this extraordinary man had landed in her life, but that it would be for only three weeks and then never again. She was about to be married and that was that.

Now, to the matter at hand.

Luci surveyed the shop in action. The customers were mostly women, a few with bored men obediently accompanying them. A couple of the women combed the racks with great seriousness, methodically considering every item as they moved down the aisle. Perhaps they were on the hunt for something in a particular size or color. That was another thing Luciana had never practiced, as the size and color of her clothes were always preselected for her.

Some of the shoppers had items draped over one arm as they worked through the offerings with their other. Another behavior Luciana had never known. Servants and handmaidens were always at the ready in the princess's life, lest she ever have the need to lift a finger.

The store carried a range from what she assumed would be office attire, to resort wear, to casual clothes.

"There are the jeans." Gio looked up from his phone and pointed her to a display case that held dozens of pairs folded onto shelves. He tugged her by the hand and led her to the assortment. One stack held the darkest of blues, azure as the midnight ocean. Others were a lighter wash. Others still had tears at the knees, a lived-in look that Luciana had never really understood when she saw it on fashion websites. The jeans styles were listed, as well. There was boot cut, straight leg, skinny and something called boyfriend.

With Gio holding her hand, seeing the word *boyfriend* spelled out in front of her made her lungs drain of air.

"Everything okay?" Gio perceived the change in her face.

"Actually, I don't think I should do this. I'm only here temporarily. I can make do with what I brought."

"Don't you want some comfortable clothes to explore the city in? If you're concerned about the cost, I accept diamonds."

This time his humor was not well received, as Princess Luciana was beginning to feel very uneasy. "I'm not comfortable doing this."

"Your subjects aren't here. No one knows you in Florence. Didn't you say you'd always wanted to wear a pair of jeans?"

As she'd told Gio on the walk to the shop, she'd had one meeting with a pair of jeans. A princess from a neighboring island, one with less old-fashioned ways, had come to Izerote to attend a diplomatic function. Luciana explained her predicament and begged the other princess to leave the pair of jeans she had brought along. Within twenty-four hours, a palace housekeeper had found the jeans in Luciana's closet, assumed that a laborer had accidentally left them behind and promptly discarded them. Luciana never even had a chance to put them on.

"I suppose I could try a pair on."

"That's right."

"What do you think boyfriend jeans are?"

Gio summoned over a saleswoman who explained the relaxed fit of the boyfriend cut. While he tended to business, she assisted Luciana in finding a couple of sizes that were likely to fit, and showed her into the changing room. It was yet another first for her to take off her clothes alongside other shoppers, each woman separated only by a privacy curtain.

She knew perfectly well that both girls and women the world over would have their own fantasies fulfilled if they got to try on Princess Luciana's ball gowns and tiaras. Yet the sound of metal against metal that the zipper made as Luciana pulled up the jeans gave her a special joy. Biting her lip, she allowed her eyes to slowly move up toward the mirror until she could get a good view of herself.

Wow. For the first time she could ever recall, she saw herself as just a young woman. Who might have borrowed her boyfriend's jeans, which fit loose around the hips and seat as they were intended to. She loved the heaviness of the denim, understanding why jeans were popularized by cowboys and miners.

But she couldn't traipse all over Florence in jeans! They were too unceremonious. Even if no one else knew she was a princess, she'd know. About to take them off and at least treasure the memory of being in this shop on this day, she decided to show them to Gio.

"Luci!" Gio nodded his approval as she exited the dressing room to model for him. She knew there wasn't anything particularly flattering about the jeans, but she wanted him to see her like a normal girl, wanted to keep them on for just a little bit longer. *"Bravissima."*

"Do they look good?" she asked in a quiet voice.

"Turn around."

Turn around? Gio Grassi, tech wizard and almost complete stranger, had just ordered Her Royal Highness Princess Luciana de la Isla de Izerote to circle around in a pair of jeans so he could examine her behind in them?

But that didn't stop her from obeying his command. And deriving a wicked satisfaction from doing so.

"Well?" she challenged.

"You look like a city girl on the go. What do *you* think?"

"They're so comfortable. And the fabric is so weighty. It makes me feel like…like my own person."

"We'll buy two pairs. You'll need tops and shoes, as well."

"No. I can't. It's not right. Trying them on was enough."

The princess glanced outside through the store window and noticed that there were two men in black suits standing near the entrance. Both wore earpieces that they spoke into. For a moment, she panicked that they were palace security from Izerote. That her father had already located her whereabouts and she was moments from being whisked back home.

If that was to happen, she steeled herself, darned if she wasn't going to first do some of what she came to Florence for.

"Thank you, Gio. I would love to buy these clothes."

"And don't worry. You're not getting anything for free. When we go to dinner, I'm going to need you to earn your keep."

Gio was happy to see that the rooftop restaurant he remembered atop a five-story building along the Arno River was still in business. With a view of the river and its many bridges, including the famous Ponte Vecchio, the trattoria was one of those secret-treasure restaurants that Florentines hoped no tourist would ever discover. Thankfully, it remained a low-key family establishment with an easygoing dress code.

Because now Her Royal Highness Princess Luciana, who had looked so dignified in the silken dinner dresses she'd worn the last two nights, was unfussy and relaxed in her new jeans, flat shoes and a T-shirt. She fit in fine with the young mothers out with girlfriends, and city workers, who unwound from their busy days with a glass of prosecco at the restaurant. Surely, no one would mistake her for nobility.

"Oh, my. This view is splendid."

As Gio took it in, he agreed. The red-roofed buildings, one after the next, lined the banks of the river and its stone bridges. Firenze was truly like nowhere else. Although it did occur to him that the sight of Luciana's face, with the sweet mouth and enthusiastic eyes as she took in the vista, was as stunning as the view itself.

At the office, he'd spent the day swamped with work. And could have put in several more hours. So he'd almost regretted having promised to take Luciana out tonight. Even though he had offered, he didn't really have time to play tour guide and rearrange his schedule. This was why he shouldn't spend time alone with women. The pheromones, or whatever it was they gave off, clouded his judgment. And he had a feeling that Luciana's pheromones had particular powers.

It had been entertaining helping her shop for those jeans. He shared her agony in buying them, though, knowing they represented more than a bit of cloth to her. In fact, his jaw tensed at the fact that something as simple as selecting her own clothes was an exception to her, not the norm.

The river glistened below as twilight was beginning to sweep the sky above, the open air taking on darkness. This was Gio's third dinner with Luciana. Considering he hadn't had dinner alone with a woman even once in the past few months, that was quite a record.

Lately, he'd been spending time immersed in development of some new biometric products. Generally when mealtimes rolled around he would ask for something to be brought in, as he was far too engrossed in his work to be bothered with leaving his desk. Or the whole team would go out for a late-night meal where beers and spicy food were eagerly consumed amid plenty of noise and clamor. He had no objection to either, although Luciana's lips, which appeared so pink in the softness of dusk, made him doubt that more pleasing company had ever existed.

Gio ordered wine and nibbles.

"You mentioned needing my help," Luciana said as she tore her eyes away from the river.

"Yes. I appreciated the suggestion you gave me about writing that press statement. To sandwich the hacking incident in between more positive news about the business. I hope the net effect was to put the matter in perspective."

"Do you think it did?"

"Somewhat. But the tech world is calling for details about the hack. Although fortunately no metadata was leaked, top secret information was breached. As leaders in the field, Grasstech always comes forward with information that could assist the entire industry."

"So you want to reveal more about what happened?"

Even though Luciana was involved in her own kind of deception, he held no ill feelings toward her like he did for Francesca, who'd misled him for her own personal gain.

Still, he had to remember never to tell Luciana anything truly confidential.

"Grasstech's advisers are pushing for this idea that I do an interview with the leading computer industry security magazine and talk about the hack from a strictly technological standpoint."

"Getting out in front of it rather than having the press snoop around is probably a good idea."

"And I have a live-stream chat scheduled with the computer science department at a local university. As you noted about my daily uniform—" he gestured down the length of his chest and then leg "—sitting bent over a computer all day, I don't give much thought to what I'm wearing. I put on a tie as a nod to my authority."

An appetizing plate of grilled vegetables and another of cheeses was delivered to the table. Both Luciana and Gio reached for a morsel.

"Are you suggesting we switch roles now? You've put me in jeans and now you want my help becoming camera ready?"

"Exactly."

"Ironic."

She smiled one of her bashful grins, as if she was sharing a joke only with herself. He supposed that the last thing she'd expected to be doing in Florence was giving public relations lessons to a techie billionaire.

"I'm all ears."

"All right, I've got an easy one for you. Take the jacket you have on right now, for example." She pointed to the blazer he wore tonight atop his starched shirt and Milanese tie. "Button it."

Gio followed her instructions.

"Now sit up very straight. Then reach behind you and tug down at the waist so that the shoulders stiffen back farther than they normally would."

Again, he did as she suggested.

Luciana approved.

"Now you have sharp, crisp lines. Very authoritative. And you can get the photographer or assistant to clip the jacket in back so it stays that way."

"I'll use that. Thank you."

This was a competent, and even confident, young woman. What a shame that her position wouldn't allow her to pursue whatever ambition she had. Gio could hardly imagine being held back intellectually. That might be a fate worse than death. Fortunately with the encouragement of his loving parents, he'd found the calling he loved in the computer sciences. Even if he had to turn to more administrative matters, he would still keep his hand in the product design he was so apt at.

"Could we have cappuccinos?" Luci asked.

"Certainly." Gio chuckled. The princess wanted a cappuccino while most of the women he'd ever known wanted far more. His money. Or his reputation. Or his secrets.

"What's funny?"

For an instant he looked at the woman sitting across from him as Luci, whom he was out with for an ordinary dinner date like many others around them in the restaurant. Where people came to talk about their days, or the tomorrows ahead of them. Where they didn't just eat a meal, but shared a human experience. They connected.

Would he ever make space for a personal life? His constant travel had been a deterrent to any long-term liaison. That was how he professed to want it, but was that really true? Or was he hiding from having to learn how to share himself with another, how to meet the demands of a relationship without diminishing his work?

There had been women here and there. If he was being honest, it was only to satiate bodily desires. Then he met Francesca. And became transfixed by her prowess of tech smarts combined with the looks of a film noir movie star from the 1940s in her dark clothes and red lips. Not unlike those old movies, it turned out she was a spy in disguise.

Gio had been duped. Perhaps his childhood was too idyllic, with parents who taught him to value honesty and candor. Trust. It was what he expected of others. Which proved to be a mistake he'd never make twice.

Peering left to right, he knew that no one in the restaurant would have any idea that Luciana was a princess. So while his pretty dinner companion had revealed her true identity to him, she still attempted to fool the city of Florence and Gio would remember a hard-learned lesson. Never let anyone get to him again.

After their delicious dinner, Luciana and Gio took a long walk along the banks of the Arno. He told her the name of each of the bridges that linked the two sides of the city. As they walked over the Ponte alla Carraia, they stopped to lean over the parapet and could make out the outlines of their reflections in the glistening waters.

They were silent for a spell in the glow of the night, after a dinner filled with interesting conversation. About the possibilities of technology. About the advances in communication, scientific research and the globalization of business. But also about the dangers of piracy and impostors on social media. The sharing of ideas made Luciana think of the great minds that had passed through this city over the centuries.

Although Her Royal Highness often sat in on meetings where matters such as improving the technology on the island were discussed, she was rarely asked her opinion. Plus, the conferences never motivated her father to take any action, and the island remained hopelessly behind the rest of the world. She wished futilely that she could bring some of Gio's heightened thinking and know-how back with her when she returned. But she'd be far too busy regrouping from her trip here, begging her father's forgiveness and marching toward her wedding day.

Still leaning over the side of the bridge, Luciana judged her image reflected in the water. She was wearing the straight blond shoulder-length wig that disguised her long and thick brown curls. Between the hair and the jeans—and, of course, Gio—her time in Florence couldn't be more different from what it was on the island. She recalled a cute expression she'd read in a magazine: people referring to a situation with the acronym YOLO. *You only live once.*

After listening to the quiet swish of the river in the dark of night, Luciana was ready to talk some more.

"You're so lucky that you developed that genuine interest in technology without your parents forcing you to follow into the company if you didn't want to."

"I am at that. My parents told Dante and I that they'd never want to sell the business but that if we decided to pursue something else, they'd let others run Grasstech."

"Your parents sound like wise people."

"You say you'd like to be a teacher. Why aren't you allowed any vocation outside of the monarchy? Plenty of members of royal families have careers."

"None of the women in my family have, and my father won't permit it. For heaven's sake, I'm not even supposed to be wearing jeans!"

She couldn't blame everything on her father. Always wanting to please him and not cause him any more pain after her mother died, Luciana had often kept her mouth shut when she should have spoken up. And so outdated customs perpetuated.

"I couldn't bear the lack of liberty."

"This is the only existence I've ever known. I don't mean to sound critical. Of course, to be royalty is an unparalleled honor and I have many experiences few other people do. It's just that all we ever do in Izerote, really, is walk in place. I fear the world is passing my people by."

"Hence, the tourism that your fiancé will bring."

Luciana cringed at hearing Gio say the word *fiancé*. Somehow it sounded even more undesirable coming out of *his* mouth.

The princess had never been allowed to date. If she had, Gio was exactly the type of man she would have gravitated toward. An intellectual. An iconoclast. Someone without walls to his imagination. Who was determined, and knew how to achieve his goals. A man who was receptive, fair, considerate and could have a laugh at the world.

What was she doing? She didn't even really know this man and suddenly she was able to list his attributes? *While you're at it, Luci, don't forget drop-dead sexy!*

In fantasy, she could envision him as the perfect man and even make him hers. But in real life, he could be in a relationship. Married, even. He could have a girlfriend, a wife and even children in Hong Kong or Mumbai or any of the other places he mentioned working from recently.

Perhaps they were waiting for him to get everything settled in Florence before he sent for them.

Somehow, she didn't think so. It sounded as if he'd come to distrust the people around him. Probably even more so after that hack. As a matter of fact, he could be running some kind of charade of his own and she'd never be the wiser. She'd be smart not to forget that Gio Grassi was merely an unexpected addition to what was already a dream, but definitely one that she would wake up from.

Once again, she had to remind herself to remain optimistic about her future. Duty had its own rewards even if it was sometimes hard to see it that way.

Gio gently nudged her arm with his elbow, sensing that sadness was beginning to take her over. She half smiled in return.

"It won't be so bad," he said softly. "It sounds as if you love children. Even if you can't be a teacher, at least you will soon have some of your own."

"Yes, but what will I be birthing them into? The isolation of the palace?"

"They'll have you. You'll teach them to understand a larger world."

Luciana's eyes blinked back tears. Everything Gio said was so supportive. And she was so aware of not wanting to give the impression that she was ungrateful. Yet she burned inside for more to her life. To challenge her brain, to stretch her soul, even to explore her body.

There was a wedding night to come when her virginity would be taken for the purpose of breeding. Yet she knew that marital relations could involve more than the obligation to her monarchy.

From reading novels and watching movies, she could fathom carnal longings. She'd had vibrations in her body that hinted at pleasure, that even promised ecstasy. The way her breath had stuttered when Gio had placed his palm on the small of her back as he'd ushered her into the restaurant this evening. The way he always offered the crook of his arm for her to take, which forced her body to brush against his, making her swoon a bit each time.

She'd implored herself to shut down those reactions to him. They were highly improper.

However, the battle was being lost.

Standing on the bridge with him right now, she could hardly contain herself. She wanted him to grab hold of her, to take her into his arms with a male urgency that was savage. That knew her not as a princess but as a woman made of flesh and blood.

Not willing to settle any longer for only the reflection of him in the river's water, she turned to face him and he followed suit. She gazed into his eyes that shone like stars in the night.

As if reading her mind, he bent down toward her face and softly kissed her lips. His touch might have been light but a thousand sensations shimmered down her body, waking every inch of her.

Not willing to stop there, she stood up on her tiptoes to bring her lips to his a second time. She felt her softness melt against his firm mouth to share another stolen kiss. Knowing that she should back away, she instead opened her mouth slightly, to know the kind of kiss she'd read about in books and seen in movies. A lover's kiss, only for him. Which joined them and made her wish it was forever.

Her knees went weak.

As hard as it was, she finally pulled apart from him. He reached to twirl a lock of her hair in his hand. And then abruptly let it drop from his fingers. "I forgot you were wearing a wig."

"It looks real but it's artificial to the touch."

"I shouldn't have kissed you. I'm terribly sorry."

"I wanted you to. I kissed you in return." They looked at each other in anticipation. Of what? "It can't happen again."

"I know."

Their eyes locked for what might have been minutes or it might have been hours.

Finally, they had to break their gaze and returned to looking down into the river.

"Do you dislike my wig?"

"I'll admit I was shocked when you removed it to show me your natural hair."

"It's as if I'm someone else when I wear it." Someone who would kiss a man she was so attracted to she might have burst out of her skin if she didn't. "I like it."

"You should keep wearing it, then, Luci. You should do whatever you want to do."

Those were words Luciana heard so seldom she could hardly make sense of them. Do what she wanted to do? Right now what she was dying to do was to kiss this amazing man again. In this most romantic of places. Under the dark skies and atop this ancient bridge.

However, she'd settle for wearing the new clothes and the wig, playing a game of reverse dress-up.

And she'd savor having heard Gio utter words she never expected to hear.

You should do whatever you want to do.

CHAPTER FIVE

PRINCESS LUCIANA LINGERED across the street from the hair salon for the longest time. Watching the activity, she observed as women entered through its heavy glass door. Other women exited, and Luciana found herself imagining what their hair might have looked like earlier that morning. How many were just getting a trim of the style they had been wearing for a long time, a hairdo that their family and friends and coworkers were quite used to? Or were some experimenting with entirely new haircuts and colors, reinventing themselves from the hair down? Would they go home to compliments from their partners, or would their kids make fun of Mommy's new look?

Were the women leaving the shop happy with their new hair, or would they look in the mirror later in the day and bemoan that they had made a terrible mistake? Would they seek consolation from their sister or best friend, who would convince them that it would grow out soon enough?

Luciana thought she could stand there all day and contemplate the women of Florence, their lives and their loves. And their hair.

Luci would dash across the street, bound through the salon door and declare exactly how she wanted her hair done. Luciana wasn't so bold. When she did finally cross the street, it was slow and tentative, half of her not believing that her arm was actually pulling the handle of the door. In one fell swoop she opened it, hunching over a bit so that no one would see as she quickly yanked the blond wig off her head and stuffed it into her jacket pocket. Her own long curls fell down all around her face.

"May I help you?" a receptionist at the front desk greeted her. She'd obviously not seen the princess's slick move to remove her wig. The dark-haired woman, with a pen in one hand and a phone in the arch of her shoulder, juggled many activities.

"I'd like to get a haircut and color," Luciana murmured tentatively above the pounding electronic music and echoing chatter in the modern shop. It was designed with beige furnishings and bamboo trees presumably to give it a Zen sort of look that was totally incongruous with the decibel level of noise.

"Say it again, sweetheart," the receptionist requested.

"Cut and color, please," Luciana said a little louder.

"I have Gabriel available."

The woman pushed a button on a console. Luciana flipped through one of the hairstyle books on the counter and chose a photo of a cut that looked exactly like the wig she'd been wearing. Within a few minutes a slim young man with bleached white hair and many bracelets on one arm approached. Luci thought him very fashionable and excitedly told her inner Luciana not to be frightened. This was a good idea.

"*Carina!* Gorgeous face," Gabriel said as he took Luciana by the hand and brought her to his salon chair, fourth in the line of eight along the long wall. The chairs were white leather with a silver-studded pattern around the edges that, ironically, made them resemble thrones. A bite to the lip helped Luci hold back a giggle. Each throne faced a large mirror and shelves that held combs, scissors and other tools of the trade. "Take a seat. We'll talk before we cut."

"That's a relief."

Gabriel lifted her mane of hair and wove it in his fingers. "Healthy. Thick and glossy. But kind of like a child, long without a style, right?"

"Yes!" Luci exclaimed. "I have had my long hair as it is for my entire life." Just as her mother had worn her own long hair. Natural, perhaps brushed back from her face with a headband or arranged to complement a tiara.

"We need something modern," Gabriel said as he examined all of Luciana's hair, "and chic, right?"

"I'll show you," she piped up and showed him the photo from the salon book. "This."

"Blond. Shoulder length. Yes, this will look splendid on you." With a quick sweep, he gathered up all Her Royal Highness Princess Luciana's hair and grasped it in one hand. With the other, he reached for a pair of scissors from his workstation and held them in the air. "Are you ready?"

"Yes," Luci answered for Luciana, who was speechless and terrified.

"I'll take off some of the length and then we'll truly begin."

"Do it," Luci eagerly agreed in anticipation. Luciana clenched both her teeth and her fists.

With just a couple of snips, Gabriel cut a good six inches from the length of hair and let it fall from his hands. He and Luci and Luciana all watched as it hit the black salon floor.

Luciana's mouth dropped open in shock.

"Can I offer you a coffee?" Gabriel asked.

"Absolutely," she answered without hesitation.

As Gabriel worked his ministrations on her locks, Luciana reflected on how this trip had turned into much more than what she bargained for. Not only was she cutting her hair and wearing pants and touring Florence at her leisure, something far more important had happened. A six-foot-three-inch something, to be exact.

Jeans fade and hairstyles grow out, but meeting Gio would linger with her for the rest of her days. Last night on the bridge was surely the most romantic interlude she could possibly conceive of. The way they watched each other's reflection in the water. How they turned to stare into each other's eyes. Then he'd kissed her. What's more, she'd kissed him back. A real kiss!

Which they'd immediately backed away from. Both understanding that nothing more could ever happen between them. Knowing that what already had happened was too much.

They'd stood in the courtyard of the villa when they'd returned from the river, neither of them wanting to go to bed. In that prolonged good-night, a piece of Luciana died. She'd realized the totality of what she would never have. This swirling dream she was dancing in could last for a few weeks, but that's all it would ever be, a milky vision to reflect back on like a photo in a memory album. That was all she'd be taking home with her.

Sleep had eluded her. It was too grand not to recall over and over again their walk along the banks of the river. The way they chatted and discoursed, even argued, about everything they could think of from politics to art history to the evolution of Grasstech. Gio's family was so progressive. They thought far and wide. They took bold chances and weren't afraid to fail.

Princess Luciana wished she'd grown up with people like that around her. Her mother had been, effectively, silenced long before she gave birth to a daughter. While in her heart she had the utmost respect for her father's decisions to preserve Izerote's natural beauty and its idyllic way of life, that wasn't what Luciana would have chosen for herself.

"Finito," Gabriel chirped with a flourish as he lifted a hand mirror to show Luciana the finished job. Luci smiled from ear to ear because it looked exactly as the wig did, but now it was hers. It belonged to her. She could float up on angel wings for her hair felt as light as a feather without the weight of its former length down her back. The color was dramatic and sophisticated. Luci complimented Luciana on looking like a self-assured young woman, no longer a little girl.

Thankfully, Gio had insisted on giving her some money to keep in her pocket, so she was able to pay for the salon services.

Gio said he'd take a lunchtime break to show her one of Florence's most visited sights, the original statue of *David* at the Galleria dell'Accademia. Viggo would pick her up in front of the villa soon. She decided to wander in what was essentially *her* neighborhood now. A bench at a small park beckoned, where she took in the noonday sun, let the rays shine through her new hair and replayed the electrifying kissing from last night.

A child's ball hit her on the leg and snapped her out of her meditations.

"Mi dispiace," a tiny voice apologized as a little boy

came to fetch the ball. Probably about four years old, he had dark corkscrew curls and huge black velvet eyes.

"That's okay. Here you go." Luciana rolled the orange ball back to the boy, who wasn't able to stop it. It passed behind him. The child stood only a few feet from the bench Luciana was sitting on and she had rolled it very slowly on the ground, so it was odd that he had missed it.

"Matteo!" A woman about Luciana's age retrieved the ball and brought it back to the boy. "Try again, bambino." The boy took the ball from her and ran toward the other six or so children in the park.

"Hi, I'm Luci. Do you care for all of them?" Luciana asked the woman.

"I'm Chiara and I suppose you could say that. I'm their teacher." She pointed to a small building attached to a church. "We've come out from the nursery school to play before the children take a nap."

Luciana watched the children, who were now chasing pigeons. She smiled at their lovely faces.

"Do you enjoy being a teacher?" she asked the young woman, whose hair was piled into a loose bun and who wore an airy blouse with a lot of stains on it. Probably everything from paint to clay to jam.

Her Royal Highness often made appearances at schools and children's charities in Izerote. Of course, when she toured a facility she was dressed as a princess and rarely given anything to do but meet the children, who stared at her as if she worked for Disney. Or she might be permitted to do a nonmessy craft with them for five minutes. Nonetheless, she treasured the visits.

While there, she might observe a particular quirk about a child. How one interacted socially, perhaps having trouble when another child was around, or crying at the slightest provocation. How much she wished she could formally study the behavior of children, to play a part in helping them grow up to be fully functioning adults.

"Of course, Luci." Chiara brushed some dirt from her own hands while her eyes never left the children. "To encourage the evolving young minds, to listen to their ideas. What could be better? What do *you* do?"

Obviously, she couldn't reply that she was a princess. "I'm finding my way," she answered wistfully. "I'd love to work with children."

The two women conversed a bit more, both keeping a vigilant eye on the needs of the children. As Chiara had just expressed, to watch each child interact during play held endless fascination for Luciana. While at university, she'd taken classes in child development, but how she longed to earn an advanced degree. To study different styles of learning, gender analysis, social conduct. To make a difference in the lives of precious, unrestrained children.

For a fleeting minute, Luciana felt like Luci, a denizen of this great city. A woman who had a direction and was at ease with herself, and who was in a secure relationship with a wonderful man.

What? Luciana caught her own thought. Even if she were free to love, Gio had made very clear that a serious relationship was most definitely not on his agenda. Last night's spontaneous kisses had probably meant nothing to him. Not only did he need to concentrate on the responsibilities of running an enormous corporation that was on top of its competitors, Gio was a man who lived out of a suitcase without entanglements. Just because he was spending time in Florence didn't mean that was immediately going to change.

Nonetheless, for just an iota longer, Luciana pictured her life as a Florentine schoolteacher in love. Imagining what she was going to cook for her man tonight and the warm embraces she'd have with him in their bed.

The boy with the big doe eyes threw the ball to Luciana again. She tossed it gently back and, again, he missed it.

"Chiara." Luciana leaned in toward her so the boy wouldn't hear. "I don't think he's seeing the ball clearly. Has he had his vision checked? I think he might need eyeglasses."

"That's a good observation, Luci. I will mention it to his parents when they come to pick him up."

After Chiara and the children left, Luci walked home to get ready to sightsee with Gio. Feeling very Luci indeed.

Although Luciana kept insisting that she wanted to see Florence as a typical tourist would, Gio was sure she'd just as soon not queue up for hours to see Michelangelo's *David* at the Accademia. Nor did he have the time to do so. Therefore, he was glad he had asked an assistant to book tickets in advance for a reserved entrance time. As it was he'd had to rearrange several meetings in order to free his schedule for a few hours. It was actually rather ridiculous that he was sightseeing in the middle of the day.

Gio himself hadn't seen what was one of the most visited locations in Europe in many years. He'd forgotten just how imposing and magnificent *David* really was until they approached the statue, ringed by tourists studying the work from all perspectives. The marble champion, who as the story went, was a young shepherd when he slew his powerful opponent, Goliath, with cleverness rather than might, stood raised on a pedestal for all to see.

"Michelangelo was only in his twenties when he carved this," Luciana commented to Gio while they both studied the details. "What an amazing achievement for such a young person."

"In addition to all of the other works he did in his career."

"One of the greatest artists the world has ever known. I've been waiting for so long to see this. Thank you for bringing me here."

"Look at how defined the eye sockets are. That gives him such a look of watchfulness."

"That's what they say about the biblical character it's based on. David has his slingshot there—" she pointed to the detail over his left shoulder "—that he used to defeat Goliath with only five stones."

They moved incrementally around the statue, carved from a single block of marble, observing every minute feature. The prominent veins in David's hands, the rigidity of his muscles, yet his bent left leg suggested the innocence of youth. The work was so well preserved and compelling that it felt as current now as it had been when Michelangelo created it in the early 1500s.

Gio felt himself relaxing. There had been a couple of stressful moments already today when he'd had to make decisions related to the employee structure of the company. People's jobs were on the line and it was up to him, and ultimately only him, to decree what was in the corporation's best interest. Which could be a ruthless job. He'd called his father at the vineyard. They'd discussed it over the phone and come to a decision.

He was especially interested in deciding on a new location for a manufacturing plant to produce his new slate of biometric products. With the dozens and dozens of offices and manufacturing sites Grasstech had amassed, Gio enjoyed bringing new and good-paying jobs to towns or villages whose citizens needed the employment.

"Do we have time to see some of the other works of art here?" Luciana asked after they'd circled David three times.

"I'm all yours."

Luciana looked at him with big eyes as a small smile fought to come across her mouth even though she resisted it with a bite to her lower lip.

Gio fought a grin, too, at the words that had come out wrong. He was hardly all hers, for heaven's sake!

Last night as they'd stood on the bridge, he didn't know what had driven him to kiss her, a move he hadn't been planning and knew he mustn't repeat. But there hadn't been a glimmer of censorship as his head bent down for that split second of contact with lips as pillow-soft as could be. Most unexpectedly, she'd lifted them to kiss him again and hadn't settled for the brief brush he had. No, she'd kissed him like a lover, bold and self-assured. With that, she'd rocked him to his very core.

After they'd lingered in the villa courtyard and finally said good-night, he'd lain awake in bed, high on Luciana. Like she was a drug that sent him levitating above his body. She was like no one he'd ever met, exhilarating and tragic all at once. Thoughts of seeing her again had popped into his head all night long in spite of his telling himself to get to sleep.

Gio had spent so much time alone. Even before the fiasco with Francesca, he'd been only casually dating, never able to see how a woman would fit into his life. A life dedicated to his mind and to creativity would be it for him.

Like many people who entered the world of computer science, he was not especially social by nature. More comfortable inside technology, absorbed in work. Like Michelangelo, who was said to sometimes lie down on the ground in his clothes and boots to sleep in small increments because he worked almost continually and barely ate. Gio understood how it was to get lost in a project, in the painstaking process of solving one problem after the next until he developed a solution.

Even with his parents' nearly sublime marriage as an example, Gio never imagined himself as someone who would settle down with a wife and children. He feared because of the attention he paid to his work that he would never be able to give a family the focus they deserved. Yet spending time with Luciana, it dawned on him that, with the right person, anything was possible.

"I want to see the slaves." Luciana brought him from his musings.

Taking her by the hand, and registering its smallness in his, he snaked through the crowd and led her to another hall in the gallery that held the works usually referred to as the *Prisoners*.

Four of them were on display here and others in museums elsewhere in the world. These Michelangelo works were considered *nonfinito*, or incomplete, although it wasn't known for sure as to whether he had left them unfinished on purpose as a way of explaining his own artistry.

"Michelangelo was quoted as saying something to the effect that he was merely a tool and that the sculptures were already there in the marble. His job was only to carve away what would allow the art to be seen," Luciana said.

"Ah, so we both studied art history at university. It was a good counterbalance for me to the world of science and mathematics."

"I've always been especially drawn to the Italian masters."

The four works were devastating. Each depicted a man who had not yet broken through and was still trapped within the marble. With a leg or a torso or a face not yet visible, they appeared to be half man and half stone.

"Some scholars speculate they represent man's struggle to be free," Luciana added pensively. Her face changed from admiration at the work to something personal and melancholy. Gio guessed it was the idea of being trapped in marble, bound, incomplete, unable to actualize one's full self, that had gotten to her on a profound level.

Out of the corner of his eye, Gio spotted two men wearing black suits who appeared to be looking their way. They didn't hold professional cameras or else he might have suspected that they were paparazzi that recognized Princess Luciana, although she'd told him that she was not a high-profile royal like some. Anyway, with that blond wig she was so enamored of and her new wardrobe of comfortable clothes, he doubted that the press would make the connection.

He dearly hoped that they weren't palace security from Izerote, a possibility that Luciana feared. That her father had been keeping tabs on her all along. That perhaps an arrangement had been made to allow Luciana a couple of days under the delusion that she was on her own when, really, she'd been surveilled by her father's missives all along. Who might pounce on her any minute, thereby ending this expedition that meant so much to her.

Although he was sure he would have detected it previously if they were being followed. Subtly glancing over to the men again, he saw they were now turned away from Gio and Luciana. Perhaps they were just undercover overseers for the gallery.

Strangely, he wanted to protect the princess. Fury bubbled in him as he watched her study the captives in marble, knowing she was in her own prison. Fury at her father and at a faraway land he didn't know, for forcing her to conform to outmoded conventions and gender rules that made no sense to Gio. If only he knew of a way to help Luciana's island of Izerote so that she didn't have to marry the neighboring king.

Why he'd come to care so much about Luciana in such a short time, he didn't know. Maybe it was his general disdain for injustice.

After Luciana had her fill of seeing a few of the other halls of art in the Accademia, they exited. "I can afford a little more time. Let me show you another tourist sight. Did you change something about your wig? It looks nice."

"This is the Ponte Vecchio." Gio swept his arm across the vista of the bridge filled with people.

"It's much different from the ones we saw last night." Luciana studied the bridge that was lined on both sides by shops and structures with windows.

"Centuries ago, it was butchers and fishmongers who sold their wares along this bridge. Now, as you can see, there are galleries and souvenir shops but mainly jewelers."

Indeed, Luciana and Gio walked past one small jewelry shop after the next. Gold, silver and other precious metals beckoned from the outward-facing glass cases the vendors used to attract buyers. Gemstones sparkled. Tourists pointed at items.

"It's an old saying that many a man lost his fortune by taking his wife walking along the Ponte Vecchio," Gio declared.

They observed as a man and a shopkeeper excitedly argued, their arm gestures and shaking heads indicating they had not yet reached a deal. A group of young women pointed at diamond rings from another vendor. Every few storefronts, instead of fine jewels, tables of figurines depicting the statue of *David* were for sale. Little *Davids* meant to sit on a desk as a memento of time spent in Florence. Naked *Davids* on cell phone cases. Luciana smiled wryly. Had she been princess of a larger monarchy, she might have ended up with her own likeness on a coffee mug.

From the bridge, they stopped to watch a sightseeing boat as it made its way underneath.

Gio bent his arm for Luciana to take, and they continued on.

A necklace caught Luciana's eye. Simple silver, its several strands of different lengths created a statement.

"Do you like that?" Gio inquired why she had fixated on that one piece.

"It's only that I have one very much like it."

"Did you sell it in Barcelona?"

"Not that one."

Suddenly, guilt thundered through Luciana's body. Had she completely lost her mind, selling palace jewels? Which technically didn't really belong to her. They were only hers to wear during her reign and would then be gracing her children and their children and so on. What right had she had to sell what wasn't even hers?

Her heartbeat sped to a rapid thump. In coming here, she'd rebelled against her father, who only wished for her protection. He was probably worried sick. If only he would have been more lenient with her, had let her travel, and had encouraged her to study and explore her curiosities. Or if she'd been more defiant, rather than always placating him. Then maybe she wouldn't have gone behind his back to take this drastic action most unfitting to her position. He must be in shock after his obedient daughter, who always thought first of pleasing him, had fled the island just weeks before her wedding! Yet she'd never meant to hurt him.

Absentmindedly, she touched her hair, still surprised by how silky and lightweight it was. Even Gio had complimented her on it today, without knowing why. She'd chosen not to tell Gio about the haircut. Not wanting him to think she'd taken on yet another form of disguise. It occurred to her that with his wealth and status, women left and right must present themselves in ways they think would attract him, whether it was their true selves or not.

Now she thought of her new hair as just another disappointment for her father. It would grow out. Just like the haircut, this crazy adventure would be a blip on her radar. Once she returned home, she'd take her rightful place. This city, the statue of *David*, Gio, would become pale remembrances that were completely incongruous with the life she was to lead.

Perhaps someday she'd return to Florence, to show her children the superlative art or to appear at an official occasion. She'd arrive on a private plane to be met by a limousine, and with bodyguards and palace personnel surrounding her like a butterfly net, she'd be escorted from one building into another. Never breathing fresh air, never strolling the backstreets, never watching children play ball in a park.

And she'd most certainly never, ever keep company with this fascinating and accomplished man who made her see herself as anything but a sequestered dusty relic on an island that no one cared about.

"You're regretting your decision to have sold some of your jewelry?" Gio leaned his head down close to hers as she fixed her gaze on the silver necklace.

"I don't know if I should have come here. I think I've made a terrible mistake."

"You won't regret this. It will help you along your path."

She looked him in the eye. "Why are you such a wise old sage for a techie?"

Gio laughed, a resounding guffaw that bounced through her, making her visualize yet again what it would be like to be married to a man with whom she could talk about big concepts and laugh with a dark sense of humor.

"You've learned about me already, *bellissima*. I have a mind for profound thoughts and no common sense in other matters. Which reminds me, I wanted to ask your opinion about the press statement for our new facility in Dallas."

Along the Ponte Vecchio, they chatted about catch-phrases and wording. Luciana was grateful she had knowledge about *something* that was useful to him. Dealing with the media was a valuable thing her father had taught her, to be careful what she said and did because someone was always watching.

Her arm in Gio's, they sauntered on. She willed the yearning that rose when her body brushed against him to subside. There was no reason to think Gio had those same stirrings in return. He was not looking for love, and would not accept finding it, either. She sensed he'd been hurt by love, although he never went into any detail about it. That kiss between them had been spontaneous, and it was she who prolonged it. Nothing was going to change between them as a result of it.

Which was perfectly okay. In fact, it was essential. He could be relied on to keep her growing emotions in check. Because hers were moving into dangerous waters.

"I really do have to return to the office," he said, "but I'd like to share with you one other important thing that both locals and tourists do after they've been exploring our city's streets."

"What is that?"

"Let me show you."

They reached the opposite end of the Ponte Vecchio. The bridge emptied out to the Oltrarno, the other side of the river, the part of the city that had many historic places to see but was much less touristy.

Her arm in his, Luciana had a feeling she would follow him anywhere. He took her down one quiet street and then made a right into another and another until she thought they were secret agents outwitting evil foes.

With this little dash into the Oltrarno, he had brought them far from the crowds, from the doggy dishes with pictures of *David* on them, and the salt and pepper shakers shaped like the Duomo.

Finally, they reached their destination. Gelateria dei Frediano.

"Gelato, Princess. All the problems of the world could be solved with the right gelato."

He held the door open for her to enter the shop. The smell of fresh cream immediately took her by storm. Patrons sat on ice cream parlor chairs around small marble tables, giving the place a historic vibe. In fact, there was a sign above the old-fashioned cash register that read Established 1929.

Luciana eagerly inspected the cold cases that held silver trays of many flavors of gelato in small batches. From the caramel color to the pale green to the chocolate-studded white, each one promised to be more delicious than the next.

"How could one ever select?" Luciana exclaimed, glancing up to Gio, who had been watching her as she deliberated at the glass cases.

"Pick several. We'll have a tasting menu."

"They all look delectable. You choose."

"Why don't you have a seat over there?" He pointed to an empty table in the far back of the shop.

After a few minutes, Gio joined her with a tray of three small silver dishes, all containing scoops of the creamy treat.

"What did you get?"

"I'll let you guess," Gio said as he sat down and placed the tray on the marble table. "Close your eyes."

"What?"

"Close your eyes so that you can focus only on the taste of the gelato."

She was both entranced and horrified at the suggestions that she should close her eyes here in a public place. But she knew that Luci would think it was fun to shut out the distraction of sight so that she could become intoxicated by the flavors. For her sake, Luciana obliged.

With her eyes closed, she was hyperaware of Gio's presence next to her. Warmth and strength emanated from his direction.

Was he going to kiss her?

After a moment of almost unbearable anticipation, the first thing she sensed was the cold metal of a spoon as it touched her lips. Gio maneuvered the spoon a little bit so that it coaxed her lips to part. "That's right," he murmured softly, his voice crawling over her and making her twitch in her seat.

She felt the first bit of the gelato move from the spoon into her mouth. The pure creaminess coupled with the sweet flavoring made her tongue circle. "Oh," she moaned after the first of it slid down her throat, "that was so good."

"What flavor do you think it was?" he asked but then didn't give her a chance to respond as he slipped another spoonful of the same flavor between her lips.

"It tastes like nuts," she answered in a voice that didn't even sound like her own. Did Gio know how much he was arousing her with his little game? That as he fed her the ice cream, a secret pulsing was starting from down inside her body, in her most intimate center? And that the sound of his voice was only making the throb pound stronger and louder?

"Nuts. Good guess. But what kind?"

To get any last bits that could help her formulate her answer, she rolled her tongue all the way around her lips to catch every drop. At that action, a whisper-quiet groan escaped from Gio's lips, causing her to open her eyes.

"No fair, Luci. Close your eyes," he ordered and she obeyed.

"Is it hazelnut?"

"Very good." He dabbed at her lips with a napkin, and her spine sharply straightened. She knew that no one in the shop would be able to see them, as the table was in a dark corner and Gio's back was shielding them from view. But she did momentarily consider how wholly inappropriate this exercise was.

It was only a fleeting thought, though, before the metal touched her lips again, making her forget who she was, what she was, as she could only surrender to Gio's spoon and what it told her to do.

"This one is easy. It has to be strawberry. The pink one I saw in the display case."

"You're good at this, Luci." They both knew why he kept mentioning her Florence nickname.

He ran the tip of the spoon along her lower lip. Her tongue followed the motion to chase any specks of the fruity goodness that might have lingered. Then he abruptly took the spoon away, and the tip of her tongue darted out to try to catch it, though it was gone. Gio's easy laugh shot straight into the base of her belly.

"Are you ready?" He brought the spoon back to tease her lips apart again. Her eyes involuntarily popped open. His smiling face and the nod he gave her was an unspoken direction to close them again. Which she did, with a slow inhale that filled her lungs with the fragrance of the shop.

To the next creamy offering, she rolled the gelato around her mouth again. "Chocolate. A dark chocolate at that."

"Taste more," he said as he fed her another bite.

"Delicious."

"Exquisite."

"Did you have some?"

"No. I was talking about…" He stopped himself.

Luci raised her eyelids. Gio wasn't smiling anymore. His brows creased and his nostrils flared. There was a flush in his cheeks.

"Is something wrong?"

"No," he bit out. "I need to get back to work."

In a split second, his mood had gone from playful to upset. She didn't understand what had happened, and truth be told, she was intoxicated from the ice cream feeding. His displeasure was making her dizzy.

He shot up and pulled her so she was standing, too. Then he steered her out of the shop so fast her feet didn't touch the ground. With a quick wave, he hailed a taxi and secured her inside. "I'll walk to my office from here and see you later at the villa."

CHAPTER SIX

"TELL HIM WE'LL ship the first hundred thousand to him by November." Gio gave Samuele his verdict during their daily briefing in his office. It was late afternoon and the sun had moved away from the windows, letting a thick whiteness blanket the sky.

"That's a reasonable commitment. But what is bothering you?" The older man leaned forward in his chair facing Gio at his desk. "You are snappy and distracted."

Why did Samuele have to read him so well? Maybe because he was like an uncle? Because he'd been with the company since the beginning? Had watched Gio and Dante grow from young children into men?

Gio gave him a snarl, though it was quickly diffused by Samuele's loving smile.

The truth was, Gio still hadn't recovered from that gelato-eating-turned-erotic encounter he'd had with Princess Luciana a few hours earlier. Not to mention the explosive kiss the night before. He reprimanded himself for his impulsive behavior. There was no way that spoon-feeding sweet ice cream into her luscious little mouth was going to have been a good idea. What he hadn't realized was just how bad a move it was. Because while he may have satiated Luciana's appetite for the Italian treat, it had left him ravenous. For her. Which was not in the plan at all.

Indeed, as he played the guessing game with her and her eyes had closed, a craving came over Gio so powerful it almost pushed him to madness. Watching her pink tongue dart out to chase the ice cream was a sight he couldn't imagine would ever get old. A voracious surge had forced itself through him as he told her to keep her eyes closed, leaving her defenseless and in his charge.

There was more he wanted from her as he visualized at least a dozen places on her body where he'd like to sample gelato from. By the time that list was made, the hunger was visible on his body, and he'd had to shift sideways in his chair to keep the princess from noticing. It was at the most inopportune moment that she opened her eyes and was able to perceive his discomfort with the arousal.

Gio studied Samuele's face, wrinkled with age but still very much alive and present.

"Samuele, do you trust Ginevra?" Samuele's second wife. His first had died young.

"Of course. Without trust there is no love. And without love, life is not worth living."

"But do you really trust her? Do you keep secrets from her, about work or about your hopes or feelings? Because you're worried that one day she might use something against you?"

"*Mio amico*, what are you talking about? Of course I've trusted both of my wives with everything. Just as your father trusts your mother."

Gio's telephone rang. "Yes. Schedule that meeting for two weeks."

"I understand. This is still about that woman in Hong Kong."

Francesca. Samuele had guessed correctly. Gio had no idea how to reconcile the disloyalty she had dealt him with the love that the men around him had for the women in their lives.

With casual encounters his norm, it had been fairly simple for Gio to make his decision after Francesca showed her true colors. That betrayal had put his company in jeopardy, his family in jeopardy. She'd been the only woman he'd ever let get close, and so he was convinced that was that. He'd never let a woman in ever again. Nor did he have any inclination to.

Sure, he could date all the women he wanted. A new one every night if he so desired. Without intimacy, without even good faith.

Ever.

Easy.

Over and done.

So why was he questioning that proclamation?

"When you meet the right woman, you'll know," Samuele continued. "It fits perfectly with your coming back to sit at this desk, doesn't it? Firenze is your home again, and she will find you here."

"I think you're wrong."

"Love has a way of showing up whether you think you're searching for it or not."

When Samuele left his office, Gio replayed his words over and over. Maybe love was meant to be for Samuele, who had the good fortune to find it again after loss. However, it wasn't going to happen for Gio.

One thing he was crystal clear about was that the mischief at the *gelateria* with the princess hadn't been a good turn of events. For either of them. Whatever force had come over him while feeding the sweet ice cream into her scrumptious mouth needed to be locked back up, and quick.

It was probably another unwise plan that he told her they'd cook dinner together at the villa tonight, as they had been going to restaurants since the day she arrived. Being at home with her would be much too friendly. After he'd thought he might lift delicate Princess Luciana de la Isla de Izerote up onto the marble table at the *gelateria* and ravish her with a passion he didn't even know he had, spending the evening alone with her might be dangerous business he shouldn't dabble in.

But she was so excited when he'd told her he would come for her in time to visit the food stalls at the Mercato Centrale, he didn't want to let her down. It certainly wasn't her fault that his gentlemanly self-control was being tested to its limits. Technically, it was her fault for having such a swanlike neck and porcelain skin and caramel eyes as fine as the gelato she'd tasted. However, the internal struggle to keep himself from again pressing his mouth into those bowed lips was his, not hers.

If nothing else was able to hold him back, there was one truth of such importance that it would supersede any other impulses he might need to fight.

He didn't know it as fact, but he'd make an assumption.

Her Royal Highness was almost certainly a virgin.

A virgin bride, soon to be married. No matter how much Luciana protested that she would never love the widower king she was to wed, Gio could never live with himself if she gave her maidenhood to a man she met on a prewedding runaway holiday. And, man-to-man, however unpleasantly she described her fiancé, Gio wouldn't carry on his shoulders any part of her deception to him.

A gruesome thought came over him. No one still utilized medieval methods of examination to ensure a princess bride's virginity, did they? He didn't know if indignities like that were even historically factual or just folklore he'd heard of, but that was another thing he surely didn't want to spend his life worrying about. Because, much as he hated to admit, he had a premonition that he'd wonder about Princess Luciana long after she left Florence. He'd best be careful to leave his fantasies at just that. Not realities he'd mull over for eternity, knowing he'd done the wrong thing.

It was simple, then. Under no circumstances would he let anything else romantic happen between him and Princess Luciana. Not tonight and not ever.

"Florence's central market," Gio announced to Luciana when they exited the car.

An enthusiastic smile crossed her lips.

"So many people." She flipped her head from left to her right.

"Yes, this is one of the busiest parts of the city."

The streets that surrounded the old market building were filled with outdoor traders selling their wares under tarped canopies to shelter from any weather. Buyers thronged three deep to peruse the offerings.

"Can we look at these stalls before we go into the market?"

"Of course."

"I've never been to a place like this before."

Gio didn't doubt it. While he had wandered through the souks of Morocco, the bazaars in Istanbul and the Far East Asian night markets, Luciana had no such experiences. Being in crowds such as this would be considered too dangerous for a princess to walk through. Even with an entourage, he supposed the princess had probably never been in a crush of shoppers.

They maneuvered into the thick of the marketplace. Unlike the food and food-related products that dominated the *mercato*, the outdoor vendors sold leather, pottery, souvenirs, scarves and sunglasses. Each stall was attended to by a merchant or two, some yelling about their wares or special pricing.

Luciana was so aware of people all around her, her eyes darting this way or that when someone touched her.

"I'm not used to being so physically close to so many people."

"You're going to be bumped into, rubbed up against and even shoved. If you're uncomfortable, let's leave."

"Certainly not," she said, giving his hand a playful tug that brought a hitch to one corner of his mouth. "I'm not made of glass, you know. I won't break!"

Gio had a moment's caution when he thought of himself as responsible for her safety. Even though no one had put her under his supervision, he considered himself nonetheless to be her guardian. After all, she was a princess in a strange land.

Judging from the happiness on her face, though, she was having too much fun to be daunted with any further warnings. Besides, while there were surely pickpockets and thieves in the area, the San Lorenzo markets of Firenze were hardly dangerous places. He'd watch over her to make sure she used common sense.

"Look at those colors." She pointed to one stall that held a selection of silk scarves hanging from hooks. Bright pinks and purples and yellows, every color in the rainbow was utilized in the dying of fabric to create them.

An emerald green scarf captured Luciana's attention. She looked around to see how other shoppers inspected the merchandise, unsure how close a scrutiny was customary.

"You can touch it," Gio prodded.

Luciana reached out to a corner of the scarf, rolling it between her fingers, then holding it up to check the transparency.

"One for fifteen, two for twenty-five." The hawk-like merchant quickly seized on her interest. He added a sales pitch, "The color is beautiful with your eyes."

Luciana let go of the scarf and they started to move to the next stall.

"Wait," the scarf vendor called out, "try it on. I'll give you a deal."

Gio and Luciana smiled at each other. She glanced back at the scarf that she really seemed to like.

"Haggle with him," Gio said to her. "That's the way of these markets."

"I can't do that."

"Of course you can, Luci."

The green hue of the scarf was apparently enough to lure her back. The merchant detached the item from the dozens he exhibited on hooks. Luciana stepped closer and the man wrapped the long scarf twice around her neck, creating a very chic style. He handed her a mirror to see for herself. "I'll give you two for twenty, a special price, only for you."

"Do you see a second one you like?" Gio whispered in her earshot only.

She shook her head no.

"Then make him an offer."

"I only want one," Luciana stated to the merchant, but in a tentative voice.

"Usually I charge fifteen for one. I'm offering you two for twenty."

"No," she said with a firmer volume that made Gio proud. "If you'll give me two for twenty, then how about one for ten?"

"You'll have the other one for a gift," the vendor persisted.

When she returned to her home at the palace, Gio knew that Luciana was not going to be giving presents she'd bought at street markets. No, instead she would be spending weeks, if not months, trying to quell the anger of her father and her fiancé after she'd run away on this trip. Souvenirs were not going to be appropriate.

"Take the scarf off and hand it back to him," Gio counseled. "Then we start to walk away again."

The merchant grunted as she tried to hand him the scarf. "You drive a hard bargain, *bambolina*." He wouldn't take it from her, insisting that she hold on to it. "Okay. Thirteen-fifty for one."

Luciana shook her head. "Twelve."

"Twelve? You want to put me in the poorhouse?" he balked with a grin.

"Twelve," she said with resolve.

"Okay, okay."

Inside the old market building, as it had been for centuries, fresh food was for sale. As he and Luciana browsed the first aisle, several stands held the ripest- and juiciest-looking produce, from dark greens to crisp bell peppers to oranges with skin so bright you could almost smell them from a distance. Another stall had dried pastas in every imaginable shape, some tinged black from the ink of squids, others flecked with a beautiful green from spinach. A big wooden sign leading to a kitchen area read Pasta-Making Classes Here.

Another merchant sold a wide array of olive oils from regions all over the country, the amber of their color distinguishing the varieties. Yet another stand was lined with a case of fine cheeses, from the creamy and runny to the crumbly hard of the finest Parmesan.

"What would you like to cook tonight?" Gio asked Luciana as he enjoyed seeing the green scarf around her neck and recalled the negotiation for it with amusement.

"Perhaps pasta and vegetables? And cut fruit afterward."

"Pasta with a sauce?"

"Last night at that restaurant by the river we had simple pasta tossed in olive oil and fresh tomatoes with basil. Let's make that."

Luciana chose a seller she thought had the most enticing offerings.

"I've never picked tomatoes before," she confided to Gio. "I'm assuming they should be dark and firm."

Together, they chose tomatoes from a big pile, showing each other potential candidates for the other to approve. The stall was supervised by an old woman in a knit hat who probably assumed that he and Luciana were a couple. Although they could be merely coworkers, or even siblings, or just friends.

Friends? Was that what they were? Gio barely knew how to understand these last few days let alone put a label on them. Friends had to start from some point but soon knew each other well, often seeing one another through the trials and tribulations of their days. He and Luciana weren't that. They were friendly acquaintances, he'd grant only that much.

As he watched Luciana sort through the bunches of basil on offer, he contemplated whether she had hoped that romance would be part of her exploration here in Italy. Maybe she had longed to know attraction and lust before the arranged marriage she was to enter when she returned home. Maybe she'd imagined being swept off her feet by a swarthy and confident Italian Casanova, a stereotype perpetuated in movies and TV shows. He believed her to be virtuous, but he did wonder if she wanted to play at courtship in this most romantic of cities.

That was something he couldn't help her with. Too risky, for one thing, if his own body's reaction during the gelato tasting was any indication. And thank goodness she'd pulled away after that passionate kiss on the bridge. Gio wouldn't have the slightest notion how to pretend to woo a woman yet be expected to know exactly when to back off and put the charade down so that he kept it safe for her.

He wouldn't step foot in that territory. If he wanted something he took it, and nothing stopped him. Maybe he was that cliché of an Italian lover, after all. Because want Her Royal Highness he did, so he had to jerk back his own reins.

Luciana brought the tomatoes and basil to the old woman so that she could weigh them and charge her.

"Three-fifty," the woman said. Gio reached in his pocket for his cash and began to count it out.

"Three," Luciana challenged. The princess was apparently using her newly learned bargaining skills, not knowing that produce wasn't usually brought to auction.

"No, Luci," he said with a chuckle, "these are set prices."

After all the groceries were purchased, Gio and Luciana made their way out of the market and onto the street where Viggo was waiting to take them home.

In the car, Luciana scrunched her nose with concern. "I should have mentioned that I don't know how to cook."

"I've been living in hotels for years. I have no idea how to cook, either. But it's just pasta, right? How hard can it be?"

At the villa, Gio used his key fob to open the doors to the main residence of the villa. Since Luciana had been staying at the compound, she'd never been inside the *big house*, as he called it.

"So this is where you grew up?"

"Here, and summers at the vineyard." Gio had described the vineyard and winery in Chianti where his retired parents now lived.

As they stepped inside, Luciana admired the furnishings in the huge sitting room that faced the courtyard. Glass doors running the entire length allowed light, and fresh air if desired, to permeate the room. The space was divided into different sections. One sitting area was close to the doors, with two sofas facing each other and some armchairs. It was done with white and pink fabrics, giving it a cheerful mood.

A dining area with a long rustic wood table able to seat twenty or so took up another portion of the room. Comfortable-looking upholstered tan chairs surrounded it. A grouping of dark green chairs was arranged in a corner by a fireplace where tall bookcases lined the walls.

Everything was done in a casual sophistication befitting this most successful of Florentine families. It made her want to meet Gio's mother, whom he credited for the interior design. Large mirrors everywhere gave the room an ambience that was stately without being at all stuffy. Art objects of historical significance sat on side tables, and Italian landscape paintings adorned the walls.

This was distinguished yet unceremonious. Stylish without taking itself too seriously. Comfortable in its own skin yet at the ready to summon strong passions.

Oh, wait. Luciana was reviewing the furniture, not Gio.

She couldn't resist a long gander at his visage as she caught it in profile in one of the mirrors. There was no doubt he was a breathtaking man. Although because he was, at heart, a scientist with his nose in a laptop much of the time, he was hardly the entitled playboy billionaire one might expect based on his family's success.

He'd mentioned that there had been women in his life he viewed as predators. Luciana didn't doubt that there might be many who saw only money and position when they looked at him. Women who were motivated by what they could get from him, be it a luxury lifestyle or a career gain. That must be tied into his reasons for staying single, not letting anyone get too close. He'd probably experienced personal betrayal, been used.

For her, being with Gio made her actually believe in trust.

And hope. And enthusiasm.

And a womanliness she had never known anything of before. Never to be nurtured in her, but it was nice to know that it existed.

Or was it torture?

She'd been having the most daring thoughts, ones that the kiss on the bridge and the gelato tasting only served to heighten. Gio made her want to explore something that wouldn't be found in a travel book. Luci, too, had begun to wonder about...

Lovemaking.

With Gio.

Could that be part of her awakening here in Florence? To know the pleasures of the flesh? That kiss had prompted a flood of desire, as if it had been shored up inside her and only Gio could set it flowing.

"This way to the kitchen." Gio jogged her out of those visions as he carried in the grocery bags they had bought at the central market. Luciana touched the green scarf still wrapped loosely around her neck. She knew that slip of fabric was going to be ultimately tucked into a back corner of a drawer in her bureau at the palace. Years from now and decades after that, she'd pull out the testament to the prewedding journey that changed her view of life, and herself, forever.

Perhaps it would have been better not to have taken this trip. Then she'd never have to live with the memories of bargaining at the San Lorenzo market or of taking in the sheer brilliance of Michelangelo's *David*. Of watching joyous children play in a piazza. And especially of Gio awakening her sexuality and forcing her to understand want. In the end, she might even hate him for showing her something she could never have.

What if she didn't go home? What if she could just stay here with him, in this beautiful villa, for the rest of her life? Would that smash her relationship with her father beyond repair?

She'd always put her father first, thought long and hard against taking any action that might displease him. Perhaps she should have better understood her own yearnings all along, and learned to negotiate with him rather than simply obey. Maybe then her need to catch her breath away from the demands of the palace wouldn't have become so desperate. Might her father in time have come to accept that she could not live her entire life denying her hopes and aspirations?

"Oh, how nice," Luciana commented when they entered the kitchen, brightening to appreciate the moment at hand. A black-and-white-tiled floor surrounded a large island workstation. Hanging light fixtures contributed to the slightly 1950s retro look, everything painted white with some red accents. Several ovens, refrigerators and an industrial-style dishwasher let her know that this was a kitchen created for entertaining. Built-in cupboards and pantries attested to the smart design of the space. A large rack that hung from the ceiling held copper pots and pans and baskets of other cooking tools.

"My grandmother used to cook up a storm in here. When all the family was here for a Sunday supper or a holiday, we were a formidable crowd. She'd have every implement in use."

"On her own?"

"My grandmother cooked everything. Mom and my aunts would pitch in to get everything on platters and served. They always left the cleaning to the kids. They said they didn't want us to get spoiled rotten. That cleaning the kitchen, which would look like a tidal wave had hit it by the end of the meal, would be good for us."

"Was it?"

"Of course. It built teamwork among the cousins. Plus, it was a big job so it forced us to develop a plan, delegate work, problem solve. Fabulous training for anything in life, really."

"I'm never allowed in the palace kitchen. It is attended to around the clock by staff. It's too risky for me to be in there. After all, a fork might fall to the floor." Luciana spit out sarcasm that surprised even her. "If I ever want a tea or something other than at mealtimes I, of course, merely press a button and it magically appears on a silver platter."

"Okay." Gio inventoried the ingredients he laid on the counter. "Spaghetti with diced tomatoes, basil, grated cheese and olive oil."

"Sounds wonderful."

"Why don't you wash the tomatoes?" he directed Luciana, who was only too delighted to have a task in the kitchen. She took note of the shiny skin and rich red color of the tomatoes they had picked. Turning on the tap at one of the small sinks, she rinsed their lovely selections and dried them on a nearby towel.

This was already great fun. She thought up a pretend scenario for her and Gio, preparing a simple weeknight supper just for the two of them. Perhaps they'd put the pasta into large bowls that they'd hold on their laps while they watched television. Both of them having changed from their workday clothes into loungewear, she'd wear striped fuzzy socks while Gio sat barefoot as they laughed at an American comedy show.

Never to be.

She watched as Gio filled a large pot with water. He carried it over to the stove and lit one of the burners under it.

"Right now, we can cut up the tomatoes and basil." He read the instructions on the spaghetti package. "When the water boils, we put the pasta in for eight minutes or until al dente."

"Why do you think it says *or* until al dente? Why wouldn't it be eight minutes every time?"

"Because the instructions don't indicate exactly how much water to use. It reads *'Fill a large pot with water.'*

If you had two pots of boiling water but of differing volumes, that could affect the time it takes to cook the pasta."

"Okay. That makes sense."

"Also, it reads *'Boil over a high heat.'* That's not very specific, as burners would vary from kitchen to kitchen. As a matter of fact, some are gas and some are electric, which would, theoretically, produce a different result."

About a half hour later, Gio and Luciana stared open-mouthed at the sloppy mess on the stove. Splatters of tomato seeds and skins, and once-green basil leaves that had now turned black, dirtied the white marble countertop.

They peered into the colander that held their inedible meal.

"I wish my grandmother had taught me how to actually cook something." Gio shook his head in disbelief. "After all, it's chemistry. I should be good at it."

"What do you think went wrong?" Luciana lifted a slimy strand of spaghetti from the floor and then let it fall into the pile with the others.

"Maybe we shouldn't have put the tomatoes, basil and olive oil directly into the boiling pasta."

"I thought we would top it with the cheese."

"I have a hunch everything was intended to go over the cooked spaghetti. Nothing but the pasta was supposed to go in the boiling water."

"Ah, that's why the tomatoes exploded."

"Why didn't I look this up online?" Gio mashed his lips together.

"We thought it was going to be simple."

He brought over a small trash can, and used his hand to swipe some of the mess from the countertop into it. Luciana assisted by dumping the entire colander's worth of food into the trash, as well.

Next, Gio retrieved a couple of soapy sponges and together they cleaned up the disaster. Luciana had to admit to herself that even cleaning held a special satisfaction for her, as it was such an ordinary part of life for most people. Maybe King Agustin would allow her to take a cooking class if she expressed interest in it purely as a hobby. If he'd permit it, she'd be sure to pass anything she learned down to her children. Surely propriety of the throne wouldn't be compromised by young people learning how to cook an egg or a bowl of pasta!

Once they were done, the kitchen took on a hush.

"Now we need to figure out what to eat."

"I'm not that hungry after this afternoon's gelat…o." Luciana could barely get the word out as she was overwhelmed again by the recollection of Gio's sexiness with his game about the flavors.

Their eyes caught each other's for an extended moment. Longing bubbled out of her like an overly filled pot of boiling water would on the stove.

He picked up the one tomato they hadn't used for their fiasco. "Why don't we slice this tomato onto toast with a dot of olive oil?"

"Do you think we can handle that much food preparation?"

"Despite evidence to the contrary."

"Let's take it out to the courtyard."

There they sat close to each other, enjoying their beautiful tomato from one plate until all the stars came up in the sky.

"Your wig catches the moon's glow." Gio fixed on her blond locks. What he didn't know is that the hair he was admiring was real.

"Does it?"

"Let me show you," he said as he picked up a section to hold in front of her face. He realized that the texture felt different. "Wait a minute."

With his wide hand, he squeezed a cluster of her hair against her scalp. Expecting some movement from the wig atop her head. Nothing shifted. Another chunk, same result.

"I knew it didn't look the same as it did yesterday."

"I had my own hair cut and colored this morning to match the wig because I like it so much."

"I thought you said your father wouldn't approve."

"I don't care anymore."

"The tigress has been let out of captivity."

"You know," she said, licking her top lip, "it's you who are to blame. First you talk me into buying jeans, then you tell me I should wear my hair how I'd like to…"

Luci—it was definitely Luci—was unable to finish her sentence because without thinking about it first, she leaned over and kissed Gio's lips.

A groan exhaled through him and ricocheted to her, emboldening her to kiss him a second time.

He took hold of the back of her head and brought her closer toward him. Their mouths touched yet again, and with that, she was sure he set her on fire. They kissed more, his scorching lips pressing urgently into hers.

Flames licked at her legs under the table and quickly worked their way up her body. She had never been so fiery.

The contact of their tongues sent the blaze upward to totally engulf her. As their kisses went longer, the moon stood still and Luciana willed daylight never to come.

Please let this moment last forever!

Both of Gio's hands traced her hair until they slid

down to her shoulders. Which he took hold of and pulled her tight to him. When his lips traveled behind her ear and down her neck, she shuddered with uncontrollable pleasure. A moan she couldn't negate or retract came forth from deep within her.

A chill swept over her when he took an instant's break from the embrace. Yet it wasn't a bitter wind that put out the fire. Quite the opposite, the pause from his kisses only fanned the flames to make her want more.

Gio stood. Why? Where was he going? Her normal brain functions scrambled, not even processing her own questions.

"You are so difficult to resist." Gio raked both of his hands through his curls and took in a slow breath.

"Don't resist, Gio."

"There will be no turning back."

"Please."

With that, he reached down and picked her completely up off the chair and into his arms. Relief overtook her at the return of his touch. Her arms wrapped around his neck as if it was the most natural motion in the world.

She couldn't have anticipated what was happening, nor deny the fact that it was what she wanted. Needed. Luciana tried feebly to protest, but Luci handily silenced her.

He brought her from the courtyard table to the front of his guest cottage. With an elbow, he bumped open the door and lifted her through the threshold. Once inside, the layout identical to her cottage next door, Gio carried her up the stairs and into his bed.

CHAPTER SEVEN

ALL GIO COULD concentrate on was the two kinds of comfort invading his senses. One was the calm presence of the morning sun through the bedroom windows, letting him know that he'd slept later than usual.

The other lay next to him in his king-size bed. Her Royal Highness Princess Luciana de la Isla de Izerote slept facing him, her exquisite features in repose without flaw. The blond hair she favored bathed her face in gold. If only he was an artist so he could capture her beauty this morning and preserve it for all eternity. Or if Michelangelo was still alive, Gio would commission him to carve Luciana's likeness into marble.

Actually, he might not need anything to help him remember this morning, as the recesses of his mind had already snapped pictures he'd treasure forever.

Gently, Gio brushed away a strand of hair that fell from Luciana's forehead across her eye. She stirred the tiniest bit from his touch. The ever-so-small curl of her lips affected every inch of Gio's body, forcing his loins into an involuntary stretch.

With the mild temperature, he didn't perceive the need to pull the blanket over Luciana's alabaster shoulders. Instead, his eyes traced slowly downward to appreciate the curve of her breasts. He'd luxuriated for as long as he'd wanted to last night with the perfection of them in his hands, in his mouth. With his lips, his tongue, his teeth, he'd taken her entire body...

He'd done what?

Gio scratched his beard stubble as reality blew in the window. Late last night, after the disastrous attempt at cooking pasta and after they'd settled for tomato on toast and a humble table wine, the evening ended here. In his bedroom.

Where he took the virginity of a princess.

One who was engaged to be married.

Who was leaving Florence in a few weeks.

And whom he'd never see again.

It was hard to decide which of those truths was more disturbing.

Last night. With their laughter over their culinary foibles and her bargaining during their shopping expedition. Her cute yawn and outstretched arms as the evening got later. Finally her, no doubt, impulsive move to lean in and kiss him. He was unable to deny her. The faint voices in the back of his mind that had told him to be careful, to keep his distance, to remember that Luciana was to be a fleeting memory, had no strength last night. They went down without a fight.

All Gio had been able to hear was his own heart hammering in his chest and his gut stoking a fervor that couldn't be contained. It was the savage need that had been unshackled at the *gelateria* and never restrained, waiting, waiting, growing more powerful every hour. With every indication that it was what she wanted, too, taboos were cast aside as he carried her up the steps to his bedroom.

Her Royal Highness arched her back in her sleep and Gio's body firmed in response. Gazing at her, forgetting was easy. That she wouldn't be his. And how that was what he wanted. No love. No trust. Not to be depended on.

Why was the bravado of his credo fading further and further into the background?

"Good morning." Luciana opened her eyes and murmured a singsong.

"Good, indeed." Gio tickled a feather kiss onto her cheek and another to her bare shoulder.

Yes, ladies and gentlemen, Gio Grassi of world-renowned Grasstech had made love to a princess.

Those two starter kisses were not enough and he trailed another dozen down the length of her arm.

Their fusion last night had been a combination that shouldn't have worked, yet did. Primitive instincts had driven him while the purity in her eyes relied on him to go slowly, to measure her for pain or fear.

"Are you sure about this?" he'd asked once more.

"Yes, Gio, yes," she'd assured.

Relief swept across her face when he fitted on a condom. After that, soulful kisses and the sweetest of smiles informed the rest of the night. His satisfaction had been incomplete until he'd made certain that she'd experienced every pleasure a woman should know.

Eager to teach her more, he bent over to cover her face with a million kisses until the blankets were flung off the bed and the sun moved later into the day.

A lazy few hours later, Gio held Luciana in his arms. "I've got to get to work. You, lovely miss, are bad for business."

Of course he was joking. Because, in reality, after

making love with her he surged with energy and creativity. Ideas popped into his head about how to finalize the design for the new motherboard chipsets Grasstech was developing.

Funny how spending these days with Luciana hadn't been reducing his attention to his work but had been enhancing it.

As agonizing as it was, he separated himself from their embrace and got out of bed.

"*Bellissima*, do you want to help me with a magazine interview? That was part of our deal, wasn't it?"

She slid her fingers through her hair, visibly surprising herself with the feel of her new do, which she had apparently forgotten, causing Gio to laugh.

"Only if you'll take me to see more sights later."

"You're coming to the office with me."

"I am?"

"Up and out." He pointed toward her guest cottage. "Go get dressed."

After he heard her pad down the stairs and out the door, he stepped into a hot shower. For a minute he regretted not inviting her to join him, as the travertine shower was easily an ample size for two. But he really did need to get to work, and Luciana plus a steamy shower plus a bar of fragrant soap was not going to add up to getting him out of the house anytime soon.

They reunited in the courtyard. Viggo was outside and quickly ferried them to Grasstech headquarters.

"We'll go in through the back, shall we? I have a private entrance to my office. Better that the staff doesn't have something to gossip about."

"Absolutely, thank you. I appreciate that."

Her eyes were a bit glazed and something about her

didn't look as princess-proper as she usually did. Gio bit back the craving that threatened when he realized that the change was due to the girl who had now blossomed into a woman.

In his office, he slid one of his small desks to face opposite his large one. That way, he could easily work with her on the interview while he mapped out the design for the chipset.

Several hours passed in a most pleasant fashion. Gio not only liked glancing up from his computer to find Luciana opposite him, but she was really quite helpful assisting him in how to phrase his answers to the interview questions.

Despite the unalterable fact that she was going to be returning to Izerote, Gio's mind wandered in a direction it shouldn't have. He speculated on what it might be like to see Luciana every day.

In her perfect world, she'd be a teacher so she wouldn't be sharing an office with him. But perhaps in the mornings, after they made love and learned how to prepare breakfast, Viggo would drop her off at school on the way to Gio's office. On days when he didn't have meetings, he could meet her for her lunch break. And after the long day had passed, they'd rush home to each other's arms, where they'd stay entwined until the morning light arose once again.

There was nothing about that fantasy that had anything to do with reality. He was just daydreaming because he hadn't wanted to be with a woman this much in…well…he couldn't think of a time.

"Do you want to say something about the origin of the hacking incident?" she asked.

He was finally ready to share with Luciana the detail

he'd withheld. "I'm not going public with this information, but the hacker was a woman I dated." If that's how it could be categorized. Dated. More like worked and slept with. There were no candlelight dinners or tickets for the theater.

"Oh." Luciana looked up from the laptop with raised eyebrows. "I don't know why I assumed it was a man."

"In grungy black clothes surrounded by computers in a dark basement, right?"

"Something like that."

"I was fooled, too."

There wasn't much more to say on the topic. It was a humiliation he'd have to live with. But it was something he'd wanted to tell Luciana. Then he busied himself with other matters.

When the sun set over the city, Luciana asked him, "So, tour guide. Where are you taking me?"

He'd already thought that through. And he'd also come to the conclusion that he had every right to enjoy himself with this delightful woman. Circumstances were such that it was never meant to be more than a fleeting affair. A coming-of-age for Luciana. Why shouldn't he bask in her company while she was here and leave it at that? He'd had short-term flings with women before. He knew how to do that. When the goodbyes came, he and Luciana would part knowing that for that short time one autumn in Florence, two people were good to each other.

So why was it his heart had a hard time believing it would be easy to let her go?

"We're going back to the *mercato*?" Luciana inquired when Viggo dropped off her and Gio at the now familiar sight. Recognizing the old market building and the outdoor stalls where she had bargained for that green scarf, she knew exactly where they were.

"Follow me." Gio took her by the hand and maneuvered through the people heading this way and that. Entering the food market, they reached the stand where they had bought the pasta that they'd managed to render inedible. Gio walked her past the sign she remembered from last time: Pasta-Making Classes Here.

Through a doorway was a small commercial kitchen. Work counters were wedged in wherever they would fit. A pink-cheeked woman in a chef's coat welcomed them. "I am Chef Katia. You are here for the class?"

Gio provided her with his name, which she checked off from a clipboard she held in her hand.

"We're taking a cooking class?" Giddiness wiggled through Luciana. With her father considering the domestic arts irrelevant to royalty, and her and Gio's culinary debacle last night, if there was ever a person who needed a cooking class it was her. How thoughtful of Gio to plan this activity.

Speaking of activities, she was still in shock about the one she'd participated in last night. She blamed Luci for talking Her Royal Highness Princess Luciana into it, but nonetheless, it was clear to her from the first kiss that she was going to make love with Gio. She'd had to experience the hunger and intensity and ecstasy that two people could share. Need insisted she act with abandon, wildness even, and to learn the profound strength of her femaleness and her sexuality.

For all she might have hoped the intimacy would bring, it was infinitely more divine than anything she could have ever have imagined.

It was hard to picture leaving Gio now. She felt so

close to him in a way she'd never have thought possible. He'd even confided in her that the company hack that caused him so much anguish was of his own doing in trusting a woman who'd systematically figured out how to work through him to get what she wanted.

The pieces fit together. How suspicious he'd been of Luciana when she'd first run into him on the street after those boys harassed her. And how he'd said that some women he'd known were predators. This one, Francesca, had really got the best of him. It was utterly horrible that she'd pretended to genuinely care for him when, really, she was out for personal gain. His work and his designs meant so much to him, there could be almost no worse betrayal than to steal that. No wonder he'd resigned to stay single.

How would it play out if she didn't go back to Izerote? Would Gio come to trust again? She envisioned a life filled with freedom and peace where they could go anywhere, do everything, be anything. As long as they had each other, nothing could harm them. Would he take that leap of faith if it was offered?

"If everyone will take a place, we will begin." Chef Katia called the class to attention and pointed to the stations she had set up on the worktables. Each area had a wooden board, bowls of flour and eggs, rolling pins, towels and other accessories.

Gio and Luciana took spaces next to each other as the chef began her instruction.

"We'll make a mound of flour and then dig a well into the center of it." Glee filled Luciana as she burrowed her hands into the flour. She loved the cool, powdery texture of it through her fingers. "Into the center, we'll crack the eggs."

Neither she nor Gio knew how to properly crack an egg and both struggled, with giggles, to remove the shells that weren't part of the recipe. Chef Katia came over and demonstrated her technique. On the second egg, both Gio and Luciana shocked themselves by performing perfectly.

After forking through the eggs as instructed, the chef taught them how to gradually incorporate the dry flour into the wet well.

"You were right," Luciana said. "This is chemistry. Cooking is the magic combination of science meets art."

"Perhaps, then, I'll have an aptitude for it, after all."

"I think children should be taught basic cooking. Not only for practical survival purposes, but it's an excellent way to learn mathematics, don't you think?"

"Teaching children is something you've given a lot of thought to."

Luciana's forehead creased. Yes, of course, she'd contemplated how she'd like to teach if she ever had the chance. To make learning engaging and fun, and a discovery.

"Can I ask you something?" Gio reached over with the side of his wrist to brush some flour that had landed on Luciana's nose. "When you marry King Agustin and you develop these resorts on the island that are to bring jobs to your people, won't those employees need child care?"

"Yes, why?"

"Shouldn't that be provided for them, organized to make it a workable lifestyle for families?"

"Yes, of course."

"Why couldn't *you* play a part in that? You've told me that issues regarding children have always been on your official agenda, so it wouldn't be coming out of nowhere."

Luciana kneaded her pasta, unable to look Gio in the

eye as she answered, "Neither my father nor my future husband would be in favor of that."

"Doesn't what *you* want matter?"

What she didn't want was to lament about the realities that awaited her when she returned to Izerote. All she wanted was to be here right now, completely in the moment, with this mind-blowing man at her side who encouraged her to spread her wings. To see how high she could fly.

"It's unbearable to me, Luci, to accept the idea of you returning to a life where you are limited."

"I must. And it's as much my fault as anyone else's. I allowed my father to lock me up in the palace tower."

"What do you mean?"

"My mother died when I was eleven. A mentally unstable man crashed his car directly into the one she was riding in, killing her instantly."

"How terrible."

"By the time I was a teenager I could tell that my father was a broken man. So I dedicated myself to him. I decided to never cause him any pain. We're all each other has."

"He wasn't able to get over her death."

"My mother was not a happy woman and kept herself distant. I never really knew her. She and my father didn't have romantic love. But the sense of duty that was instilled in him meant he should have somehow protected her from harm, and he couldn't forgive himself for not being able to."

"So now he goes to every length to shield you?"

"He tries to protect all of Izerote from *everything*, which is why time has stood still for our people. And he keeps me as some sort of symbol of that. And I let him."

"I give you credit. I think if it was me, I would run away never to return."

"It's not all bad. I don't take for granted that I live a life of privilege."

"Do you?"

Those two words dangled in the air.

After crumbly messes of flour mixed with egg had been miraculously converted to smooth balls of shiny dough, they were set aside to rest. The cooking students were invited to have a glass of wine and sample olive oils during the break.

Across the market floor, past the produce vendors with their stacks of ripe fruits and vegetables of every hue, Luciana eyed two men in black suits who seemed to be watching her and Gio. They both wore earpieces. She'd seen a couple of similar-looking men when they were shopping for jeans. Was it paranoia, or was she being followed? It wouldn't surprise her if her father knew her whereabouts. Perhaps he didn't trust her note that promised she'd return to the island in time for her wedding. And who could blame him?

"Gio, inconspicuously turn around. Do you see a couple of men over there looking at us?" She gestured with her head in their direction.

But when they both subtly turned to check, the men were gone.

Chef Katia called them back into the kitchen. She showed them how to roll out the dough with a rolling pin and then feed it through a pasta machine. The process looked easier than it was. Luciana and Gio hand cranked their creations through the rollers. Eventually, they ended up with even sheets of pasta that they proudly showed each other. "You should be able to see the outline of your fingers underneath," Chef Katia instructed.

Luciana tested hers by lifting it up in her hand. Gio leaned over and laced his fingers through hers so that they could see their hands holding each other's through the veil of the thin pasta. They pivoted their hands this way and that, grooving on the sight of their fingers under the dough. At the sight of their hands beautifully intertwined, Luciana bit her lip.

Chef Katia demonstrated how to cut their sheets into thin strips that were ready to be tossed into boiling water. She had pots of water ready for those who wanted to cook and eat their pasta then and there. Some students, like Gio and Luciana, instead put theirs into plastic bags to take with them.

"Let's go home and try again," he said, making Luciana think about something different from dinner.

On the ride back to the villa, Gio put his long arm around her shoulders. She adored the smell of him, always clean and fresh. Her head rested so nicely against his solid and wide chest. When they were together, she was truly *with* him. Maybe that was what it was like to be in love, in harmony both physically and mentally.

Could she stay like this? Or could he come home with her where they'd demand the life they were entitled to? Why couldn't he be by her side at the palace, sharing dreams and passions?

Way down inside, she knew that was more make-believe. What had passed between them last night was only another souvenir for her memory box. The ex-virgin princess had simply got a taste of forbidden fruit, a secret she would carry to her grave. But that was it. It most definitely shouldn't happen again. It couldn't. It was too dangerous. She knew it and sensed that Gio did, too.

So why was it that after they'd successfully cooked and eaten a delicious pasta dinner, Luciana found herself sitting on Gio's lap in the courtyard? Why was she kissing and being kissed with an urgency that nothing in her life had ever demanded before? And why did it feel unquestionably right rather than wrong when, once again, he laid her down on his bed, his potent body hovering over hers as he showed her rhapsodies she had no knowledge existed?

CHAPTER EIGHT

GIO WALKED WITH a spring in his step like a schoolboy as he rushed to meet Luciana after work. He had told her to meet him in front of the Basilica Santa Maria Novella, the Gothic landmark church near the train station. It was hard to believe how much had happened since that fateful day when she'd arrived by train and he interceded to protect her from those thugs who were attempting to steal her jewels. He'd lived a lifetime since then and was astonished as he acknowledged how big a part of his life Luciana had become in such a short time. That wasn't like him. Yet all he wanted to do was both talk to and listen to her, and he'd had more conversation with her in the past few days than he'd probably had in a year.

Which was why he couldn't get to her fast enough. He hadn't told her where he was taking her, wanting to keep it a surprise. As had become their pattern, they'd meet at dusk while visitor attractions were still open for an hour or two longer. Where he was taking her today wasn't a typical tourist stop, but it was somewhere he thought she'd like.

Can't get to her fast enough. What crazy thoughts he was having. This wasn't supposed to be happening to him, caring whether or not he was with any woman, let alone a special one. Emotions were escaping his control. Sucked into an unexplainable whirlpool, his hours and days were delineated by time spent with Luciana and time waiting to return to her side again.

None of this was in character for him. He dealt in logic and probabilities, in calculus and abstracts that allowed him to understand a technological plane that would mystify the majority of people in the world. Feelings knew no logic, no mathematical equation that could be proved without doubt. He was in an uncharted operating system, and did not know his way around.

Which must have been why his heart skipped when he saw Luciana in the church square. She was wearing the *comfy* jeans, as she had come to call them, making him think of a carefree young woman on a metro bus. She looked like a proper Luci, a girl who dressed in whatever whim dictated, whose day was her own. Not one who lived by the regimented precision she had described on Izerote.

Was Luciana talking to someone? Yes, she was conversing with a woman who had a mop of hair pulled up in a bun. A few young children were running around them in a circle. Had she struck up a conversation with a stranger, or had the woman approached her?

One of the children pulled on Luciana's leg and she bent down to talk to the little girl. The expression on Luciana's face was one of pure dedication as she appeared to be answering the child's question. Gio noticed her easy manner with the girl, just as a boy grabbed her hand from the other side. Instead of being flustered Luciana divided her time between the two children, until she and the other woman were laughing by the time Gio approached.

"This is my friend Chiara. I think I told you we had met a few days ago."

"Oh, yes, the teacher. Nice to meet you."

"And you." Chiara called out, "Antonio, stop torturing that pigeon."

The boy ran closer and Luciana said to him, "Sweetheart, when you touch the pigeons you scare them. They don't like to be petted like dogs and cats do."

"Okay." The boy shrugged his shoulders.

"Chiara was taking the kids out for a walk and we ran into each other."

"Luci is actually wonderful with the children. She's been helping me."

"I don't doubt it." Gio glanced to Luciana, who looked like the ultimate Madonna with cherubic children circling her.

"I have to go. Their parents will be picking them up soon. Nice to meet you, Gio."

"You, too."

After watching Chiara and the children scurry away from the square, Gio pecked Luciana's cheek. "How was your time at the Uffizi Gallery?"

"Magnificent, of course. Where are we going tonight?"

Gio led her down a street off the church's piazza. They reached the front of a very unassuming building with big brass doorknobs.

"What is this?"

He turned the knobs and opened the doors. "The Firenze Profumo Farmaceutica. It's one of the oldest pharmacies and cosmetic shops in the world."

They entered the formal salon.

"Oh, my gosh." Her eyes lit up as she took it all in.

They had stepped back in time. Heavy burgundy drapery with gold pull cords lined the walls. Elaborate chandeliers hung from high frescoed ceilings, casting a yellowish light. A few red velvet benches were placed here and there atop the tapestried rug. Behind one long glass counter, three attendants assisted customers.

"The smell is incredible." Luciana inhaled the floral and spicy aromas that permeated the entire space as they walked farther in.

"The Dominican friars established this in the thirteenth century," Gio explained.

Luciana was drawn to the rows of glass cases. They held a dazzling array of perfumes, colognes, creams, lotions, shampoos and soaps. Some were in re-creations of bottles that matched the era when the particular product was created, such as the Acqua di Caterina from the 1500s, commissioned exclusively for Caterina de' Medici of the famous Florentine family. Other products were in simple bottles, pots and jars bearing the label of the *farmaceutica*.

"Come this way."

They passed into an interior parlor.

"What's this?"

The room had a large glass table in the center on which sat dozens of small amber bottles with droppers. One wall was filled with books. "Those were written by the friars, the original recipes for their preparations," Gio explained. Glass doors opened to an herb garden. "They make balms and ointments and tonic remedies here."

"How do you know about this place?"

"The de' Medici family, the leaders of the Florentine Renaissance, were proponents of medicine. In fact, their name is where the word *medicine* is derived from. Florence has always been a place to celebrate the healing powers and versatility of botanicals. My grandmother and hers before her and probably relatives even before that shopped here."

"How lovely of you to bring me."

"This is the room where they develop perfumes. I thought you might like to create a fragrance that's uniquely yours. When you smell it, you can remember your visit to Florence." *And me*, Gio thought but didn't say aloud. He hoped she would always remember him, as heaven knew he'd always remember her. More than he thought he should if his prediction proved correct.

Walking the streets of Florence with her had become natural now. When he wasn't with her, he felt off. Not quite right. Incomplete. Together, they seemed to grab something out of thin air and form it into something real and weighty.

A lone tear escaped from Luciana's eyes.

"Why are you crying?"

"I'm not. I'm just so touched that you thought of this. About making a perfume."

A middle-aged woman with her hair pulled tightly back and wearing a white lab coat entered the salon. "*Buona giornata*, I am Imilia and I will be assisting you today." She pointed to one set of the glass dropper bottles on the table. "These are some of our essential oils. Perhaps you'd like to start with one of those for our top note and then we'll add on to customize a fragrance."

Imilia laid several strips of testing paper on the table. From each bottle she squeezed a drop for them to smell.

After a few, Luciana was clear that she liked orange blossom.

"Now we'll choose a central note and a base note or two."

Gio loved seeing how seriously Luciana took the task, smelling the test strips several times before she eliminated any of them.

Selections were eventually made.

"Perfume is best aged. The scents will meld over time."

Gio whispered into Luciana's ear, "Think of me six months from today when the perfume has mellowed but my memories of you won't have."

As soon as those words fell out of his mouth, Gio regretted saying them. Soon enough Her Royal Highness Princess Luciana de la Isla de Izerote would not only leave Florence, but would leave him. Forever.

There was a king to wed. Heirs to produce. Her fates were decided. It was cruel to encourage her to remember him. Quite the opposite would be kinder. If he really cared about her, he'd hope she'd forget him the minute she left Italian soil.

How could he have allowed them to make love? Two nights in a row, no less. Even though he knew she wanted to as much as he did, he should have resisted. So what that their lips fit so seamlessly to each other's? So what that Luciana's lissome body went boneless against his, meeting his angles with her pliable curves? And so what that now they anticipated each other's movements, each of them in constant undulation around each other as if they were no longer independent beings?

She was never to be his.

No matter what, they couldn't make love again. What happened couldn't be undone, but Gio could keep from making matters worse. It was the least he could do.

Monarchy aside, Luciana was an inexperienced young woman. He should have been the stronger one. Defended her. The last thing he'd want to do was hurt her.

Nothing everlasting could ever be between them.

Could it?

Imilia asked if Luciana would like to name her fragrance and have a personalized label for the bottle.

"Let's call it Luci," she answered without hesitation. Of course. Luci being a different person from Luciana. The bottle of Luci that she'd no doubt keep hidden would bear witness to secrets the princess might never tell another living soul.

From the bottle that would bear her name, she rubbed a few drops of her fragrance onto the inside of her wrist, which she brought to her nose. Then she presented it to Gio to reconfirm that the scent was appealing. He lifted her delicate wrist, his fingertips memorizing every one of the tiny bones under her porcelain skin. The blend of the orange blossom, cloves, cinnamon and bergamot was a heady and pleasing combination.

Before he could stop himself, he topped off the examination of the inside of her wrist with a kiss. Just what he'd meant *not* to do. And without realizing ahead of time that the barest amount of physical contact would reverberate through his body and make him want to do things to Princess Luciana right then and there that would have the Dominican friars rolling in their graves.

"Chiara!" Luciana waved when, out for another walk in the Santa Maria Novella piazza, she spotted her new friend and the kids.

"Luci. Come sit. The children are playing." Chiara

pointed to a bench that allowed her to keep a close watch on her charges.

"So is that handsome Gio your lover?"

"No. He's just a friend." Luciana didn't know how to answer. Yes, she had made love with him. No, he was not her lover in any true sense of the word. Yes, she wished more than anything in the world that he was.

The princess would return to Izerote changed in more ways than would be visible to the eye. Hair cut and dyed, she'd have to face her father's scrutiny over something as petty as her appearance. He'd never know that she'd been forever altered internally, as well. That she'd known the earthquake of a man and a woman in the throes of passion, the planet moving beneath them, modifying the universe so that it could never go back to exactly how it was before. More important, not her father nor her future husband nor any other living soul would know that she herself had shifted like the tectonic plates under the earth, and would never be the same again.

"I saw how your eyes shined when he met you here yesterday," Chiara continued. "And he had the face of a man who thought he was the luckiest one alive when he found you in the crowd. Smells like lovers to me," she said in a cute lilt that made Luciana laugh.

"It's complicated."

"Isn't it always?"

Two of the boys were having a duel with the plastic spoons that they had been using to eat a snack. Jamming their implements at each other in a way that was going to lead to someone getting hurt. Chiara called out, "Boys, it is a gentleman's duel. Take two steps backward and bow to each other."

Which they did, eking a smile out of the two women.

"Do you have a boyfriend?"

"I go out with a nice enough guy, but he's not *the one*. My eyes don't flicker when I'm with him like yours did with Gio. I'm leaving Firenze soon, so it's best not to get serious."

The words banged between Luciana's ears. Of course when someone was planning to leave the place where they were, it was best not to allow any meaningful relationships to develop. That was so obvious Luciana would bet that even these children having spoon duels would understand. Any idiot would.

Except her, apparently. She did know that her feelings toward Gio had passed serious days ago and now had moved into critical. Which was not good.

"When are you going?" Luciana tried to distract herself by asking about Chiara's impending move.

"I'm half there now and half here on the days I work. I commute by train." Chiara had told her that her family, her mother and two sisters who were also teachers, were opening up a school in Salerno. A town in the south near Naples, it was a four-hour train ride from Florence. "To open a school is not a way to make a lot of money, but it's what we love. So I go down as often as I can to paint walls and buy furniture and network with the people who live there."

"Do you have commitments from families that are going to send their children to the school?"

"Oh, yes. We already have forty students enrolled."

"That's amazing!"

Luciana admired Chiara. Not only had she pursued her goal of becoming a teacher, but now she was opening her own business at it.

"What about you?"

To the outside world, they must look like two friends sharing a chat during lunch while the children in their care play. Perhaps that outside world might see Luciana as a teacher, too. Passersby would think them two young gals who were dishing about boyfriends and aspirations.

"If Gio isn't your lover, what are you doing with him?"

Waltzing through the cloudy haze of a beautiful dream she never wanted to wake up from?

"I'm only in Florence for a short time," Luciana uttered softly. "I'm leaving, too."

"Ah, Gio was your passionate Italian fling?"

Princess Luciana winced at that characterization, thinking it cheapened the situation. Although perhaps that's exactly how she would recollect it decades from now.

"You're sad to leave him."

Chiara had no idea how right she was. But Her Royal Highness would have so much to distract her when she returned to the palace. There would be dull diplomatic lunches to attend, boring dedications to make appearances at and a man she barely knew to marry. How would she find the time in her schedule to pine for the magical man in Florence?

"I am."

"Have you rubbed the snout of Il Porcellino?"

"Not yet." Luciana knew about the legend of the bronze figure near the Mercato Nuovo. Lore had it that if you rubbed the nose of the boar, it meant you would return to Florence.

Luciana would do that before her trip was over, although her wish would be bittersweet.

Because even if she was to return, it would be too late for her and Gio.

"You don't want to go home, Luci?"

"I don't, and yet I can't stay here."

"Do you want to come work for me in Salerno?"

"Do I what?" Luciana could hardly believe the words she was hearing.

"Work for me. I can't hire you as a teacher until you earn a degree in early childhood education. But you can assist us. The children clearly love you."

Laugh or cry. Both options were equally viable. Princess Luciana de la Isla de Izerote had been offered her first job. In her chosen profession. In some families, that would be cause for celebration. In hers, it was a disgrace. *Laugh or cry.*

Even though she was supposed to have another two weeks in Florence, her departure was imminent.

The proverbial clock ticked.

Walls closed in.

There'd be no escape.

"A job."

With every blink of her eyes, she saw flashes of red.

Warning lights.

Danger signals.

Because Princess Luciana could not ignore that, once again, across the piazza, she noticed two men in black suits staring directly at her as they spoke into earpieces. Her stomach sank to her knees as the reality became impossible to dispute.

Chiara handed her a business card, which Luciana numbly slid into her jeans pocket alongside the pocket money Gio had insisted she carry.

"You can think about it. Let me know in the next few days."

* * *

Was she really thinking what she was thinking? The events of this past week made Luciana doubt every stronghold she'd ever embraced. Heady concepts like responsibility and sacrifice, honor and privilege, obligation and liberty were now all under question. Anything and everything was up for grabs.

Would she really be able to pull off the idea that was fighting for a place in her rational mind? It made sense and it made no sense at the same time. When Viggo dropped her off at her requested location, Luciana had been so lost in her dilemma that she'd hardly noticed the drive. She asked him to wait and stepped out of the car.

The Piazzale Michelangelo was a public square on a hill that afforded a breathtaking view of the city. From the river and its bridges to the bell tower of the Badia Fiorentina to the Duomo to the Tuscan mountains beyond, its breadth was spectacular. Overwhelming to take in all at once, the panorama had been known to make people weep. No different for the princess. Tears rolled down her face in a steady stream, chilled by the hilltop breeze.

The first tears were for Gio, whom in any scenario, she'd be torn from like a bandage that rips away the skin underneath it when it is removed. Other tears represented trepidation about what she was planning. If she failed, she'd have made even a bigger mess than what she'd already created. If she succeeded, there would be no turning back.

There were tears for the mother she barely knew. Who was unable to rise to her own duty. Although she didn't cause her own death, her spirit was laid to rest before her marriage at age eighteen. Part of Luciana's decision would be in her mother's honor.

Still different tears were for her father, whom in spite of all of this, she loved dearly and risked wounding. A young man himself when her mother died, he was ill-equipped to parent an eleven-year-old girl and turned to fear of loss as his only guidance.

And, because it had transformed her so drastically that no matter what road she took it could never be one she'd already traveled, she cried for Florence, which she'd miss every day of her life.

Luciana got back in the car and had Viggo drop her off at her next destination.

Chiara had been right. Il Porcellino was quite the tourist attraction. The open-air Mercato Nuovo was in full swing near the bronze boar, and the whole area was alive with Florentine bustle. As she'd seen elsewhere in the city, budding artists used colored chalk to draw replicas of famous paintings onto the pavement of city streets, putting out tip cups for passersby to show their appreciation. Many of the chalk renderings were excellent. Luciana took note of the young artists and wondered what their lives must be like, living and practicing their craft in this inspiring place.

Visitors queued up to touch the famous boar, and the princess took her place behind a tour group, all of whom wore matching plastic nameplates around their necks. English, German and Japanese were just three of the languages she heard around her. The bronze *porcellino*, or piglet, was covered in a green-brown patina except for its snout, which had been polished to a sheen by all the attention bestowed on it.

While she waited, she pivoted her head as far as she could to the left and then all the way to the right to take in the scene at the Mercato Nuovo until she found what she knew she would. Past a vendor specializing in wallets and belts, two men in black suits watched her. She couldn't tell if they were the same men from the piazza with Chiara earlier today, but it didn't matter.

She'd seen men in black suits outside the clothing store when she and Gio were shopping for jeans. There were two at the Mercato Centrale when she and Gio took the pasta-making class. Then today at the piazza. Part of her had been trying to deny the reality of what they represented. Now as her breath tightened and a blush burned her cheeks, she could pretend no longer.

King Mario de la Isla de Izerote had found her. Maybe he'd had her followed all along. She no longer believed that she was going to get the full three weeks of escape she had planned before returning to Izerote and her wedding. Today was her seventh day. A hunch in her gut told her it was her last.

This schedule was probably designed by her father. He, no doubt, instructed his security detail to have her located and surveilled but if she seemed safe, to let her have her silly little fun. Rage inched up her throat as she fully comprehended what must have happened. That she hadn't even had the small measure of freedom she'd hoped to cherish for the rest of her life. All she'd been granted was a longer chain than usual.

When it was her turn to touch the bronze boar's nose, she stroked it as lovingly as she would have had it been Gio's face. She threw her arms around its neck and held herself close. Because she was in love. With Luci, the young teacher who had the most marvelous boyfriend in the world.

If rubbing Il Porcellino's snout meant she would return, she'd rub it a hundred times before she let go.

Thank you, Florence.

Thank you, Gio.

Finally, she backed away to let the people who were waiting have their turn.

As she did, poison blackened her insides when she heard an unfamiliar male voice behind her say, "Princess Luciana, may we speak with you for a moment?"

Luciana didn't turn around to acknowledge him.

"And we'd like to speak with the gentleman you've been keeping company with."

Those words sliced like a lash across her back. The most unbearable consequence of her actions would be if Gio was brought into the chaos she'd made. He had plenty of his own issues to deal with. He'd been nothing but kind to her and deserved better.

Blood vessels throbbed through Luciana's skull. What she was scheming was her only hope. A far-fetched Hail Mary. Worth a try because, at this point, she had nothing to lose.

She suddenly bulleted forward and dashed into the outdoor marketplace.

If she could just get away from these security men right now, she'd carry out her plan immediately. Making an abrupt right turn, she tore through an aisle of merchants who were all selling tablecloths and bed linens displayed on hooks so that the fabrics danced in the afternoon wind. As the bedsheets swayed, Luciana was able to maneuver quickly between one and around another until she got to the other end of the market.

A quick glance backward confirmed that she'd done it. The men weren't trailing her!

With no time to wait for Viggo, whom she'd asked to return in an hour, she hailed a taxi to return her to the villa. Which she slipped into, seemingly unnoticed. As she bounded up the stairs of her guest cottage, her heart thundered. The ticking bomb was about to explode. Time to hurry.

She picked up the phone on the night table beside her bed. It had been seven days since she'd held a phone, the hard plastic harsh and now unfamiliar in her hand as she punched in a number. "Chiara, it's Luci."

After the call, she yanked her suitcase out of the closet and tossed it on the bed, unzipping it to unpack the items she had left buried inside. The ones she had hoped never to need. The ones that were now her last chance.

"Luciana?" Gio's voice called up to her bedroom from the courtyard a half hour later. "Luciana?"

What was he doing home? It was hours before he was to finish work and join her for their usual early-evening sightseeing. They were to finally tour the Duomo, which she had been greatly looking forward to.

"I'm up here," she yelled through the open doors to the Juliet balcony, hoping not to have to see him.

"I was so worried," he continued shouting up. "Viggo said he went to pick you up but you weren't there."

"I'm fine, Gio. Go back to the office."

Luciana had already written him a note to leave on the table in the courtyard. An in-person goodbye was more than she could handle.

"Come to the balcony, Luciana."

"No, Gio. Please go back to work." It was agony to tell him to go, but if he knew what she was planning, he'd try to stop her.

"Luciana! Luciana!"

The low timbre of his bellow was too much for her to fight. She'd allow herself one last time the sight of his exquisite face and the tall muscular body that had educated her in ecstasies she'd never expected to learn.

With a last check in the mirror before she'd have to tell Gio the truth, Princess Luciana confirmed that her look was complete. When she'd arrived in Barcelona after stowing away on that supply ship leaving Izerote, she'd bought not one but two disguises. Her *just in case* would be put to the test right now.

The boy's brown suit fit her about right, appropriately shapeless to skim over any womanly curves. The white shirt and brown shoes matched it. And the dark wig cut above the ears gave her the appearance of a teenaged boy, perhaps on his way to a school interview or reluctantly forced to get dressed up for an occasion. No, the delicate skin and regal bones of her face were not very masculine, but she knew that some boys had fine features. Walking down the street, no one would give her a second glance.

She stepped out onto the Juliet balcony to face Gio.

"The men who have been following you?" Gio asked upon seeing her in the ensemble.

"How did you know?"

"I saw them, too. I didn't say anything because I hoped you hadn't noticed. I didn't want to ruin your precious time here with the news."

"I can't go back to Izerote, Gio. Not after everything that happened here. Not after you."

She inhaled the full view the balcony afforded. The old buildings, the chirps of birds sharing a song with the horns of taxicabs. The splendid mixture of the ancient and the modern that was this city. And the high-tech billionaire here who'd keep her heart.

Luciana moved away from the balcony and back into her bedroom. Closing her suitcase, with the bag of jewels that were her only currency inside, she made her way down the stairs and out to the courtyard where Gio stood waiting.

"Where are you going?"

"Chiara offered me a job at her new school in the south, near Naples. If I can get away without being caught, maybe I have a chance. I'll disappear there. I'll find a way to contact my father and tell him that I'm not coming home."

Desperation had driven her to the unconceivable.

"Don't leave," Gio implored. "We'll figure it out. There has to be a way."

"There is none. Not when they're closing in on me. On us. As it is, I've dragged you into this further than I ever meant to."

His hands circled her wrists, handcuffing her in his grasp. "No. You're not leaving."

"Maybe someday I'll be able to return. I rubbed the nose of the boar. Maybe a Florence miracle will be ours."

"I'll help you. I'll drive you there. At least then I'll know exactly where you are. When it's safe we'll be together again."

"No. They'll follow you. Go back to the office. When they question you, say I disappeared without a trace. Say you don't know anything."

"You've never been on your own. I'll worry about you every day of my life. I can't let you go."

"Let me go, Gio. For both of our sake. You have your company to protect. And I can't have you take the place of my father. I have to try something of my own or else I'll never know what freedom is."

She lifted up on her tiptoes and craned her neck so

that her lips would reach his. For one goodbye kiss that contained the sun, the moon and all the stars in the sky.

Then she broke away from him, grabbed her suitcase and fled out through the entrance tunnel that led to the street.

Chiara was to meet her at the train station, so Luciana rushed in that direction, disguise in place. But within seconds, a black car screeched to a stop beside her on the street. The two men who had been following her at the bronze boar got out of the car.

"Princess Luciana, at your father's request we are here to take you home."

Speechless and unsure what to do, she covered her mouth with her hand. In her heart of hearts, she knew she'd never be able to outrun these men, and even if she did they—or others like them—would be back again the next day. It was a foolish attempt. Her father had decided that it was time for her journey to come to an end. Just as she always figured he would.

She looked back toward the villa. Gio had chased after her and stood a few paces behind. The two men glared at him, and then one of them took hold of Princess Luciana's arm. The other opened the passenger door of the black car. He stated flatly, "Time to go."

Using no small amount of force, the man began to marshal Princess Luciana into the car. In doing so, her wig came off in his hand. The blond lob that had now become her real hairstyle spilled around her face as tears pooled in her eyes. She turned back one last time and called out, "I love you, Gio! I love you."

With that, she surrendered into the back seat and the door was closed after her. The two men got into the front seat, and from the clicks and beeps she heard, she knew she had been securely locked into her motorized jail.

Her Royal Highness Princess Luciana de la Isla de Izerote jerked around to look out the back window as the car pulled away. Gio ran toward her, sprinting after the car, picking up his own speed as the vehicle did, too. But when the car took a big lead over him, the last thing she saw was his mouth saying something to her. She'd spend the rest of her life wondering what it was.

CHAPTER NINE

"I LOVE YOU, too, Luciana! I love you, too."

Gio stared blankly out of his office window replaying the words he had screamed at the top of lungs yesterday as the black car drove his heart away from his body.

Yesterday. When the world was a different place. Because Luci was in it. Luci, the whip-smart, fun-loving, sensual breath of fresh air that had shaken Gio to his core, was gone forever. Oh, certainly Princess Luciana de la Isla de Izerote still lived and breathed. To marry and bear children, and hopefully remain healthy and strong for decades to come. But the part of her that had spent this enchanting week with Gio had disappeared into thin air as quickly as she had arrived.

What was she doing right now? Begging her father's and her fiancé's forgiveness? For stealing seven days? Who could blame her for wanting that? How could that be considered an offense? Gio's fists clenched at the injustice.

For her.

For him.

She was supposed to have three weeks. He'd been planning to take her to his family's vineyard in Chianti. To show her the charming coastal towns of the Cinque

Terra. The lush terrain of the Emilio Romagna region. Perhaps a few days in Venice.

Cruelly, their time together was cut short. But the week they'd had changed the course of his life. Because once you loved, you could no longer pretend that it wasn't important. That it was something you could live without. That it wasn't worth the risk.

That it wouldn't destroy a person once it was gone.

Destruction wasn't an option for Gio. Family loyalty demanded that he run this empire. The responsibility was on him.

He turned his concentration to work. As he drafted a public statement to announce the next generation of DDR SDRAM that would render everything currently on the market obsolete, Princess Luciana's suggestions to him came to mind. She'd remind him that it wasn't technical mumbo jumbo that the public would respond to. It was people being their genuine selves that made an impression.

How right she was. His fingers flew over the keys as he typed. Grasstech might be a leader in the computer industry, but it was a company started by one man and now under the care of his sons. With thousands of employees throughout the world, each of whose diligent work contributed to the company's success. For the new RAM, Park Baek Yeol in Seoul had worked for years on its development. Adil Pannu's group in Mumbai tested hundreds of designs until they found one that could be produced at much less expense than its predecessor.

Once Gio had crafted a statement he was pleased with, he was ready to share it with his marketing team. After hitting the send button, he shut down his computer for the night.

As he was leaving the office, Samuele locked in step with him in the corridor. "*Mio amico*, we must decide where we are going to manufacture the biometric products. This is an enormous undertaking for us. Have you given it any thought?"

"I will, Samuele. Thank you. I want you to know how much I appreciate you."

"Why are you so wistful?"

Gio couldn't bring himself to explain about Luciana. Not yet, anyway.

At home, he pushed open the door to the villa. There was no doubt that the envelope on the table in the courtyard was for him. Luciana had left it, hoping to make a clean exit without having to say goodbye. Luck, or serendipity, spoiled her plot. As bad as it was to watch her being driven away by her keepers, it would have been far worse not to have bid her farewell. After she'd been transported long out of sight, he'd shuffled back to the villa but couldn't bear to read her note.

Recognizing the Grasstech logo embossed on the top left corner of the envelope, Gio nodded to himself. Of course, even in order to leave him a message, she'd had to borrow an envelope and probably the piece of paper it was written on. Which of his pens had she used? Anything he had was hers for the asking, yet it brought a crinkle to his face that she hadn't brought royal stationery with her from Izerote. No, she was too busy bringing wigs and palace jewels in her attempt to clinch time without her tiara for just one holiday.

Gio slid his finger under the flap to open the envelope. Having never seen her handwriting, he was awed by its feminine and stately precision. Every line symmetrical, every word incorporating as many swirly flourishes as it could hold.

Ache pushed through him as he appreciated the beauty in the way Luciana had written his name.

Gio.
You have no idea how much you have given me in addition to your generosity. You have shown me a modern world full of excitement and potential, where ambition and innovation are celebrated.
I vow to you now that I will find a way to teach that to my children, and to tell them about the brilliant man in Florence who taught it to me.
You are the only man I will ever love, and I will love you until my dying day.
Yours forever, Luci.

Uncharacteristic mist filled Gio's eyes as he peered up to the Juliet balcony of Luciana's guest cottage, knowing only too painfully that she wouldn't be appearing. Because darn if the words he yelled as he tried in vain to catch up to that car weren't true. He loved her. And now that he knew what love was, he was sure it was something he'd never known before.

With Francesca, until she betrayed him, there was lust. And the commonality of working in the same industry. A similar lifestyle. Work came first, and there was never any worry about dividing his energies.

But his heart never lurched out of his chest at the mere thought of Francesca. He'd surely never had sunny visions of a home built together and children to share it with. A foundation that sparked his creativity. Celebrating successes and enduring challenges as one, an entity stronger than the sum of its parts.

Luciana made those possibilities dance through his head. In fact, he couldn't stop obsessing over them. So much so that those visions had bent to include royal life. It would take adjustment, but he could see himself accepting the obligations and rules that would come with being at the princess's side. They'd find a way to protect some amount of a private life for themselves. Love gave everything potential.

After sitting down at the courtyard table to pick at the pasta left over from their cooking class, Gio let his mind travel to faraway places. To the island of Izerote. To imagine what his heart was doing at this very moment. To miss her.

When he had wallowed for as long as he could stand, he forced his mind to turn a corner. The next issue on his agenda was where the biometric products were to be produced. He could give them to one of the India plants, although the crews there already had plenty to do. In fact, he'd like to shift some of the ongoing manufacturing he had operating out of Mumbai to somewhere else. The Tokyo plants were overworked, too. A new location might be what was in order. The components were all small parts that didn't require massive production equipment, so that opened up a lot of options.

The strangest germ of an idea popped into his mind. With some research and phone calls, he began to envision a prospect. The next morning, he summoned Samuele to his office and included his father at the winery in the discussion via FaceTime. Gio announced where he was taking new manufacturing.

If he had his way.

Which he was about to find out.

"Samuele, I have no idea how to reach my destination. Book a trip for me."

"Your Royal Highness, may I ask you to lift up your arms?" Three dress fitters swarmed around Luciana. She obliged, although the tight lace sleeves of the wedding gown didn't allow much flexibility of movement. "Just a bit higher, Princess, please. Most appreciated."

With the three-paneled mirror set up in front of a dais that provided easy access for alterations to the gown, Luciana was on display like a pirouetting ballerina in a child's wind-up jewelry box. One tailor slowly circled the bottom of the gown, pinning it for a perfect hemline. The other two attended to the rest of the fit.

"Would you prefer us to add a large lace flower at the waistline?" one of them asked. The question caught Luciana by surprised as it was the first one anyone had asked her since she was returned to the palace yesterday. Every last detail of her upcoming wedding had been decided on by the royal wedding planners and her father. She supposed that having disappeared for seven days she had further forfeited her right to any say in the matter. Although she was the bride, she felt like a mannequin that was only one element in the whole of the affair, of equal importance to the cake or the table settings. The fitter held a lace rose to the waistband of the gown. Then withdrew it for comparison.

The dress was so undeniably hideous the princess didn't think it much mattered whether yet one more adornment was added. At her father's request, the design had been modeled on the one worn by her great-great-grandmother at her own wedding. While a style that was hopelessly out of date could have a kind of retro charm, this one did not. She was reminded that the unbearable confines of this gown were what propelled her to finally stow away on that supply boat, and to take her fateful trip to Italy.

A stiff collar led to a fitted lace bodice and sleeves. The silk layer under the lace extended upward almost to the neckline, eliminating any hint of sexiness or even femininity to the décolleté area. Past the waistband, the skirt portion was full-on poof, round with gigantic petticoats that made her think she might be wearing a hot air balloon. Perhaps she could float up toward the clouds and be carried away.

A veil was affixed to her head. It was long enough to hoist beachcombers from Barcelona onto Izerote. The ensemble was finished off with uncomfortable matching pumps with decorative buckles—yes, buckles—encrusted with crystals.

"Princess?" The fitter was still waiting on her opinion about the lace rose at the waistband.

Luciana lazily shrugged her shoulders. She was defeated. Gio was right. She'd never been independent and she never would be. Why should she decide if the gown should have a flower on it? Let the dresser choose.

The royal planners had buzzed themselves into a tizzy as soon as the princess had been delivered back to the palace, with everyone told that she had been temporarily called off the island to lend her support to an urgent humanitarian crisis. A palace public relations spin, in action. But which, in essence, was accurate as far as she was concerned. Although, even if they knew the truth, she wouldn't have expected any sympathy from anyone at the palace about her own human need to soul search before she dedicated the rest of her life to the service of the crown.

Returning wasn't so easy, as she'd been changed by her journey. So her new goal would be to become more like her mother. To shut down, check out, not have an opinion about anything. She'd keep the life she wished she led alive in her mind, but walk through her real one.

"Kindly allow me a few minutes of privacy with my daughter." King Mario de la Isla de Izerote's stomp, then voice, reverberated off the walls as he shooed away the wedding staff. They assisted the princess down from the alterations dais before taking their leave.

Surely Luciana's father was the person least able to understand why she had to go to Florence. In fact, he hadn't even welcomed her back last night, merely sending a representative to convey his relief at her safe return. His wrath was to be one of the prices she'd pay for her defiance.

It was worth it, though, she confirmed to herself with a bite of her lower lip. "Father," she exhaled bravely.

"What have you done to your hair?"

"I had it cut and colored."

"That much is obvious."

As was expected of her, Luciana had always shown her father the utmost respect and deference. She loved him. If only he'd been a perceptive enough parent to see that spending her life isolated on this island where time stood still was a fate his daughter couldn't bear.

"I didn't mean to cause you worry," she stated with her head slightly bowed so she wouldn't have to make eye contact. "That's why I left you a note promising my return."

"It would have been proper protocol to ask my permission, not to stow away on a supply boat."

As she suspected, she'd been surveilled from the very beginning of her voyage.

"If you were following my every move, Father, why didn't you allow me the three weeks my note to you promised?"

"I received information that you were keeping company with a man. There was an incident involving *gelato*," he spat, as if it were a bitter taste in his mouth, "that my operatives interpreted as highly improper. I decided it best to sever that liaison as soon as possible, in your own best interest."

The princess brought her hand over her mouth in absolute mortification.

After a painful silence she said, "My best interest. I've tried to be a perfect daughter and a perfect princess."

"Is your idea of a perfect princess who is soon to be married one who cavorts around Florence with a man who isn't her fiancé?"

"That wasn't something I had planned." Nor was falling in love.

"Perhaps. But it was most undignified. We all have rules we must abide by, girl."

"I'm not a girl."

"You have acted like one."

No, he was wrong. For the first time in her life, Luciana had been a steel-eyed, rock-solid adult. Gio had taught her that. In seven short days, she'd learned more about being an adult from him than she had in her entire life.

Amazing Gio. Who thought for himself. From big-picture revelations to infinitesimal technological solutions. How often during her too-brief time with him had he asked her what she wanted and, if she didn't know, challenged her to find her answer? He shaped her into the woman she would now be. Which ruined her at the same time. As it was the man before her now to whom she was truly bound.

"It doesn't matter anymore. We live like museum pieces. We're fossils. I'll just turn to stone like mother did."

"Don't you think I know what you're feeling? I'm not so old that I don't remember what it was to be young. To crave drama and abandon. But I came to accept, as my forefathers did and as you will, too, that the honor and onus of the crown is far more important than any selfish goals that might try to lure us away."

Deep down, Luciana knew that her father was not the enemy. She could blame her fates if she wanted to. What good would that do her in the end?

"You will marry. And bear children. Your days will be full. These longings you have will pass. In time, you'll forget them."

"I don't love King Agustin." She loved Giovanni Grassi. And although she would never see him again, she would hold her love for him like a precious jewel in her hand until her last breath.

"And your mother did not love me." King Mario spoke a truth they both already knew. "Duty, Luciana. You'll truly be an adult when you stop battling your destiny."

Luciana shifted her eyes to the three panels of the dressing mirrors. There she stood in the ugly wedding gown she was to wear when her father would escort her down the aisle. Her father, who'd endured a loveless marriage that produced only one, ungrateful heir. A man who had to receive the middle-of-the-night phone call that his wife had been crushed to death in a car accident. Who did what he thought was his best with his only child.

"King Agustin will bring the jobs to our island we so desperately need," he reminded.

"Eroding our natural resources with tourist resorts? Is that really what's good for our subjects in the long run?"

"Without industry, we have no means to employ our people. It might not be the most inventive idea. However, it's what we're being offered."

Luciana studied her father's reflection in the three mirrors. His hair was still more pepper than salt. Shoulders that had always stood straight outlined a king with many decades left on the throne.

"Father, we have to think bigger."

"There is no other way."

There simply had to be. Despite her outward resignation, a whisper inside her heart told her she would not walk down that aisle to marry the widower king.

That evening after she'd changed into her nightgown and slippers, Luciana unpacked the suitcase she'd brought to Florence, refusing to let an assistant do it for her. As if they were as fragile as eggshells, she placed the two pairs of boyfriend jeans, the emerald green scarf from the San Lorenzo market and the bottle of Luci perfume in the back of the bottom drawer of her bureau. On top of them, she stacked a pillow and a blanket in the hope that her treasures wouldn't be discovered.

Slipping on her dressing gown, she stepped out onto the terrace of her sitting room. From this vantage point she could survey the north side of the island, facing toward the Spanish mainland.

It was a quiet night on the island, as always, with the

crash of the waves against the rock bluffs the only sound to be heard. The sea was rough, water bursting over and over again upon itself with turbulence similar to what she felt in her own center.

No matter how hard she tried, Luciana could not get her mind off Gio. It would eternally haunt her to ponder what it was that he had mouthed to her as the security detail forced her into that black car and squired her away from him. She knew what she hoped he had said. The same words she had screamed out to him, the last words she would ever speak to him.

What was he doing at this very moment? She allowed herself to imagine that it wasn't a palace terrace she looked out from tonight but, instead, the wrought iron Juliet balcony overlooking the courtyard of his villa. With its fragrant lavender and colorful flowers. That he was standing in the midst of it, gazing up at her, his sparkling eyes bright in the dark of night. Beckoning her to come down to him. To his embrace, to his kiss.

The moon tonight was high above the sea. Its distance made her think of a movie plot she'd heard of in which a woman had to be separated from her child. To ease her young son's mind, she promised him that every evening they would each look up to see the same moon. That no matter their distance, because they could both see the moon that would mean they were together.

Oh, Gio, please be looking at the moon. Please be with me tonight.

After staring at the sky with Gio in her heart for as long as she could take it, her eyes drifted to the hills and valleys of the island. To the west sat two abandoned factories, side by side. The eyesores were a constant reminder of the failures of Izerote, one of the reasons why

the island's leadership could not provide enough employment for its citizens.

Those two factories had been built by a manufacturing
company with the utmost in environmental protections as
to not disturb the pristine ecosystems of the island. En-
gineering and construction were costly in such a remote
location. Materials were brought by boat and with the use
of the small airstrip that allowed private planes to fly in.

What the business investors had failed to take into
consideration was that the machine tools they were manufacturing were heavy in weight and that shipping the
finished product back to Barcelona for distribution was
so costly all of the profits were eaten up. Within two
years, the factories closed and the employees were again
out of work. It was not only a catastrophe for the local
economy, it was an embarrassment to the king and his
advisory team.

If only those factories could be repurposed. If only a
small, lightweight product could be manufactured or assembled there, an enterprise that would learn from the
mistakes made in the past.

An idea stirred within Luciana.

It might not work. She might not get the necessary
parties to agree. Without much knowledge on what the
operation would involve, it might be an impossibility.

But what if the impossible was possible? What if?

Her mind swirled with a million thoughts and as many
questions. She'd get them all answered. Tomorrow.

By the time dawn broke, she'd spent all night typing
everything she'd thought of into her laptop. Ready to take
action. She stepped again out onto the terrace to greet
the day, assuming that if Gio had seen the same moon,
her love would share the sun with her, as well.

Good morning, my exquisite Gio. Can you help me again?

Wasn't it rather early in the morning for a small airplane to be landing onto the island's airstrip?

As the private plane he'd hired descended for landing, Gio got his first glimpse of the island of Izerote. Luciana had not exaggerated when she'd explained to him just how remote her home was. After the flight to Barcelona, Gio transferred to the small aircraft that shuttled him the rest of the way. Finishing the glass of blood orange juice the lone flight attendant had presented to him earlier, he surveyed the island from the window beside his seat.

Untouched mountain ranges covered much of the terrain. From his vantage point, he spotted three small coastal towns and two more inland. They appeared to be like most towns in Europe. Gio could make out a center area in each, the commercial core dense with buildings erected closely together. Surrounding those in something of a ring were the residential areas with the structures a bit farther apart, homes with small yards. And farther out still from the town center were the more rural properties, some with plots of farmland.

He even saw livestock dotting the green fields. Although not much, according to Luciana, who had explained that most of the food for the island's inhabitants was shipped or flown in. Which explained why goods and services were very expensive, thereby contributing to the reasons many of the citizens were moving off the island. A complex set of issues faced this tiny land. He hoped to be part of the solution.

In a valley, he saw two large buildings that looked like factories. From what Gio could see, they appeared to be empty. If that was the case, his purpose here could be even more easily accomplished. He vaguely remembered Luciana telling him about some ill-thought-out industry that had gone into business here only to fail. That disaster pushed her father even further toward deciding on the arranged marriage between Luciana and the widower king from the neighboring island.

Which was about to be called off, if he had any say about it.

When the palace finally came into view, Gio's pulse quickened. Somewhere within those walls was his love. Picturing Luciana still asleep in a royal bed, no doubt blanketed in the finest of fabrics with her lovely head upon the fluffiest of pillows, filled him with happiness. He could hardly wait to bring his lips to hers. To taste her sweetness. To hold her softness against him.

There were many obstacles to cross before he'd have her in his arms again. But he'd get there.

After touchdown onto the island, Gio located the hired car that had been reserved to take him to the palace. Thank heavens for Samuele at the office in Florence, whom Gio could always count on to get the job done. Samuele had also spoken with palace staff to make an appointment for Gio to speak with King Mario, as a formal meeting with the monarch seemed the most appropriate method of introduction.

Once at the palace entrance, the driver opened the car door for Gio to step out. He took in what he could see of the palace grounds. The whole of it was rather small, befitting the size of the island. Nonetheless it had the foreboding of a fortress with its surrounding barricades of stone.

Upon giving his name at the security gate, Gio was

directed to the offices of the king. He passed through entrance doors into a reception foyer. A large oak desk stood in the center. A telephone bank and computer suggested that the desk was useful to operations, although its chair was empty at the moment. Gio took stock of the computer equipment setup and deduced that Wi-Fi was available. Which answered one of the questions he had regarding the idea he'd come to speak to the king about.

A wooden door to Gio's right opened, and a young man in a jacket bearing the palace insignia on the breast pocket emerged but was called back before he exited. He didn't see Gio, and spoke loudly enough to whoever was behind the door that Gio was able to hear them.

"I'll take care of it, King Mario," the attendant continued while Gio eavesdropped. "Also Your Highness, Mr. Giovanni Grassi should be arriving shortly for your appointment. Palace Intelligence has just informed me that Mr. Grassi is the gentleman Princess Luciana had kept company with during her sojourn in Italy."

Uh-oh. Gio had hoped that the king wasn't going to find out the connection between him and Luciana prior to their meeting. He was sure that, as an overprotective father, he would disapprove of Gio after finding out he had been touring Florence with his daughter. Gio wanted to first discuss his plan with the king before he got on to personal business. And, indeed, there were urgent personal matters to discuss. But if the king knew who Gio was at the outset, his anger might bias his ability to hear him out.

"Very well, Your Highness, when Mr. Grassi arrives I'll let him know that you were unexpectedly called away and that your schedule is full for the foreseeable future."

Gio needed to think fast.

If this attendant saw him in the foyer and Gio introduced himself, he'd be escorted out of the palace grounds immediately. Now that the king had gotten word of Gio's association with Luciana, the original course of action was ruled out. He had to find a safe place to reevaluate.

"Thank you, King Mario." The attendant uttered his last words before he closed the door on the king's office.

Not knowing what else to do but disappear before he got caught, Gio hurried down a corridor that led away from the foyer. In his dark blue suit and carrying his Italian leather attaché case, he looked like a legitimate palace visitor. If he encountered anyone along his way, he could feign being lost on his way to an official conference.

Mentally taking note that the corridor was leading him west and then north, he decided that what he needed to do was find Luciana. She'd shelter him and then they'd speak with the king together. Not to mention the fact that every second he'd been apart from her since she left Florence two days ago had been torture. By her side was where he wanted to be as soon as possible, for now and for always.

When he observed a housekeeper wheeling a cart of bed linens up ahead, he assumed he had reached the residential section of the palace. He was on the right track. Trying first one then another, he finally found an unlocked door and ducked into a room before the housekeeper saw him. From behind the closed door he listened until the cart was rolled past.

Tapestries depicting nature scenes adorned the walls of the room he found himself in. Antique or antique-style furniture sat in the center of the room, which appeared to be a parlor. The decor was as oppressive as Luciana had described, mismatched pieces that wouldn't have even been stylish in their day. Even the telephone on the claw-footed table was of an old style, connecting to the wall through a cable. Plenty of lighting suggested that the electrical systems were fully functional, though. He wondered about the wiring on the rest of the island.

Glass doors opened from the parlor onto a stone terrace. Gio stepped through and out into the fresh air, quickly taking note of where security cameras were placed so that he could avoid them. The sea breezes were bracing. As he made a careful assessment, he could see that one terrace led to the next and the next all in a row, each separated by a wall.

Leaning forward and around to the adjacent terrace he saw that it was empty, and was able to get a footing and swing himself over to it. Keeping from view, he peeked into the windows of the room there. Another parlor area with no one inside. He made his way to the next terrace, then peered into that sitting room.

Luciana! He'd know his love anywhere even though he saw her only in profile as she sat at a small desk typing into a laptop. Blood surged through his veins at the sight of her, and he could hardly wait to reunite with the kindheartedness and intelligence that lay beneath her staggering beauty.

The blond hairdo she was so proud of was pulled into a ponytail. She wore one of her conservative dresses, this one in brown, and looked ready to shake hands and have her photo taken at an official function. Maybe this was how princesses dressed every day, whether or not they had an engagement to attend. He'd have much to learn about palace life in the future.

Not wanting to scare her, he rapped lightly on one of the panes of the glass door. When she glanced up and recognition slowly took hold, tears leaked out of her eyes.

He'd kiss away each one.

She sprang out of her chair and rushed to open the door. Throwing her arms around his neck, she fluttered a hundred kisses all over his face and pulled him into the room, shutting the door behind her.

He swallowed his breath with a mixture of relief, yearning and joy beyond any jumble of emotions he had ever imagined possible. One disastrous scenario that had run through his mind before coming was that once he arrived, she'd not want any more contact with him. That she was ready to move forward with her fates and would not be open to his plan. Her response assured him otherwise.

"Gio," she cried, kissing him passionately on the lips and then holding him tight. "My Gio."

CHAPTER TEN

AFTER THEY COULD momentarily tear themselves away from celebrating their reunion with hugs and kisses, Gio explained how he had wanted to meet with her father but that the king had refused. "I want to manufacture my biometric products here. I'll establish a production plant and a development center on Izerote."

Luciana could hardly believe Gio was really here, flesh and blood, in her sitting room at the palace. Florence seemed a world away. Her mind ping-ponged in a hundred directions. "I had the same idea! I was reminded of these factories we have on the island, and then one thought led to another. That maybe it would be good for both your business and for my people. I was going to contact you."

"With a different solution to create jobs on the island, surely your father won't force you to marry King Agustin."

Tears trickled down Luciana's cheeks again. Because Gio had thought of a way to save her from marrying a man she didn't love. How fundamentally considerate he was, even though she didn't doubt that this arrangement would benefit him, as well.

But after the shock of his arrival subsided, she reminded herself that Gio wasn't here to give her the rest of her life with the man she loved. He was on Izerote to do business. He'd made it clear that he wouldn't devote himself to a woman and was not interested in building a family. There was no cause to think he'd changed his mind simply because they had been physically intimate.

She thought of her last minute in Florence. How, as she was being escorted into the car that would take her away, she yelled out to Gio to tell him that she loved him. She'd never expected to see him again after that, but she'd wanted him to know. And she'd needed to hear herself say it out loud, if only once in her life. Gio had mouthed something back to her that she hadn't heard. What was it? She couldn't bring herself to just come right out and ask.

"I spotted the factories from the plane," Gio said. "Can we go see them?"

He needed all of the information he could gather in order to prepare a presentation for her father. She had to think of a way to let him see those factories and decide if they were usable for his enterprise.

She dared not disappear again. And she couldn't very well call for a palace driver and exit her sitting room with Gio in tow. Hmm…

Recalling that fateful night when she'd climbed off her terrace to hike down to the shore where she'd stowed away on the supply boat, she remembered that her path took her straight past the factories. Gio could go that same way, and she'd go by car and meet him there.

"Good thinking, Princess." Gio planted a passionate kiss onto her lips before he hopped over the terrace wall like a swashbuckler in an old movie.

When Luciana told the driver where she wanted to go,

he balked. "Your Highness, I don't believe there is anyone on the premises there anymore."

"Thank you, Nico. If you'll just proceed, I'll take it from there." It turned out Gio must have brought a little of Luci with him from Florence. Because the princess was finished with acquiescing to what everyone, including a palace driver, thought she should be doing.

Regardless of the outcome of her plan with Gio, there was no turning back. If she refused to marry King Agustin, what could he and her father do? Throw her in jail? That didn't scare her. She was already in one.

Telling Nico to return for her in an hour, she found Gio on the property inspecting the buildings. Windows on all sides allowed them to get a good look into the inside of the factories. Gio was pleased that they were in good condition, and he could tell from the solar panels and lighting design that the structures were built with energy efficiency. He made guesstimates about the size of the work floors and how many assembly stations he could set up.

"This is really quite perfect," he said as he took her hand, his palm bathing her in instant warmth. Even if they were to be tied together only in business, Luciana thanked the universe that she'd at least have Gio in some way if they could bring this to fruition. Her world was a better place with him in it, even if he wasn't going to be at her side like she wished he would.

"Yes," she echoed. "Perfect." *Well, almost.*

They walked together to a grassy embankment behind the factories that overlooked the coast. She studied his profile while he looked out to the waves.

It was incongruous, his handsome face on *her* island. The magnificent curls blowing in *her* sea breeze.

"Luci," he said, using the distinction in her name. "I didn't come to this idea only because it would be good for my corporation. Or even to help you get out of your forced engagement to King Agustin."

"You didn't?"

"No, *bellissima*." He turned to her and took hold of both of her shoulders. His strong hands traced their way inward to her throat and then rode upward to caress her jaw, until he held her face in his hands. "My actions are not merely intended to keep you from another man. I'm here because I want you. I won't say I want you to belong to me. Because you belong to yourself. You're more than capable of standing on your own two feet. And I want to walk beside you. I want to catch you if you fall. I want you to catch me, too."

He placed a light kiss on her lips. Luciana shivered with cold abandon when he let his hands drop from her face. Then her spirit soared again when he went down on one knee and looked up to her with a sparkle in his eyes that she'd swear was more beautiful than all the gemstones in the world.

"I thought I would never partner with someone. That I wouldn't make time, that I wouldn't trust. Until I met you. You fill me up rather than deplete me. I don't know if you heard me declare my love to you in Firenze as the car was taking you away from me. I love you. I have never loved before. And I never will again. My love is only for you."

She covered her mouth as the shock settled in. "But I am bound to live here in Izerote. Someday I will be queen."

"I've lived all over the world. I'll make my life here in order to be with you. I can adapt. Home is where you are. Our wills are strong. We can make this work. Your Royal Highness Princess Luciana de la Isla de Izerote, will you marry me?"

Luciana fell to her knees to meet him eye to eye. Mouth to mouth. "Yes, Gio, we *will* find a way. You are my one true love, too. Of course I'll marry you."

The clack of King Mario's boots against the wooden floor was thunderous even from behind his closed office door as Luciana and Gio approached.

"Princess." The attendant in the blazer with the palace insignia whom Gio had avoided earlier now marched toward them. "Please allow me to notify the king that you wish an audience with him."

"Thank you, Joaquin, but I refuse to make an appointment to speak to my own father," Luciana rebuffed him as she opened the office door.

Gio slipped in behind her and closed the heavy door until he heard it click shut.

"Luciana." The king looked up from his audible pacing across his office floor.

"Giovanni Grassi," Gio introduced himself and hurried to meet the king face-to-face, thrusting out his hand for a proper handshake.

King Mario merely looked at his hand and continued on his walking course.

"Bow," Luciana mouthed to Gio.

Bow? Gio couldn't believe such an antiquated custom was still used on this remote little island that, frankly, had no relevance on the world stage. He knew that bowing to royalty was protocol in formal settings, but he somehow expected a man-to-man shake would be more appropriate to this private meeting.

The king returned to his paces.

It was with a grinding of his teeth that Gio bowed his head. "It's a great honor to meet you, sir."

He wasn't sure if *sir* was an acceptable address, but Gio was doing the best he could.

King Mario sized him up, his approval or disapproval impossible to read.

Gio decided to forge ahead with a preemptive, "Your Highness, I do apologize that our acquaintance begins so unusually. After I received the intelligence that you were unwilling to meet with me, I took a bold action in conferencing with the princess."

The king finally stopped his pacing and stood facing Gio, crossing his arms over his chest. "Indeed."

"I hope that when I, when we—" Gio gestured to Luciana, who stood beside him "—fully explain our proposal, you'll agree that the plan benefits all concerned."

"So, you and my daughter have already mapped out the future of Izerote? Mr. Grassi, you've known of the existence of this island for exactly how long?"

"A week, Your Highness. Please allow me to explain."

King Mario said nothing, merely nodding his head once. Princess Luciana straightened her spine and made herself taller, which Gio took as a positive sign of her willingness to stand up to her father.

Fortunately, from the minute Gio had had this idea, he'd been compiling scores of information. As he talked of his plan to bring the manufacturing of his biometrics to Izerote, he was able to emphasize Grasstech's eco-friendly practices that Luciana had told him were very important to her father. They were the sticking point that had caused him to reject other propositions in the past for enterprise on the island.

The strategy appeared to be working because King Mario listened attentively. "And depending on your preferences, if you so choose we could operate the factories on a twenty-four-hour cycle, with three sets of staff working eight-hour shifts, allowing us to employ thousands of your citizens."

"Not to mention that Gio will be able to bring the highest level of technology into our homes and throughout all the other businesses on the island," Luciana chimed in.

"At my expense, sir. We'd seek to modernize Izerote on a full scale."

Luciana surprised Gio by taking his hand. Which felt so right, Gio's chest swelled.

King Mario took note of the hand-holding.

The act was a declaration of independence that was difficult for her father. Just the same, Gio was proud of his beloved for doing it.

"I suppose you two have got all of *that* figured out, as well," the king stated flatly as he gestured to their hands in each other's.

"We do."

"I love Gio, Father. I knew it from the moment I met him."

"Your Highness, I will admit that I'm an informal man. My employees address me by my first name. Most of the time I'm wearing a pair of jeans and sipping a cappuccino as I hover over a computer." Although he had donned his finest dark blue Savile Row suit to meet the king today.

Luciana smiled at the comment about the jeans. Gio's mind paraded back to their time in Florence when Luci had first bought the pairs of baggy jeans that she was so thrilled to wear while they took in the sights.

He and his love locked eyes, making the world disappear. With her gazing at him like that, the affection and closeness they'd come to share, Gio could conquer the world.

"I'm well aware that as a commoner, sir, I have a lot to learn about palace etiquette. Therefore, again I beg your forgiveness if I'm not following royal decorum when I ask you for your daughter's hand in marriage."

"You are already engaged." King Mario's glare could shatter glass.

"To a man that I don't love."

"Perhaps you will in time, child."

"I'm not a child and I could never love King Agustin. Because I love Gio and there would never be any room in my heart to love another. Father, I know that you and Mother didn't have the kind of romantic love that only the lucky few are destined for. But I've been chosen. Don't you think that brings its own duty? Even though you didn't have it, don't you want that for me? I believe my mother would have."

The king's face transformed dramatically, morphing into one of a much softer man, changing into a loving father.

"I know this is a lot to take in all at once, Father. May we please sit down together?" She pointed to the dark wood conference table and chairs in front of the bay windows. "We want to tell you so much more about our plan for Grasstech on Izerote."

An hour later, Gio didn't know whether King Mario had admitted defeat or had been simply won over by his and Luciana's enthusiasm. There had been enough of the occasional half smiles and several nods indicating his comprehension of the plan that Gio was satisfied.

He wanted to conclude the meeting while things were still going well.

Just one more part of the endeavor needed to be outlined. "King, there's a final matter we need to discuss."

"How do I look?" Gio buttoned his jacket and modeled for Luciana as they prepared for the public address.

She lifted up on tiptoe to give her handsome fiancé a kiss on his mouth before she applied her lipstick. "My love, you look as fine in your bespoke suits as you would in a tuxedo or in swim trunks." And added with a wink, "Or in nothing at all."

"I can't believe how nervous I am. I've spoken in public many times before."

"It's the palace balcony bit. Intimidates the best of us."

Allowing a royal dresser to approve them as they passed through the corridor, the princess and her soon-to-be husband were escorted to the inner chamber that led to the official balcony. Luciana could hear the murmur of the citizens on the grounds below. It was a din she'd heard often enough to be able to estimate that it was a packed crowd with most of Izerote in attendance.

She had to admit to some jitters herself, as she generally appeared beside her father as a porcelain doll who merely waved and rarely spoke. Today, she had a lot to tell her subjects.

King Mario joined them and they were announced as His Royal Highness King Mario de la Isla de Izerote, Her Royal Highness Princess Luciana and honored guest Mr. Giovanni Grassi of Florence.

Gio looked to Luciana for instruction, and she pointed for him to step out onto the balcony. The crowd below stretched as far as the eyes could see. With the palace grounds not able to hold the mass, people stood all the way back to the entrance lawn in order to get a glimpse of the royal family when they took to the balcony. Their appearance was met with loyal applause and cheers.

Luciana peered down to the people and worked to spot individual faces in the crowds. A young father held his toddler up on his shoulders, the boy's arms wrapped around his neck. Teenaged girls looked up to Luciana with palpable admiration. An older couple linked arms.

Truly, Luciana loved Izerote. The untamed natural beauty. The cordiality and goodness of its people. She slanted her eyes sideways to steal a glance at Gio. With this man by her side, she could do her duty to these citizens. As a pair they would not only change the island for the benefit of these deserving people, they'd leave a future of stewardship and prosperity for generations to come. Luciana again focused on the little boy atop his father's shoulders in the crowd.

"Princess." King Mario leaned in to speak only to his daughter. "You've forced me to see how much my own fear has suffocated you. I love you, daughter. You've become a wise woman. You'll make a fine queen someday."

"I love you, too. Dad." The corners of both of their mouths tipped up in a private almost smile that they alone shared.

King Mario then thrust his shoulders back and faced his subjects.

"Thank you, citizens of Izerote, for joining us today," he spoke through the standing microphone placed on the balcony. The crowd cheered. The king explained the arrangement he'd made with Grasstech to create jobs and futures for the island's population. He invited Gio to speak.

"My father began Grasstech forty years ago," he began, "at a time when computer technology was ancient compared with what it is today. He founded the company with the command to his employees to think deep, to think wide, to think far outside of the box. King Mario has told you a bit about what we plan to do here in Izerote. But, in reality, that is only the beginning. We don't yet know how high we can fly, how fast we can soar. I can hardly wait for us, together, to find out."

The throng roared with approval. Luciana filled with pride at Gio's inspiring words.

Now it was her turn to stand in front of the microphone. She peeked over to Gio, then took her place in the center of the balcony, righteous and strong.

"I am pleased to see so many children here." She pointed to six or so in her sight. "Because any actions we take today affect them tomorrow. Gio has outlined our plans to bring living wages and enduring jobs to our people. As parents, and as future parents, we understand that in order for us to be successful in our work, we need to know that our children are being meaningfully looked after. That's why I'm pleased to announce the formation of the Luci Foundation, a new initiative that will create free, quality child care for our youngest citizens until they are old enough to go to school."

Many in the audience applauded, especially the women.

Luciana bowed her head to her father, who, after she and Gio laid out their intentions for this element of the plan, had consented.

"In addition to devoting myself to you as a monarch," she continued, "it has always been my own personal dream to work with young children. To help parents raise confident, happy, creative and secure children who will grow into the big-thinking adults Gio just spoke of. I ask you today to support me in my quest. I would like to continue my education to earn an advanced degree in early childhood education so that I can lead the Luci Foundation with experience and expertise, and work together with you to bring Izerote the progress and prosperity I know we can achieve."

Her speech was met with ovations of endorsement.

In reality, Luciana had always known that her father was wrong when he insisted that the citizens of the island did not want advancement and modernization. It was only he who feared it. The protective king didn't want to put his people, or his daughter, in danger and thought that by keeping them sheltered and separate he could better safeguard them.

She and Gio would teach him. Slowly, in a way that was comfortable to him.

Her lovely Gio had already broken the ice when after the meeting in the king's office yesterday, the conversation turned friendly and Gio taught his future father-in-law how to check the weather and the world's stock markets on his smartphone.

King Mario handed something to Gio, who nodded knowingly. She'd spied them having a private tête-à-tête this morning but didn't know what the topic was.

His Royal Highness moved to the microphone. "Our family has another announcement to make. Princess Luciana has made a change in her personal plans. She will not be marrying King Agustin de la Isla de Menocita. I spoke with the king this morning and he wishes everyone on our island peace and prosperity in the future."

A hush of shock swept across the gathering. Luciana swallowed hard, knowing that she was perhaps disappointing people with this news. She was compelled to take over the microphone from her father and speak candidly.

"Are any of you in love?" she asked her subjects. Bellows and yelps came from different areas of the grounds. Couples kissed. Others smiled. "I hope you'll agree that there's no predicting love. Quite unexpectedly, I have fallen in love. To a man I wish to marry. Although he is a commoner, I hope that you will accept him and learn to love him as much as I do. Together, we will earn your trust. Ladies and gentlemen, Mr. Giovanni Grassi is not only the genius mind who will help us take our island into the next generation and beyond, he is also the man I will marry and bear children with."

Gio stepped forward and opened his hand. It held Luciana's great-grandmother's wedding ring. She remembered the family stories about Esmerelda being the only one in her lineage who fell in love with her husband after an arranged marriage.

Luciana mouthed *Thank you* to her father.

Her fiancé placed the ring on her finger.

The princess took his hand in her left and her father's in her right. The three faced the crowd, who went wild with well-wishes.

Gio and Luciana had their first official kiss as an engaged couple, which was welcomed with resounding cheers that echoed all the way to the blue skies above.

* * * * *

SPECIAL FORCES
FATHER

VICTORIA PADE

To my editor, Elizabeth Mazer,
who kindly, tactfully and with humor embraces
my characters, kicks them in the shins and
complicates their lives in ways that make better
books. I have so, so enjoyed our collaborations
and would give much for it to go on and on.

Chapter One

"It's princess hair."

Really bad princess hair, Dani Cooper thought as she looked at herself in the hand mirror that her four-year-old hairstylist Evie Freelander brought her.

But she said, "Oh, I feel like a princess now."

"That's not princess hair," Evie's twin brother, Grady, decreed when he looked up from his coloring book to assess his sister's work. "Princess hair looks pretty."

"It's pretty because Dani is pretty!" Evie insisted.

"Thank you," Dani said with a laugh, turning her head from side to side to get the full view of her long dark mahogany hair. Evie had attempted to braid four different clumps of it and then secured those clumps with neon hair clips haphazardly around her head.

Dani had applied light makeup that April morning to accentuate her golden-brown eyes, her thin nose and her full lips, and that was still in place this evening, but she was glad no one outside the Freelander home would be seeing her like this.

"Okay, clean up now," she said. "It's time for our ten-minute dance party to get the wiggles out, and then it's pajamas and your wind-down for bed."

"Dance party!" Grady shouted, quickly putting his markers in their box while Evie made a face and fell back on the sofa as if in a faint.

"Can Grady help me?" she moaned.

After three years as the twins' nanny, Dani knew this routine. "Nope," she answered Evie. "Grady is picking up his stuff and you need to pick up yours. Or we'll dance without you!" she finished with a cheery reminder of what the consequences would be.

Evie groaned again, sat up as if it was a chore for her and gathered the mirror, toy hairbrush and what remained of the clips to put away.

"I'll meet you in the dance room," Dani called after them when they headed for their rooms to return their things.

The Freelander house was a large, starkly contemporary structure of glass, steel and concrete. It sat far back on a huge lot at the end of a cul-de-sac in one of Denver's upscale gated communities in the Cherry Creek area. The distance from the street allowed for some privacy despite the undraped windows that comprised almost the entire front of the house.

The twins' mother had taken ballet lessons several times a week as her workout and the in-home studio occupied one of the front-facing rooms. The kids liked to cut loose there. They got a kick out of the echo. So that was where Dani let them have their dance parties.

As she went into the dark room she could see outside, where the curved drive was illuminated by in-ground lighting. But the minute she turned on the lights the windows reflected only inside the room.

She got the music started just as the four-year-olds ran back in.

"Ready?" she asked them before all three of them launched into some free-form jumping, footwork and wiggling around that amounted to wild gyrations more than anything that resembled dancing.

Their ten minutes were nearly up when the doorbell rang.

Dani's friend Bryan had said he might stop by tonight after the kids were asleep, so she hadn't yet turned on the security system. He was early.

At the sound of the doorbell the dancing stopped and, as Dani turned off the music, both kids went to the window, where they bracketed their eyes with their hands and pressed their faces to the glass to see out.

"It's a so-dyer," Grady announced.

"A soldier?" Dani repeated the word he'd mispronounced.

"It is," Evie confirmed.

With the twins following behind, Dani left the studio and went to the marble entry hall, certain that the eight-foot-high steel front door was locked. Beside the door were an intercom and a small screen that displayed the images picked up by the camera outside.

"You're right, it is a soldier," she mused, convinced by the officer's service uniform and the straight, stiff military stance of their visitor that made him look as if he were at attention out there.

She pushed the button on the intercom and said, "Can I help you?"

"I'm Liam Madison. I got a message from someone named Dani Cooper. I'm looking for the Freelander house…"

Ohhh, she knew the name Liam Madison.

Not the man but the name.

But since she didn't know the man and she was very protective of the twins, she said, "Do you have some identification?"

He produced a military ID, complete with a picture, and held it up to the camera.

Holy cow, he was handsome!

And that was only his ID picture.

She'd been distracted by the uniform, but when he took the ID away from the camera lens she took in the sight of his face, realizing that he was definitely hella-handsome. He also was, indeed, Liam Madison, and since it was Dani who had reached out to him, and the twins who were in need of him, she unlocked the door and opened it.

"Hi," she said simply, taking in what neither the four-inch security screen nor the ID picture had done justice to.

Not only was the guy gorgeous, he was also over six feet tall, broad shouldered, toned and muscular. His hair was closely cropped and the color of unsweetened chocolate. His face was a masterpiece of chiseled bone that gave him refined cheekbones, a sharp jawline, a sculpted chin and a nose that was kept from being completely perfect by a bit of a boney bridge. He had slightly thin lips, and the bluest eyes she'd ever seen, streaked by silver to make them even more remarkable.

"I'm Dani Cooper," she introduced.

"Ma'am," he said formally to acknowledge the introduction.

"This is a surprise," she said.

"I was granted an emergency family leave and just got off a plane at Buckley Air Force Base."

"Even though you're a—"

"Marine. Yes, ma'am."

"*Is* he a so-dyer?" Grady asked, hiding behind Dani while Evie stood to one side of her.

"Soldiers are army," he corrected.

He got points for understanding the word, but getting so technical with a four-year-old only made Dani smile.

Just before she remembered what Evie had done to her hair and how she looked meeting this man for the first time.

But if he'd noticed that she was unsightly there was

no evidence of it. And there was nothing she could do about it now, so she merely said, "This is Grady and this is Evie," nodding to each child in turn. "Guys, this was a friend of your mom's. His name is Liam."

Any mention of their late parents sobered them and this was no exception.

"Say hello," she prompted when neither the kids nor Liam Madison responded to the introduction.

"H'lo," both children parroted, eyeing him somberly the way they did all strangers.

"Nice to meet you," the marine said as much by rote as the kids' greeting had been.

It occurred to Dani just then that she'd kept their guest outside long enough. She invited him in and dispatched the twins to put on their pajamas.

"Get your blankets for wind-down and I'll bring your yogurts and milk in just a minute," she instructed as Liam Madison stepped across the threshold to stand at attention inside rather than out.

Hella-handsome but not warm and fuzzy. Dani was familiar with that military-instilled rigidity.

As the kids bounded out of the entry she closed the door, motioned behind her with a thumb over her shoulder and said, "Why don't we talk in the kitchen? I'll be able to hear them better from there."

The marine nodded curtly and followed her as she led him in the same direction the kids had gone, to the rear of the expansive house.

"Can I get you something to eat or drink?" she asked along the way.

"Thank you, no. But you could tell me who you are, exactly."

Like the rest of the house, the kitchen was industrial,

and she offered him a seat on one of the metal bar stools at the stainless steel island in the center of it.

He didn't accept the offer, remaining standing at one end of the island while Dani went behind it and got out bowls, spoons and glasses, and then took yogurt and milk from the fridge.

"I've been Evie and Grady's nanny since they turned a year old and switched from a baby-nurse. Well, I've been their primary nanny. There was one who came in at bedtime for overnights, and another for the weekends. But after the accident—"

"What kind of accident?" he interrupted. "Your message said that's how Audrey and her husband died but you didn't give any details."

Dani had no idea what kind of feelings this man might still have for Audrey, so she trod lightly when she answered. "It was a car wreck. I don't know what you know about Owen, Audrey's husband…"

"When she ended things with me she just said she'd met someone else," he said matter-of-factly, giving no indication that he had any lingering resentments. Or tender feelings either.

"Owen Freelander was an acclaimed architect. He designed and built this place—it was his showpiece. His crowning glory just before he retired."

"Retired?"

"He was a lot older than Audrey. He'd just turned sixty-eight a few weeks before the accident."

"Sixty-eight?" the marine repeated in surprise. "Audrey was a year younger than I am so she was thirty-one… Her husband was thirty-seven years older?"

"He seemed like a young sixty-eight, but there was definitely an age difference. And even though he also seemed healthy, he had a heart attack driving home that night three weeks ago. He died when he lost control of the car and hit a tree. Audrey was critically injured. She only lived for two days…"

Still unsure how the marine felt about her late employer, Dani paused a moment and then said, "I'm sorry."

"It's a shock—this whole thing is a shock—but I haven't seen or heard from Audrey in over five years. I didn't wish her any harm but I moved on a long time ago. I don't think I'm in line for condolences."

Dani nodded as she finished spooning yogurt into bowls. "Audrey lived just long enough to tell me about you, to ask me to try to contact you to take the twins."

"Because I'm their father?"

The guy seemed tough as nails until he said that, and Dani heard an underlying note in his voice, clueing her in to how dumbfounded and unsettled he really was by the prospect.

"She told me that she knew she was pregnant when she broke up with you but there was something about a phone call when she hadn't been able to talk to you for months? Whatever you said to her made her know that was how it would always be?"

"I'm Force Recon… Reconnaissance… That's US Marine Special Forces. When I'm on a mission I'm out of touch. I can't be reached. That's how it had been for a while before I had the chance to call her, after we'd seen each other the last time. It's how every mission is, how my next mission was going to be. And I never know how long a mission will take. Plus I couldn't ever tell her where I was or what I was doing either. She couldn't know anything," he explained. "No one can."

"Well, I guess that conversation, learning that, convinced her that she didn't want a relationship anymore with someone who wasn't available to her. She'd found out that she was having twins. She'd met Owen and he wanted her to marry him. He was even willing to claim the babies as his own. Owen's name is on the birth certificates as Evie and Grady's dad." Dani said that last part gently because she also had no idea how it might affect him.

He scowled but she wasn't sure whether that was out of anger or hurt or what. But since he didn't say anything, she went on answering his initial question about who she was.

"Anyway, Audrey told me that you—not Owen—are the twins' father. She knew she wasn't going to make it and neither Audrey nor Owen had any family to turn to for the kids. She said you were all they would have left and that I needed to let you know about them. To try to contact you through the marines..."

He was still just frowning, saying nothing, so she merely continued.

"There wasn't even a guardian named in their wills, so when Audrey passed, Evie and Grady became wards of the state. But I just couldn't see them go into foster care. I sent you that message right away and talked to Owen's attorney so he could approach the court to ask that I be named the twins' temporary guardian. I told the judge what Audrey had confessed about you, and that I'd sent you word, and asked that they let me do whatever needed to be done so Evie and Grady could at least stay at home, with a familiar face, until this gets sorted through. So that's who I am—formerly their nanny, now their guardian."

"We're ready," Evie called.

"I'll be right back," Dani said, taking a tray with the bowls of yogurt and the glasses of milk across the kitchen to the stairs that led to the children's portion of the house. It was four steps down from the main floor and devoted to the twins' bedrooms and a nanny's suite she was using. There was also a play area and a living room complete with the kids' own entertainment center.

"Is that man still here?" Grady whispered as she got them set up to watch the animated shows they were allowed before bed.

"He is. We're talking in the kitchen if you need me."

"He's kinda scary," Evie whispered, too.

"You don't need to be scared of him. Remember he was a friend of your mom's. She wouldn't have been friends with him if there was anything to be scared about, would she?"

There was no answer, so Dani said, "She wouldn't have been. I think he's just a little sad that she's gone—like we all are."

Their expressions were skeptical but they were more interested in getting to the cartoons, so she started those and left them to watch while she returned to the kitchen and Liam Madison standing where she'd left him.

"So…" she said when she got there, hoping to prompt him to say something.

"It's been over five years. Not a word, not a hint that I have kids…" he said.

"Yeah…" Dani debated whether or not to address that. Then she decided that he needed the whole story so she said, "Audrey told me that she'd planned never to tell you. She said when she met Owen he was at a time in his life when he regretted that he'd put everything into his career and didn't have any family. She said you weren't in a position to be a dad, and she had been afraid to raise kids on her own. She said Owen could be there for them all, that he could take care of the three of them, and that was something she needed. Something she wanted—to be taken care of…"

"That sounds like her," he acknowledged. "She wasn't the most strong or independent person."

And there he was, as strong as they came and exuding the ability to protect. Knowing the kind of woman Audrey had been, Dani could see how she would have been drawn to that. Until she'd had to face the fact that he wouldn't be around for long periods of time to fill that role.

Dani watched the marine take a deep breath and exhale slowly. "When I got your message I called my older brother. He's here, in Denver. He got me a lawyer. The lawyer says the first thing that needs to be done is to prove that I *am* the father. There needs to be a DNA test."

"The court will need that, too, or they won't even consider giving you custody... If custody is what you want..."

He didn't confirm that *was* what he wanted.

Instead, in a clipped, just-stating-the-facts voice, he said, "The timing tracks. I know it's possible that I fathered Audrey's kids. I don't know that anything would have ever worked out between Audrey and me—there weren't any plans, and we were just having fun—but if those kids are mine..."

There was resignation in that, but he wasn't jumping for joy at the possibility.

"I'll do what's right," he ultimately admitted.

"And what's right might just be finding them a good, loving home with people who want them..." She felt the need to say it. After all, she was there to make sure the kids ended up in the best home possible, and she wasn't convinced that even a biological father was the right choice if that man wasn't thrilled with being a parent to them.

"I've thought about it, though," he went on. "And even if they aren't mine... Well, I considered Audrey a friend—"

A friend with benefits, apparently, Dani thought. But she didn't say it.

"—and I know she didn't have anyone. So even if her kids aren't mine, I want to make sure that they're taken care of in the best way possible. That they aren't just left in a bad situation."

That was commendable.

"And if they *are* mine," he continued, "I should get to know them."

"That's probably a good idea," she agreed. Especially since Audrey hadn't seemed to have any doubt whatsoever that the twins were his.

"So... I don't know... What would you say to me maybe coming here to stay with the three of you? That way I could help out with them, too, learn some of the ropes, just in case..." His dark eyebrows arched suddenly, showing how baffled he was by this whole thing. "This place is huge and I can bunk anywhere you'd be comfortable with... If you would be comfortable with sharing a place with a complete stranger."

Dani had to think about that. He was right. She would be agreeing to share a house with a complete stranger. A big, muscular, handsome-as-all-get-out stranger. None of which told her that he was a person she could trust.

On the other hand, Audrey really hadn't left any question that he was the twins' father. He'd come from who knew where the minute he'd learned that he might have kids. And while he was obviously shaken by the news, he was still willing to take responsibility whether or not the kids *were* his, to make sure they were well taken care of.

None of those things spoke of character she shouldn't—or couldn't—trust. At least enough to put him in one of the rooms on the upper levels of the house.

And she did think that it would be good for the kids to get to know him. It would be a good idea for her to check him out, too, in case it came to handing Evie and Grady over to him.

"I think it would probably be okay," she said then. "I'm staying in a room downstairs near the kids, but there are four empty bedrooms up another floor from here, and a guest suite that's in that sort of box that sits a level higher than that—"

"I wondered what that was. It looks like a tower for an air traffic controller."

"I know. It's nice, though. Plush. Plus the view is something to see and there's a deck to go out onto. The kids and I went up there to watch the city's fireworks display last summer and it was like being in the sky at eye level with them. Unless you don't like heights…"

"I'm fine with heights," he informed her as if there shouldn't have been any question.

"There's also an elevator up to it if you don't want to climb all the stairs," Dani added.

"I think I'll be fine with the stairs, too," he said in the same way he'd said he didn't have a problem with heights.

And of course he would be all right with the stairs with thighs the size of tree trunks inside those uniform pants, she thought.

But what she said was, "Do you want to stay tonight?"

"My brother and his fiancée are expecting me tonight. I haven't seen any of my family in over ten months, so I need to check in. But tomorrow—"

"Sure, you can just move in whenever you're ready."

He switched gears then. "According to my lawyer we can go to a doctor or to a lab for the DNA tests—it's just a couple of mouth swabs—but it has to go through channels in order for the court to accept it. The twins must have a doctor, right? I was thinking that if their doctor would do it—somebody they know—they might not be scared. If something like that would scare them... I don't know."

But he was thinking of them, of how to make things easiest on them, and Dani appreciated that. "I can call their pediatrician first thing in the morning and set it up. I'll try for an appointment tomorrow so we can get it in the works," she offered.

"Good," he said with a nod and the return of those arched eyebrows that seemed to give away whenever the possible reality of being a dad struck and rattled him. "I got a cell phone when I hit the States. Let me give you the number."

He did and Dani gave him hers, assuring him that she would let him know if they could get into the doctor the next day.

"Otherwise, what's a good time for me to move in tomorrow?"

"The kids' preschool is closed for spring break this coming week and next so I'll let them sleep until they wake up on their own—eight o'clock at best. After that tomorrow is pretty open."

"So maybe we'll just play it by ear?"

"Sure."

He nodded, keeping his focus on her so that Dani again remembered how weird she looked and wished she didn't.

But he still didn't remark on it or question her about it. Instead, after seeming to apply her appearance to memory, he said, "I'll take off then, get to my brother's."

He glanced in the direction of the lower level and said, "Should I say goodbye or something?"

Dani almost smiled at the confusion in his voice that said he was at a complete loss of what to do with kids.

"It's up to you. If you want to. But they get pretty engrossed in their cartoons at wind-down and I wouldn't expect too much from them."

"I like that you just said I'm a friend of their mother's, though. I wasn't sure who to say I am…"

"Yeah, let's just start there. They've had a lot to deal with since the accident. Keeping things as simple as possible seems to work best."

"And if I *am* their father…we'll figure out how to say that?"

"We'll cross that bridge when we come to it."

"If we come to it."

So he had some doubts. She supposed he was entitled to that after Audrey kept him in the dark.

Dani walked him to the front door, opening it for him and realizing only then that there was a big, black rented SUV parked in the drive just outside the dance studio, so he must have seen what was going on in there when he arrived.

And thinking about how she just cut loose during dance parties with the kids—all while her hair was in the state it was in tonight—was a little disheartening and a whole lot embarrassing.

But she decided against saying anything and only said good-night.

Then she watched him walk out to his rental, unable not to notice that his backside was as good as his front.

But it didn't matter. The guy had a lot to deal with,

and she was only there to care for, advocate for and protect the twins.

And once that was taken care of, she had decisions of her own to make. Big ones.

So the way he looked didn't make any difference.

Chapter Two

"That was some hard-core sack time—eleven hours straight. You must have been beat."

"I was coming off about thirty-six hours without, so yeah," Liam confirmed to his older brother, Conor, on Monday morning over coffee and the bacon and eggs Conor had made. "Sorry, though, for being the lousy houseguest who comes in the door and just crashes."

"No problem, I understand. And so did Maicy."

Liam had barely said hello to the woman his brother was now engaged to and shared a house with—Maicy Clark. They'd grown up with Maicy in the small Montana town of Northbridge. Conor and Maicy had only recently met up again, resolved old issues and rekindled their romance.

But after a brief greeting when Liam had arrived from the Freelander place the night before, he'd begged off to get much-needed sleep.

"I was just glad to hit the rack," he said. "But now that I have, the first thing I need to hear about is Declan."

Liam hadn't known anything unusual had been going on with his twin until a week ago when he'd returned from his latest mission—the same time he'd received the message from Dani Cooper about Audrey. The message waiting from Conor had been old and it had only relayed that Declan had been wounded in action.

After receiving the two communications, Liam had immediately called Conor. But even then his older brother had said only that Declan was all right. Liam could tell Conor had been holding something back but he hadn't been able to get him to say more. Because their phone time had been limited, Liam had needed to move on to the other news that had rocked him. Since then Liam had been in transit and unable to make more contact.

Last night Conor had only repeated that Declan was okay, but now Liam wanted to hear the details.

"It happened two days after Mom passed—after I'd called you about that. But when I tried to get hold of you to tell you about Declan, you were already out of reach," Conor began.

Their mother had died in October. It hadn't come as a surprise. She'd been in a steep decline physically and mentally for over a year by then. In some ways it had been a relief to Liam to hear it on the eve of his mission because at least he'd left knowing she wasn't suffering any longer.

"Mom died, I left, Declan got hurt—all in three days?" Liam said, giving a succinct timeline.

"Yeah, it was a helluva three days," Conor said, showing some of the strain it had put on him.

"So what happened?" Liam prompted.

"Declan and Topher were in a Humvee when they drove over a buried IED."

Topher was Topher Samms. Like Maicy, Topher had grown up in the same small town with the Madisons. Both Liam and his twin brother, Declan, had considered Topher their best friend. The three of them had even gone through Annapolis and joined the marines together.

"Is Topher okay, too?" Liam asked, suspicious that this was the first he'd heard his friend's name mentioned in the incident that had injured Declan.

"I'm sorry, Liam," Conor said, his words, tone and expression enough to convey that Topher hadn't made it.

That news was another blow to Liam, who closed his eyes and leaned on forearms he set on the table on either side of his breakfast. He let his head fall between his shoulders and took a steeling breath that he held until his lungs burned, all while Conor gave him that moment.

It was a lengthy one as he tried to digest that his and Declan's old friend was gone.

When he could, he exhaled, sat up straight and opened his eyes again.

"Tell me about Declan," he said curtly because it was the only way he could keep emotions in check.

"It's been rough," Conor finally admitted. "There was more than once that we came near to losing him—"

"But we didn't. You didn't let that happen."

Conor was a navy doctor and navy doctors treated marines.

"He's family so I couldn't take an active part in his care, but I took all the leave I'd accumulated so I could go with him from hospital to hospital, to make sure nothing was overlooked—he was in bad shape at the start. But yeah, he pulled through and even kept the leg I wasn't sure was going to make it with him. I did some shuffling and he's on his way here for rehab, so I can keep track of that, too. You'll be able to see him."

"So he really will be okay?" Liam said, still needing some reassurance.

"His body's healing," Conor seemed to hedge. "I'm a little worried about his head—"

"Brain injury?" Liam asked.

"No, thank god there wasn't that. But I think he's carrying a lot of baggage about Topher. Declan was driving the Humvee. As bad as he was hurt himself he did everything to try to save Topher. He even carried him away from the burning Humvee—although seeing Declan and how bad he was, I can't begin to guess how he did that."

"He'd have done anything to help Topher," Liam said, knowing his twin, knowing it was what he himself would have done.

"But Topher took the brunt of the explosion. He died before anybody could get to them. Declan won't talk about it—not to me, not to the counselors I've sent in. I'm afraid we're still facing some rough waters there. But physically... He has some scars, he may have a limp, but yeah, he's gonna be okay."

Liam was grateful for that at least. "I do want to see him. As soon as he gets here. But in the meantime, can I call him?"

"Sure, I got him a cell phone. I'll get you the number when you're ready."

"Yeah, I'm ready now," Liam said. "I'm not going to be staying here..."

He explained the arrangement he'd made to move into the Freelander place.

"You're gonna start playing dad even before you know for sure?"

He told his brother his reasons for that.

"Did you see the kids?" Conor asked.

"For a few minutes. The nanny—that's the Dani Cooper who sent me the message—told them I was a friend of their mother's. They weren't too interested."

"And what did you think? Did you feel any kind of instinctive connection?"

"Uh, no, I didn't even know what to say to them. I was just glad I wasn't alone with them and that the nanny is pretty smooth."

And even though he meant Dani Cooper was smooth

in her dealings with the kids and the awkwardness of him showing up the way he had, it was suddenly the nanny's skin he was thinking about—flawless peaches-and-cream skin so smooth he'd wanted to run the back of his hand over it to see if it felt like it looked...

He reined in the odd wandering of his mind and said, "They're cute kids, I guess... They have dark hair like ours. Blue eyes—"

"Like ours? The color Kinsey thinks ties us to the Camdens?"

"No, theirs are more the light blue that Audrey's eyes were. There might be a little resemblance between the girl and Kinsey when she was a kid, though—I kind of thought I might have seen that."

"So they really could be yours."

"I told you that anyway. That week with Audrey before I deployed was a wild one. Audrey was a partyer and we were drinking like there was no tomorrow. And not always being safe...stupid as that is."

"But that was five years ago and she never came after you for child support, for anything. Seems like if the kids were yours she would have at least wanted you to pitch in with some money."

Liam repeated what the nanny had told him about Owen Freelander and described the house that made it obvious there hadn't been a need for more money.

"It doesn't surprise me that Audrey would have gone with somebody who was offering what this guy was," Liam said. "Marriage, money, to take care of her and claim her kids as his own to provide for, too. And actually, the more I think about it the more sense it makes that the guy was so much older than she was—"

"She had daddy issues?"

"Maybe. She saw herself as a helpless kitten, I know

that. She was raised by older parents with money. There were nannies and people paid to take care of her every need. Her parents spoiled her rotten and I had the impression that when they died she started searching for replacements to take care of her and spoil her the way she was used to. Finding herself pregnant? With twins?" He shook his head. "There's no way she would have wanted to do that by herself. I'm kind of surprised that she didn't terminate the pregnancy at the get-go."

"Never an easy thing to do."

Liam conceded to that. "And I don't think she really understood what it is I do—we met when I was here, doing that training. That lasted two months, looked more like a normal job—"

"But then you deployed…"

"Right. And even though I'd warned her how it would be when I did, I don't think it really sank in with her until she actually experienced it a few times. I know when I finally did call her that last time—the call that, according to the nanny, was when Audrey made the decision to take this Owen guy up on his offer—she was pretty upset that there hadn't been one word from me in a long while." He tried to get some breakfast down but the appetite he'd woken up with had disappeared, so he just pushed his plate away.

"Sooo…how are you doing with the idea that these kids could be yours?" Conor asked.

Liam shook his head. "I'm just kind of in a daze," he admitted. "Like your message about Declan, the one from the nanny—now guardian—only caught up to me a week ago. I almost thought it was some kind of bad joke. Audrey was dead? She'd left twins that are mine? The kids have no one else and now need me to step in or risk being separated and put into the foster care system?".

He shook his head again. "It sure as hell *seemed* like it must be a joke. But then I got to a computer and found an obituary for Audrey that didn't say how she died but said she was survived by four-year-old twins. Four years plus however many months since they turned four, add nine more—that puts it somewhere in that five-years-ago time slot that I spent with Audrey. And here I am."

"Still, you just said yourself that Audrey was a partyer... You are going to test the DNA the way the lawyer told you to, right?"

"Oh, yeah. This afternoon. I got a text from the nanny saying she scheduled an appointment with the pediatrician to do it."

"And what about the nanny?" his brother asked.

Yeah, what about the nanny...

That mere mention of Dani Cooper brought the image of her into his head again.

Not only did she have great skin, she was something to look at all the way around. Exquisite caramel-colored eyes. High cheekbones, a straight nose. Pretty, luscious lips. And a delicate bone structure that gave her a kind of sophisticated, unapproachable beauty.

Or at least it would have seemed sophisticated and unapproachable if her long, dark brown hair with its rich reddish cast hadn't been in some kind of weird style that he couldn't imagine she'd done on purpose. But the style was so weird—and silly—that it had softened the distant, classy beauty.

And she had one damn fine body to go with it—trim without being too skinny, not tall, curves in all the right places.

One damn fine body that she'd been using to gyrate like a crazy woman with as much abandon as the kids when he'd first pulled up to the house and could see what was going on inside.

And yeah, he had to admit that even though the kids had been the reason he was there, even though he'd been sleep deprived and freaked out at the thought that the kids might actually prove to be his, it was still the nanny who had caught his attention. And held it for a while, sitting in his rented SUV, unable to take his eyes off her.

But what about the nanny—that's what his brother had asked.

"What do you mean?" he answered with a question of his own because all he could think about was the way she looked and he didn't think Conor was asking about that.

"You said she was the guardian now," Conor reminded him.

"Right. I guess she's been their nanny for a few years, and when Audrey and her husband died she had Audrey's husband's attorney go to court to have her named as the kids' temporary guardian so they could stay in their own home for now."

"That's nice of her. That's got to mean she went from taking care of them as just her job to being completely responsible for them and playing single parent 24-7?"

"Yeah, that's the way I'm understanding it."

"That's above and beyond the call of duty."

"Yeah," he agreed, realizing that he'd been so busy thinking about how she looked that he hadn't given her credit for that. And he should have.

"Are you going to start trading shifts with her?" Conor asked then. "Taking care of the kids part of the time so she can get away?"

"Oh, god no!" Liam said, feeling a rise in his stress level at that idea. "I figure if the court appointed her as their guardian she has to stick around, right? And she needs to—I don't have a clue what to do with them. I mean, I said I want to get to know them, that I thought it would be good for them to get to know me, in case I am their father. That it would be good for me to learn the ropes. And that if by some chance I'm not their father, I want to make sure they get well taken care of for Audrey's sake. But I can't be left alone with them."

His brother's expression was amused and sympathetic at once. "Okay. But you know that if you *are* their father eventually that could happen?"

"I... Yeah... But that isn't right now. Right now the nanny will be there and I'm just planning to lend a hand. To follow her lead. I can't be left alone with them," he repeated.

His brother grinned. "So you're really terrified of them?"

"Wouldn't you be?"

"I had to do a rotation in pediatrics so I've had a little experience," Conor said of his training as a doctor.

Liam got up from the kitchen table and took his plate to the sink to rinse it and do what he could to calm his nerves over a prospect he hadn't considered before this: being left alone with twin four-year-olds.

Once he felt as if he had some control, he turned back to his brother and said, "I just have to do what I have to do. Whatever that is."

"Sure," Conor agreed. "And I'm here for you, if there's anything I can do."

"You can take me shopping for some clothes," Liam said. "I don't have any civvies with me—I pretty much just threw what I needed to travel in a duffel and took off. And I think the uniform makes me a little intimidating to the kids."

"Whose names are?"

"Oh, yeah, they have names," Liam said, sounding overwhelmed and at sea. "The girl is Evie. The boy is Grady."

"Evie Madison. Grady Madison. I guess that works," Conor mused.

"Yeah, let's not get ahead of ourselves," Liam cautioned, thinking that he could only handle so much at a time.

And also thinking how grateful he was that Dani Cooper really would be there to hold his hand through what seemed like the most daunting mess he'd ever been in.

Well, not to literally hold his hand.

Although there was something about that idea that made the thought of going back to the house to face what he had to face much easier...

"That man from last day is coming back and we have to go to the doctor with him?" Evie said, questioning what Dani had just told her and her brother.

"The man who was here last *night*," Dani corrected. "Remember his name is Liam, and yes, he's coming with us to the doctor."

She was combing Evie's long hair and putting it into pigtails while Grady watched.

"But we aren't sick," he pointed out. "Why do we have to go to the doctor? Are we gonna hafta have shots?"

"No, no shots and nothing that will hurt. You won't even have to get undressed. All you'll have to do is open your mouths and let the nurse touch the inside of your cheek with a cotton swab."

"But why?" Evie persisted.

"It's a test. Remember last time you guys had sore throats? The nurse used a cotton swab to get some stuff from back there and sent it to be tested to see if you had strep—"

"I didn't like that," Evie said.

"Me either," Grady chimed in.

"I know, but this will be easier than that. Here, let me show you." She took three cotton swabs from the medicine cabinet, demonstrated what would be done on herself first and then persuaded them to let her do it to them.

"See? This one is no big deal. But then they can send the swab to a laboratory to test it and tell all kinds of things about you."

"Like what?" Grady asked suspiciously.

"It could tell that Evie is a girl and you're a boy. It could tell the color of your hair and eyes—"

"I can tell you that," Evie reasoned.

This wasn't easy to explain to inquisitive four-year-olds.

"It can also tell you stuff that you can't see—what's inside of you that makes you you and who your family is. Like if I had the test, it could tell me that my grandmother was my grandmother."

"So it's gonna tell us if we have a grandmother?" asked Grady.

"Well, no, we already know your grandparents are all in heaven, too, but it might tell us if you have any other family you don't know about."

"You think we do?" Evie asked.

"Maybe," Dani said. "And that would be kind of nice to know, wouldn't it? That there might be someone else in the world who would love to know you guys are their family?" And she hoped that would somehow prove true—that if Liam Madison was their biological father, he'd eventually make his way through what had seemed like shock last night and embrace the news and the kids and become a loving, caring parent to them.

"I s'pose it would be nice," Grady agreed marginally.

"Then would we hafta leave the glass house to live with them?" Evie asked.

They'd referred to this place as the glass house since moving six months ago from what they'd called the brown house—the house they'd lived in while this place was being built.

"I don't know," Dani answered honestly.

She didn't want to go beyond that so she changed the subject.

"Okay, how about if you guys do some of the new puzzles while we wait for Liam?"

It felt a little odd saying Liam Madison's name with such familiarity but it was for the sake of the kids. She wanted to give the impression that he really was a friend to them.

Dani sent them into the common area just outside their bedrooms. Once she knew they weren't going to fight she went into the room she was using and checked her own appearance.

She'd gone to a few extra lengths today to make up for the way she'd looked the night before. She wore a pair of her good jeans and a blue T-shirt over a tank top edged with a row of lace that showed above the T-shirt's square-cut neckline.

She'd also gotten up early so she could pay special attention to her hair. Rather than a quick blow-dry, she'd let it air-dry so she could scrunch it and bring out the natural waves. Then, instead of keeping it contained in some fashion the way she ordinarily did for working with kids, she let it fall free to the middle of her back—what

Grady had deemed *real* princess hair when he and Evie had seen it this morning.

She'd also applied a pale eye shadow to accentuate her eyes and a little mascara to go along with her blush and lip gloss.

But even though it was all what she might have done for a casual, daytime date, that wasn't the reason she'd put in the time and effort, she told herself as she checked to make sure the hours that had passed since then hadn't left her in need of touch-ups. She just wanted to improve upon the bad impression she was afraid she might have made on Liam Madison with her hairstyle by Evie the previous evening.

As nanny—and now as guardian—she had to play two roles. To the kids, she had to be a disciplinarian in a warm, caring manner so that her young charges could be at ease with her. But to the adults in their lives, she had to present a more professional image. A more professional image that she might not have presented to Liam Madison the night before.

So today she wanted to compensate. It didn't have anything to do with the fact that Liam Madison was a fantastic-looking man.

So fantastic-looking that the image of him had stuck with her, even as she'd tried to fall asleep last night. And it had still been with her the minute she woke up this morning and the whole way through her shower and all that extra primping.

But picturing him in her head merely came along with thinking about him actually doing what Audrey had wanted him to do—coming to the kids' rescue. It wasn't about anything personal between the two of them. And there wouldn't be. They had one thing and one thing only bringing them together: the current care and future well-being of Evie and Grady. And once what would happen to them was established, Dani would move on.

It came with the territory of being a nanny.

Yes, she did get a little attached. It had happened with kids she'd nannied for much shorter lengths of time before Evie and Grady. It was especially true of these twins because she'd been with them for a little over three years now. And they were great, smart, adorable, funny kids who she'd needed to provide for more than she had others whose parents were more involved than Audrey and Owen had been.

Add to that that she'd gone through weighty loss with them—both the loss they'd suffered and a particularly difficult loss she'd suffered herself at almost the same time—and now she was their stand-in parent, so a bond had definitely formed.

But still, her attachment to them had to have a limit because it all came with the knowledge that Evie and Grady were *not* her kids. That she *would* have to move on and leave them behind. It was something she never lost sight of. And since her sole connection with Liam Madison was through the kids, she'd be moving on and leaving him behind, too.

So the fact that he was great-looking was insignificant and the fact that she couldn't stop carrying around the image of his great looks in her mind was also unimportant and meaningless.

Besides, she reasoned with herself as she turned upside down to brush her hair from underneath to add some fullness, even if they'd met at a party, locked eyes across a crowded room and been drawn together last night, nothing would have come of it. Too much had happened recently that had left her in no position for anything.

She'd ended her engagement to Garrett after too long indulging his need for control and living under his thumb.

She'd lost the grandmother who had raised her, the grandmother she'd loved dearly.

And then Audrey and Owen had died.

Now she had to make sure that Evie and Grady would be okay.

Plus her grandmother had left her with the biggest decision she'd ever faced—a decision that could not only affect everything for her from now on, but that could also affect numerous people and their jobs.

And if all that wasn't enough—which it was—Liam Madison was in the military.

She knew only too well what that could mean because her own father had served. And suffered for it.

So no matter how fabulously handsome the guy was, she had a laundry list of things that all added up to one really big *no* when it came to Liam Madison, and made those good looks and the fact that she couldn't stop carrying the image of him around in her head totally and completely irrelevant.

She straightened up and flipped her hair into place, feeling a strong resolve settle over her at the same time.

She'd enjoy the view of Liam Madison but that was it. The nurse at the pediatrician's office had said DNA results took about five days. There would likely be a few more days before a final decision was made for Evie and Grady, and she would do whatever she could to help them transition to any new situation once that decision was made. After that she'd pack her bags, move on and leave that view behind.

Simple as that.

"Evie says this piece is for her puzzle but it's not for

her puzzle. It's for my puzzle!" Grady hollered from the other room.

The doorbell rang just then, making Liam Madison ten minutes early but giving Dani an excuse to sidestep the kids' conflict.

"That'll be Liam and we need to get to the doctor's office so we'll sort it out later. Get your shoes on," she said to the twins before snatching one last glimpse of herself in the mirror and then hurrying to the front door.

Denying along the way that what she felt was eagerness to see the big marine again.

"Is *he* really gonna stay here?" Grady whispered to Dani that evening when the four of them returned home. Liam Madison was outside, retrieving his things from the back of his rented SUV to move in. Dani was in the kitchen with the kids.

"He really is going to stay here," Dani confirmed. "He'll be up in the guest room. It's what your mom wanted."

"Because he's her friend?" Evie said in disbelief.

"Yes. And because she wanted you all to get to know each other, and he wants to help out with you guys."

"I don't think so," Grady added his own skepticism, which had some foundation based on the way today had gone.

But rather than confirm the little boy's doubts Dani instead said, "I want you guys to be kind of patient with him, okay? I don't think he knows much about kids."

"I don't think he likes us," Evie amended.

"I don't think we like him," Grady added under his breath.

"We all just have to give each other a chance," Dani said, making it a quiet command. "That's *why* we get to know people—so we can find things about them that we *do* like."

"He doesn't smile," Evie observed.

"He's like a robot. But not a fun robot," Grady contributed.

There was no disputing either criticism because both things were true during the time they'd known the man.

"It'll get better," Dani assured, hoping she was right. "Now go put on your pajamas and I'll cut you some *yellow* cheese and tomatoes and avocados to go along with your yogurt since you didn't have much dinner."

"I want my adocados in salad," Evie informed.

"And the magic word is…" Dani said.

"Please," Evie complied.

"Please," Grady said, too, even though Dani hadn't been instructing him. "But I want my adocados sliced."

Then they headed downstairs. But they were both eyeing the front door the whole way, not looking pleased with the addition that was about to be made to their household.

Dani couldn't blame them.

It had been a long—and stilted—four hours since Liam had arrived that afternoon.

The first stop had been the pediatrician's office where—after a half-hour wait during which the twins had played with the office toys and Liam had sat silent and straight-backed in one of the waiting room's chairs—Evie's and Grady's DNA had been taken.

Unfortunately, between the time Dani had called and made the appointment—when the receptionist had said that yes, they would also take Liam's DNA—the doctor had nixed that. Apparently the receptionist hadn't been clear on just how strict the office policy was against addressing anything to do with an adult. Instead they'd been given an address for a lab they could go to for Liam's swab.

The lab had been a twenty-minute drive from the doctor's office. A twenty-minute drive during which Liam had not made conversation beyond asking for Dani's navigations.

The lab had required another long wait in a small area with only three chairs and no office toys for the kids. Dani carried coloring and activity books in her purse but there also wasn't a table the kids could use. So she'd set them up on the floor, out of the way of incoming and outgoing patients. Then she'd sat in one of the empty chairs but couldn't persuade Liam to take one of the others.

"The kids should sit in them," he'd said, standing as if he was on lookout, and seemed embarrassed that the kids weren't using the remaining chairs.

After his test, Liam had suggested taking them all to dinner at a restaurant his brother had recommended. At the restaurant there had been another lengthy delay before a table opened up for them—during which the kids had again colored, this time using the seat of a chair as a desktop—something else that Liam eyed as if the irregularity made him uneasy. From his position again standing like a sentry.

Once they were led to a booth Liam had sat at one end of the table while the twins had huddled on either side of Dani as far away from him as they could get.

They'd agreed to grilled cheese sandwiches from the uninspired children's menu and while they'd waited for their food, Grady had devolved into entertaining himself by tormenting his sister. That caused a small ruckus when Evie fought back, and while Dani managed them, Liam seemed not to know where to look, staring over their heads like a Buckingham Palace guard.

By the time the food arrived the kids were just plain contrary and had taken one look at the grilled cheese sandwich and refused to eat it because the cheese was white instead of yellow. And even after Dani had persuaded them just to try it, Evie had gagged on her bite and Grady had let his roll back down his tongue and onto the plate, delivering the verdict that it was yucky.

They did eat the french fries and fruit that came with the sandwich, so that was something, but through it all Liam Madison's discomfort and embarrassment had been palpable.

And the twins hadn't been all that happy themselves when they'd learned during the meal that Liam was going to be coming to live with them.

Dani had been grateful that they hadn't said anything rude, saving their comments for Dani alone now that they were home and Liam was out of earshot. But the news had so sobered them that there was no mistaking they were not thrilled with the idea. From then on they'd become as quiet as Liam, so the car ride home had been stony all the way around.

And that was how a weary Dani had left it. She'd exhausted every effort to engage Liam in things with the kids, she'd failed at getting the kids to interact with Liam, and for the time being she just gave up.

But this needed to work, she told herself now that they were back at the Freelander house. If Liam was Grady and Evie's biological father, she really needed him to save them from the system.

Just then Liam came in the front door carrying a large duffel bag.

Dani left the kitchen and went into the entry as he closed the door behind him, trying not to notice how good he looked in the khaki slacks and white shirt that had replaced the uniform of Sunday night.

"Stairs or elevator?" she asked.

"Your choice," he said.

"Usually I'd take the stairs—this is the first house I've ever been in that has an elevator—but let's use it tonight. It's quicker and I need to get back and fix the kids a snack. But maybe once you've settled in and they're watching their shows we could talk a little?" she proposed.

"Even in civvies they're still scared of me, aren't they?" he guessed.

Dani almost laughed but she fought it. He was a massive wall of man, all granite-hard muscle held in an unyielding demeanor that made him seem totally unapproachable, and he thought it was his *clothes* that were off-putting to two little kids?

"I don't know that they're scared exactly..." she hedged as she showed him to the elevator and they got into the small space.

He not only looked great, he smelled great, too, and the clean scent wrapped around her in the confines of the elevator as she pushed the button to close the doors and send them up.

But like looking good, smelling good was inconsequential, she reminded herself, instead addressing only the issue at hand. "I don't know what your situation is—"

"Unmarried. Uninvolved."

He thought she was asking him if he was single? Well, *situation* could be interpreted that way. And she *had* been wondering...

"And childless, right?" she added. "Well, other than potentially the twins?"

"Childless," he said as succinctly as he'd said everything today.

"And without much experience with kids, I'm kind of assuming..." she said to introduce the subject she was getting at as they arrived at the guest suite and the elevator doors opened directly into the room.

"No experience. None," he confirmed emphatically.

"So I'm hoping maybe you wouldn't mind a little advice," she said diplomatically.

"Advice…"

There was the tiniest inflection to his voice that confused her. It could have been amusement that said he didn't think he needed her advice. But it could also have been flirtatious. From underneath some heavy cover. Something that hinted he might have hoped for something better when she'd suggested they talk.

But she couldn't for a minute even entertain the idea that that's what she'd heard, so instead she decided he'd found some humor in something and merely went on.

"Advice, yes. Unless you don't want it."

"I don't think there's any question that I need it, right?"

"You do," she said.

He cracked the smallest of smiles, lending some credence to the thought that he'd found something funny in her offer. The smallest of smiles that crooked up only one side of his mouth and drew a sexy line around the corner.

"Show me what I need to know up here," he said as they stepped off the elevator, "and then I'll come down and we can talk."

"Good," Dani said, still not quite sure how receptive he was going to be.

But she didn't like being far from the kids for long so she quickly showed him around and instructed him in making the television rise out of a credenza at the foot of the bed and controlling the blackout draperies covering the three glass walls of the suite. She pointed out the control panel for the sauna before leaving him to go downstairs again.

As she did it struck her for the first time that she and the oh-so-hunky Liam Madison were now going to be living together.

Well, not living *together*, but sharing the place.

And there was something about the thought that suddenly felt a little titillating.

It shouldn't have. Not only wasn't there anything personal about it at all, but she already shared an apartment with her friend Bryan so there was nothing really out of the ordinary about a living arrangement like this.

Of course Bryan was her best friend and gay, but still, he was a guy and that's all Liam Madison was. A guy.

An incredibly hot, sexy guy...

Who she couldn't seem to take her eyes off of.

Who would be undressing just upstairs.

Showering just upstairs.

Sleeping just upstairs...

She actually had goose bumps, she realized as she reached the kitchen.

That would *not* do!

No thinking about him any differently than you think about Bryan! she directed herself firmly.

But still, the thought of living even in these not-so-close-quarters with him made her slightly tingly.

She just tried to ignore it.

And hoped that it would pass when the novelty of this situation did.

Please, please, make it pass...

She'd just delivered the twins' snack and turned on their wind-down shows when she and Liam arrived back in the kitchen at the same time.

"Since we're in show-you-around mode," she said as she put things back in the refrigerator, "this is the fridge— feel free to help yourself to anything in it, of course. Plus we need to take a trip to the grocery store tomorrow so you can add whatever you like."

She went on to show him the walk-in pantry and the coffee machine that was housed in its own compartment near the sink, and where the utensils, cups, bowls and plates were. She demonstrated the toaster, blender and food processor that—like the television in the guest room—rose at the push of a button from separate compartments underneath the stainless steel countertop. Then she opened both the dishwasher and the trash compacter to unveil them since they were indistinguishable from the stainless steel cupboards.

"This place is like a space station," he observed when the tour of the kitchen was complete.

"Owen was a sci-fi fanatic so he would have taken that as a compliment. But yeah, most of it is sort of out there. Except for downstairs. That's the kids' area and it's just pretty normal, bedrooms and bathrooms, and that space you can see from here is where the kids can play or watch TV."

"Is there a workout room by any chance?"

"Next to the ballet studio. Come on, I'll show you. You can use it." Because clearly he didn't have that body without working out.

When she'd shown him that, too, they again went into the kitchen, where Dani sat on a stool on the side of the island that allowed her to see into the lower level to keep an eye on the twins. Liam stood in the center of the room, still stiff and formal.

"Okay, what am I doing wrong?" he asked.

Dani did laugh that time. Just a little. "Audrey said you're military through and through. But really, you have to loosen up. Like, for instance, you're home now, not waiting for somebody to give you orders. Sit down and relax." Relax—it was something she'd said far, far too many times to her former fiancé. Futilely.

"Sorry. Force of habit. Especially when I'm out of my element. And believe me, this whole thing qualifies," he said, glancing at his surroundings to include the house and then casting another, somewhat pained look down the four stairs where the kids were.

Dani felt a little sympathy for the man who looked like he could handle anything thrown at him. Apparently looks were deceiving.

But he did join her at the island, taking a seat on a bar stool around the corner and down three from her.

"Better?" he asked.

"Sure," she said, although he still did not look as if he felt at home.

"Have I blown it with the kids? Do they hate me?" he asked then.

"I think that maybe they don't know what to make of you," she answered, soft-pedaling. Then, continuing to tread lightly, she said, "Grady says you're like a robot."

"Is he a sci-fi fanatic, too, and that's a compliment?"

"Sorry, no," Dani said, suppressing another laugh.

"So, what do I do? I don't know the first thing about kids."

"Well, you were one…weren't you?" she joked, unsure how he would take it but trying anyway.

"Once upon a time, yeah," he answered, showing a hint of humor in the reappearance of that crooked smile.

"So maybe you could just think back, put yourself in your own shoes when you were a kid, remember adults in your life that you related to and why for starters. Grady and Evie are kids, just like I'm sure you were. They like to play and they like it when you play with them—"

"Or color with them like you tried to do at the restaurant?"

Oh, he was dishing a little out by reminding her that that attempt had failed.

Dani just laughed again. "Okay, they aren't *always* receptive, especially when they've reached their limits. But—" she pointed a finger in the direction of the refrigerator where there were three crayon drawings displayed "—the middle one is mine from this morning when they *wanted* me to color with them," she finished victoriously.

Liam flashed her a full smile that seemed to say he liked that she could take a little ribbing. And that made him all the more attractive. And appealing. Damn him…

"And you can talk to them," she went on. "Directly to them. Today you just talked to them through me."

"But will they understand if I talk to them the way I would talk to anybody?"

Dani tried not to reveal just how silly that sounded. "They will. They mispronounce some words themselves, but they have a better-than-average vocabulary for four-year-olds. And if they don't understand a particular word or phrase, they'll let you know. Then that gives you the opportunity to expand their vocabulary. But they're not babies. Think of them as just small people. Today you didn't say word one to either of them after you said hello."

"To be fair, they didn't talk to me either."

"Uh-huh, but kids don't talk to people who seem unfriendly."

"I seem unfriendly?"

"Oh, yeah."

"I'm a nice guy," he defended himself, seeming to really drop some of his guard in that defensiveness.

Dani laughed once more. "Okay. But you have to come out from behind the military shield and show it because that isn't what they've seen of you. You're more like the secret service on duty with the president's kids. Except that you aren't completely hiding that it bothers you when they do what kids do—like running to catch up to the hostess seating us at the restaurant."

He made a face that acknowledged that he'd found that inappropriate. "And the stuff with the grilled cheese sandwiches…" he added, showing his disapproval.

"I know. But like I said, they're *kids*. You use moments like that to teach them that spitting out a bite of food is bad manners and what to do in polite society."

"That's what you did."

"While you looked like you just wanted to crawl into a hole."

"Yeah, all right, I did," he conceded. "So, where should I go from here? Shall I, like, ask them to throw a ball with me or something?"

"Why don't you just start by being yourself…well, the self you must be with your own family or your friends. Just let your hair down a little, speak to the kids to acknowledge them and kind of roll with things until you get a feel for them and what they respond to."

With the mention of hair his gorgeous blue eyes went to her hair for just a moment—the first time it seemed he'd noticed that it was different than it had been the night before.

Then he redirected his gaze and in a tone that was slightly controlled again, he said, "Yeah, okay, I'll give it a try."

"They like to have a book read to them before bed. I can ask them if they'd let you do it and you could start with that…"

"Tonight?" he said as if she'd suggested something terrifying.

"You need to prepare yourself?" she teased him, dishing out a little of the goading he'd served her.

"I do," he confessed.

She let him off the hook since the simple suggestion seemed to have rocked him all over again. "Okay. Sure."

The ending song for the show the twins were watching sounded faintly in the background and Grady called, "It's over."

"Which is the cue for the bedtime book," Dani said.

"And you have to get back to them," he finished for her. But this time his tone seemed to hold some disappointment. "I should probably go up and unpack anyway. *Prepare* myself for tomorrow—they'll still be here tomorrow, right?" he joked.

"They will be."

"I don't know how early things start around here but I like to run at sunrise—"

"Not *that* early."

"And then I have an appointment at eight in the morning with the attorney my brother hired. I haven't met with him yet. How does that work with you and the kids?"

"They'll usually sleep until seven thirty or eight so why don't you just do your run, then go to your appointment and we'll see you after that."

She told him the code to the security system in order for him to leave without incident.

"And what about breakfast?" she asked. "There's bread for toast—"

"I saw cereal in the pantry, milk in the fridge. That'll do."

Dani nodded. "If you need anything or have any questions about things around here, just holler. Or text me. There's an intercom all through the house but it's kind of complicated. You have to know the place pretty well to know which button connects you to which room."

"I'm sure I'll be fine. Unless I hit the wrong button up there and launch myself into orbit."

Another joke. She liked that he had a sense of humor. "You're safe. I put duct tape over the launch button so you wouldn't hit it accidentally," she joked back.

He took a breath that expanded his impressive chest and sighed it out. "Guess I'll start the great climb then," he said as if he was at the foot of Mount Everest.

"You can use the elevator," she goaded.

"I'll pass. I've never been in a house with its own elevator either. Seems weird."

Dani nodded.

"I'll see you tomorrow and try to loosen up," he pledged.

She nodded again.

"And by the way," he said with a beautifully devilish smile, "your hair looks better today."

Dani laughed, glad to finally have her weird hairstyle of the previous evening acknowledged.

"Thanks. I did it today instead of Evie."

"I don't think the kid has a future ahead of her as a stylist."

Dani laughed yet again. "I don't think so either."

Then she watched Liam Madison walk out of the kitchen, hoping that tomorrow he might show the twins more of the human side he'd finally shown her tonight.

And enjoying the sight of tight buns in khakis as a secret reward to herself for a day that hadn't been any fun until just now.

Chapter Three

"Bryan! Did you see our socks?" Evie asked by way of greeting Dani's best friend as the twins rushed him Tuesday morning when Dani let him in.

"Let me see 'em," Bryan Dreeson instructed, peering down at their feet. "Oh, my gosh! Those socks are great! Red Minnie and Mickey? Why don't they make them in my size?" he lamented.

"Let's see yours," Grady said as he bent over and pulled up one leg of the attorney's suit pants to reveal snazzy argyles. A love of flashy socks united Dani's friend with her charges.

"Pretty," Evie judged with awe.

"And he brought you one of his special quiches for breakfast, too—"

The twins cheered and jumped around like crazy people, laughing at themselves as they did.

"Okay, okay," Dani said to contain them as she closed the front door behind her friend. "I want you to go down and finish getting dressed while I talk to Bryan, and then you can have breakfast."

Bryan's family had lived in the house next door to her grandparents. Being the same age, Dani and Bryan had grown up together and been best friends since soon after Dani had gone to live with Nell and Nick Marconi.

Bryan had called the night before and told her that he would stop by on his way to his office this morning to bring her papers. He was an estate lawyer and had handled the trust Dani's grandmother had left.

"Mmm…fresh tomatoes, spinach and cheese," Dani said as she carried the quiche to the kitchen. "The kids love this. And so do I."

"Because it's delicious," Bryan said with no humility whatsoever.

"Are you eating with us or have you already had breakfast?" she asked as they got to the kitchen and she set the quiche on the island.

"I waited so we could eat together. And I'm desperate for a cup of coffee!" he said dramatically, going to the cupboard to get a mug—a familiarity that had developed since he became a frequent visitor after Dani had taken up residence here and left the apartment they shared.

"I have to warn you—I didn't make the coffee and it's really strong. Gramma would have called it battery acid."

"The marine made it?" Bryan asked. They talked almost every day and there was nothing in Dani's life that Bryan didn't know about, including every detail of the situation with the twins, her efforts to contact Liam, his arrival and request to move in and that Monday had been designated as the day for that.

"The marine or elves. It was here when I got up," she said.

"Am I gonna get a look at him?" her impeccably dressed blond friend whispered over his shoulder as he poured the dark brew.

"I haven't even seen him this morning—he's an up-before-dawn guy. He says he likes to run at sunrise. Then he had an appointment with a lawyer to deal with paternity if the DNA proves he's the father," she said just as softly so the kids didn't overhear anything.

"Too bad. I wanted to see if he lives up to your description."

"If he lives up to my description? How did I describe him?" She'd thought she'd described him as average. Even though he was actually far, far above average.

"You made him sound so hot that steam was coming out of my phone," Bryan claimed.

"I did not," Dani denied as she got out four plates, silverware and a knife to cut the quiche.

"You sooo did," Bryan countered. "Down to every tiny little freckle—"

"He doesn't have freckles."

"And you should know because you didn't miss a thing. You had me drooling and hoping he plays for my team."

"Evie and Grady are probably his so I don't think he plays for your team," she whispered again.

"And wouldn't you be crushed if he did," Bryan teased.

"No," she said. Maybe a little too emphatically because it made Bryan laugh.

It also provoked him to give her his fashion once-over. "Your hair is down. Instead of yoga pants or rolling-around-on-the-floor-with-kids jeans you have on a nice pair, and that come-hither pink sweater set? You are dressed for more than work," he deduced before adding, "It's all right if you kind of like this guy, you know? This has been a rough few months. You're due for a little good."

"Well, it isn't going to come out of this," she responded confidently without denying that, like yesterday, she'd primped more for work than usual. But she'd told herself that she had a busy day ahead and that that was the reason. Not Liam Madison.

"Then I'll keep hoping that he's gay," Bryan challenged.

"And I'll tell Adam on you," she countered, referring to Bryan's longtime boyfriend.

The exchange made them both laugh. It was the kind of back and forth they'd shared since childhood.

As Dani cut slices of Bryan's homemade quiche he took papers out of his briefcase and slid them across the counter to her. "Gramma's trust," he said. He'd always called her grandmother Gramma the same way Dani had even though there was no relation. "Since you're the only beneficiary all ownership has been transferred to you."

That sobered her. "Already."

"It's been six weeks since she passed. We did the trust instead of a will because it would be quicker and easier at the end and wouldn't have to go into probate like a will. And there's the proof—no court, no court costs, over and done. You're now the sole owner of the house and Marconi's Italian Restaurant."

Essentially that had been true ever since her grandmother had died, but still, the finality and reality of it, of the loss of her grandmother, landed heavily on Dani all over again.

Dealing with that made her go very quiet and when Evie came up the stairs with a request that she fasten the buttons in the back of her dress, Bryan intercepted her to do it while Dani got down glasses for the twins and poured milk.

Then Evie went downstairs with a promise to Bryan that he was going to love her shoes and Dani took a deep breath to fuel herself to go on.

"Your cousin wants to buy the house," she said.

Bryan had several cousins. One of them was newly married and she and her husband had rented the house that Dani had grown up in. The house that had belonged to her grandparents and passed to her when her grand-mother died.

"I know Shannon loves the house, but I told her not to pressure you about buying it," Bryan said. "It could be a nice home for you, you know? When some time passes."

"Or I could sell it and use the money to renovate the restaurant," Dani said. "Or I could sell them both…" It was a conversation they'd been having since her eighty-year-old grandmother's death.

So many changes were in the wind. Too many. All of them weighing on her.

And Bryan knew how overwhelmed she was, how torn she was about whether or not to let go of the house she'd grown up in. About whether or not to accept the end of her time with the twins as the end of her own career as a nanny so she could take over where her grandparents had left off with the restaurant. About whether or not to sell the business that had been the lifeblood of her family. The business that had kept her grandparents alive in some ways. The business that couldn't go on as it had without Dani. About whether or not to genuinely close the door on the people and life she'd always known. And loved.

"Gramma would have been right about this coffee—battery acid!" Bryan said.

Dani knew he was attempting to distract her from her own thoughts and from drifting into the doldrums and grief that were just below the surface.

"Let's try a little cream and sugar," he suggested. "I can't believe Hottie Marine actually drinks this black."

"'Hottie Marine'?" she echoed. "That's the best you could come up with?"

"We haven't even met," Bryan defended himself. "Would you prefer Lovely Liam?"

"Oh, that is waaay worse."

Bryan passed her on his way to the refrigerator for the cream and nudged her with his shoulder. "You okay?" he asked seriously, knowing her well enough to understand what she was feeling.

"Sure," she answered.

"Lot of decisions on the table—go at them one at a time."

"I will. But I'm not doing anything about my own future until I know the kids will be okay."

He kissed her cheek. "That's why I love you, lady."

And that small comment brought tears to her eyes that she had to blink back.

"So tell me more about our marine," he encouraged.

But the twins were finished dressing and both came into the kitchen. Grady was in red-and-white star leggings with a salmon-colored T-shirt—he called it his toucan shirt because of the long-beaked bird on it—and sparkling blue tennis shoes that lit up when he stomped his feet, which he demonstrated for Bryan. Evie wore her predominantly navy blue flowered knit dress with green striped leggings under it and her own light-up, sparkling pink running shoes.

"Wow! You guys are colorful!" Bryan said as if he was impressed.

"Dani let us pick out our own clothes because it's our bacation and we don't have to wear umiforms."

"And what a great job you did," Bryan commended. "Now come and eat my quiche and tell me how good it is," he added.

The twins eagerly went to two of the bar stools to climb up and do as he'd instructed.

And Dani wished that Liam was there to watch her friend and maybe pick up a few tips on how to build rapport with the twins.

Although, for some strange reason, she'd been wishing that Liam was there since she got up this morning.

And it didn't have anything to do with the kids.

"You say it *pit-sails*—not *piz-els*. And these are ours that get saved for us. They're the broken ones Dani lets us have," Grady informed Liam.

Liam had been alarmed that the kids had gone behind the bakery case at Marconi's Italian Restaurant and begun to help themselves from a drawer below it. He'd warned Dani that they were getting into the Italian waffle cookies, pronouncing the name the way it was spelled on the sign where stacks of them were displayed for sale.

"It's okay," Dani assured him. Then to the twins she said, "But not too many. You can each have two broken pieces and put the rest in a bag to take home." Then, using a tissue to take an unbroken one from a stack, she handed it to Liam. "They're traditional Italian cookies—my grandmother's recipe with anise oil and anise seed. It tastes like licorice and the cookie itself is buttery and crispy and light...if you've never had one."

"I like licorice," he said, accepting the *pizzelle* from her. After tasting it he inclined his head and gave his approval. "Good."

"Really good," Evie confirmed. "You can have some of ours."

That was a positive sign.

It had been a full day.

Liam had arrived home just as Dani was telling the twins after lunch that they had to have a rest time even if they weren't tired enough to take a nap and herded them to bed.

When naptime concluded they'd gone to the grocery store, where Liam had observed the process without really participating and with an expression of bewilderment when he'd realized that on every aisle the same exchange took place half a dozen times: the kids asked for everything that struck their fancy whether they knew what it was or not. Dani said, "Not today," and they responded, "For our birthday can we have it?" To which Dani had said yes every time.

"Why not just say no?" he'd reasoned.

Rather than answering that, Dani had shown him why not. She'd said a flat *no* the next time, when they'd asked if they could have the Chinese noodles in the black-and-red package that had caught their eye.

"For our birthday?" Evie had asked on cue.

"No," Dani had answered, earning a rash of begging and insistence that even though they didn't know what the Chinese noodles actually were, they *loved* them and wanted them.

"Okay, maybe for your birthday," she'd conceded, and they'd been appeased and agreeable enough to move on.

"That's just weird," Liam had commented.

And once more Dani had responded, "They're four."

After returning home to put groceries away they'd gone to the park. Although Liam had remained reserved at the grocery store, at the park he'd offered to push Evie and Grady on the swings.

Unfortunately the offer had still been so stiff and formal—similar to her former fiancé Garrett's attempts—that they hadn't been responsive and had insisted Dani alone do it.

But there was one thing they always wanted to do at the park that Dani wasn't physically capable of, and it had occurred to her that tall Liam could do it—especially when she had factored in his expansive shoulders and the biceps

that stretched his pale yellow polo shirt to the limits. And
made her look at him more often than she'd wanted to.

She'd suggested that maybe Liam could take turns
holding the twins up, one at a time, so that they could
reach and cross the monkey bars.

She'd had to warn Liam not to let go of them once they
were up there, to keep holding them as they reached from
one bar to the next without actually bearing any of their
own weight, but he'd done it—several times because the
man seemed to have the stamina of an ox.

It hadn't broken down any huge barriers between the
three of them, but Dani thought it had at least made a dent.

Then they'd moved on to dinner. Tuesday night was
fast-food night for the twins—the only time it was allowed, as she'd explained to Liam.

Tonight Dani had insisted on paying, and had told Liam
that when the court had granted her guardianship of the
twins, it had also allotted her funds from the estate for
their care. Since Tuesday night chicken nuggets were part
of the routine, she thought that qualified.

As they did every Tuesday night, the kids had wolfed
down their food in order to get to the play area afterward.
While they were gone Dani had explained to Liam that
the next stop was the Italian restaurant that she was responsible for and needed to check in on.

Which was how they'd come to Marconi's, using the
employees' entrance in back and prompting a return of
the reserved Liam as he'd watched the kids charge in,
greet and be greeted warmly by the kitchen staff, then
proceed into the restaurant itself and to the bakery case
to help themselves.

"They're just at home here?" he asked Dani when he'd
finished his *pizzelle*. He was observing Grady and Evie
getting a brown paper sack from a shelf under the cash

register and carefully emptying the container of broken *pizzelles* into the bag on their own.

"They've been here a lot. Especially lately," she answered before introducing Liam and Griff, her manager, and then consulting with Griff before the day could come to a close.

Liam again seemed very ruminative on the short drive between Marconi's and the Freelander house, saying only, "They can be kind of loud, can't they?" when the kids began singing preschool ditties in the back seat.

"They can," she agreed. "But it's happy noise," she added, worrying that he was going to be so stern or sound sensitive that he wanted to stop four-year-olds from singing.

On the alert for his response, she saw him glance in his rearview mirror at them and held her breath, hoping that he wouldn't tell them to be quiet.

But ultimately all he did was shrug, return his gaze to the road and say, "Yeah, good point."

It might not have been singing along but it was something, and Dani was grateful for it as they pulled into the driveway to the tune of "The Wheels on the Bus" coming from the back seat.

"He didn't do funny voices," Evie complained an hour later when Dani was tucking in the little girl. It was the same grievance Grady had voiced a moment before when Dani had put him to bed.

She'd persuaded Liam to read the bedtime story and the kids to let him. "Remember what I told you—he's just learning about you guys. He probably didn't know you like that book read with funny voices. You had a good time with him at the park, though. You finally got to do the monkey bars."

"Yeah, that was fun," Evie recalled as she arranged her doll next to her. "And he likes *pizzelles*."

"He does," Dani confirmed with some amusement that that was a plus. But at that point she was willing to take any encouraging sign she could get.

"I don't wanna go to that camp, though."

"Oh, no, that's just what Liam called it," she said. After reading the book, Liam had asked them if they'd like to do a boot camp workout with him sometime. Grady had given a reluctant okay—though Dani was reasonably sure he had no idea what he'd agreed to—but Evie had refused outright. "Liam was just asking if you wanted to exercise with him. Kind of like when Bryan comes over and we do yoga."

"I like Bryan."

But not Liam—that seemed to be the unspoken part of the sentiment.

"I think you're going to like Liam, too. He's just different from Bryan. Maybe you could watch him and Grady when they do the workout and decide if you want to do the exercises, too."

Evie put the doll named Baby in a headlock and rolled onto her side without responding to that. Dani didn't push it; she just smoothed Evie's hair away from her face and said good-night.

Then she left the four-year-old to sleep and went up to the kitchen to find Liam making a hoagie with some of the groceries he'd bought himself.

It didn't surprise her. He hadn't eaten a hearty dinner. But she was glad to see him making himself at home, reasoning that the more comfortable he was with his surroundings, the more comfortable he might become with the kids.

"I make a good sandwich," he bragged as she joined him. "And there's plenty. Can I interest you?"

Ohhh…too many things about him had interested her as the day and evening had gone on. Dani had been struggling with it. But at that point he was only talking about the food in front of him.

"No, thanks. But if you'd told me you were hungry when we were at the restaurant, we do a really good Italian sub—mortadella, Genoa salami, *capicola* and prosciutto with provolone, ricotta *salata* and roasted red peppers on buns we make ourselves."

"You're putting my ham, turkey and Swiss to shame."

"I'm just saying that I could have saved you the trouble."

Dani took two knives and two carving boards out of a drawer, handing him one of the boards and a carving knife to cut his sandwich, and keeping the second board and a large knife with a serrated edge for herself.

As he sliced his sandwich and wrapped big, capable-looking hands around one portion of it to take a bite—hands she inexplicably thought were the sexiest hands she'd ever seen—she went to her purse and took a large compressed cardboard tube out of it to set on her own carving board.

Liam was watching her and, after swallowing his bite and washing it down with a swig of the beer he'd opened, he said, "I know you wouldn't tell the kids what that was for when you took it from the restaurant, but how about letting me in on it? And what is it anyway?"

"It's just the roll the giant commercial plastic wrap comes on. The staff kept it for me." She measured its length and made a mark that divided it in half. "It's for a craft project for Evie and Grady," she added as she started trying to saw through it with the serrated knife, finding the quarter-inch thickness of its walls as strong as wood and not as easy to cut as she'd expected.

"Hold on," Liam said to stop her. "You need a saw to do that. Is there one around here?"

"I don't know."

"I poked my head into the garage this morning— there's a worktable out there—let me look and see if there might be a saw," he offered, taking another bite of his sandwich for the trip.

He disappeared through the door that connected the garage and the kitchen, was gone for a while and then came back with a small handsaw.

"There's all kinds of tools out there," he informed her. He didn't give her the saw, though; he took another bite of his sandwich and reached for the tube and second cutting board. "Let me do it."

Dani watched as one of those sexy hands gripped the tube and the other wielded the saw, making forearms and biceps alike bulge as he worked.

Her mouth was suddenly a little dry and she didn't like that she was imagining feeling the strength of those arms around her, those hands on her body, so she went to the refrigerator for a bottle of seltzer water.

In that short time, he'd cut the tube in two—something that she knew she'd have been working on for half an hour to accomplish.

"There," he said, sliding it back to her and continuing to eat as he stood on one side of the island.

Dani went to the opposite side and sat on a stool despite the fact that she knew she should busy herself elsewhere rather than stay there just to enjoy the view. And the company.

"So how'd I do today, Teach?" he asked then.

"I think you had a couple of wins," she said without much conviction.

"In other words, not great," he said with a wry chuckle.

He'd been clean-shaven through the day, but in the last few hours a shadow of beard had begun to appear, and she noticed that now it had turned into very sexy scruff.

She didn't know why her mind kept going there but she curbed it and forced herself to concentrate on tutoring him.

"You were a *little* looser but…are *you* scared of *them*?" she asked, recalling that he'd thought they might be afraid of him the night before but now wondering if it was the other way around.

"Shhh! Marines aren't scared of anything," he barked facetiously.

"So you are!" Dani goaded. "A great big macho marine scared of two munchkins."

"They're just not what I'm used to. I'm used to order and discipline and rules and regulations and adults who follow them. But kids…they're all over the place."

"But in a fun way," Dani said.

"Just seems like anarchy to me."

Dani laughed. "That military stuff again," she groaned. "You have to switch gears. But you did gain some ground with the monkey bars. They always want to do them and I can't hold them up like that. And you liked *pizzelles*—"

"Even though I said it wrong and earned a reprimand."

"But the fact that Evie was willing to share with you was something."

"And then I screwed up reading to them tonight— Grady said tomorrow night you need to do it. But I don't know what I did wrong. I *can* read," he ended defensively.

Dani laughed. "Sorry. I do dumb voices that they like.

But still, you did better today than yesterday. And you'll get there." She hoped.

He sighed. "Guess I'll keep trying anyway."

He got points with her for that.

"Now tell me about you and this restaurant," he said as if that had confused him as much as the kids did. "You're a nanny named Cooper but it seemed like maybe you *own* a restaurant called Marconi's?"

"Yeah…" She steeled herself for talking about this. "My mom was Antoinette Marconi, daughter of Nick and Nell Marconi and a full-blooded Italian, so I'm Italian on her side. I'm French, English, Irish and German on my dad's. I'm the variety pack."

"Proved to be a good mix," he said with approval in his voice and in the blue eyes that were taking her in.

Dani tried not to notice. Or to be pleased. But she was.

She forced herself to move on from it, though.

"When my grandparents got married they used their wedding money to start the restaurant," she told him. "It's been our family's business ever since for the last sixty-two years. My grandfather ran it and my grandmother cooked—right up until the day she died six weeks ago."

"You *just* lost her—I'm sorry."

"Thanks. Me, too. But I'm grateful that she went peacefully, in her sleep. And I keep reminding myself that she had a long life. She was eighty—"

"And still working?"

"Making meatballs right to the end," Dani said, the humor helping.

"Making meatballs at the *restaurant*?" he said, getting back to what had started this.

"At the restaurant. My mom grew up there. Worked there. She met my dad there. He was a customer and then he worked there, too, before he did a stint in the marines."

"Your dad was a marine," Liam noted with respect and camaraderie.

"He enlisted just before my mom realized she was pregnant with me. He served for four years."

"Good man."

"He was," Dani said sadly before she returned to the subject. "I basically grew up at the restaurant the same way my mom did. They kept a crib and a playpen in the corner of the kitchen when she was a baby and then again when I was. I had chores there from when I was little. I went straight there after school. I worked in the kitchen cooking with my grandmother. I bused tables, waited on customers. I learned to read from the menus. I learned math running the cash register and at my grand-father's side doing the books. I earned money for college there. And even ever since, I've pitched in when Gramma needed me…"

The enormity of the tradition weighed on her suddenly the way things had that morning, too, and she sighed. "And now I'm all that's left of the family, so…it's mine. Lock, stock and barrel. Officially as of this morning."

"This morning?"

"Gramma and I have been all that's left of the family for the last fifteen years since my grandfather died. She'd put everything in a trust that left me the restaurant and the house. As of this morning the trust was dissolved and everything was turned over to me for real."

Her voice had cracked as she'd talked and apparently he'd caught it because he said, "My mom died just a few months ago. It isn't easy…"

"No, it isn't. I'm sorry for your loss, too."

"And now there's only you? No brothers or sisters? No more parents?" he asked gently.

"Like I said, my dad was a marine. He served in the

Persian Gulf during Desert Storm and came back with some problems."

"He was wounded?"

"Not physically, but mentally, emotionally… He had really bad PTSD. I know sometimes people don't think that's as serious, but they're wrong. I was the twins' age when he came back and even I could see how much he was suffering. Sometimes he wouldn't know where he was. He'd think he was still in combat. And even when it wasn't the outwardly noticeable stuff, he was so sad… That's how it seemed to me, but I know it was depression. Bad enough that my mom was afraid to leave him alone."

"Afraid he'd hurt himself," Liam said as if she wasn't telling him anything he didn't already know. "I've seen PTSD in a few of my men. Had to send them home."

"He didn't have any family, but my mom and my grandparents did everything to try to help him. He'd have a few good days here and there, but then it would just hit him again, sometimes worse than other times. My mom bought him a boat because he'd always liked to go boating and that did help—there was something about being out on the water that calmed him. So every chance they got, they took the boat to a lake and spent time on it."

"Here? In Colorado?"

Dani knew what he was thinking. "Yes. And no, it wasn't a good solution during the winter months when everything around here freezes over. So when Dad got bad and things here were frozen, they hitched up a trailer for the boat and took it somewhere warmer—Arizona or California or Texas—somewhere they could still get out on the water for a while, until he felt better again."

"What about their jobs?"

"My dad was on disability. He couldn't be around a lot of people or noise. Sometimes he helped my grandfather with the paperwork or did some maintenance around the restaurant when it was quiet, but that was about it. The restaurant was my mom's job and my grandparents understood the situation, so they were okay with her taking off when she needed to."

"Did you go on these trips?"

"No, I stayed with my grandparents. If my dad needed the boat that meant he was in really bad shape, and I think my mom and my grandparents must have agreed that it was better if I wasn't around him then. It actually saved my life because when I was six my folks were killed in a boating accident."

Liam's dark eyebrows arched. "Oh... I didn't see that coming. You don't hear about a lot of those."

"Yeah," she agreed. "Although it might as well have been on the road—there was drunk driving on New Year's Eve involved. The holidays had been particularly rough for my dad that year, so the day after Christmas he and my mom headed for Arizona with the boat. We got the call on New Year's Day. Some college kids rammed full throttle into my parents' boat. No one survived."

"And your grandparents raised you from then on?"

"They did. I was lucky that way. I keep wishing that Evie and Grady were that lucky."

He didn't comment on that. Instead he said, "But you didn't stay at the restaurant like your mother—the restaurant that was going to be yours one day—and you became a nanny?"

"My grandmother wanted me to have a college education. She said there was nothing that said I had to stick with the restaurant, and she knew I loved kids—she liked that I seemed to have a knack for working with them. She thought I should be a teacher. I went with childhood development instead. My degree is in educational psychology.

I thought I'd still go into the schools, but I was actually recruited by the nanny service just before I graduated and I kind of liked the idea of working more one-on-one with younger kids, so I signed on."

Liam had finished his sandwich and begun cleaning up after himself just as the buzzer on the dryer gave the alert that the laundry was done.

"I better get that folded," she said. "Grady was devastated that his favorite hoodie was in the wash today and I swore it would be ready for him tomorrow."

Dani went downstairs into the laundry room, took the clothes out of the dryer and then brought them in a laundry basket to the couch in the central open space of the kids' lower level of the house.

She didn't expect Liam to follow but not only did he, he also sat on the coffee table and dipped into the basket to help her fold the kids' clothes.

She almost told him he didn't have to do that. But then she realized that he might soon be in the position of doing the twins' laundry, and decided to let him get some experience at that, too.

"And now the restaurant is yours," he said, picking up their conversation as if there hadn't been any change of venue. "Does that mean you're switching careers?"

"I don't know..." Dani answered with a hint of a groan that relayed only a fraction of her own quandary. "So much has happened... I was still reeling from my grandmother dying when the Freelanders were in the accident. My time with the twins will end when the court decides where they go from here, and I guess I'll have to decide where I go from here, too."

"Can you do both—take on a new nanny job and keep the restaurant going? I mean, you went in to check on things tonight and it sounded like you were making plans to go in more this week to do some things, and you're still taking care of the kids…"

Dani shook her head. "I'm in sort of a grace period. Everyone is going to extra lengths at the restaurant so running it isn't falling completely on my shoulders at the moment. But for the long haul? The restaurant is a full-time job even with a manager as good as Griff. And there are some issues with the building itself—we've known for a while that renovations need to be made and those are definitely outside of Griff's job description. Plus now I'm the only one who knows a lot of the recipes that have kept us going—Gramma was very protective of her recipes," Dani said, laughing a little at the memory of just how vigilant her grandmother had been about keeping those recipes their family secret. "There's just no way I can do both the restaurant and nanny or even work in a school."

"So you loved working with kids enough that your grandmother pushed you out of the restaurant nest to do it. But now, without you, there won't be any more of a restaurant that has to mean a lot to you."

"It does mean a lot to me," she admitted. "And not only does it mean a lot to me, it means a lot to that whole neighborhood, that whole community. Over the years it's become the heart of it. Marconi's is the go-to place for wedding and baby showers, and the weddings and wedding receptions themselves—people around there fight for dates to have their events there. You wouldn't have believed the size of my grandmother's funeral. It was standing room only—that's how important she and the restaurant have been to those people. And even since then there's been an outpouring of sympathy that's come along with notes and letters and phone calls begging me not to make them lose the restaurant, too."

"Carries a lot of weight."

"And that isn't even the biggest thing," Dani went on. "I also have to factor in that the restaurant is people's livelihoods—Griff, a few of the waitstaff and at least half the kitchen staff have been with us literally for decades. They're like family—"

"And if you close the doors they're out of work," Liam finished for her.

The laundry was all folded and Dani set it in piles in the basket to put away, leaving her and Liam merely sitting across from each other without much distance between her on the sofa and him on the coffee table. But he stayed there, looking at her with his full attention.

"So you're under just a little bit of pressure," he said with a small sympathetic smile, obviously trying to lighten things up. "On top of stepping up for Grady and Evie," he added.

It was only then that Dani realized she'd just vented to him in a way she usually only vented to Bryan. And she barely knew Liam.

"Oh, I'm sorry to dump all that on you!"

"It's okay," he assured in that strong male voice, laughing a little. "It kept me out of my own head for a while—which, these days, is a good thing because believe it or not there's a little stress that comes with the idea of becoming a father out of the blue," he said facetiously.

"No, it was out of line."

"It really wasn't. I'm just kind of amazed that you're in this tough time of your own life and you're still here doing what you're doing for the twins."

"I can take care of myself. They can't," she said simply, deflecting the praise that embarrassed her.

He smiled again, a small, thoughtful smile that brought something softer to his expression and drew her focus to his mouth. To his oh-so-supple-looking lips. Making her wonder—out of the blue—what it might be like to have him kiss her.

She didn't know what had happened to send her thoughts there but she yanked them back into line a split second later and sat up as posture-perfect straight as he was.

"It's getting late," she announced. "I've been up since early this morning and you had already made coffee by then, so you had to have been up even earlier. You must be tired."

She heard nervousness in her own voice but thinking about kissing him was so out of left field that it *had* unnerved her.

If Liam noticed her sudden fluster he didn't show it, but he also didn't deny that he was tired—despite the fact that he didn't look it. And there was something in his eyes that made her think he knew what was unnerving her.

Oh, she hoped not!

Unless maybe it was on his mind, too…

No, no, she couldn't go there, she told herself sternly.

Then he got to his feet and stepped away from the coffee table and the sofa—and her.

And she could only hope that wasn't because he'd had any inkling of what she'd just been thinking about.

"I need to have breakfast with my sister tomorrow morning," he said. "I was at my older brother's place Sunday night and I've talked to Kinsey on the phone, but I haven't seen her yet—"

"Sure," Dani agreed too quickly. "It's supposed to rain and be cold tomorrow so I planned an inside day. That's what the tubes you cut are for, to keep the kids busy. And I thought we'd watch their favorite movie while I set some dough to rise. They love it when they get to make their own pizzas, so that'll be dinner tomorrow night."

He smiled again, though this time there was mischief

around the edges. "You're gonna make me learn to cook, too?"

"I don't know if putting toppings on a piece of dough counts, but I have faith that if four-year-olds can do it, so can marines," she goaded him again.

"Fighting words," he warned with mock affront, helping Dani get over the stress that her wayward thoughts had caused her.

"You'll just have to prove yourself," she challenged.

"In so many ways these days…" he groaned, making her laugh at the reemergence of his anxiety over the situation with the kids.

Dani picked up the laundry basket and headed for the twins' rooms. "We'll just see you when we see you tomorrow," she concluded casually.

Then she warned herself to keep it casual as she slipped silently into Grady's room to put away his clean clothes.

Reminding herself firmly that casual did not mean ever experiencing how Liam Madison kissed.

Not ever.

Chapter Four

"It's a good thing I ran an extra mile before I came over," Liam moaned on Wednesday morning.

"It's been two years since you've had my waffles. Might be another two before you come home and get them again..." his sister tempted good-naturedly—unlike in the past when she would have said it sadly.

Liam was happy for that particular change in her.

It had been hard on Kinsey to have all three of her brothers in the military. On the rare occasions when they'd been able to visit her she'd made the most of it, but their time together had been tinged with the fact that she didn't know when she would see them again.

Those long absences had also left all the responsibilities for their parents on her—which Liam, Declan and Conor regretted. Coupled with friendships that had been sacrificed to the care of their parents during their declines, Kinsey had been desperate to gather more people, more family into her life. Family that would be accessible to her rather than halfway around the world when she needed them. Liam understood that.

But now she was engaged to Sutter Knightlinger and Liam knew that helped her not feel the loneliness and abandonment she usually did over the looming reality of him—or Declan—returning to duty.

But, according to Conor, neither Kinsey's engagement nor the ending of Conor's own military career were enough for her to cancel the quest she'd been on in recent months.

And Kinsey proved that when she pushed her own plate away and said, "Did Conor tell you that the Camdens are asking for DNA from us now?"

The Camdens.

Ten of them, all around the same ages as Kinsey, Liam, Declan and Conor. Raised by a grandmother called GiGi. Running an empire founded by their great-grandfather. An empire continued and expanded by his son and GiGi's husband, Hank, and then by Hank's sons, Howard and Mitchum Camden, who had, between them, produced the ten people who oversaw it all now.

Mitchum Camden was also the man Liam, Kinsey, Declan and Conor's mother had revealed on her deathbed was their father.

It had been a revelation that had sent Kinsey on a path to have herself and her brothers recognized as Camdens and taken into the fold.

Something none of her brothers were enthusiastic about.

"He told me," Liam answered her question.

"Will you do it?" Kinsey asked.

Liam stood and poured himself another cup of coffee without saying anything.

Then he rejoined his sister at the small kitchen table in the alcove of the apartment that she was beginning to pack up in anticipation of moving in with her fiancé.

He looked squarely at her, sighing heavily. "I don't know, Kins. Can't you just let it lay? You're getting married. You'll have a mother-in-law. Conor and Maicy live in Denver now. They'll probably have kids. You'll probably have kids. *I* may have kids…" That had come out more ominously than the rest but he went on anyway.

"Our own family is growing. Before you know it, you'll have more than you know what to do with. Why keep on with that other family?"

She rolled her eyes in exasperation. "You guys," she complained. "You're all so stubborn!"

"About this? Yeah!" he confirmed. "Why the hell would we want to be Camdens? Or even acknowledge any link to them? They've got money coming out of their ears that they accumulated off the backs of people they basically swindled and conned and ripped off. That's not what any of us are about."

The Camden name was now highly respected, redeemed by the current generation. But it had always been widely rumored that the fortune amassed by the predecessors of Camden Superstores had been ruthless, devious and scheming, that there was very little done by any of them to be proud of. Or to be proud to be associated with.

"At least Conor soft-pedaled it a little," Kinsey complained about Liam's blunt depiction.

"What's to soft-pedal? It's the truth. Robber barons— that's where H.J. Camden and his son and grandsons have their place in history. And you think I want any part of that? I fight for people *not* to be trampled over, Kinsey."

"I know," she said. "But the Camdens who also came from Mitchum are our half-siblings, the ones who came from Howard are our cousins, GiGi is our *grandmother*— they haven't done what the other ones did—"

"But you want to make one of those 'other ones' our *father.*"

"I'm not trying to *make* him our father. Mom did that."

Liam sighed again and shook his head. "I don't know what a father is to you, but to me it isn't what that guy was. To me it's what Hugh was. If it was what that guy was I wouldn't be here now, would I? I'd have just blown off the fact that I might have kids the way he did. Or thrown some money at them and gone on about my business."

"So this is really striking a chord for you," Kinsey said quietly.

"How could it not?"

"Okay. But, Liam, take away the father part. The past. That's over and done with and there's no one left to answer for it or to punish for it or to hold accountable. And what's left? We could have half brothers and half sisters. We could have a grandmother. Isn't that something that we shouldn't just ignore?"

"It seems like they've done a pretty good job of ignoring us."

"I'm sure they didn't have a clue that we existed until I brought Mom's letter to GiGi. If you could have seen the look on her face when she read it and found out about us, you'd know it was a shock."

"And did she open her arms to you? No, she left you twisting in the wind. Then they had us *investigated* like the criminals *they* come from. Now they want DNA proof?"

"You want DNA proof that the Freelander kids are yours."

"Not the same thing!"

"Exactly the same thing."

"These kids and I—and the court—need clarification so we all know where to go from here. I don't need clarification of who my father was—it was Hugh Madison, not the sperm donor. And if these kids are mine then I'll do whatever it takes for them. What do you think is going to happen if you force the Camdens to know for sure that Mitchum Camden was our father? They probably just want to know what they're up against to keep us away from their money and their stores. Maybe from them."

"I made it clear to GiGi when I saw her that we don't want anything from them—"

"And I'm sure she believed you," he said facetiously.

"If Audrey's kids do end up being yours, are you gonna wish you never knew?" Kinsey challenged.

"Would I rather not know that I have kids out in the world? You have to be kidding to even ask me that."

"And I certainly want to know if they're my niece and nephew. Mom would have wanted to know she had grandchildren. When I think about it, it's horrible to me that she didn't, that she could actually have had three and a half years with them before she died. But you think that we shouldn't give information like that to the Camdens? That we should just gloss over the fact that they're *our* family because it didn't have such a great start?"

"We're their dirty little secret. Living, breathing proof of the lowlife things one of them did. My situation is different."

"You're already having your DNA tested," Kinsey reasoned. "All you'd have to do is get a second copy of the results for me to send to them."

She really wasn't letting up on this.

"And then what, Kinsey?" Liam asked. "Are you picturing a big family dinner the next time I'm in town?"

"The Camdens have those every Sunday. They're really nice."

Liam put his forehead in his hand and shook his head, thinking that he had enough to deal with without this on top of it.

"And if the twins are yours, then they're Camdens, too. Shouldn't everyone know that?" Kinsey added.

"Oh, geezez…" was all Liam could say to that because intertwining these two loaded issues just made it worse. But he knew his sister wasn't going to let up so he looked at her again and sighed once more. "I'll think about it. But if I do it, it won't be because I want to or want any part of that family. It'll be because you want me to. It'll be for you." For all she'd done, she deserved to have what she wanted, even if he thought it was ill-advised.

He stood and took his plate to the sink. "Let's clean this up. I should get back."

"To being a dad?" Kinsey taunted, finding some humor in it.

"Yeah, I'm not really being that. I'm just trying to get them not to hate me."

"They don't hate you," Kinsey assured him, bringing her own plate and taking over at the sink. "Why would they hate you?"

"I'm not good with kids."

She laughed. "What, you? How could that be, Mr. Tact… Mr. Storm Trooper… Mr.—"

"Yeah, I get it. I don't 'soft-pedal,'" he said, using her earlier complaint. "I'm trying to, though. With them. But apparently it doesn't come off that way and I just seem like some kind of tight ass who needs to *relax*. Today I'm gonna do the boot camp workout with the boy—"

Kinsey laughed. "And that's your idea of relaxing and getting a four-year-old to like you?"

"We always liked doing that with Hugh," Liam defended.

"You and Declan and Conor liked doing that with Hugh," she amended. "Not me."

"Yeah, I asked the girl to do the workout, too, but she wrinkled her nose at me as if I'd suggested dipping her in dung."

"Uh-huh. I understand that."

"Dani says I have to think of something to do with her

that *she'd* like to do. But I don't have the foggiest idea what that would be."

"Uh-huh," Kinsey repeated.

"Hugh never did anything special with you," Liam said, defensively again.

"No, he didn't," Kinsey confirmed pointedly.

And then it struck Liam. "And you didn't feel about him the way we did, did you?"

The tone in his sister's voice had caused Liam to recall that and wonder suddenly if the lack of attachment Kinsey had felt to the man who had raised them was part of what made her so determined to connect with the Camdens now.

"I loved Hugh," she said. "But I wouldn't say that I felt close to him. He was all about the military and whipping us into shape for that. When I wasn't interested in being whipped into shape or in going into the military, it seemed like I became incidental. You guys were who was important to him."

"And you think Dani is right and the girl will feel like that with me if I don't do something else with her," Liam said.

Kinsey shrugged. "I think that Dani—that's the nanny's name?"

"Nanny and acting guardian."

"Yes, I think she's right. If you want Evie to feel closer to you than I felt to Hugh, you'll have to figure out how to bond with her by doing something other than the boot camp workout."

Liam just sighed again.

"And this Dani?" his sister said. "You call your potential daughter and son 'the girl' and 'the boy,' but the nanny is 'Dani'—like you like her…"

"She's great," he said without hesitation, but also with-

out affection, giving credit where credit was due. "She's
great with the kids. She's going above and beyond the call
of duty for them at a time in her own life when things
are tough, when someone else would have bailed to deal
with her own stuff. And she's patient with me. She's not
putting any pressure on. She's trying to help me wade
through the waters with the kids."

"Is she pretty?"

Beautiful.

"It doesn't matter. I have enough problems. I could be
the father of two four-year-olds and I don't know what
the hell I'll do if I am. You think I'm dumb enough to
add to that with some kind of hey-let's-get-it-on-during-
the-short-time-I'm-here hookup?"

His sister grinned at him. "Oh, you've thought about
it."

Damn but he had…

Last night, after doing nothing but talking to Dani,
folding laundry with her, he'd gone up to that space-age
guest room and spent much too much time thinking about
her…

But it had been a long time since he'd hooked up with
anyone and that was why it was on his mind, he'd decided
both last night and again this morning. When it—and
she—had still been on his mind.

It was only natural that after a long hiatus from sex,
plopped down in shared quarters with someone who
looked like Dani did, someone sweet and funny and
nice, that the idea of starting something physical with
her would occur to him.

But there was no way he would act on it. He was here
for one reason and one reason only—to find out if he'd
fathered the twins and go from there. If the twins *were*
his, he had a whole can of worms to deal with. If they

weren't, then they were still the kids of someone he once cared for. He had to see what he could do to make sure they were taken care of in the best way by someone else—and he didn't have any idea how he'd do that either. The last thing he was going to add to this mess was the complication of any kind of personal relationship or hookup.

"I think about a lot of things," he said in response to his sister's remark. "But I don't have anything if I don't have self-discipline."

"A direct quote from Hugh," Kinsey said with a laugh. "If you had self-discipline you wouldn't possibly have two kids."

"Oh, that's low," he said, laughing himself.

"Is your self-discipline strong enough when you're staying in a house with a pretty nanny who's 'great'?" Kinsey said skeptically.

"Yes," he answered unequivocally.

Because while Dani Cooper might be beautiful and great, while he might be finding himself looking forward to being with her—with and without the kids—while he might, at that very moment, be champing at the bit to get back to the Freelander house with more thoughts of spending the rest of today with her than with the kids, it didn't mean a thing.

He'd come here on a mission. And a marine on a mission didn't let himself be distracted even by flowing dark hair or big toffee-colored eyes or skin like cream or a smile that made something in him heat up the minute he saw it.

A marine on a mission kept to the straight and narrow to complete that mission.

And that's exactly what he was going to do.

Whether his sister scoffed at his ability to pull it off or not.

* * *

"Now *this* was a good idea!" Liam said as Dani brought their pizza into the dining room from the wood-burning pizza oven in the kitchen.

"I thought we earned it. Plus sometimes letting the kids cook ruins my appetite and I like to have my own dinner after I've put them to bed."

Which she'd done about an hour earlier, before focusing on the meal for herself and Liam while he went up to the guest room to shower.

He'd come down dressed in jeans and a plain white crew-neck T-shirt that looked better on him than any jeans or T-shirt had ever looked on anyone. At least that's how it had seemed to Dani when she'd glanced up from preparing a salad to feast her eyes on the T-shirt that hugged broad shoulders, well-defined pecs, bulging biceps and a hard, flat stomach. And jeans that, when he'd gone to the fridge to get himself a beer, had shown her that he also had a derriere to die for.

Plus he was clean-shaven and smelled like a tropical breeze, and suddenly her appetite for food had switched to an appetite for something that involved him instead.

Which she'd curbed the minute she'd realized what she was hankering for.

She'd been reining in a multitude of wayward thoughts about him for the last twenty-four hours, striking her like lightning bolts since that craziness had gone through her mind last night about kissing him.

She didn't know what was wrong with her but she knew she needed to fight it.

"Heart-shaped pizza and star-shaped pizza with ketchup instead of tomato sauce, ground beef, salami, black olives, slices of *orange* and *yellow* cheese?" he was saying as she again thought about how incredible-looking he was while running a pizza cutter through their own pie to slice it. "And they actually ate it."

"They did," she said with some horror of her own. "No accounting for a four-year-old's palate. But they also ate broccoli and sliced tomatoes—"

"Why do they call tomatoes 'red potatoes'?"

Dani laughed. "I have no idea. They just do. But anyway, they ended up eating a pretty good dinner, so that's all that counts."

"But yeah, it was really unappetizing," he confirmed as she served him a slice of pizza. "But this…this is pizza."

Homemade dough she'd had rising for hours, sauce, four kinds of Italian cheese, sausage, pepperoni, mushrooms, olives and red onions, which were not only for flavor but also so she could think about onion breath if kissing came to mind tonight.

"So give me my report card for today," Liam said after tasting the pie and getting slightly rapturous over it, judging it the best he'd ever eaten.

"You improved," she said, knowing he was referring to his behavior with the twins.

It had been a full—and rainy—day of entertaining them. By the time Liam had returned from his breakfast with his sister, they'd already used the tubes he'd cut the night before to make dragons and they'd been chasing each other around with them, growling through the tubes that had tissue paper at the opposite ends to billow out like flames.

After lunch and their naps—during which Liam had gone to the workout room beside the ballet studio to lift weights—he'd again invited Evie to do the boot camp workout with him and Grady. She'd declined but he had engaged the little boy in the clearly toned-down exercises they'd done downstairs while Evie had helped Dani make pizza dough.

Dani had been a little worried that the barked-out commands that went with the boot camp workout might put Grady off. But Grady had actually seemed to like the gruff praise and encouragement that went with it, and had, in fact, gone to great lengths to earn it.

"You definitely made some strides with Grady," Dani informed him. "Plus he liked that you watched their movie with us." Though Dani had found it difficult to concentrate with Liam sitting just within her peripheral vision.

Liam made a pained face at the mention of the movie. "That was a *lot* of singing."

Dani laughed. "That's what they like best—the animated musicals. And then it was good that you took them outside to splash through puddles when the rain stopped."

"That was supposed to be close-order drill—to move a unit from one place to another in an orderly manner."

Dani laughed. "Uh-huh. And Evie wasn't into that when it sounds like so much fun?" she said facetiously.

"Yeah, she just did the splashing. With her back to us to make sure we knew she wasn't going to march."

"Yeah, I don't think you're going to make a miniature marine out of Evie."

"She actually kind of seemed mad at me today."

And he really had tried with both kids.

"She and Grady are close. Sometimes they get a little bent out of shape if the other one plays with someone else. Grady would have done the same thing if you'd been doing stuff with Evie instead of him."

"But I wasn't leaving Evie out. I tried to get her to do what we were doing," he defended.

"I know—"

"Only we weren't doing anything she wanted to do,"

he guessed. "My sister thinks you're right, that I have to figure out some other girlie way to win her over."

"It doesn't necessarily have to be 'girlie'—although she does convince Grady to play dress-up and dolls and castle with her. But she's actually a little more of a daredevil than Grady is, too. Remember yesterday it was Evie who was the first of them willing to cross the monkey bars."

"I should take her bungee jumping?" he joked as he polished off his first slice of pizza and took a second.

"She'd probably like it but I wouldn't recommend it," Dani said. "It helps that you made a few strides with Grady, though. That's kind of broken the ice with them, and it might help bring Evie around a little—"

"An if-you-can't-beat-'em-join-'em thing?"

"Sometimes it works like that, yes. But I don't think it will be through your workout or marching drills," Dani said, barely able to suppress a smile at what he thought might lure a four-year-old girl to participate. "She does always need a prince when she plays castle." And boy, did his looks qualify him!

"So I should go up to her and say let me be your prince?"

He was joking and Dani did laugh at that. "A little subtlety might work better. When you see her playing with the castle you could just ask her things—what each room is for, who the dolls are, just show an interest. Then maybe kind of slip into the role with the prince doll. The prince doll could ask the princess doll to go to the ball. Evie *loves* it when there's a ball."

Liam made another pained face and frowned at her. "Do you know what I do for a living?" he asked as if she must be clueless to suggest what she was suggesting.

"Not take princesses to balls?" she joked.

"Not hardly."

"Well, buck up, Marine, because if you want to win Evie over, you might have to."

He groaned and Dani laughed again.

Then she said, "You talked to your sister about the twins?"

"Some. Kinsey pointed out how she wasn't as close to our adopted father as my brothers and I were because— like Evie—she wasn't interested in being turned into a marine. And with Hugh it was that or nothing."

"You were adopted?" Dani asked, curious about his roots. Well, curious about everything about him, although she was trying to convince herself that was only to evaluate him as the twins' potential parent.

"We weren't adopted from out of the system because we were in need of a home or anything. We lived with our mother on a farm in a small town in Montana called Northbridge. The man our mother married adopted us."

"You mentioned an older brother and your sister—"

"And I have a twin brother, too."

That surprised her. "You're a twin?"

"Yeah. I've heard they run in families so that probably ups the chances that Grady and Evie are mine."

That was what she'd been thinking.

"Declan is my twin," he went on. "We're in the middle. Conor is the oldest. He *was* a navy doctor but he just re-signed his commission to go civilian after a restart with his high school sweetheart. Kinsey is the baby of the family. She's a nurse, and she's getting married in May."

"Are you and your twin close?"

"Yeah, we're close."

"Are you identical?" Could there really be *two* guys running around looking like he did?

"Identical," he confirmed. "We got a lot of mileage

out of confusing people when we were kids. I think it's a little easier to tell us apart now."

Because Liam was a big, muscular marine and maybe his twin wasn't?

At least that's what Dani imagined because she couldn't fathom that even his identical twin would be quite as impressive a specimen as Liam.

But what she said was, "What does he do for a living?"

"He's a marine," Liam said as if that should have been a given. "We've both been overseas for a while, but in different units. Although right now he's stateside, too, recovering from what I'm told was a pretty serious injury that he almost didn't make it through."

"You were told?"

"Special Forces missions cause me to drop out for periods of time—I can't be reached, I can't reach out to anyone else. I heard about my mom dying just before I was set to follow my latest orders. I've been underground since then. Declan was hurt in an IED explosion two days after Mom's death and I was already in the field. I found out about it the same time I heard about Audrey and the twins—when the mission was complete and I came up for air again a week ago."

"That's a lot to have waiting for you."

"A whole lot," he agreed. "Now Conor and Kinsey have told me what's been going on and how Declan is, but I haven't been able to connect with him yet even by phone. I came straight here to deal with this situation when I hit the States, and he's in transit to Denver for more rehab so we keep playing phone tag. But no matter what, I'm not really going to be able to rest until I can see him for myself."

"They're saying that he's going to be okay, though, right?"

"That's what they tell me," Liam answered with some reservation. "But like I said, I need to see him for myself. And, now that we're talking about this, Conor called while I was showering and left a message that Declan just arrived in Denver. He'll need to go through admission at the rehab center and they won't let me see him tonight or I'd go, but... I know I keep bugging out on you in the mornings and I'm sorry about that, but Conor can get me in to see Declan tomorrow morning—"

"Oh, go! For sure," she said. Not that he was asking permission, but she certainly didn't expect him to put off seeing his injured twin just so he could help make oatmeal. By moving in and making the effort with Grady and Evie, he was already doing more than she thought most men would *before* being sure they actually had fathered the twins. Or even just to safeguard the orphaned kids of an old flame. She certainly wasn't going to condemn him for not being here every minute.

She took another half slice of pizza and let him know that would be her last if he wanted to finish the pie.

"I do," he said without question, taking his third full slice.

After eating a little more salad Dani got back to the rest of what they'd been discussing, hoping for additional information. "What about your biological father? Did he die and leave your mom with four kids?"

Liam hesitated in answering that and she wondered if he was still thinking about his twin or if she'd just asked a question he didn't want to answer.

But after a few minutes he said with disgust, "The guy who I guess was my father just left my mom with four kids."

That didn't sound good.

Before she could say anything, he sighed and confessed, "That's not exactly true. He did die—in a plane crash with a bunch of his family. But even before that he left my mother on her own with us. And if he hadn't died, I'm sure he would have gone on leaving her alone with us, just dropping in when it suited him."

Liam's expression was stern and as disapproving as his voice. "Apparently we're the product of an affair," he explained. "My mother kept it hidden until she was dying at the end of last year. That was when she told Kinsey that we're the secret family of Mitchum Camden."

"Camden? Like the Superstores?"

"Yeah," he said unhappily.

"Oh," Dani repeated because that was quite a revelation and she really didn't know what to say.

But once again she didn't have to come up with anything before he went on, as if he needed to get it off his chest. The chest her eyes wandered to periodically because it was just so fine…

"In the romantic version," he was saying, "my mother told my sister that Camden was torn between her and his wife. And even though my mother knew it shouldn't go on, and so did he, they couldn't stop themselves. My mother was pregnant with Kinsey when he was killed in the crash. Who knows how many more of us there might have been because she said she didn't think she would ever have been able to actually end it with him."

The way Liam said that did not make it sound romantic but Dani refrained from pointing that out and instead said, "And in the unromantic version?"

"I don't see anything romantic about lying to and cheating on the woman he was married to and had a family with. I don't see anything romantic about using the feelings my mom had for him to string her along on the side, to get her pregnant three times. I don't give a damn if he supported her and left us money or not. I don't see anything romantic about leaving her to answer for four illegitimate kids in a small town that couldn't have looked kindly on that!"

He definitely needed to vent.

"You said they 'couldn't have looked kindly on that.' That sounds like you didn't experience it?" she asked.

"Declan and I were two years old when he died, so no, I don't have any memories of Camden or of anything before Mom married Hugh and he adopted us. To me, we always looked like any other family. But I grew up in that gossipy small town and now that I know the truth I also know a situation like that couldn't have been good for her until Hugh made an honest woman of her."

"What did your mom tell you about your biological father when you were growing up?"

"Nothing. She said Hugh supported us, looked after us all and that to talk about another father was disrespectful and hurtful to him. So she wouldn't do it. She saved it for the end," he muttered somewhat under his breath. "None of us ever pushed it because there was nothing about Hugh that didn't make him our father."

"Except that you call him Hugh," Dani pointed out.

"Actually we called him Gunny. He retired as a master gunnery sergeant from the marines, the highest rank for enlisted, and Gunny is what he preferred. If we said something about him outside of the family we called him our father, but Mom always just referred to him as Hugh. She never said 'your dad' or 'your father'—maybe she was hanging on to the memory of Camden in that. So whenever Declan or Conor or Kinsey or I had anything to say about him to each other, we called him Hugh, too."

"But you still thought of him as your dad. You loved him and respected him," Dani observed, making the assumption from the change in his voice and attitude when he spoke of Hugh as opposed to when he spoke of his biological father.

"I did. He was a good man," Liam said readily. "Tough and stern—a marine to his core—but kind and fair and decent to my mom and to all of us, too. The same way he would have laid down his life for his country, he would have laid down his life for any of us. Come to think of it, probably everyone in Northbridge knew that, too, and that's why there were only a few snobs who went on snubbing my mom, while everyone else let go of her past and the fact that we were the products of it."

Tough and stern, kind and fair and decent—that seemed to describe what Dani knew so far of Liam, too. Now she knew where it came from. And also maybe why he was there to look out for the twins even if they weren't his—the way his adopted father had looked out for kids he hadn't biologically fathered.

Liam had polished off what remained of their dinner and even though Dani could have gone on talking to him much longer, she knew that she should put an end to the evening. While she wanted to get to know him well enough to feel confident in handing over Evie and Grady to him should that day arrive, she was finding that the more she learned about the kind of man he was, the more she liked him. And that made things difficult on an entirely different level for her.

So she stood and stacked their plates on the pizza stone to take into the kitchen, saying as she did, "It's getting late."

"Yeah, and I want to check in with Conor, make sure Declan got in all right tonight," Liam concurred, following her with his empty beer bottle and her water glass in hand.

She'd cleaned the kitchen while their pizza cooked so there was very little left to do. She took care of the pizza stone and washed off the dining room table and counter-tops while Liam put their dinnerware in the dishwasher.

Still, he didn't seem in any hurry to make his phone call because, rather than leaving her, he instead leaned a hip against the end of the island, effectively cornering her cozily in the L of the surrounding counter she'd just finished sponging off.

"So, what should I do tomorrow after seeing Declan—come home in a horse-drawn carriage like a fairy-tale prince to soften up Evie?" he asked.

"Only if it's a 'wipe' horse," Dani said with a laugh.

"I don't know what a 'wipe' horse is…"

"That's how Evie says *white*. She's very big into white horses right now. But I don't think you have to go quite that far."

"Thank god because I don't know where I'd get one!" he joked, cracking a smile that put lines at the corners of those amazingly blue eyes and—like the night before—turned that mouth that could be very sober into something so much more appealing…

Then, in a voice that was deeper, quieter, he jokingly confided, "I'm not always such a clod. Sometimes I actually *do* succeed with girls."

That had to be an understatement because just looking up into that face made her wobbly inside, and she didn't have a doubt it did that to everyone. How could it not?

In order not to give herself away, though, she played it cool and said, "Yeah, I kind of figured that."

But suddenly kissing was on her mind again. More than the night before when it had merely flitted through her brain.

Tonight it took firm enough root for her own lips to go a little slack in anticipation. Or was it invitation?

She wondered if he might have shaved because he'd considered kissing her.

She wanted him to.

In fact she was thinking about it—wanting it—so much that for a moment she wasn't sure if he was leaning forward just slightly or if she was hallucinating because she wanted to believe he was.

She tilted her chin even as she chanted to herself, *Onion breath, onion breath, onion breath...*

But the truth was he still only smelled like a tropical breeze...

He *had* leaned forward but she only knew it for sure when he straightened up again, taking himself out of range.

Which of course was what he should have done, and Dani responded with a higher raise of her chin that she hoped conveyed he'd made the right choice.

Even as something inside her was deflating because he hadn't gone through with it and kissed her.

Then he turned and went to the far end of the island as he said, "What's on tomorrow's agenda?"

Back to business.

"The kids have swimming lessons and sometimes I let them stay to splash around for a while and practice when the lessons are over—it helps wear them out. Then I promised them dinner at Marconi's afterward. I need to check in, take a few minutes to measure and mix some of the ingredients for a soup I need to make this week. It has a lot of different parts so we only do it once a year and I have to get things started for it. Plus Griff, my manager, called today and said the leak in the pipe downstairs is getting worse and I need to take a look at it."

Liam nodded. "Italian food again tomorrow night then," he said.

"Our grill man makes the best rib eye around and a great burger, too, so you don't have to eat Italian."

"It wasn't a complaint, Variety Pack," he said in a voice that she thought almost sounded affectionate. "I never get my fill of Italian."

There seemed to be some deeper meaning in that as his gaze stayed steady on her face, drinking it in.

But then—like with that lean in a moment before—he snapped out of it, said he'd see her tomorrow and left.

And alone in the kitchen, Dani took a deep breath and exhaled, telling herself to be glad that he *hadn't* kissed her.

Her life was already complicated and unsettled enough.

His life might be on the verge of the massive complication of parenthood coupled with a career in the military that meant his life was always unsettled.

And while they might be together for the time being, it was going to pass fast and they weren't going to have anything to do with each other once it did.

Which would make kissing a really dumb thing to do.

But he *had* been about to do it…

Somehow she was sure of it.

And despite knowing it was for the best that he hadn't, when she turned off the lights and set the security system before heading for bed, she was fighting some heavy-duty disappointment.

Chapter Five

"Liam…"

"Oh, my god, Declan, you look…" Liam blurted out in answer to his brother's greeting when he walked into the room at the rehab hospital and set eyes on his twin being helped from a bed into a wheelchair.

Looking at Declan had always been like looking in a mirror—not only were their features that similar, but they'd always been the same height and build. As teenagers they'd competed when it came to working out, measuring biceps, pecs, waists, thighs and calves to compare who was gaining more muscle mass. Even striving to win that contest, they'd always been within a fraction of an inch of the other.

But now Liam was faced with the signs of his brother's injuries. Declan had lost weight and muscle. He was pale; his cheeks were sunken. His eyes were dull and lifeless. He looked weak and vulnerable—something Liam had never seen in him—and it shocked him.

"He looks great now. You should have seen him before," Conor interjected, sounding like a cheerleader. "Plus you have to remember he was traveling yesterday. That wore him out. That's why today is a rest day and he won't start therapy until tomorrow."

"That's what we were just talking about," said the man who had helped Declan into the wheelchair. He introduced himself as Declan's physical therapist.

The physical therapist left them and Conor motioned to one of the visitor's chairs for Liam while he did his own examination of Declan.

He checked the jagged scar on the back of Declan's left hand, testing the movement of his fingers and the strength of his grip. He studied a nearly healed wound on Declan's left temple, by his hairline. Then he moved on to what was clearly Declan's worst injury—his left leg and knee.

A massive brace kept the knee stationary and his leg extended. Conor unfastened the brace to expose evidence of multiple wounds that—like his head wound—were almost healed, along with the scar of an incision that ran from mid-thigh to mid-shin.

Conor had Declan show him how far he was capable of bending the knee and asked him to move his toes. Then Conor tested the feeling in his toes and foot before replacing the brace, all while Liam watched his twin comply and show pain only in the flinch of his eyebrows.

The exam gave Liam a few minutes to come out of the shock of seeing Declan like that. But as he adjusted, he also began to think that Conor had understated the problem when he'd mentioned Declan's mental state. Declan's spirits seemed alarmingly low.

Of the two of them, Liam had always been more by-the-book, serious natured. Declan was the smart-ass jokester with boundless energy constantly looking for action, fun and excitement.

Now, not only did he merely comply with Conor's requests without any effort to speak to Liam along the way, he also made no jokes, no puns, no comments at all. He was more poker-faced than Liam had ever seen him, completely expressionless and detached, as if he was there physically but totally removed otherwise.

Conor finished his exam and Declan watched the brace

being replaced as if it were being done to someone else. Then Conor said he wanted to talk to the physical therapist and left the room.

When they were alone, Declan looked Liam squarely in the eye and said in a gravelly, barely audible voice, "We lost Topher."

"Conor told me," Liam answered the same way.

They'd both been almost as close to Topher Samms as to each other. In many ways—since Conor was four years older—they'd been closer to Topher than to Conor.

The Samms farm was next to theirs, so the three of them had been together from the cradle up. They'd gone to Annapolis together. They'd gone into the marines together. Had Liam not become Special Forces, he would have joined Declan and Topher in requesting to be assigned to the same unit. For Liam, losing Topher was very nearly as bad as it would have been to lose Declan. And Liam knew that for Declan, too, losing him wouldn't have been much worse than losing Topher.

"I tried but I couldn't save him…" Declan confessed, the crack in his voice the only sign of emotion that Liam had seen since entering the room.

"Course you did," Liam said without a doubt.

"The front wheel on his side of the Humvee must have hit the IED. Topher took most of the blast. It blew the Humvee onto its side…my side… I was driving…"

Liam could see that his brother was looking for absolution. But he also knew that there was nothing to absolve him of and even though Declan had to have heard that any number of times, he still couldn't forgive himself.

Still, Liam had to add his own. "Wasn't you who planted the IED, Dec. Couldn't see it to avoid it. Not your fault."

His brother's eyes filled and damned if Liam's didn't,

too. So a moment passed in silence as they both dealt with that before Declan said in barely more than a whisper, "Feels like my fault. Should have been me."

"Hey! Don't give me that bull—"

"A pregnant wife…a little girl…that's what I took him away from. Why the frick am I the one left when he needed to come back to them?"

"Geezez, Declan, there's no answer to that! Because it was his time and not yours? I'm just glad I didn't lose you both, for god's sake! But it sure as hell wasn't your fault and it sure as hell shouldn't have been either one of you!"

"Uh, this is a hospital," Conor said as he came back into the room.

It was Liam's voice that had been raised and, like with Evie and Grady, he was afraid he was desperately mishandling this.

He took a breath and recalled advice Dani had given him for the twins, trying to put himself in his brother's shoes.

Forcing moderation into his tone, he said, "Okay, it's bad enough that we lost Topher. I'm seeing you in this shape for the first time. You can't make me think about losing you, too…"

Liam needed another moment to regain his control.

When he had it, in his most authoritative tone he said, "You are *not* to blame and if I have to have that tattooed on your arm or tell you that a million times, I will. And you and I both know that Topher would be saying the same thing to you. We talked about this—the three of us—we knew what we were taking on, not one of us was doing it because of the other two. We agreed that it was to serve a cause greater than ourselves, no matter what the risk. I meant that. Didn't you?"

Declan shrugged and inclined his head slightly, arching an eyebrow that confirmed it without enthusiasm.

Still, Liam was going to take what he could get. "I know Topher meant it, too. He was willing to do it *for* that pregnant wife, that little girl of his. It sucks that they're all making the worst sacrifice they could have, but he went in with his eyes open—the same way we did—and now we have to go on. We have to deal with what's left, Declan. We move forward from here—you and I—exactly the way Topher and I would have if it had been you, exactly the way you and Topher would have if it had been me. It's what we promised each other and it's damn sure what we're going to do. Because it was Topher, that means we'll do whatever we can, whatever needs to be done for the family he left behind."

It didn't seem as if that had any impact on Declan. He only acknowledged it with a single raise of his chin.

"Liam is right," Conor contributed in support. "You honor Topher's memory and do what you can to help his family, to make sure they never want for anything."

Still Declan just sat there. He didn't say anything. He again showed no emotion.

"Letting yourself be another casualty won't help them," Liam felt the need to point out. "Work on getting back on both feet, getting yourself in shape again, getting the hell out of here. Then we'll tackle what Topher left behind. We'll make sure we do everything for them that Topher would have done for us if the tables were turned."

Another slight raise of Declan's chin was his only response and that seemed to have nothing behind it but a feeble attempt to humor both Liam and Conor.

But their conversation was cut short just then when a nurse came into the room.

"I asked your doctor to take some more X-rays," Conor

explained, nodding in the direction of the nurse. "I want to make sure everything is healing the way it should be before we get started with this rehab. It'll be intense and I want to know the leg can take it."

Yet another scant raise of Declan's chin and nothing more.

"I'd say you could wait for him," the nurse said as she unlocked the wheels on his chair and maneuvered it in the direction of the door, "but after X-rays he has his entrance interview with Dr. Noone and that takes quite a while. But it's up to you. The cafeteria is one floor down."

"No, he needs to rest, too," Conor said.

"We'll be back another day," Liam told Declan.

Declan merely nodded but didn't say goodbye as the nurse wheeled him out of the room.

Liam took a steeling breath and stood. Only when he and Conor were out in the hall and headed in the opposite direction to leave did he say, "He's not good."

"Physically—after what he's been through—he's doing great."

"It's not that I'm worried about. When have you ever known Declan to be like that? Flat—it's like he's not there."

"I know," Conor said. "No wisecracks, no jokes—"

"Hell, he barely talks! He's like an empty shell—except for the stuff over Topher. It's like there's nothing there *except* guilt. And that crap about how it should have been him? Geezez, is he gonna hurt himself?"

Conor breathed a sigh that made Liam think his older brother was finally letting his own concerns for Declan show.

"He hasn't made any threats of that," Conor said. "But I wanted him in this rehab for their psych department— it's one of the best and I've got him on their radar. I've been told that there are a couple of other guys rehabbing here who are carrying some similar baggage so there's a plan to start a group, get them together with Declan, see if maybe he'll open up with them better than he does with a shrink. Or with me. Or even with you, apparently—I was hoping it might be different with you—you know, the twin thing—but I guess not."

"I don't know… I just… I didn't know whether to kick his ass or hug him and try to make him cry it out."

"Yeah. Neither one would have worked any better than what you did—I've tried both. He's buried under his own demons right now. Since I'm in Denver to stay I've also set it up with the shrink to counsel me—he can't legally tell me anything specific to Declan because of privacy laws, but I'm just trying to figure out the best way to approach him, to deal with it, because I don't know what to do either. My area is the body, not the mind. The shrink says it'll be a process, the same as his leg—one step at a time."

"With a guarantee that he'll be himself again when it's done?"

They'd left the hospital and were at Conor's car, facing each other over the top, so Liam saw his older brother's weak shrug. "There weren't any guarantees on his leg. There aren't any guarantees on this. We just do what we can and hope for the best."

Was she gawking?

Well, she was, but was it obvious? Dani glanced around to see if anyone had noticed.

She was sitting on the bottom bleacher beside the swimming pool where Evie and Grady were just finishing their swimming lessons.

Dani didn't always agree to the extension in the pool the twins regularly begged for. Swimming was not high on her list of likes. But today when their pleading had begun, Liam had offered to do it.

And he'd just come out of the men's locker room.

While he'd worn clothes that gave hints about the body being covered, nothing had prepared her for seeing him in only a pair of swim trunks.

And what those swim trunks didn't cover was most definitely something to gawk at.

Not only was his face movie-star handsome, he had the body to go with it. There was a full six-pack of abdominals below pecs that could have been sculpted from granite. Expansive shoulders and biceps were pumped up into boulders under his taut, smooth skin. His legs were long and also well honed, with thighs that looked thick enough to power lift a house. And viewing it all together, Dani had to force her jaw not to drop.

This is a public place, not a bedroom! she silently reminded herself.

Bedroom? Had she actually just put Liam Madison and bedroom together in one thought?

That was bad.

She couldn't do things like that, she told herself firmly. Not even in her mind. She couldn't do things like think of Liam in conjunction with anything to do with the bedroom and she also couldn't do whatever that had been when they'd almost kissed last night.

But now that thoughts of the bedroom and kissing were creeping in, it told her that she really needed to work on putting it all to a halt.

The twins were and had to be the center of the universe for them both, with nothing else added to the mix. She was Evie and Grady's guardian; he was potentially their father. There was no way she should ever, in a million years, let herself feel the attraction she was feeling for the father of kids she was in charge of. It was one great big no-no and she was going to stop it. Now!

She unscrewed the top to her water bottle and took a big gulp to cool down the sudden flush she was feeling, wishing she'd worn clothes that were lighter weight than the jeans and double layer of T-shirts she had on. At least she'd put her hair up today—that helped.

But even over the bottle she couldn't take her eyes off Liam as he got into the water, where the swimming teacher was just saying goodbye to Evie and Grady.

And the camouflage of the pool water didn't help much because he was in the shallow end, so his incredible upper half was still there for her to see in all its glory. And Dani thought that if she really wanted to cool down she might have to pour her bottled water over her head rather than drink it.

But then she took a look at Liam's face alone, his expression, and that actually helped more than the water or the stern talking-to.

He was gorgeous. And yes, there was something about that time after the kids went to bed at night when he wasn't trying so hard, when he seemed to drop his guard, something about talking to him and having quiet time alone with him, that felt like there might be a little connection happening.

But she'd been looking for signs of Liam's military service taking any toll on him mentally or emotionally. And today she worried that one might have appeared.

This morning, when he'd come home from seeing his family, he hadn't come searching for her and the kids. He hadn't jumped right into their day.

Instead he'd immediately gone upstairs to the guest room without so much as a hello or an announcement that he was back. He'd just come in the front door, climbed the stairs and stayed secluded for well over an hour.

And as that time had grown, Dani had had sort of a flashback to when her father had vanished into the bedroom or bathroom in dark funks, lost in himself and his memories and whatever else his PTSD had caused him to suffer through, putting and keeping distance between himself and everyone else.

She'd worried that was what Liam had been doing up there.

Yes, seeing his injured brother for the first time had likely not been easy. And had he merely come back from that more quiet than usual that wouldn't have alarmed her. It was that full-on withdrawal that pushed a button in her.

Dani had told herself that was only her own baggage coming to the surface and she'd tried to stay positive. She'd also considered that maybe Liam hadn't felt well and had needed a short nap or something with no deep-seated meaning behind it.

She'd told herself that maybe he'd brought something in with him and he was going to come down with a surprise for the kids—a toy he'd needed to assemble or a project he'd needed to prep.

She'd told herself that there was probably a simple explanation and everything was fine.

But then he'd finally come downstairs. And when he had, it wasn't with an assembled toy or a project for the kids. And he wasn't the Liam who had been trying so hard to make friends with the twins. He wasn't the Liam she'd spent the last few nights talking to, getting to know and even thinking about kissing.

He'd been—and remained all day long—the Liam she'd first met. Stiff, solemn and nearly silent. A sentry standing in the wings just observing, barely giving an indication that he was even there. Seeming more than down-in-the-dumps over his brother but impossible to engage, to draw out of himself and his withdrawal. Like her dad.

She'd tried including Liam as she'd played with the kids, teasing him, joking with him, but nothing had worked.

Just the way nothing but time on the boat had worked on her father's funks.

She'd ultimately decided her focus needed to be on Grady and Evie, and she'd left Liam to whatever it was that had caused this switch, hoping that it might just right itself.

Soon! she silently commanded, watching him now. After all, he was in the pool with the kids—wasn't that a time and place to lighten up?

But no, there he was, still stiff and solemn, his handsome face stony, just going through the motions.

And even worse, he was insisting that the twins do only what they'd just learned, refusing to let them vary from the drill. Exactly the way Garrett would have and that set off another alarm in her.

Liam was being completely inflexible. He was trying to maintain strict control over the kids, the situation.

But if you don't bend, you break... Dani had said that to Garrett so many times.

Garrett was a police officer. A tightly wound police officer who had not unwound when he was off duty.

But trying to convince him to try, to try for her sake and for the sake of her young charges when he was around them, had been to no avail.

That constant drive for control had ultimately destroyed her relationship with him. Thinking about their relationship now, Dani knew two things: she never wanted to be involved with another man like that, and if Liam didn't bend a little now, after an entire day of the detached wooden-soldier act, he was going to lose the headway he was only beginning to make with those kids.

"It's okay if they just play," she called to him, hearing an undertone of anxiety in her own voice, both because he was reminding her of her former fiancé and because similarities to her father's sudden lapses into withdrawal stressed her out. Plus there was so much riding on Liam for the twins' sake.

"I thought this was to practice what they learned," he called back, frowning at her, again reminding her of both her father's intensity and Garrett's.

"That's the reason they give to stay in the pool. It isn't what they really want to do. But it's okay," she repeated. "They had their lesson. You can just have fun now."

For a moment his expression showed complete disapproval of that notion, and yet again she thought of the strict adherence to things that her former fiancé had demanded.

She held her breath. Fearing the worst. Hoping for better.

Come on, Marine, these are little kids... Pull it out of the fire...

Their eyes were deadlocked, and Dani really did feel as if she were facing men of her past as she willed Liam to come out from under whatever it was that had a hold of him today. But still, she feared that he would stand his ground, get angry and insist on dominating the situation.

Garrett would have.

But then Liam nodded. His expression remained somber and he still didn't relax, but he did seem to accept her encouragement to move on because he broke off eye contact with her, returned his attention to Evie and Grady and said, "So, what do you guys like to do in the pool?"

It was a question asked without any real invitation to

change course, but Dani told herself it still opened the door for the twins to let him know what they wanted.

She went on watching, unsure if Liam had already put them off to the extent that they didn't want to swim anymore.

But apparently staying in the pool was important enough to them to give Liam a second chance because they told him what they liked to do.

And to his credit, he complied and took turns bracing them with his big hands under their backs to keep them afloat so they could pretend they were boats sailing in circles.

Dani breathed a sigh of relief.

He could give a little. He had put what the twins wanted before whatever was going on with him. So he wasn't as bad as her dad had been. Whatever demons he was fighting today weren't debilitating and he was still able to deal with the kids patiently.

And he *had* let go of that inclination to keep a tight rein on things in the pool, too. Even if it had taken some intervention, he'd still allowed Evie and Grady the freedom to play and just be kids—another thing that would hopefully make him okay as a father.

As much as she wished for it, she couldn't expect perfection. With Evie and Grady's future at stake, Dani had to hope not only that Liam would prove to be their father, but that he could at least be an okay father to them. And while seeing what she'd seen today wasn't heartening, it hadn't robbed her of all hope for that.

But it did temper the impact of his gorgeousness.

Because while there was no arguing that the man was hotter than lava, Liam reminding her of her father and Garrett was an eye-opener.

Liam *was* a marine, in the line of work that had caused

her father's problems. There were no assurances that Liam wasn't on the same path.

And when it came to the reminder of Garrett? The similarities she'd seen between the two today?

She couldn't ignore that either. She'd already come up against enough of the issues that Garrett's high-pressure job had caused to know she wasn't the person to be with someone whose occupation caused rifts in their personal life.

The reminders of her dad's and Garrett's issues added even more reasons to resist Liam's almost overwhelming appeal.

But watching him sail Grady in a circle gave her a slow three-hundred-and-sixty-degree view of that torso, those muscular arms and that full expanse of back, and she decided his appeal wasn't *almost* overwhelming.

It was completely overwhelming.

So it was a good thing that she had a whole list of reasons to resist.

"What was the name of what I ate tonight?"

"Evie and Grady's favorite pasta—*cavatelli*. But for some reason we've always shortened that to *cavatils* so that's how they say it and it sounds different than it looks on the menu," Dani answered Liam's question later that night when the kids were in bed.

He'd followed her to the laundry room, where she was taking the swim things out of the washing machine to hang the suits and toss the towels into the dryer.

He leaned a shoulder against the doorjamb. "Ah, that makes sense—I did see that cavatelli thing on the menu. They were really good," he praised. "And you *make* those?"

"Not me in particular. It *is* Gramma's recipe but not

one of the secret ones, so it isn't something I have to do myself. Ours are a little different than what they usually are because we put ricotta in the dough."

"They look like tiny hot dog buns."

Dani laughed. "That *is* what they look like."

"And the kids, you might have to put them on the payroll. They handed out menus to customers, brought out the silverware wrapped in napkins. All very seriously."

Dani laughed again. "I know. They call it 'playing restaurant' but they really get into their roles."

"And you just let them have run of the place even with the customers?"

Was that more of a need for control coming through? Because Garrett had also disapproved of the kids being allowed to do even those small things.

"I told you it's always been a family restaurant. They aren't doing anything I wasn't doing at their age. Most customers get a kick out of it but when we have the occasional one who doesn't, Carmella intervenes and keeps the kids away from them."

"Carmella…" he said, putting some lilt into the name. "She's, what? About a hundred?"

Dani laughed. "She's eighty-six."

"She told me working keeps her alive."

"I know, she tells everyone that. She's a fixture there. She and my grandmother were close. I wasn't sure Carmella would stay after Gramma died, but she told me she didn't know what she'd do with herself without that place to go to every day. And everybody loves her, so as long as she wants to work, she works." Unless Dani closed or sold the restaurant.

But she didn't add that.

Instead she was just glad to see that Liam's mood had improved.

That improvement had first started at the pool. Grady refused to play it, but Evie's favorite game was to get out of the water, go to the pool's edge and jump into waiting arms.

Dani's safety stipulation was that the little girl *not* get the running start she really wanted. But even doing it right from the edge, Evie still loved the challenge of trying to increase her distance each time. Her gusto for the leap, her cries to warn that she was coming and her glee when she was caught—and maybe that it had helped break the ice between Liam and Evie—had caused the first slight lift in Liam's curtain of gloom today.

Then, at the restaurant, the curtain had risen a little higher when Carmella had been undaunted by that still-stoic manner of his. The warm, elderly woman had treated him the way she treated everyone—as if he were her cherished grandchild who'd come for a visit. She'd doted on him, teased him, flattered him and eventually succeeded at improving his mood even more.

When Dani had finished in the kitchen she'd called the twins to the table where Liam was stationed and the four of them had eaten dinner. The kids had chattered freely and Carmella had joined them at the table whenever there was a lull, so the meal ended up with a lot of happy talk and laughing. Liam didn't join in, but it did seem to take his disposition up another notch.

By the time they'd left Marconi's, he was still quiet, but his low-spiritedness seemed to have gone away. And now here he was, seeking out her company rather than retreating to the guest room's isolation again the way Dani had thought he might.

"I've been in homes that aren't as homey as your restaurant—my own, for one," he said.

"Your *home* wasn't homey?"

"Not like that, no. At my house growing up it was strictly kids should be seen and not heard. Coupled with Hugh's military attitudes, we were taught to stand straight, only speak when spoken to, follow orders without question—"

"In other words, do what you were told," Dani translated with another laugh. "That's what all parents want."

"Sure, but…there was just a different atmosphere. Watching you with Grady and Evie, watching things tonight at the restaurant, it's all… I don't know, open and warm and inviting and indulgent in ways that my upbringing didn't have. You all act like kids are special."

"Kids *are* special," Dani said as she finished with the swimming gear and they went into the kitchen, where she opened the dishwasher to empty it.

"Like I said, that isn't how I was raised. Everything was more reserved. More conservative. We knew my mom loved us but there were no spontaneous hugs like Carmella dishes out at the drop of a hat, like you do with the kids all the time—"

"Italian families can be very affectionate," she conceded.

"And your whole restaurant has that feel to it—like one big Italian family. With the kids being little shining stars right in the middle of it instead of being…well, seen and not heard," he went on. "In my family kids treated anything like Evie and Grady were, are, considered spoiled."

"I was spoiled rotten by my grandparents, and I grew up in the 'atmosphere' you saw tonight, but there was still discipline and rules. I had to behave, but I knew I was the apple of everybody's eye and it was great. I feel bad for kids who don't have that. It's actually one of the reasons I like being a nanny. I like the idea of bringing that into the lives of kids who maybe *are* expected to be seen and not heard, or kids whose parents don't have the time or inclination to make them feel the way I did growing up. I like to be able to give them the kind of attention I had."

"Yeah, I suppose now that I think about it, Hugh training us for the military got Conor, Declan and me a lot more attention than most of our friends got from their parents, so that's probably part of why we liked it. But it just wasn't all so…touchy-feely."

"Sooo…if you end up being the twins' dad, which way will you go as a parent?" She felt the need to ask.

"Huh…" he mused. "I haven't thought about that. You mean, like a parenting *style*, right? It never occurred to me to *choose* what kind of parent I'd be. I just thought… you know…you just *do* it…"

Dani handed him glasses to be put in the cupboard. "You aren't just *doing* what you're doing now without putting any thought into it," she said. "You've been working on the relationship you want to have with the kids. The kind of parent you are will determine that, too. My friend Bryan was raised with the sort of attitude you're talking about—not military but definitely not 'touchy-feely.' He's gay and it made it kind of hard to come out to his family. In fact, he came out to mine before he came out to his. I always thought that was sad. And he and his father don't even speak now."

"Yeah, that's not good," Liam agreed.

Talking about Bryan reminded Dani about the call she'd had from him today. Since she wanted to let seeds she planted about choosing the kind of parent to be take root, she changed the subject.

"Bryan called me this morning to tell me there's been an offer on the restaurant."

Liam's brows pulsed together. "I didn't think it was up for sale. I thought you were on the fence about that."

"I am and, no, I haven't put it up for sale. But an offer came in anyway. Bryan is an attorney and he represents us. He also represents another small chain of Italian restaurants around here. That's where the offer came from."

"A chain? So they'd change things to fit in with that? They wouldn't leave it the way it is?"

She shook her head. "But it's a good offer because they want the secret recipes, too, to add to their own menu."

"Are you going to take it?"

"I haven't had time to think about that. I'm just kind of in shock at the amount right now. And it seems so soon…"

"After being at that place I can imagine how tough a decision it is to part with it. It's more than just a business—"

"It's family in itself."

"But stick with it and you have to stop working with kids," he repeated what she'd told him before.

"Or sell and feel like I'm really losing what's left of my grandparents."

He nodded, giving credence to her dilemma. "But it seems to me that since your grandmother steered you into doing your own thing, she'd understand if you sold out so you could go *on* doing your own thing."

"True," Dani conceded.

It didn't make the decision for her but talking to him did help ease a little of the pressure she was feeling. She appreciated that. As much as she appreciated talking about this with someone as coolheaded as he was.

But she didn't want to deal with it right then so she made a joke to get them out of the conversation. "And if I sell, that leaky pipe in the basement could be someone else's problem."

"That leak is nothing. You just need a section of pipe replaced and I can do that."

"You can?"

"I'm no master plumber but I can shut off your water and do that. I'll fix it tomorrow while we're there making that weird bomb soup you and the kids kept talking about."

"Billi bomb soup—it's a family recipe but I promise there are no real bombs in it," she joked again, realizing that she was suddenly feeling better on two counts: Liam was back to himself and it was good to have another perspective on the restaurant, especially now that there was an offer on the table. It was also good to have someone who could lend a hand with a problem there.

But a temporary reprieve from thinking about the offer put her mind back on Liam and his mood today as they finished with the dishwasher and moved on to the dance studio.

The twins had taken a box there that contained the pieces to ten puzzles. They'd wanted to put them together on the flat, open floor. But that had turned into throwing the pieces at each other to see how many they could land—like a snowball fight—and now the pieces needed to be organized.

As she and Liam sat cross-legged on the dance studio floor with the mess between them, she ventured into new territory that she realized was prying but couldn't resist now that his sullenness seemed to have passed.

"So…what was going on with you today? You were kind of…off…" she said cautiously, wondering if mentioning it would reproduce his bad humor the way it would have with her father. Or if it might set off the kind of temper and defensiveness it would have roused in Garrett.

But in Liam it didn't do either of those things. He didn't deny it and said with some regret in his tone, "Yeah… I'm sorry about that."

An apology. Dani thought that was encouraging.

"Seeing Declan this morning hit me kind of hard," he admitted then.

"You said he was doing okay." When Liam had finally come down from the guest room she'd asked him if everything was all right with his brother. But he'd assured her his twin was all right.

"Physically he *is* on the mend," Liam went on, explaining what he'd found on that initial visit. Then he said, "He's in a bad way mentally, though."

Liam told her in detail what his brother had said about their friend, filling her in on who that friend was and their history with him. As he did, the glumness reappeared full force to deepen his voice before he finished and fell silent as they exchanged puzzle pieces.

"I'm sorry," Dani said in condolence for his friend.

"You hope there won't be casualties. But you know there always could be," he said solemnly, his tone telling her that his brother wasn't the only one to have feelings over this loss.

But he didn't talk about his own feelings. He went on talking about his brother. "I've just never known Declan to be as low as he is. He's not himself and that got to me more than even the physical stuff. I'm worried about him, and I don't know what to do to help him."

"From what went on with my dad I know that can be really tough," she commiserated when she heard the frustration and concern in Liam's voice. "I think you just hang on tight. Hear him out when you can get him to talk. Listen for clues to what he needs from you. My mom used to say we needed to do that with my dad, that sometimes we could figure out what to do from listening."

Liam laughed humorlessly. "Something else for me to figure out?" he moaned. "Something else that isn't simple?"

Dani laughed the same way he had. "Life and people get complicated."

"Yeah," he agreed.

For another moment he didn't say more as they finished putting the puzzle pieces back into their boxes. Dani wondered if his melancholy had so much of a hold on him again that he would retreat to the guest room now.

It shouldn't have mattered to her. But it did. She didn't want him to go yet. And she needed to steel herself a little for the possibility that he would.

Then, rather than getting to his feet and leaving her behind, he shifted positions, bending one knee and hugging it with both long arms.

He was wearing jeans and a yellow sport shirt. His sleeves were rolled to just below his elbows, exposing thick wrists and powerful forearms that his big hands wrapped around. And for some reason, something tingly rushed through Dani that brought with it madly inappropriate thoughts of those arms around her. Of those hands on her skin.

She mentally fled from the images and tried to quash the tingling, forcing her eyes upward to his face.

Which wasn't the best of solutions because that gave her the view of his smoldering good looks as he smiled a bit sheepishly and obviously came out of the gloom again.

"You're pretty good medicine for what ails me, though," he said. "You and being around the kids and the restaurant and Carmella." He paused again and looked into her eyes with those stunning blue ones of his. "But mainly you."

"I didn't do anything," she claimed because she didn't feel as if she had.

"You picked up the slack I left all day long. You kept things cheery enough that I don't think the kids even realized I was moping." His smile stretched into a grin. "You also helped by giving me that nudge at the pool so I didn't blow it with the kids again by being a taskmaster. In fact you let me treat Little Miss Daredevil Evie to that jumping-into-the-pool-thing and I think I made a little progress with her because of it—today of all days. Without you I probably would have just made them like me even less. I kind of felt like we were partnered up and you had my back." He shrugged. "Just being around you is... I don't know...good," he added as if he needed her to know that.

"Well, sure, because there *is* my magical superpower force field," she joked in response.

He laughed a genuine laugh of his own—which was the only thing she did think of as an accomplishment with him today.

"So *that's* what it is about you—a superpower force field," he responded, playing along.

"You forgot magical," she corrected matter-of-factly. "It's an upgrade."

"*Magical* superpower force field," he amended, still amused. Then those blue eyes of his took on even more of a sparkle of delight and, as she watched, his smile somehow turned very sexy. "I saw you in here that first night, you know?"

She didn't know what he was talking about. "You saw me?"

"Sure. With the lights on in here, from outside in the dark you can see everything. You were in here with the kids, your hair was all whacky from Evie doing it and you were going as wild as they were."

Dani suddenly remembered that she and the twins were in here that night when he'd arrived.

"Oh, dance party! We were getting the wiggles out," she recalled.

"Yeah," he said with an even bigger grin. "That's also not something that would have ever gone on at my house growing up. But I enjoyed watching it…"

There was heavy insinuation in his voice, which had gone deeper when he'd said it, infused with more intimacy.

"You were spying," she accused.

"It wasn't like I could have missed it," he defended. "Go out and see."

"If I do, will you dance?" she goaded.

He laughed again. "Not a chance."

"Then we won't be even."

"It was quite a sight," he teased. "I wouldn't say you have a lot of rhythm…"

"We were just playing."

He shook his head, denying that, clearly giving her a hard time. "You were totally into it."

"For the kids!"

"Nah…your eyes were closed and you were cutting loose."

"I *know* my eyes weren't closed."

"They were," he insisted with another laugh. Then, in a voice that changed to match that intimate look in his own eyes, he said, "You were a sight to see…"

He was looking at her so intently there seemed to be something to see now, too. And out of nowhere a memory of her own bout with voyeurism flooded her with the vivid image of him walking out of the locker room at the pool today.

Oh, that body.

Those cobalt blue eyes that were holding hers…

He unclasped one hand from the opposite forearm and reached slowly across to slide it behind her neck—so slowly she thought he was giving her ample time to slap it away if she wanted to.

But she didn't want to. Not when everything she'd been fighting the last two nights, at the pool today, just now at the simple sight of those hands and arms, all came out from hiding again.

He leaned forward. Pressure from that big hand on the back of her neck urged her forward slightly, too. And there was nothing Dani could summon to make herself not go there, not accept it when his lips met hers, not kiss him back the same way he was kissing her.

And she *was* kissing him back—eyes closed, lips parted just a little, with only enough sway to answer his— as everything instantly became about that kiss. That kiss was good enough to wow her into oblivion.

Before it ended a moment later, for no reason, even though she knew it should never have happened at all.

"I know," he said quietly. "You're gonna tell me I shouldn't have done that. That there's no place for it in the situation we're in. And you're right." He shrugged one of those broad shoulders. "But I couldn't help myself." Then he smiled with only one corner of that supple mouth she just wanted back on hers. "Must be your force field pulling me in."

"I'll see what I can do to turn it down," she said, deciding to go along with the gag so she didn't tell him that, regardless of whether he *should* have kissed her, regardless of the situation they were in, she just wanted him to kiss her again.

"Thanks, that would be helpful," he joked.

He got to his feet and held out a hand to help her to hers.

And it didn't make any difference that she knew without a doubt that she shouldn't take it. She took it anyway, unable to deny herself slipping her hand into his, feeling the strength in the arm that pulled her up.

Once he had she wished mightily that he would pull her all the way to him and kiss her again while she melted against that big masculine body.

But he didn't. Instead he was a perfect gentleman and as soon as she was on her own two feet he let go of her hand.

Sending a ripple of disappointment through her.

But that really was the way it needed to be, Dani told herself, bending over to pick up a wooden puzzle box and holding it in front of her like schoolbooks to keep her own hands from reaching out to him.

She headed for the door, leading the way out of the dance studio.

"I'll go to the hardware store in the morning and get what I need to replace your pipe," Liam informed her as he followed. "And then it's a day at the restaurant?"

"It is," she confirmed, heading for the entryway and the staircase that would take him up to the guest room.

Up to the guest room alone, she reminded herself when her mind wandered up there with him.

"And Evie and Grady are going to teach me how to make the bomb things," he was saying over those wandering thoughts.

Dani smiled. "They do think they're experts. We made a small batch just for us a while ago when we got snowed in and they learned how."

"They don't seem confident in my abilities," Liam said as he stopped at the foot of the steps.

"But *I* have faith in you."

"Thanks," he said with another laugh.

She didn't pause for more than that, though, afraid

of what she might do if she put herself in kissing position again.

Instead she left him there with a "See you tomorrow," and kept on going as if nothing had happened between them.

But even after his answering "See you tomorrow," she didn't hear him climb the stairs.

She thought she could feel his gaze staying with her down the passageway to the kitchen and until she turned into the stairwell to get downstairs.

She didn't glance back to see if she was right, though, because it was bad enough that she was thinking of that kiss and how good it had been.

And worse than that, she was fighting the inclination to instigate more of them, and it was all she could do to keep herself on track.

Chapter Six

"Okay, go to work. I'll be back tomorrow at zero seven hundred," Liam said on Friday morning when a nurse came to retrieve Declan's breakfast tray and take him to physical therapy.

"You're serious about that?" Declan said.

"Every day as long as I'm around. Conor got it okayed and I'll be here for breakfast with you. Conor'll come, too, when he can—doing a new residency to switch from ER to orthopedics has him tied up a lot—but I'll be here come hell or high water. Count on it."

"Okay," Declan said, agreeing without a fight.

The ease of that concession surprised Liam but he thought there might be the faintest hint of something not quite as disheartened in that single word.

Declan had shown no enthusiasm when Liam had arrived this morning and announced the breakfast plan that he'd put into play through Conor last night after talking to Dani. And it wasn't as if Liam's presence had seemed to lift his twin's spirits.

But now, while that barely uttered word might not have seemed like anything to get excited about, to Liam it was the first encouraging sign from his brother.

Liam left Declan to the nurse, glad he'd taken seriously what Dani had said the night before.

After talking to her he still hadn't known exactly how to help Declan. But he'd thought about what she'd said about her father, about her mother figuring out how to help her father, and he'd tried to translate that into something he could do.

He'd decided that for now maybe he should just be there for Declan. Spend more time with him than he'd planned or thought he might be able to, and maybe that would give Declan the opportunity to begin to open up. Even if that didn't turn Declan around, it might at least give some clue to something more Liam could do to help. Like Dani's mother hitting on the boat idea to help her father.

If nothing else, he was going to make damn sure that his brother knew Liam was thankful not to have lost him. That one way or another he wouldn't let him go down with the ship. And he was going to do that by starting every day at that rehab hospital with Declan.

From the rehab center Liam headed for the hardware store, feeling better than he had the day before when he'd left his twin.

Seeing Declan for the first time yesterday had been frustrating and discouraging and left him with a sense of powerlessness—something that he rarely experienced.

Now, despite not having a clear mission with all the details figured out, he at least had a plan to put into motion. Having even an undetailed plan of action helped him feel slightly less useless.

And again it was thanks to Dani.

He wasn't sure what he would do without her right now, he thought as he got on the highway. Somehow she'd become his guiding light as he trod through the current murky waters—first with the kids and now with Declan.

Just talking to her offered him comfort and support and relief, and then to top it off she gave him insights on how to handle it all. When he was stewing over Declan yesterday, even knowing that he *could* talk to her when he was ready to, that she was a great listener, that she would give her perspective without being pushy about it, had helped. And he was grateful.

"But that wasn't gratitude at work last night when you kissed her," he muttered.

No, it hadn't been gratitude. It had been something much harder for him to swallow—a soft spot.

He didn't have many weaknesses, but it was becoming clear that she might be one. Kind of a big one because he'd never in his life kissed someone he knew he shouldn't kiss.

Being friendly, getting to know her, learning from her, and even confiding in her was one thing. He was Special Forces—when there was a mission that required skills he could provide, he was called in. When it came to kids and what to do for a depressed brother—missions that were out of his skill set—he needed someone to turn to who did have those skills. That was just standard operating procedure.

But going from friendliness and her expertise and insights to kissing her? Definitely not SOP.

But what the hell was the universe thinking to send him a guiding light like Dani? A guiding light with long, thick, lush hair, glistening eyes and skin that looked like silk and made him want to see if it felt like that, too? A guiding light who was smart and funny and quick-witted? Girl-next-door sweet, kind and simmeringly sexy, too, to tempt him to forget all his troubles and escape into her instead?

Because being with her *did* offer an escape. Being with her helped him to sort through all this stuff he was up to his eyeballs in right now. She made him feel like he could come at things better on the next pass, and once she accomplished that, he could just enjoy being with her.

And he *did* enjoy being with her…

Which had culminated in kissing her because that was the normal course of being with someone who made him feel so much.

But he still shouldn't have done it. He knew that and there was no excuse for it except the driving need that had shot his discipline to hell.

Okay, sure, another time, another place, and he would be saying full steam ahead when it came to her.

But now?

He had to figure out how to help Declan. He had to figure out what to do if he was Evie and Grady's father. He had to figure out how to *be* a father if he was. And if he wasn't, he had to figure out how to help get those kids taken care of better than just being loaded into the system. Because now it wasn't only wanting to look out for kids left by someone he'd once been close to, he was beginning to care for the kids themselves.

So he had enough to work through without adding a new relationship with a woman to it all. A woman with a lot on her own plate.

This was just not the time, and he had to put his discipline, his training, into effect.

As he went into the hardware store the certainty that he could control himself went with him.

And lasted long enough for him to get what he needed and return to his rented SUV.

Then there she was again, on his mind.

And for some reason he was thinking about how nice it had been kissing her.

So damn nice…

And she hadn't stopped it, he thought as he got behind

the wheel. In fact, if *he* hadn't stopped that kiss he thought she might have kept it going.

What did *that* mean?

Maybe that he could provide her with a little escape from her own problems?

And if that was true, maybe it wasn't such a bad thing…

No, no, no, it was a bad thing, he insisted to himself.

They were both just in the middle of too much other muck. And even though escaping it when they felt good in that moment, it was liable to make things a lot more complicated down the road. And that was a stupid thing to do.

So he wasn't going to do it, he resolved again.

Sure, he couldn't keep his eyes off her whenever they were together and he couldn't keep his mind off her whether they were together or not.

But he did need to keep his hands off her.

And there was no question he was going to make sure he did.

"Dani?"

"Garrett!" Dani responded, stopping short when she heard her name called from across the parking lot and looking up to see her former fiancé coming in her direction.

She, Liam and the twins had just come out of an indoor trampoline park at the mall.

"That's Garrett," she heard Grady whisper to Evie with some guardedness.

"I know," Evie responded, impatient with her brother for thinking she didn't recognize the man. Then to Liam she whispered, "He's Dani's friend," with some warning in her own tone.

Liam didn't say anything and Dani didn't have time

for an explanation before Garrett was right there, not so much as casting a glance at Liam or at the twins, acting as if she were alone.

"Hi," Garrett said in a tone that seemed to question the wisdom of approaching her.

Her former fiancé—an attractive boy-next-door blond who couldn't compare to Liam's good looks—was dressed in a suit and tie. The tie's knot was loosened, and since Frank Gregson—another Denver Police Department detective and Garrett's partner—was keeping his distance in the background, Dani assumed they were working. Despite the fact that it was after seven o'clock on Friday night.

She hoped that their being on the job might make this quick, and since Garrett was completely ignoring Liam, she wasn't sure if she should introduce the two men.

Would it seem to Garrett that she was throwing another man in his face if she did?

She knew him and she knew an introduction wouldn't benefit Liam. Garrett had been jealous of even her friendship with Bryan and had been awful to him. So maybe it was better to just get this over with as soon as possible and keep Liam out of it.

"I'm surprised to see you," she answered in a neutral voice, not happy to run into him but also not wanting to make this first meeting since their breakup any more awkward than it already was.

"We got a call about an abandoned car left here. It belongs to a runaway we're looking for, so we have to check it out," he informed her mechanically before going on to say, "I haven't seen you since your grandmother died... I wanted to give my condolences."

"Thanks," Dani said as if his sentiment had been more sincere than it was.

"I thought about going to the funeral. But I didn't know if I should...what with your grandmother being one of our issues," he said somewhat under his breath and unable to conceal a tinge of hostility.

Dani didn't say anything to that and her silence caused him to finally acknowledge Grady and Evie by casting them a cursory glance. He still didn't say anything to them, though, before he looked back at Dani and said, "I saw the accident report. I didn't think you'd still be doing this."

"It's complicated," she said, having no intention of getting into the details.

"And—" he tossed an insolent nod in Liam's direction "—already? Really? Or maybe I just didn't know about him before?"

The accusatory tone made Dani bristle but more than that, out the corner of her eye, she saw what it did to Liam. He was a big man but he seemed to have gotten even bigger. Even taller, stronger, sturdier. He seemed to have subtly become even more of a force to be reckoned with.

What he didn't do was anything antagonistic or combative or hotheaded, though, and she appreciated that. And the sense that he was there and ready should he be needed.

Dani took a breath to keep her own temper in check and opted to introduce the two men in hopes now of keeping things civil. "Liam is here for the twins," she added.

Neither man offered a hand to shake or any friendly overture. There was a mutual glare but that was all.

Then she prompted Evie and Grady to better manners than Garrett had shown them and said, "Say hello, guys."

Evie and Grady muttered discontented hi's and Evie reached up to take Liam's hand while, on his other side, Grady leaned firmly against Liam's thigh.

Dani wasn't sure whether it was a declaration of loyalty or merely to gain more distance from Garrett. But either way she was glad to see that the twins had gravitated toward Liam. It seemed like an indication of acceptance of him. And she was even happier when Liam reached his free hand to Grady's shoulder, as if to let him know everything was okay.

"Guess I should get back to work," Garrett said. "Without your grandmother you must have more free time... maybe we can have dinner some night?"

Seriously? First he was going to show her one of the things about himself that she'd liked the least, and then he was going to ask her out? The man was clueless.

"I'm actually busier now than I was then," Dani said softly but succinctly, still bristling at every mention he made of her grandmother.

"Take care of yourself," he said as if the question had never been asked or answered.

"You, too," Dani countered.

He turned back to his partner and they headed to a different section of the mall while Dani took a moment to compose herself under the silent scrutiny of Liam's blue eyes.

Then she bucked up and said, "It's late. Let's go have our soup and see how we did today. I'm hungry. You guys must be, too, by now."

"Soup!" Grady cheered, his exuberance released again by the removal of Garrett's oppressive presence.

"Do I get my heart billi bomb?" Evie asked.

"You do," Dani confirmed before glancing at Liam and finding curiosity in his expression that she had no intention of addressing. Instead she said, "And we get to see how Liam did making his first billi bombs."

"His snakes were too fat," Grady goaded.

"I showed him how to make them skinnier," Evie defended as they went the rest of the way through the parking lot to their car, the kids competing while the adults said nothing.

Billi bomb soup was a multistage project. Before taking the twins to the trampoline park as their reward, Dani, Liam, Evie and Grady had spent the day at the restaurant.

While Liam had repaired the leaking pipe in the storage basement—with the assistance of Evie, who was interested in the project and the tools in the toolbox, while Grady preferred kitchen duties—Dani had mixed the dough for the billi bombs.

With a table set up at the end of the kitchen far away from the stoves and ovens and anything else that could hurt the twins, Dani and the kids had tutored Liam in the making of billi bombs from the dough that was a cross between a macaroni dough and a bread dough.

With even the kids observing health code rules of washed hands and gloves to handle food, bits of it were rolled into thin snakes—a job Evie and Grady enjoyed. Then the snakes were sliced with pastry cutters into small sections. Except for the one section that Evie insisted be left long enough to form a heart shape for her own personal billi bomb.

As the sections accumulated, the kitchen staff deep-fried them.

Dani, Liam and the twins also helped roll the meatballs, which—unlike the restaurant's usual meatballs—had to be made the size of marbles before they were also fried.

In the meantime, the kitchen staff simmered a soup that was a combination of chicken and beef stock, a small amount of tomato juice, multiple vegetables, plus raw chicken and cubes of beef.

When the billi bombs and meatballs were all fried, they were added to the soup. The whole thing needed to simmer until the hard-as-rocks billi bombs turned into soft dumplings—which required hours.

Despite the fact that Evie and Grady enjoyed themselves at the restaurant all day, Dani still made sure there was some playtime to follow. So while the soup cooked—and as a means of regaining appetites ruined through a day of munching—Dani had planned time at the trampoline park to be followed by a late soup supper.

So when they left the mall, they returned to the restaurant to eat.

Knowing they would be back, Carmella had extended her own long day in order to eat with them. And once again the meal was a warm, genial event during which the kids talked and laughed and contributed as much as the adults did, all of them enjoying the fruits of their day's labor in the soup that Liam had three bowls of and declared the best thing he'd ever eaten, worth all the trouble and teasing he'd taken for kitchen technique surpassed by four-year-olds.

Four-year-olds Dani thought he'd gained ground with by working alongside them and taking their instruction as seriously as it was given. By listening to their chatter and asking them questions and overall having a day similar to many she'd had with her mother and her grandmother in that same kitchen, making that same soup.

Full of soup and weary from the day, the ride home from the restaurant was quiet as the kids crashed and neither Dani nor Liam said much.

Dani knew what was keeping her quiet. And since Liam had not had a repeat of yesterday's doldrums and had been himself again until they'd run into Garrett in the parking lot, she had to assume it was that accidental meeting of her ex keeping him quiet tonight, too.

Since she'd mentioned the desire to wash off the cooking smells after giving the kids baths for the same reason, Liam offered to do the twins' bedtime routine so she could have a little while to herself to shower.

Dani was pleased to see further proof of the headway that had been made between Liam and the twins when they both agreed that he could read their bedtime story and even chose books that didn't require funny voices to make it easier on him.

That freed Dani to retreat to her own room.

After her shower, she wasn't sure if Liam had gone to bed, too. Just in case he hadn't she put on a T-shirt and a pair of polka dot pajama pants presentable enough for a co-ed encounter, and went out to see if her evening was over or not.

She found the kids asleep and no sign of Liam on the lower level, in the kitchen or in the workout room. But when she went to the front door to set the alarm, she nearly bumped into him as he came down the stairs.

Apparently he could shower much quicker than she could because he'd changed into sweatpants and a T-shirt and smelled of that tropical breeze cologne that went right to her head.

And mingled nicely with the tiny spritz of perfume that she'd used on a whim after applying a light dusting of blush and just enough mascara to keep herself from looking washed-out.

"I thought you might have gone to bed," she said when she happened upon him, making sure that she made it sound as if it didn't matter to her one way or another.

"You promised me your restaurant's special pink-grapefruit Italian ice. Isn't that why we brought it home—to have after the kids went to bed?"

"It is," she confirmed. "But when I came out and you weren't around I thought maybe we'd overworked you today and you couldn't stay awake."

He grinned cockily as they headed for the kitchen. "You thought today overworked me?"

"It wasn't what you're trained for," she pointed out.

"Yeah, I still think I *might* be able to push myself a little more," he said, as if the thought that today had tired him out was amusing.

"As long as you're up to it," she joked when they reached the kitchen.

Dani went to the freezer to take out the container they'd brought home as Liam said, "It's so warm tonight that I left my balcony doors open. Why don't we go out on the patio and use one of those four fire pits back there?"

Maybe because the thought of the two of them curling up on the overstuffed cushions of the seating around the fire pits was a lot different than eating standing at the counter? A lot more cozy and intimate—things that should not be fostered between them since he'd already kissed her?

But could she make herself say no?

No.

"The fire pits are gas-powered. Why don't you turn on one of them while I dish out the Italian ice?" *And try to make sure that's the only thing you turn on tonight...*

"Meet you out there," he said, flipping switches until he'd turned on the lights that lit the ballroom-sized patio. Then he opened the sliding glass doors and stepped outside.

That was when Dani realized they were both in stockinged feet tonight—she in fluffy ones and he in gray athletic socks—and that seemed like something else adding to the cozy intimacy that worried her a little.

As she spooned Italian ice into two bowls she thought about returning to her room for shoes before she joined him.

But it had been a long day of double-duty while cooking for the restaurant and still managing the kids—triple-duty when she factored in teaching Liam how to do both of those things, too—and she was finally done for the day. She could relax and have some downtime. Some shoeless time. She didn't want to give that up.

And it was silly, really. So what if they were both in lounging-around clothes and only socks? Being more and more comfortable with each other was bound to happen under the circumstances. After all, they were living in the same house, spending most of every day and evening together. They were even beginning to form a pattern for their own wind-down after the kids were in bed. No shoes were just another increment to that. It didn't mean anything. It wouldn't lead to anything. It was just no shoes, for crying out loud.

And actually, it was good Liam *was* loosening up, she told herself. The return of the wooden soldier yesterday had been alarming. But today he'd been back to an even keel and if that culminated in feeling free to pad around in his stockinged feet, great! If he ended up with the twins, she wanted to imagine the three of them hitting the end of every day that way—at ease enough to kick off their shoes.

She was just making a mountain out of a molehill because there was something that much more alluring about a leisurely Liam. But she wasn't going to let it get to her.

Vowing that, she took their dessert and the monitor for the twins' rooms outside.

The stainless steel fire pits were in each corner of a square sunken conversation pit and she descended the steps to where Liam was standing.

Handing him one bowl, she set the monitor on the tiled patio floor above them. Then she took the other bowl with her to the seating provided by ledges extending from the walls of the pit, where cushions on the seats and up the sides made it more comfortable.

She opted to sit very near one of the conversation pit's corners. He joined her, sitting at a forty-five degree angle and not all that far away. Making it even cozier.

Dani tried not to notice and took a bite of her ice at the same time he tasted his.

"Oh, that's sour!" he complained after the initial taste made him pucker.

"It's not sour. It's tart," Dani corrected. "That's why I like it and why it's good for your digestion."

"You should have warned me. I was expecting sweet. I don't know if I can take this."

"Wimp," she teased. "There's ice cream if you want that."

"I'm okay. This is the first thing I *don't* like from that place, though. That soup… I want that every day!"

"I'm glad you liked it. It'll be the special all weekend and it will pack the place."

He repositioned himself slightly so that he was angled toward her and stretched a long arm across the top of the pillows behind them before he said, "So, you probably know what I'm gonna ask you…"

Of course, he wanted an assessment of how he'd done with the kids during the day.

"You're just fishing for a pat on the back," she accused. "You know you made strides today."

His eyebrows drew together into a split-second frown

of confusion before he seemed to grasp what *she* was saying. "No, I didn't mean… I know it went well with Evie and Grady—I could tell that when they both wanted to sit by me at dinner. I was going to ask about *Garrett*." He said the name with scorn. "The kids said he was your friend but I don't think so…"

Of course he would be curious about Garrett, Dani thought, belatedly getting on the same page.

"I should probably apologize for him," she said. "He was rude to you. But I appreciated that you didn't make a big deal out of it."

"One of the most important things a marine learns is self-discipline," he said, as if that carried a lot of weight for him.

Garrett would have called it self-*control,* and it had been something he'd said a cop needed to maintain at all times.

But what Dani had thought of as a strength, an asset, at the start of her relationship with Garrett had instead shattered it because it wasn't only himself that he'd been obsessed with controlling.

Now here was Liam touting self-discipline the same way and, while she was glad it had been in effect tonight so Garrett hadn't been able to provoke him, it raised a red flag for Dani.

Self-control and self-discipline. A police mind-set and a military mind-set. Liam and Garrett were different men but she knew she needed not to lose sight of their similarities. Those things in Garrett that had impacted her relationship with him and altered it.

"Anyway," she said, "I appreciated it."

"But that still doesn't tell me who he is," Liam persisted before he drew back slightly and said, "Not that it's any of my business if you don't want to get into it."

But he *was* curious, Dani could see that. And Garrett wasn't a secret. So why not explain? And remember the cautionary tale she needed when she was sitting across from someone who could be carrying around the same tendencies…

"Garrett and I were engaged," she said.

Liam's eyebrows arched at that. "Oh. I was thinking that he might be some kind of stalker or something—some guy who's been trying to get you to go out with him. That maybe you used your grandmother as an excuse not to and that's why he thought he might have a shot now that she's gone."

Dani raised her own eyebrows at him. "You've done a lot of thinking about it in the last couple of hours."

Liam broke into a grin. "Just because I wasn't sure if you needed some kind of protection from him, you know…if he *was* a stalker," he claimed.

Dani didn't buy that for a minute. Garrett was imposing but he wasn't threatening, and he'd taken the brush-off of his invitation to dinner without a problem. But it was flattering that Liam was curious about the other man so she didn't call him on it.

"Garrett is a Denver police detective and he isn't stalking me. The breakup wasn't fun, but tonight was the first time I've seen him since."

"How long ago did you end it?"

"How do you know it was me who ended it?"

"I could tell. Plus he didn't seem stupid enough to let *you* go."

Dani tried to like his response less than she did.

"So how long ago did you end it?" he repeated.

"Three months ago."

"Three months ago… Not long before your grandmother died. I thought it was a lot for you to deal with losing your grandmother and still dig in here with the twins right after that. But, on top of it, you were fresh out of a breakup, too? That makes it even worse."

Dani acknowledged that with a nod. "There's been a lot of big stuff in a short amount of time, yeah."

"His being a cop explains a couple of things he said, though—what he was doing at the mall, seeing the accident report…" Liam observed.

She thought that Garrett being a cop explained most things about him. "His being a cop is also why it's especially good that you didn't react to his spitefulness. For Garrett, his position gives him a sense of power that can go a little wonky. He considers the slightest thing people say or do to be disrespecting his authority. And it's not beyond him to escalate situations and then charge someone with assaulting an officer if the other person reacts badly. He's bragged about doing that, laughed about how he has the upper hand if someone doesn't take what he's dishing out."

"And he was dishing it out because he assumed we were dating or something and he was jealous. He probably would have enjoyed a reason to arrest me," Liam said with some humor. "Did your grandmother not approve of him? Is that why she was an issue?"

"We were together quite a while—over three years—so Gramma kind of followed the same route I did with Garrett. It was all good at the start and then it evolved into not so good."

"And she ended up chasing him with one of those big kitchen knives at the restaurant?" Liam joked.

Dani laughed. "Is that wishful thinking? No, Gramma never did anything like that. In fact I don't think she ever knew she *was* one of our issues. I hope she didn't."

"So how *was* she an issue?"

Dani finished her Italian ice and set her empty bowl next to his on the fire pit, trying not to notice as Liam propped an ankle on top of the opposite knee and brought a stockinged foot to her attention again.

A really big stockinged foot that really did make this feel more intimate than she wished it did.

Still, she tried to focus only on their conversation about her relationship with Garrett.

"Being a cop is a stressful job," she said. "Garrett is good at it and, like I said, he likes the power, but the day after day of it changed him over time. Not that he wasn't a pretty serious person from the start, because he was. But it got to where he wasn't ever *not* super serious. And along with that, what he saw on the job made him… I don't want to say paranoid, but he really kind of was. At least about me—"

"About you?" Liam asked, sounding as if he didn't know what she meant.

"At first it was only small things, so I just kind of adapted to it to humor him because it seemed to make him feel better."

"Were you thinking he was like your dad somehow?" Liam asked.

"Some. I mean my dad's PTSD came from what he'd seen and experienced, and yeah, I think Garrett's stuff comes from what he's seen and experienced, too. Only my mom had to deal with the aftermath. With Garrett I thought I could prevent some of his anxiety before it got any worse if I just did what he asked. Small things—like if I called to check in with him or let him know I'd made it home safely. I just saw it as making him comfortable by doing things that weren't a big deal to me. But it sort of fed the beast rather than kept the problems from getting worse."

"He did get worse?"

"He did. Especially after we got engaged. He started wanting to know my every move every day. He said he investigated people who went missing and those cases turned out best when he had a clear picture of where that person was before disappearing, but that too often no one who knew them knew what they'd had planned."

"So you gave him your schedule every day."

"In detail. It was kind of a pain, but I did it. All the while telling him I could take care of myself, hoping he'd see that, relax, not need it so much. But that didn't happen. Then he started telling me that I *couldn't* do things—"

"Such as?"

"Meet a friend somewhere he said was a seedy part of town. Or that I couldn't close the restaurant on Griff's nights off so my grandmother could go home early."

"And that made your grandmother an issue?"

"My grandmother, the restaurant, the fact that we ran a business that was open late in the evening and could be robbed… By the end he was saying that the only time he could feel like I was completely safe was when I was with him." She sighed with the memory of it all before she went on.

"And when it came to Gramma it was even more than his concerns for safety," she admitted. "He doesn't have any family and he really didn't understand that it can involve demands on your time—especially as people age. The last year or so that we were together he just…" She shrugged. "He got madder and madder that my grandmother needed my help. He said it was unreasonable."

"He thought you should tell the woman who raised you to take a flying leap when she got old enough to need the roles reversed?"

"He just didn't get it," she said.

"And how did Grady and Evie get to know him?" Liam asked.

"He was our 'protection detail,'" she said, rolling her eyes. "That's what he'd say if he had time off when I was with them, if I was taking them somewhere. So he went to museums with us. The zoo. But it wasn't good for the kids."

"Why?"

"Garrett was definitely in the seen-and-not-heard camp when it came to kids, so if they didn't sit like little statues or if they made noise when he was with us, he thought they were 'totally out of control'—his words."

"When they were just doing normal kid stuff?"

Dani was glad that he was coming to understand what normal kid behavior was. "Yes!" she said with some praise in her tone. "And when they argued—"

"Which they do a lot," Liam said with a small laugh.

"Because they're siblings and siblings fight—"

"Oh, yeah—my brothers and I had some knockdown, drag-out battles. And there were plenty of tussles with Kinsey, too," he said.

"But again, Garrett was an only child and he didn't understand that it was normal. So when they argued it was a big deal to him. He said I didn't have any idea how many delinquents he had to arrest because they thought they could run wild. And if I didn't have a firmer hand I was creating two more."

"I guess that could come from some job anxiety spilling over. But Grady and Evie are not delinquents in the making."

And Liam was clearly feeling a little defensive over them—something else she was pleased to see.

"No, they aren't," she assured. "And a few times he

stepped in when it wasn't his place to, scared them and we had to have it out about that."

"Doesn't sound like he would have made much of a dad either," Liam observed.

"That was another thing I started to see," she admitted. "We did *not* agree on how to raise kids and when it came up over Evie and Grady it was an eye-opener."

"And why they don't like him much."

"They couldn't be comfortable around him, that's for sure. Not that he put any effort into *making* them comfortable, because he didn't."

Liam smiled crookedly. "You couldn't teach him how to do better, the way you're trying to teach me?"

Dani laughed. "He wasn't open to suggestions." And Liam was—he really did get kudos from her for that. Yes, the military stiffness seemed to come more naturally to him, but he was trying to mend his ways, to learn how to better handle the kids, relate to them.

"So what was the final straw?" Liam asked.

"Oh, it was more like everything just came to a head. I was trying so hard to appease him and that was wearing on me. Then we had a big fight about Gramma because she had a cold and I wanted to stop by and see her after he and I had dinner to check on her—"

"He didn't want to?"

"No. He said I was babying her and somehow that evolved into a talk about how, yes, if the day came when she couldn't live alone, I would want her to live with us, and *that* set him off royally! Then the day after that he went to the zoo with the kids and I for the second...or maybe it was the third time so he should have known how it went...but he lost it over them running from exhibit to exhibit and yelling to each other when they got excited about things they saw. That led to another fight later that night about raising kids and… I just knew," she said with finality and some sad resignation. "I gave back the ring."

"How did he take it?"

"Not well," she understated.

"How'd you take it?" he asked, studying her face.

"I'm kind of ashamed to say that it was more of a relief to me than anything. By then the tension in the relationship was so bad that I was more on edge with him than in love with him. When I returned the ring I felt like I'd set myself free."

"And seeing him again tonight? Did that change anything?"

Dani shook her head slowly. "I hated the way he acted tonight. To you, to the kids. I was glad all over again that I'm not involved with him anymore. I did care for him. I wouldn't have been with him as long as I was or accepted his proposal if I hadn't. But he kind of wore that out. He wore *me* out. And when he did I realized that I couldn't be happy with a personality like that. I need things a lot more easygoing, mellow, flexible."

"I can see that," he said kindly.

For a moment he let it all lay, as if giving her a chance to put it behind her again.

Then the expression on his handsome face turned mischievous and his smile had a wicked hint to it as he said, "So you're into flexible, huh?"

The innuendo made her laugh and really did lighten things up.

"And you're into order and regimentation," she accused, to remind both of them.

His smile grew. "Not *all* the time," he contended. "Especially since meeting you, flexibility is my middle name."

Dani laughed again. "Oh, that's you all right, Mr. Flexibility."

"Haven't I been?" he said, challenging her to deny it.

"You *are* working on it," was all she allowed him.

"Don't burn me because of yesterday," he defended himself. "Yesterday was a bad day—I think I should get a pass on that. Everybody's entitled to one of those now and then."

"Okay, you're right," she conceded because he *had* had good reason to withdraw yesterday and he had also rebounded from it with no lingering effects.

"And you said yourself that I did good today," he persisted.

"You did," she agreed.

There was a slight pause as more of that devilish smile appeared. "You know," he said, "the kids get rewarded for that…"

"I brought you Italian ice. You didn't like it."

"I didn't, no," he said, his voice deeper. "But I did so well today I really think I should have a second choice."

Something in the air around them was suddenly electric and there was a look in those gorgeous blue eyes of his that was warm and lazy and so sexy it made the surface of her skin nearly quiver.

She shouldn't be encouraging this, but she'd wanted him to kiss her again since the minute his lips had left hers the night before. Now that she had the chance for it, she couldn't deny herself.

So she said, "Okay. What else would you like as a reward?"

That oh-so-divinely-wicked smile became an oh-so-divinely-wicked grin. His gaze dropped to her lips. And just when she thought he was going to kiss her, he said, "Another bowl of that soup," and made her laugh instead.

Enjoying his own joke, he grinned even wider.

But somehow not even humor blunted the electricity that was firing between them and he kissed her.

He reached one big hand to the back of her neck to bring their mouths together in a kiss that seemed like it should have been playful in that moment. But instead it was instantly infused with something that said *finally* or *at last*, as if they'd both just been waiting for this since the previous night's kiss.

Which had been very nice. But this one was far more.

His arms wrapped around her so he could pull her completely to him. His lips parted and when she followed that lead, his tongue made its way to hers.

The kiss *was* playful but with a lot of heat and spice that caused mouths to open even wider and carried Dani away into a make-out session that was all the more heavenly with the fire burning beside them.

She turned into putty in those arms that were holding her against the solid wall of his chest. She could feel the contained strength of biceps that cradled her while the things he did with his mouth, with his tongue, drove her to distraction.

One of her own arms had gone around him at some point when she wasn't even thinking about it but her other was caught between them, her hand in a loose fist. A loose fist she realized that she could open to press her palm to his chest.

But it was *his* hand on *her* chest that she really wanted and, even as their kissing gained intensity, that thought shook her a little.

Making out with him was one thing. But wanting it to go to the next step? Considering how to get there?

That was going too far, she told herself.

So rather than pressing her palm to his chest to enjoy

the feel of it and to give him a hint, she used it to gently push him away as her tongue retreated from his and the kiss became only a nice kiss again.

Another push separated their mouths and Liam took a deep breath, sighing it out before he opened his eyes to look down into hers once more.

"Now *that* was a reward," he said, his voice deeper still.

"I thought you wanted soup?" she challenged.

He smiled. "Your soup is amazing," he said rapturously. "But not quite as amazing as you are."

His arms eased reluctantly from around her and he sat back. Then he said, "I'm thinking that gaining flexibility is shooting the hell out of my self-discipline."

He used an index finger to move her hair away from her shoulder and she sensed if she didn't do something he was going to kiss her again. And if he did she knew she'd let him. But since she wasn't sure where things might go from there, she decided she'd better avoid it.

So she stood, turned off the fire pit, gathered their bowls and the monitor and went inside.

A few minutes passed before Liam came in, too, closing and locking the sliding doors behind him.

"Tomorrow," he said, much like he had every other night, "you're making me go to the *Butterfly* Pavilion?"

Dani laughed at him. "There are spiders and tarantulas and all kinds of bugs, if that makes it seem more manly to you."

"I don't know how a place called the *Butterfly* Pavilion can be manly, but if you say so… And you're okay with my plan to have breakfast with Declan every morning?"

"Absolutely," she said as she put the rinsed bowls into the dishwasher. "I think it's a great idea. It'll give you the chance to spend time with him and I think that can only help."

"I hope you're right. I'll be home not long after the kids have breakfast. Evie even agreed to try boot camp workout tomorrow," he added, sounding proud of himself for accomplishing the agreement.

"Grady has been bragging about how he can do a push-up and she can't."

Liam laughed. "You should see his push-up."

"Oh, he showed me. Mostly his rear end goes into the air and nothing else really goes anywhere."

"Yep. He's really good at it," Liam added drolly.

And that brought the evening to its conclusion, but they both just stood there for a moment longer.

A moment during which Dani was just willing him to come closer and kiss her again even though she told herself to cut it out.

Then she summoned a force of will, pulled her shoulders back and said, "It's late."

Liam nodded but he didn't say anything. He just kept looking at her as if he couldn't get his fill.

"Thanks for replacing the pipe today," Dani added.

"Happy to do it. Thanks for everything else—everything you do with the kids and to help me with them, and for what you've done to help me with Declan—"

"And for the soup," she joked because his gratitude embarrassed her.

He only smiled softly at her, reaching a hand to run his knuckles tenderly along her cheek this time. "Definitely that," he added in a quiet voice and a tone that said soup wouldn't have been on the list.

But just when she thought he might pull her in again, kiss her again, he didn't. After that featherlight stroke of her face he just took his hand away and said good-night.

Once he'd left her alone in the kitchen Dani closed her eyes and took the deepest breath she could, holding it, hoping to suffocate the things he was stirring in her.

But it didn't help and she headed to her room, giving herself a lecture on all the reasons why nothing could ever work out between them.

Because nothing could, she told herself.

But somehow that didn't seem to matter tonight.

Chapter Seven

"I don't want nuffink for dinner." Grady pouted, stubbornly crossing his arms.

The little boy was having a hard time Saturday. Fresh out of bed this morning he'd asked when his mom and dad were coming home. Dani had had to remind him again that they wouldn't be. He'd been acting out ever since, which meant stubbornness and picking fights with Evie, who had become oversensitive about everything after the conversation, too.

It hadn't made the trip to the Butterfly Pavilion pleasant and even getting ice-cream cones when they were finished with the bugs had been more of an ordeal than a good time.

Now Dani, Liam and the twins were at the apartment that Dani ordinarily shared with Bryan, invited for dinner by Bryan and his boyfriend, Adam.

"Dinner is a little while off anyway. Why don't Liam and I take you two over to the park across the street and maybe we can work on your appetite?" Adam suggested. Then to Liam—with a nod toward Dani and Bryan—he said, "These two are going to want to chat so we might as well get out of here and let them."

"Is that okay?" Liam asked Dani.

"It's okay with me if it's okay with you. You know how things are going today," she answered, both because the twins were not being cooperative and because Liam hadn't yet been alone with them even under the best of conditions. She wasn't sure whether he was up for that.

But he surprised her by saying, "I think I can handle it."

Adam was a former air force pilot so the two of them had found common ground talking about the military. Dani turned her attention to the kids, urging them to go to the park.

Neither child was eager, but it helped when Bryan enticed them with the possibility of a small gift if they went, played hard and then came home hungry for the salmon he was making especially for them.

When they'd left, Dani went into the small kitchen with Bryan to help with dinner.

"You let him take the kids?" her friend observed.

"I'm practicing today," she informed Bryan. "There's a good chance that he's their dad and that we'll all find out very soon. If it's true, they'll be a family that I'm not a part of. So I thought it might be a good idea to start letting Liam get a feel for that. I've been hanging back all day."

Bryan chuckled. "And you picked a day when the kids are being difficult?"

Dani laughed. "Not purposely, but if he's their father he'll have those days to deal with, too. I'm letting him get that experience in the mix. I'm actually glad Adam wanted to take them all to the park. It'll give Liam a real taste of things without me."

"And how are you doing with it—the hanging back and watching Evie and Grady go off without you?"

"Okay," she said tentatively. "I've been with those kids since they were barely a year old. I know they aren't mine and I've always known that the time would come when I'd say goodbye to them. It won't be easy. But…"

Okay, it really wasn't going to be easy because there

was suddenly a lump in her throat that she had to swallow before she could go on.

"But the more time I spend with Liam and get to know him, the more I hope that he *is* their father because it helps to at least be able to picture who I'll be handing them over to. From the start of this I've dreaded the idea that I might just have to pass them off to the unknown of the courts and foster care, and believe me, this is not as hard as that."

"If he isn't the dad maybe you and I will have to get married and try to adopt them," Bryan said with half humor, half seriousness. "I don't think I can stand to see them disappear into the system either."

"Let's just hope we don't get there."

Bryan gave her the ingredients to make herbed butter for him while he prepped the salmon. "And how are you doing with the idea of watching Liam go away?" he asked in a lighter vein.

"It'll be a relief—my eyes will get a rest!" she joked.

But she'd realized today she wasn't particularly thrilled with that prospect either.

She'd refused to analyze it, though, and had merely taken it as a warning and forced herself to hang back even more. And while she was hanging back she'd gone over and over in her mind exactly why she should be perfectly fine with Liam riding off into the sunset. The sooner the better.

She'd actually thought she had herself convinced and her attraction to him reined in until they'd gone home between having ice cream and coming to dinner.

Then, as if she couldn't contain herself, she'd changed out of her kid-friendly clothes, putting on her best butt-hugging jeans and a lightweight, black wrap sweater that she ordinarily wore a tank top under for modesty's sake. And tonight she hadn't.

She *had* tied the sweater tighter at the side of her waist so the resulting V neckline was higher than when she had something underneath it. But still, there was slightly more enticement without the underneath layer.

She'd also taken her hair out of the ponytail she'd had for the day and used the curling iron before brushing it and leaving it loose.

Then she'd added a hint of eye shadow, a second application of mascara, and blush and highlighter, too.

And not only hadn't she been able to resist dressing for him, but trying to rein in her attraction to him hadn't been too successful when Liam had come down from the guest suite after having showered and shaved, and bowled her over once again. Tonight he was wearing a pair of jeans that fit jaw-droppingly well and a white crew-neck sweater just tight enough over those broad shoulders and every muscle of his massive chest and flat stomach to tease her.

But still, she'd spent the drive over here swearing last night's kissing was the last time she was going to let that happen, and that she was going to put more distance between them from here on. She was going to do it or die trying!

"I can understand your eyes needing a rest," Bryan said with another laugh. "I thought you were exaggerating about how great-looking he is, but you weren't!"

"Told you so," Dani said with a laugh.

Despite talking on the phone every day, they'd both been too busy to get together since Bryan had delivered the papers for her grandmother's trust on Tuesday morning. He'd suggested this dinner so he could meet Liam because Dani had confided that her resistance to Liam's appeal was eroding. It had made Bryan all the more determined to meet him.

"I thought you were crushing on him and that's why you made him sound so good," Bryan added. "But, sweetheart, how is your tongue not hanging out all the time?"

"I told you what's going on so you would talk me *out* of it," she reminded him. "Gushing over him doesn't help."

"I don't want to talk you out of it," Bryan said matter-of-factly.

"Bryan…" she chastised with her tone.

"I don't," he said, standing his ground firmly. "Until he came around, if you weren't worrying about one thing, you were worrying about another. What to do with Gramma's house. Whether to keep the restaurant and give up nannying, or sell the restaurant. The twins and what's going to happen to them—"

"I'm still worried about all of that. I still have to make decisions about the house and the restaurant and my own future. I still don't know what's going to happen to Evie and Grady—"

"But the thing is, even though all that stuff is weighing on you, since that guy has been there I think he's kind of balanced out some of the bad. He's lifted you out of the thick of it. And I think that's just what you *need* right now."

She couldn't deny that Liam had become some sort of counterweight. That it was not only nice to have him around so she didn't always have to be a mock single parent, but also so she could talk to him about even her own problems. Nice to have their evenings alone after the kids were in bed…

But she also couldn't deny that *shouldn't* be the case. Or at the very least that she couldn't let that become something bigger than it was. That she couldn't come to expect or rely on him to the point where she felt any kind of loss when this was over.

"So last night…" Bryan was saying into her wandering thoughts. "Kiss or no kiss?"

She'd told him yesterday about the brief one on Thursday night, lamenting that it had happened and why she shouldn't let it happen again. She'd sworn to him that there was absolutely, positively *not* going to be another kiss.

Now her only answer was a grimace that made Bryan laugh yet again. "How was it?"

"Ohhh…incredible," she complained.

"Was it *only* kissing?"

"Yes. But a lot of it. And—"

"Hot?"

She shrugged.

Bryan laughed again. "Better still!"

"It's not," she insisted. "It's bad and stupid and I don't know why I keep letting it happen!"

"Because you like him. Don't you?" her friend challenged.

"I don't *dis*like him." It was the most she would admit to.

But there *was* more she could have admitted to.

Not that it was anything serious—how could it be when they'd really only just met?

But still, something odd was going on with her. In the mornings when she got up she kept watch on the clock, literally counting how long she thought it might be before he'd be there. More eager than she wanted to be for him to show up.

And when he did? There was the weirdest warm rush that went through her the minute she set eyes on him. A warm rush that didn't even have anything to do with those blazing good looks of his. A warm rush that was like…

She didn't want to think this, but it was like something was missing until he walked in and then all was right again.

It really was nuts. She'd never felt that about anyone. Not even Garrett, who had been a huge part of her life for a long time. Who she could have *married.*

But maybe it was just that counterweight thing, she told herself. Liam gave her the sense that everything was going to be all right.

"I know why you're letting it happen," Bryan said in answer to her comment. "It feels good and it's fun. And I think that's why he was sent to you—like the donuts that appear every Friday in the break room at work. I have no idea where they come from or who goes to the trouble or pays for them. It's just a little job benefit that I gladly accept."

Dani laughed again but with some confusion. "Liam wasn't 'sent to me.' I had to have the marine corps track him down. And that was for the sake of Grady and Evie."

"So it was the marine corps that sent him to you," Bryan concluded neatly. "They've sent in the troops—that's why you should go for it."

"Simple as that?" she said.

"Yes. A little simple, no ties, no expectations, purely biological release. With one of the hottest men I've ever seen. Something to ease all the stress you're under and put a smile on your face, so when you're old and think back on it, you can have one sweet memory of an otherwise awful time."

Dani laughed again. "Wow."

"Oh, yeah, I'm betting there will be a lot of wow," Bryan said.

"You know that some kind of fling is not me," she countered.

"I know it hasn't been. And it won't be after this. But this one time? Let it be you."

"Bryan..." she chastised again.

"I'm serious! You like him. You've earned it. What harm is there? Unless..." He paused to look at her just as he was about to put the salmon under the broiler. "Do you *more* than like him? Is this something that could end up hurting you?"

She didn't think so...

But what she said was, "He's a marine like my dad was. And he has a mind-set that isn't much different than Garrett's—"

"I know he had a bad day when he saw his twin for the first time, but I thought you were leaning away from the idea of PTSD."

"I am. But still...when you come from that world anything could happen to cause it anytime."

"But it's not there now. And the mind-set thing? You know Adam can be a little like Garrett, too, when he's in military mode and he's all earnest and conservative and straitlaced. But he isn't *always* in military mode the way Garrett is *always* a cop, policing everything and everybody. From what you've said about Liam he's more like Adam with that stuff than like Garrett."

Dani didn't refute that but she also couldn't be completely sure it was and would always be true. Instead she said, "And there's the fact that I did only break up with Garrett three months ago and am not ready for anything else yet—especially with the house and the restaurant and my career future all waiting for a decision. Until I've sorted out what I'm doing all the way around, I can't be starting something new."

"Donuts on Fridays is not 'starting something new,'" he pointed out. "It's just a job benefit. It doesn't happen every day. It could end and we'd all just go on the same. But we enjoy it now, when it's happening..." he finished in a singsong voice.

He seemed to give her a moment to be tantalized by the idea before he said, "And what if you *could* enjoy a little *job benefit* in the form of Liam but you don't? You'll always wonder what it might have been like. You'll build it up in your mind to something that nothing else and no other man might ever live up to. Think of it as doing a service for the Mr. Right you finally do end up with. And for yourself so you don't spend the rest of your life disappointed with him."

"What if I did it and no one for the rest of my life *can* live up to him?" she said, as if this was a purely academic debate even though she thought there was a chance that Liam might always be in a class by himself.

"Or maybe he'll be so bad at it that he'll cure you of lusting after him the way you are now."

Dani laughed. "I am not lusting after him."

"Oh, you sooo are. So just take care of it. You take care of everything else for everybody else. No matter what reason convinces you, do this for you. Trust me—and I know you do—you will regret it if you don't, not if you do."

Dani just shook her head at that notion as if her friend was out of his mind.

But secretly she wasn't convinced that he didn't have a point.

"Oh, you didn't go to bed. Or run away from home," Dani said.

After getting the twins to sleep Saturday night there had been no sign of Liam. The day and evening with Evie and Grady were so fraught with four-year-old melodrama that she'd thought he might have just retreated. But when she'd gone to the front door to activate the security system she'd spotted him in the formal living room off the entry, in the direction opposite the dance studio and workout room.

He was lying flat on his back on the floor underneath the enormous skylight in the ceiling. The only illumination in the room came from the moon overhead and the glow of the exterior lighting coming in through the two walls that were completely glass. But everything in and about the space was white—the walls, the leather sofas, the molded coffee and end tables, the unlit lamps, the white-on-white artwork—so everything was fairly visible, including Liam even though his white sweater blended in.

His hands were on his ultra-flat stomach but he took one away to pat the white shag carpet beside him. "Felt like I spent most of the day hunched over. I needed to stretch out," he explained. "Try it. Puts everything in line again."

She wasn't sure what it put in line again, but it was quiet now that the twins were asleep, and peaceful there in that big open room with so much of the outdoors coming in through all the glass. And despite knowing that the best way to fight Liam's appeal would be to simply say good-night and go to bed with a good book, Dani looked forward to this time with him too much to deny herself. Especially after a day with pitifully unhappy kids.

So once the alarm was set she joined him.

But she didn't lie down the way he was. She sat near his upper half, resting her weight on one hip and hand, and curling her legs under the other hip.

He rolled to his side to face her, propping himself on his left elbow and forearm. "I've had days in combat that were easier than today. And I've run into insurgents more agreeable than those two downstairs," he said.

Dani laughed. "Kids are entitled to bad days, too." But she'd been happy to see that, through even the worst of it, Liam had been steady and calm and patient; he'd never lost his temper.

"Yeah, I can't imagine what must go through their little minds," he agreed. "It's lucky they were used to round-the-clock nannies so maybe it's not so unusual for them to go a long time without thinking about their parents. And lucky that they live in the moment. But when whatever brings it up for them that Audrey and her husband aren't coming back…that's gotta scare and confuse them."

"Definitely living in the moment is a plus. They don't know yet that their own lives won't go on the way they always have, the way they are. So far they've taken in stride that I'm their only nanny now, and it hasn't occurred to them that it might not just go on forever."

"They don't need to be prepared for it not to?"

"Sure. But until I know what to prepare them for, there's no sense in worrying them with the possibilities." As much as it was worrying her that she might have to hand them over to the system. "I want them to have whatever sense of security they have with me for as long as they can. I want to protect them as long as I can."

Liam smiled and made a small sort-of-chuckling sound. "I don't know if it was the court or Audrey who picked you out of the nanny pool to be the primary caretaker now, but whoever did it was smart."

"It was Audrey first—right after the accident she asked me not to leave them with anyone else. Since she was still alive they didn't need a guardian, just a round-the-clock nanny. Technically it was the court who formally named me guardian. But it helped convince the judge that I should have guardianship because I'd been Audrey's choice as round-the-clock nanny to begin with."

Audrey was not a subject they'd talked about beyond the current situation. It was slightly strange to Dani that he'd been involved with someone she knew. But it wasn't as if she and Audrey had been close. Dani had been told to call both Audrey and Owen by their first names but, beyond that familiarity, Dani's relationship with them had been strictly as their employee.

But talking about Audrey now brought it home to Dani that Liam *had* had a relationship with the other woman and made her wonder about it.

"How did you and Audrey meet?" she ventured.

"At a wedding," he said without seeming to have any reservations about telling her. "My sister was living here then, too—that was before she went back to Northbridge for a year to take care of Mom until she died—and I came to Denver for a training and to see her. Kinsey's boss was getting married, she needed a plus-one, and I was it. Audrey was a bridesmaid."

"I'm surprised she didn't have me contact your sister about the twins or about getting hold of you."

"Kinsey worked with the groom. She didn't even know the bride. She met Audrey through me and only at the wedding when I introduced them after *I'd* met her. Usually Kinsey took time off work if one of us came to see her but she couldn't for that one and, since she was on overnight shifts, I spent days with Kinsey and evenings with Audrey without any overlap."

Dani was reasonably sure he meant that he'd spent *nights* with Audrey but appreciated that he was downplaying that aspect. Although rather than feeling any kind of jealousy, she had difficulty actually imagining them together. In her mind, Audrey went with Owen.

"After that," he was saying, "Audrey and I stayed in touch for about eight months long distance. But there was no reason for her and Kinsey to see each other or talk. Kinsey didn't even know I'd kept in contact with Audrey, and Audrey was a little scattered—I doubt she remembered my sister's name. They definitely didn't run in the same circles. Audrey was a trust fund baby and my family is anything but."

"I wouldn't have expected Audrey to want a long-distance relationship," Dani said with some surprise. The Audrey she'd known had required a great deal of attention from her husband, to the point of competing with Grady and Evie if Owen showed much interest in them.

"I don't know if you'd call it a relationship so much as acting out a fantasy," he said with what sounded like reluctance. "The uniform can inspire that in some women. I've always avoided them and since I met her when I was in civvies, it didn't occur to me at first that that was part of it with Audrey. I guess that was dumb because she said she could tell I was military the minute she laid eyes on me, even in a suit."

"You *do* have that air about you. I think it's in the posture."

"Well, by the time I realized that was the draw, we'd hit it off. And she was fun, she had the money and the desire to travel to wherever in the world she could meet me when I had leave, so I just kind of went with it. I figured that the most it would amount to was having a little company on leave and that's always nice. We did a week in China, ten days in Japan, then the last time it was a week in Spain. It was after Spain when things changed."

"Because she was pregnant. But she really didn't give you any idea that she was?"

"None—even thinking back on it there was nothing. It was just a Dear John call. I'd had them before."

"Were you brokenhearted when she called it off with you?"

"No," he answered without having to think about it. "I liked Audrey. But it was just fun and games with us. That's all either one of us was interested in. And I've been doing what I do for a long time. I didn't have any illusions. I knew the odds of Audrey falling into something with someone else when she hadn't even heard from me in months on end was pretty high. That just goes with the territory."

"So you weren't in love with her?" Dani knew she probably had no business asking but for some reason it made it easier for her to keep her perspective—that the love of Audrey's life had been Owen, and that Liam's time with her late employer was little more than a lark. A long-ago lark.

Not that it should matter one way or another, she was quick to remind herself.

"I wasn't in love with her, no," he said, again without having to think about it. "And she wasn't in love with me either. From the start we agreed to no strings attached. So when she called things off it wasn't a huge surprise and I wished her well—and meant it—and just went back to business as usual."

Then he switched gears and Dani thought it was a signal that he didn't want to talk about his relationship with Audrey anymore.

"What about you?" he asked. "Were you and Audrey friends—"

"I was just the help. She was friend*ly* and pleasant to me, but we didn't talk about anything except the kids. It was only at the end when she told me about you—or anything personal—and that was out of necessity."

He nodded as if that made sense to him.

There didn't seem to be more to say about their mutual acquaintance but Dani was still curious about his past. She said, "You've had a lot of Dear John calls?"

"I didn't say 'a lot,'" he amended with a laugh. "I haven't had a lot of *relationships*. The longest one was with my high school girlfriend—Kristi Williams—before we went our separate ways for college and lost touch—"

"That easy? Your first love and you just 'lost touch'?"

"No, there was some teenage angst and heartbreak, but that's what first loves are for, aren't they?" he said with a smile that spoke of a tender spot for that memory and made Dani like him all the more for it.

"And between your first love and Audrey? Since Audrey?"

He grinned. "I don't have a Garrett story," he said. "I've never been engaged or even come close. I haven't ever even had the *exclusive* talk. There have just been women I've connected with the way I did with Audrey. I'd see them before and then again after a few mission gaps until something made things fizzle. But I'm not sure those count as full-blown *relationships*."

"Do you juggle women?"

"No!" he scoffed, again without hesitation. "I've had runs with one woman at a time while they last, until something happens to change things."

"Such as?"

"There was a warrant officer in another unit who reached the end of her tour and went home. There was a navy nurse restationed to Africa. A couple of civilians who met other guys while I was away—one of them had even gotten married during the ten months I was unavailable. There was a photographer with a news crew who was just long gone when I got back from a mission." He shrugged. "No matter what's going on on the personal side, I get my orders, disappear for two days or two months or—"

"Ten months," she recalled.

"And when I come out from under, things can be the same or anything can have changed. That's just how it goes."

But suddenly she was thinking about him being Grady and Evie's dad again. "Ten months," she repeated. "That's not only long enough for one of your civilians to meet and marry someone else, it's a long time in the life of little kids."

He sobered, frowning. "Yeah. I've been thinking about that."

"You're career military."

He nodded slowly. "Have been..."

"Will that change if the kids are yours?"

He took a deep breath and shrugged. "I'm not really sure. But it *is* why I want to do tomorrow's family day at rehab. Conor and Kinsey are going. Kinsey wants to talk about her wedding. And the Camdens, I'm sure. But I was thinking maybe I should talk to her and Conor about the twins, too."

"In case they *are* yours."

"Actually, even if they aren't," he said.

"Oh?"

"I've been thinking about what to do with them if the DNA comes back and says I *am* their father, about taking them to live on bases overseas, about babysitters and nannies, missions I can't control the length of... I don't know that that would be the best thing for them and I think maybe I need to talk to my brother and sister about leaving the kids here with them, about having one or both of them be guardians while I'm deployed... *If* I stay in the corps or until I can transition out..."

"Is that something your family would do?"

"Honest to god, I don't know. This is nothing any of us has ever dealt with before. I'm just going to feel them out about it. I can't really make the decision about whether or not to stay in unless I know if I'll have help. And while I'm feeling them out about what happens if I *am* the dad..." He hesitated before he said, "Today I thought that maybe we should also talk about taking them on even if I'm not the dad."

"In what way?" Dani asked.

"I don't know, I'm just throwing ideas out there," he admitted. "All I know is that when I came here I was figuring that I'd do what I could for them, even if I'm not their father, because I knew Audrey and wanted to help the kids she left behind. Maybe because I was a kid who got help from someone who wasn't related to me and I owe a little payback for that. But somewhere along the way the little buggers got under my skin all on their own and made that a bigger deal to me."

"And that occurred to you *today*? When they were at their worst?"

"Yeah," he answered with a wry laugh. "Today especially, I guess, because I saw them upset about Audrey and her husband being gone. Saw them kind of scared, and..." He shook his head. "I have to fix that for them, whether they're mine or not."

"How?"

"I don't have a clear picture. But I just got to thinking that if I *am* their dad I'm gonna need help. If I'm not, *they* need help. Kinsey is looking for more family. She'll be married next month. There's Conor and Maicy... I know couples have to be attractive volunteers to take in kids. Add me to the mix—a friend of their mother and the person she picked to give them to—toss in a couple lawyers lobbying for it and maybe we could persuade the courts to let us be joint guardians or an extended foster family or whatever it might take so that all together we could look after them. I don't know. I'm just hoping we can maybe take the first step to putting our heads together to work something out."

"It would be great if you could..." Dani said, unsure if what he was suggesting was possible. But unconventional or not, it was still the best solution she'd heard for the twins if Liam didn't turn out to be their biological father. And just the fact that he was willing to try made her feel as if there was hope for Grady and Evie avoiding the system.

He had no idea how much that meant to her. So much that she got excited enough to say, "I'd help! Regardless of where I end up going from here, I'd actually like the chance to stay in contact with them."

It made her feel worlds better to think that might be possible after having been so close to the twins for the last three years. To think that she might not have to merely hand them off and never see them again.

"That'd be good, too. You're important to them. We'll just all have to see what we can do—the takes-a-village thing," he concluded.

But coming from him Dani had faith. And she just wanted to throw her arms around him and kiss him and show him how much she appreciated just what a good man he kept proving to be.

Which she knew she couldn't do.

So she got a grip on herself and decided it was better to return to the lighter topic of the evening—his love life.

To that end, she said, "So, you know not to get too attached to any woman. Audrey wasn't alone in that."

"What I know is to enjoy the moment and everything

in and about the moment," he said, taking the hand she wasn't leaning on and holding it cradled in his, rubbing his thumb in circles on the back of it. "I guess I have to have a four-year-old's mentality for that."

"And when that moment is over you're not sorry? You've never tried to hang on or *asked* a woman to wait for you?"

"There have been one or two I've been a little sorry not to see again. But no, I've never asked anyone to wait for me."

"Because there's never been anyone you care enough for to try to tie up, or because you don't think it's fair to ask that of them?"

His gaze was on their connected hands. "Both, maybe," he answered. "I know plenty of guys in Special Forces who are married or engaged or have girlfriends. But I've just kind of always played it by ear. Like with Audrey. When I came up for air on a mission I'd contact her. If she still seemed on board, great—"

"But when she wasn't, that was okay, too."

He answered that with another shrug.

"Have there been some women you don't contact when you come up for air?"

He grinned. "Haven't you had guys you don't want to see again after a date or two?"

She laughed. "Sure."

"Me, too," he said with a laugh of his own.

There was something that gave Dani the distinct impression she'd reached the end of his tolerance for talking about his past, though.

Proving that she was right he suddenly acquired a more playful air. He used that hand he was holding to pull her down to him as he raised up on his elbow enough to meet her halfway and give her a sweet, savoring kiss before he ended it and said, "Last night got to me kind of bad."

"Too much soup?"

He laughed a throaty, sexy laugh. "No, not too much soup. *You.* Wanting you got to me kind of bad..." He shook his head and his expression showed some amazement at just how much before he said, "It started me thinking that being here right now with you and not making the most of it might be the worst thing I ever let happen..."

"'Making the most of it...'"

He grinned crookedly and an even greater sparkle came into those already sparkling blue eyes of his before he kissed her again. And, in the midst of it, let go of her hand to wrap both arms around her and pull her to lie on the floor with him.

She could have protested but between what Bryan had said to her earlier and what Liam had just said about getting the most out of the moment she didn't force herself to. And it *would* have taken some superhuman force because kissing him was exactly what she wanted to be doing.

So kiss him she did, lying there on the floor with him, her arms around him, too, and her tongue answering the call of his with the same fervor it had the night before, thinking that maybe sometimes there didn't need to be a tomorrow because today—tonight—was too good to pass up.

And kissing him *was* too good to pass up because the man could kiss better than anyone. His tongue was perfect and adept and knew all the right things to do.

His body against hers was also sublime—all rock-solid muscle and strength and power, pliable under fingers that pressed into his back and palms that rode expansive shoulders in a massage that had him writhing ever so slightly.

Her breasts against that hard chest made her nipples

strain for more as he rolled just enough to put her flat on her back, coming partway over her.

His mouth opened even wider then and his tongue played a more forceful game with hers as one of his hands found the tie at her waist, pulling it free so that her top fell open, exposing her lacy bra.

Still, she wasn't inclined to put up any opposition. Or close her top. Instead she adopted a little boldness of her own and slipped her hands under his sweater to touch that smooth skin she'd ogled at the swimming pool.

His hand sluiced slowly away from her waist where the tie had been knotted, stealing his way up inch by inch until it was just to the side of her breast.

Was he waiting for encouragement or torturing her?

Dani knew only that it was definitely torture to have his hand so close to where she wanted it without him finishing the trip.

She arched her spine just enough to relay the message but all he did was curl his fingers into the side of her bra and slide them to the outer swell of her breast.

Oh, he was torturing her all right!

So she took a deep enough breath to expand into the cups, her taut nipples poking into the lace.

He seemed to know exactly what she was doing because he chuckled faintly, deep in his barrel chest, and brought the backs of his fingers forward to catch one of her hardened nipples between them, squeezing gently but enticingly but still not giving her what she wanted.

Damn him!

She raised a knee and let it fall to his thigh to do a little more enticing of her own. That did it—he took his fingers out of the cup of her bra, pulled it below her breast and replaced the cup with the most wonderful palm to nestle into.

And regardless of how cool he'd been playing it, that first contact of his full hand to her breast evoked a guttural groan from his throat as his mouth and tongue turned that kiss into something too erotic to bear.

All while his big hand showed her some other tricks he knew and left her nearly quivering in all the best ways.

She suddenly became aware that her leg had somehow wrapped around him and brought him tight up against her, where she could feel the substantial proof that he was as worked up as she was.

And, oh, did her hand itch to reach down and learn all there was to know about that part of him, too!

But then she realized that she had to call her brain back from the brink and put it in charge again before this went completely out of control.

She had kids only a few rooms away that she was responsible for. Kids who could wake up and come looking for her at any moment.

She couldn't risk them finding her like that. Finding her and Liam like that. Let alone doing more than that— which was where this was headed. Where everything in her was crying out for it to head.

And when he reached to unhook her bra she knew it had to stop.

So as much as she didn't want to, she ended that all-consuming kiss and whispered a raspy, "No, we can't. The kids…"

Liam's hand halted its journey and he plunked his forehead to hers, sighing a heavy sigh of resignation. "Like I said, I want you, Dani…"

He laid his hand on her side again but for a time he stayed where he was, as if it was no easy task to bring himself back from the same brink she'd been on.

Then he let her go and fell back to lie on the floor the

way he had been when she'd joined him, his eyes pinched shut in misery.

It gave Dani the opportunity to sit up, fix her bra and retie her top. She stood, taking one long look at that incredible male body she'd just been up against and wanted so badly still.

Liam did a sit-up and got to his feet, too, sighing resignedly as he faced her, rested his forearms on her shoulders and again put his head to hers.

"The kids have a sleepover tomorrow night," he said quietly.

"The Tyler twins' birthday," Dani confirmed.

"That starts at four in the afternoon," he said, repeating what she'd told him on the way home from dinner with Bryan and Adam. "And I'll be gone all day before that. But I was going to see if you'd let me take you to dinner after my day with my family and the kids are gone—a grown-ups only dinner, just you and me…"

"You were?" But was he still?

"Will you go?" he asked more clearly.

"Okay," she agreed.

"But I'm gonna be straight with you…lay my cards on the table…" He paused. "If, after dinner, I'm in this house with you and there aren't any kids…"

He took yet another deep breath and exhaled before he confessed, "The only chance I have of keeping myself in check is if I take you to a nice dinner, bring you home, kiss you at the front door and go to my brother's." Another pause. "So I'm leaving it completely up to you. And I want you to think about it in the cold light of day," he commanded, putting so much weight on that that it made her laugh.

"I mean it," he insisted. "I don't know where anything

is going from here. You don't either. And I don't want
you to be sorry—"

"I'll think about it," she told him.

He took his forehead from hers, tipped her face up
with a gentle nudge of one knuckle under her chin and
then kissed her like there was no tomorrow, nearly making her knees buckle right out from under her.

Before he stopped and stepped away.

"I'll pick you up at seven," he said wryly, that mouth
she was still starving for crooked up at only one corner.

Once more she wasn't sure what he meant—if he intended to get ready somewhere other than here and then
arrive to take her to dinner as if it was an ordinary date,
or if he would only descend from the guest suite and pretend to pick her up.

But either way she got the idea and said, "I'll be ready."

With that settled and her instructions to consider
whether or not to let him stay tomorrow night, Dani left
him in that starlit living room, stealing one last glance at
him before she went.

But even without his instructions, she knew there
wasn't much that was going to be on her mind other than
whether or not to finish what they started tonight.

And right then, with every inch of her body shrieking
to be back in his arms, she wasn't sure exactly how she
was going to make a rational decision.

Cold light of day or not.

Because it still wasn't her brain in charge.

Chapter Eight

"Okay, here's my new *unworn* sport coat, your new shirt and slacks ironed by Maicy and the spare key that you may or may not be using tonight…" Conor announced when he came into the guest room of the house he shared with his fiancée. Liam had just showered and was in nothing but a towel.

It was late Sunday afternoon. Liam, Conor and Kinsey had spent the day with Declan at the rehab center until Declan had claimed fatigue and ended family day.

Leaving the center, Liam had enlisted his sister and brother to go shopping with him to help him pick out something to wear to dinner tonight with Dani. During the shopping trip Conor had offered to loan Liam his newest purchase of civilian clothes—a sport coat—so they'd focused on buying pants, a shirt, tie, shoes and socks to wear with it.

Then Liam and Conor had dropped off Kinsey and gone to Conor's place, where Liam was prepping for his night out.

"Thanks," he said as Conor hung everything on a hook on the back of the door.

Liam went into the adjoining bathroom to shave and Conor trailed along, going as far as the bathroom door, where he leaned a shoulder against the frame.

"I thought you and Declan and I would talk more about whether or not to go along with the DNA tests for the

Camdens before any one of us gave Kinsey an answer," Conor said. "You kind of blew that today."

Liam had told their sister that he would give her a copy of his DNA test when it came through this week. "Yeah, but I know what a big thing I'm asking of her—and of you—when it comes to the twins, and it didn't seem fair to ask it and then turn down what she wanted from me. I made it clear that just because I'm handing over the DNA test, though, it doesn't mean I'll have anything to do with the Camdens."

"Yeah, but you and Declan are identical twins, so your DNA will prove whether or not Declan is half Camden, too—which takes away the choice for him—"

"He didn't care. I talked to him about it over breakfast yesterday morning. I was almost hoping it *would* get a rise out of him but not even that did."

"And that leaves me as the holdout," Conor said.

"I thought you'd basically decided to do it anyway. To give in since Kinsey had been giving you the hard press. You said you were tired of fighting it."

"Yeah, but still, you kind of forced my hand."

"I didn't mean to, that whole Camden thing just seems minor to me right now, when there's so many bigger things to deal with. I agree with you—I don't think anything is gonna come of it. I think Kinsey is barking up the wrong tree to think that they'll want anything to do with her even if she proves Mitchum Camden was our father. But you said yourself there's no stopping her. So I just figured I was getting on board with you—why fight it anymore? Besides, *we* all know we had the same father. We'll know anyway when Kinsey finds out for herself. Why not just give this one to her and forget about it?"

Liam saw his older brother's reflection in the mirror as he lathered his face. He could tell Conor wasn't mad about his agreement to let their sister send his DNA to the Camdens. Conor was just letting him know he didn't appreciate that Liam had agreed before the three brothers had reached a formal consensus.

And Liam didn't see any point in dwelling on it, so as he picked up his razor he changed the subject. "So you'll talk to Maicy tonight about the twins?" Liam had talked to Conor and Kinsey about some possibilities over the rehab lunch.

"I told you I would."

"Tonight, though? You won't wait?"

"Tonight. I won't wait. But I'll just be telling her the basics. You don't expect any kind of decision, right? I mean, we can't really make one when you don't know if you're asking us to be short-term or long-term guardians if the kids are yours—which are two pretty different requests. And if they aren't yours…that's a whole different ball game altogether, especially not knowing if you'll be around. Because if you won't, then it's just us becoming foster parents."

Hearing it laid out like that, Liam realized that his brother had a point, that this morning with Conor and Kinsey he'd tossed a lot of possibilities out at them. It was just that *something* had been eating at him about including his brother and sister in a future with the kids and he hadn't figured out what it was.

"Yeah, sure, you're right," he said. "I got wrapped up in Evie and Grady's situation and didn't think my part all the way through. I can't ask you guys to make a decision when I haven't. When everything is still up in the air until I know if I'm their father or not."

"And maybe because you *are* wrapped up with these kids, you might not want to only facilitate and leave them in other people's hands—whether they are yours or not," his brother suggested.

Liam raised his chin in acknowledgment. "This whole thing—"

"I know—it landed in your lap and you want to rescue them no matter what. That's what you're trained for. And I'm not saying no to anything because I can see this has hit home for you. These kids have come to mean something to you. But you have to get what *you* want—and what you're going to do—straight in your own head before we can know what role we'll play."

"Sure," Liam agreed.

"So work it out and in the meantime I'll ease Maicy into the possibilities, so she can be thinking about things, too. But that's as far as it can go for now."

"Yeah, I can see that," Liam agreed again.

It was Conor who changed the subject then. "And tonight? The twins are at a sleepover and you aren't sure if you'll be having one of your own with the nanny?"

Conor's tone and expression had lightened and it allowed Liam to once again put off thoughts of his own future and just concentrate on what he'd been looking forward to all day: tonight.

"That's about it," Liam confirmed. He wouldn't have told his brother as much, but since he might need to bunk at Conor's, he'd had to reveal more than he'd wanted to.

"So, it hasn't been all about the kids this last week," Conor said.

"It's been *mostly* about the kids," Liam hedged as he went back to shaving.

"But tonight you're having a little R and R with the nanny."

"Tonight I wanted to take Dani to a nice dinner to

show her how much I appreciate all she's done for Grady and Evie and for me, teaching me what to do with them."

"Uh-huh," Conor said knowingly. "And you're hoping to show her *appreciation* all night?"

"I gave her the option of not being alone with me in the house with the kids gone so it didn't look bad."

Conor laughed before he said, "It's good that you're looking out for these kids whether or not they're yours. But when it comes to the nanny? What you *appreciate* about her doesn't have jack to do with the kids or what she's taught you. It's you who wants to teach her a few things," he said, his tone heavy with insinuation.

Liam said only, "It's up to her whether I stay there tonight or not."

Conor laughed more. "But you're so damn hot for her that if she sends you back here I'm gonna have to hose you down."

Yeah, that is actually true...

But Liam wasn't going to admit it. "It's a crazy situation," he maintained.

"You said yourself that she's pretty and nice, that you have a good time with her. Hell, you can barely say a sentence without 'Dani this' and 'Dani that.' The two of you have been in close quarters, stuff is getting stirred up, you came straight out of a mission so who knows how long it's been since you've been with a woman—I don't see anything *crazy* about that all leading to what you're hoping it leads to tonight."

"The amount of time I've been without a woman or that we've been in close quarters has nothing to do with anything."

Maybe the close quarters had a little something to do with it; they'd spent a lot of time together in a situation that bred intimacy.

"And she's more than just pretty and nice," he felt compelled to add for some reason. "She's also just great—easygoing and sweet and kind and smart and insightful and patient with those kids. She brings out the fun in everything—including in me. Being with her is the best R and R I've ever had even without getting her in bed because when she and I are alone together, everything else just fades…"

"Wow," his older brother said, making Liam realize he really had gotten carried away with the accolades. And maybe revealed more than he'd intended.

So much more that it had sobered his brother. "The stuff with the kids…you don't just want to impress the nanny, right? 'Cause I was just giving you a hard time about her, but the nanny is a bigger deal to you than I thought…"

"Dani and the kids are two separate things."

"But you *do* want to impress her."

"I'm not trying to win her over by taking care of these kids, no. I'd still feel the way I feel about that—about them—whether Dani was watching or not."

"But there's more happening with Dani than you've let on," Conor concluded as if solving a mystery. "Are you sure the game hasn't changed for you all the way around?"

Liam frowned at his brother in the mirror.

Conor responded to that scowl by saying, "All of a sudden you could be a father and even if you aren't, you're feeling responsible for two kids. There's a girl you're *more* than just hot for. These kinds of things can get you completely off course, you know? Maybe you have more to rethink about the future than just the twins."

"The kids are enough," Liam said to squash his brother's implication that there was something serious going on with Dani.

"And that leaves the nanny as what? Just a little perk?" Conor goaded.

Liam couldn't let that pass because it sounded disparaging of Dani. "She's not a *perk*."

Conor smiled smugly, as if Liam had just proven his point. He pushed away from the door frame to head out of the bedroom, saying over his shoulder, "Game changers, Liam. Game changers."

But Liam was just glad his brother was leaving so that he could get ready for tonight in peace.

Dani, Evie and Grady spent Sunday buying birthday presents for the Tyler twins, then wrapping them and packing for the party. The party that there were endless questions about since it was their first sleepover.

Dani answered all the questions and offered even more information so they were clear that they would be spending the entire night sleeping in their new sleeping bags at the Tylers' house with their friends.

The four-year-olds were excited about it but leery, too, and needed reassurance that if they didn't want to stay when it got dark, Dani would come and get them. Which Dani promised them she would.

All the while hoping that didn't happen.

Not that she was absolutely certain she was going to spend the night with Liam, but she didn't really want that option taken away. Just in case.

The Tyler house was near the entry to the gated community, the first house inside the gate, and was even larger than the Freelander home. Huge, in fact. When Dani brought the kids in they discovered that the enormous recreation room had been transformed for the party. There was a small bouncy house and a ball pit and activity stations along with a tent that looked like a circus tent set up for sleeping under a canopy of twinkling stars.

Between the atmosphere and the fact that everyone else there was a familiar face from preschool, Evie and Grady jumped right into the festivities and barely said goodbye to Dani, giving her hope that they would make it through the night.

After dropping off the twins, Dani rushed to the apartment she shared with Bryan to get clothes for her dinner with Liam.

Bryan was out so she was able to waste no time gathering everything she needed before hurrying back to the Freelander place to get ready, the whole while in heady anticipation of a genuine date with the man who was a constant, vivid presence in her mind even when he was nowhere around.

She brought her phone with her into the bathroom as she showered and washed her hair, just in case there was a call about the twins. She also kept it close enough so she could hear it while she blow-dried her hair to only slightly damp. Then she put a few rollers in it to dry the rest of the way.

The dress she'd chosen was a sleeveless party dress in a bronze hue that Bryan said brought out the toffee tones of her eyes.

It was light and airy, made with strips of delicate chiffon in wispy ruffles layered together. For the bodice the layers were laid over each other diagonally to form a deep V neck in front. A banded waistband accentuated her midriff, and the circle skirt went just to her knees, formed by vertical layers of the scant ruffles.

With her hair completely dry by then she took out the rollers and brushed it upside down, then flipped it to fall in full, come-hither waves around her shoulders.

Sling-back sandals with nothing but sexy little criss-cross straps over the base of her toes to hold them on completed the outfit, and as she took one final look at herself in the full-length mirror in the closet, the doorbell rang.

It was the stroke of seven. Since Liam's rented SUV hadn't been there when she'd arrived home and she hadn't heard him come in, she assumed he'd dressed at his brother's place and was now at the front door to pick her up.

Making sure to slip her phone into the small evening bag that matched her shoes, she tried to walk to the door at a moderate pace. But there was still a quickness to her step because she just couldn't wait to get to him.

She opened the door and there he was, tall and straight, dressed in a light gray sport coat, darker gray slacks, a crisp white shirt with a grayish cast to it and a charcoal tie. Clean-shaven, his hair neat but not slick, she was struck again by how drop-dead gorgeous he was, and it required a minute for Dani to take it all in.

A minute he spent giving her the once-over before a grin slowly spread across his supple mouth in flattering appreciation.

"Ohhh, *very* nice…" he breathed.

"Thank you," she said. "You clean up pretty well yourself," she countered, even as she was thinking that as great as he looked, it was no better or worse than the first time she'd opened that door to him. The man just couldn't look bad.

"I made reservations for seven thirty, so if you're ready…" he said.

She took a deep breath to calm herself down because she was more excited for this evening than she had been since the first date she'd gone on when she was fifteen.

You're being silly, she told herself. *It's just dinner with some guy you've seen and had dinner with every day for a week.*

But still, as she stepped over the threshold and pulled the door closed behind her, it felt different.

"I love this place!" Dani said as they were seated at a table in the chic Sushi Sasa, a Japanese restaurant in Denver's hip Lower Highland area.

"I know," Liam said. "I didn't have any idea where to take somebody who owns a great restaurant herself, so I talked to Bryan on the sly when we were there last night. He told me."

Dani appreciated that Liam had gone to that length. She'd never had anyone consider that aspect of dining out with her before.

"Do you like sushi?" she asked.

"I learned to when I was in Japan."

"So you'll know how this compares to the real thing."

"Compares, maybe. But I'm not an expert," he hedged.

They ordered drinks then—a lychee martini for Dani and Japanese beer for Liam. Over appetizers that Liam ordered, they discussed what else to have.

When they'd made their selections, Dani said, "How did your day with your family go?" Although she was most interested in how his family had responded to his request for help with the twins.

"It went okay," he said without much zest before adding, "Not great, but okay. I made a couple of mistakes."

"What did you do?"

"The first one was that I brought up what to do with Evie and Grady when we were with Declan."

"And that was a mistake…why?"

"He's wrestling with guilt over Topher's death, and

VICTORIA PADE   183

part of that involves the little girl and the new baby Topher's wife is pregnant with—"

"And there you were talking about two other kids
who've lost parents," Dani said, predicting what he was
getting at.

"Yeah. Talking about making sure the twins are taken
care of, about making it a family effort—in front of
Declan—was stupid of me when I had a similar conversation with him the first day I saw him, about us doing
whatever we could to help Topher's widow and kids."

"Did he feel like taking care of Grady and Evie was
instead of that?"

"I'm not sure. Maybe a little. Maybe he thought I was
asking for Grady and Evie to have priority—"

"If they're part of your family they kind of will, won't
they?"

"Yeah, that's probably inevitable—which Declan probably realized. And I think it might have made him wonder if we'll forget Topher and his family, which we won't,
but... I don't know. He got a lot quieter and seemed to
shut down more—if that's possible. I should have thought
about what it might mean to him and talked to Kinsey
and Conor when we weren't with Declan. But I was in
such a hurry to see if I could get them into this, I didn't
think about that." He sighed, sounding rife with self-
disgust. "And actually I guess the second mistake qualifies as jumping the gun and not thinking everything
through, too."

Dani finished a sip of her martini with raised eyebrows
that asked for him to expound.

"Conor pointed out that I'm asking things of him and
Kinsey before I can be sure what it is I'm asking, that I'm
sort of pushing for them to make a decision...a commitment...even before I have any idea what I'm going to do."

Liam went on to explain and as Dani listened she realized that she'd jumped the gun, too. It hadn't occurred to her that Liam hadn't made any decisions about himself or his future with the kids. She, too, had been so eager for a comfortable solution for Evie and Grady that when it seemed like he'd come up with a plan of action providing it, she'd just been relieved.

"He's right, isn't he?" she said about Conor's point of view and balking at being pressured to make some kind of commitment to the twins before Liam had.

"He is."

"So what happens to Evie and Grady is still up in the air," Dani said, feeling as if a little of the wind had been taken out of her sails.

"It's less up in the air if they're mine. Then it's a matter of if I'm asking my family to look after them just until I can get situated to take over myself, or if I'm asking for something more indefinite."

"But if they aren't yours…"

"Conor is right and I don't really have any business asking him and Kinsey to become foster parents on their own at this point. Conor didn't shoot down the idea. And neither did Kinsey. They both said they'd talk to their other halves. But I can see now that it's a different—a bigger—suggestion. And at first it seemed like a good idea, but I have to admit that when I said it, it felt kind of…off. I don't really understand it. I guess I have more thinking to do."

"Sure," Dani said, disheartened. And worrying all over again that her young charges' future was hanging in the balance.

"I'm not just giving up, Dani," Liam said, as if he saw the reemergence of her stress over the kids' future. "But

I do have to make up my mind about what I'm willing to do myself before I can go to my family again."

Dani nodded, and as she studied him across the table she could only hope for the best. Again.

Their sushi arrived and after pointing out what was what, their waiter left and Liam said, "Has this been mistake number three today? Has talking about this now wrecked tonight?"

"It didn't help," she said with a humorless laugh.

"I'm sorry. I wanted tonight to be a treat—just you and me, free as birds. I didn't mean to bring it down."

At least he knew how to apologize in a tone that made her believe he genuinely meant it.

As they began to try the sushi he said, "Did I hear you and Bryan talking about the offer on the restaurant last night?"

Dani could tell that he wanted to get them past the last topic, but it must not have occurred to him that this one wasn't going to lighten things up.

Still, she went with it and said, "Apparently dragging my feet making a decision caused the offer to go up. By a full 50 percent."

"That's a lot."

"A lot," Dani confirmed.

"Does that sweeten the pot or thicken the plot?" he asked.

"Both," she said with another laugh. "It's too much money *not* to consider. I need to *really* be sure I want to run the restaurant before I can say no to it. I don't want to be making meatballs one day and fantasizing about all that money that could be sitting in a bank account as a big fat cushion that would have let me work with kids instead and wishing that's what I'd done."

"Would your grandmother be happy thinking that selling the restaurant *would* be the cushion that lets you go on working with kids?" he suggested.

"Maybe," Dani admitted.

"So you have as much weighing on you as I do," he concluded, taking another California roll.

Dani took one of those, too, thinking that maybe it was impossible for either of them to have even a temporary reprieve when they were both facing so many heavy decisions.

Then Liam said, "But tonight we're free birds! Let's give ourselves a break from the rest so we can come at it fresher this week when it's all going to hit the fan."

It all *was* going to hit the fan this week when the DNA results were in, when Grady and Evie's future would again be a court decision that Dani feared could land them in the system. When those results either made a father out of Liam or would put his vow to help the kids to the test.

He didn't give Dani the opportunity *not* to switch gears, though, because in a genuinely lighter vein he said, "I told you who my first love was. Tell me about yours."

She'd been so excited about this dinner tonight. She couldn't let it be ruined. So she played along. "You mean after Bryan?" she said, only half joking.

Liam's eyebrows shot up. "Bryan was your first love?"

"I was almost seven and he was very sensitive to my feelings over losing my parents."

"So you fell *romantically* in love with him?" Liam said.

Dani laughed. "It *seemed* romantic at seven," she contended.

"And now?"

"I love Bryan like a brother. Maybe more because we don't have any sibling rivalry. But there's nothing romantic about it."

"Okay, so your *second* first love," Liam prompted

while they continued to work their way through the platter of sushi.

"That was a crush when I was ten on the delinquent son of the carpenter who my grandparents hired to build the booths at the restaurant. The carpenter owned a small farm and the handyman stuff was the supplement to the farm's income. I don't remember what the handyman dad's name was, but the delinquent son was Neville—"

"How much of a delinquent can a ten-year-old named Neville be?" Liam teased.

"*I* was ten, *he* was sixteen. And he was enough of a delinquent that he'd been kicked out of school, so his dad brought him to work as his assistant. That's how I got to see him. He was a *very* bad boy," Dani said as if she was dishing up a torrid scandal. "He had all the cowboy stuff going—a few muscles from the farm work and he wore Western shirts and tight jeans and pointy-toed boots and a cowboy hat with sweat stains—"

"You were turned on by sweat stains?" Liam asked with another laugh.

"Oh, yeah, it seemed so *manly*," she gushed. "And he was cute and insolent and just simmering with teenage angst and anger and rebellion—" Dani sighed at the memory. "I followed him around like a puppy."

Liam laughed and those joy lines she liked so much formed at the corners of his eyes. "Now *that's* a love story," he judged facetiously.

They ate their sushi but Dani opted for leaving most of the spicy tuna rolls for Liam because they were a little too hot for her.

After that Liam amended his inquiry into her past again and said, "How about the first love that was *reciprocated*?"

"That didn't happen until ninth grade. Parker Fitzpatrick and it almost caused a rift between Bryan and me because Bryan loved him, too. But Parker loved me."

"*Loved* loved?" Liam asked with innuendo.

"I did not lose my virginity to Parker, if that's what you're getting at. But we did go together until junior year…"

"When it ended badly?" he guessed from her ominous tone.

"When he decided he might have developed a crush on Bryan after all."

"Ooo…" Liam said as if absorbing a hit.

"Yeah. That was as hard on me at that point as me being with Parker was on Bryan at first," Dani said as she finished the salmon sashimi.

"And where did the confused Parker ultimately land?"

"Gay. He and Bryan dated for a while and the whole thing kind of shook my self-image for the rest of high school, especially when some not-so-nice kids made me the butt of jokes about how I turned guys gay…"

Liam's laugh was sympathetic again. "Am I just on a roll today when it comes to making mistakes with what I say?"

Dani laughed, too. "No. That was all too long ago to bother me anymore. It just isn't as pretty as your first love story with the one hometown girl you dated until you both went to college. My past is a little more checkered."

"I don't think it qualifies as that," he judged.

Dani took one last California roll and announced that she'd had enough, leaving the remaining variety of three rolls for Liam, who took them onto his plate as he said, "Did you rebound in college?"

"That followed a more regular dating zigzag path that wasn't particularly noteworthy."

They'd both finished eating by then and even though

Liam tried to talk her into dessert he didn't succeed, so he paid the check and they headed back to the Freelander house.

Along the way they discussed how the sushi had compared to what he'd had around the world and Liam rated it in the top five.

Then they were home again and he was walking her to the door where he'd already assured her he would leave her if that was what she wanted.

When they reached the front door he said, "Well, this is it..." and he did kiss her.

It was a leisurely kiss with lips parted but with no claim to more.

Before he ended the kiss and grinned down at her.

"That *felt* like an invitation..."

It should have—she'd put her heart and soul into it.

"Was it?" he asked in a quietly husky voice.

She asked herself the same thing.

But as she stood there looking up into those blue eyes in the glow of the outdoor house lights, drinking in the sight of his dark hair and chiseled features, she was thinking that tomorrow everything could change. DNA results could come in and the future would take over.

And what Bryan had said about her regretting it if she *didn't* see things through with Liam was true. Because there was no question that she wanted him. More than she'd ever wanted anyone.

A single sweet memory to take with her out of what had been such a rough time these last several months...

So she smiled back at him and said, "I think it is an invitation."

"You can't just *think*," he warned. "You have to be sure."

She stood on tiptoe and kissed him to show just how sure she was.

Then she turned and punched in the code to unlock the door and went inside, casting him an expectant glance over her shoulder to let him know to follow.

He laughed in a way that said game on and stepped over the threshold, closing the door firmly behind them before he grasped her upper arm and spun her into a third kiss that made the other two pale in comparison. His mouth opened over hers and his tongue mounted a sexy assault so fierce that he had to catch her head in his hand to support it against the onslaught.

But Dani gave as good as she got, clamping a firm hand of her own to the back of his neck.

His other arm went around the small of her back and hers went to his chest, where that sport coat suddenly seemed far too bulky. So while her mouth went on answering the call of his, she let him know the jacket had to go by snaking her hands underneath it to his shoulders and pushing it partially off them.

With his cooperation, she managed to remove it. Then she tossed it onto the table beside the door.

She returned both of her hands to his neck then, one rising higher into his coarse hair while they went on kissing like two people meeting again after a long and lonely separation.

But only until Liam went from kissing her mouth to kissing the side of her neck as he said in an even huskier voice, "I found sheets in a linen closet upstairs and changed the ones on my bed this morning before I left…"

Dani laughed. "Oh, did you…" she said.

She felt him smile against her skin before he flicked the tip of his tongue to it. "Just in case," he said.

"I do love clean sheets…" she responded softly.

That was all he needed to hear to grab her hand and take her up the stairs to the guest room, a step ahead of her the entire way, unwittingly providing her with the chance to check out his great rear end.

The guest room was awash in moonlight coming in through its glass walls and the skylight overhead. But Liam flipped the switch that mechanically closed the curtains all the way around them for privacy, leaving only the starlit sky overhead visible and bathing them in just enough illumination to satisfy her desire to see him.

He closed the bedroom door behind them, too. Then he leaned that strong, straight back against it, and while his eyes held her in the heat of his gaze, he got rid of his shoes and socks.

Dani took that same opportunity to step out of her sandals, feeling somehow more vulnerable in her bare feet and missing those two inches of height as he came close again and his over-six-foot frame dwarfed her.

But while he was imposing, there was nothing threatening in him raising only one hand to gently brush the backs of his fingers on her cheek while he leaned over and again kissed the side of her neck ever so lightly.

"You have no idea how much I want you," he said, as if it was taking everything he had to contain himself.

Dani tilted her head to allow freer access to her neck, bringing her own hands to the top button of his shirt to unfasten it.

With only those delicate kisses and a scant flicking of his tongue to her neck again, he reached around to lower the zipper on the back of her dress, taking his time to unclothe her as she did the same with him, sliding his shirt off once she'd finished with the buttons and pulled it free of his pants.

It didn't take much for her dress to float down around her ankles a moment later, leaving her in only her string bikini panties and the lacy demicup bra that went with them.

He wrapped his arms around her and pulled her close as his mouth again found hers.

Oh, it was so delicious to have his warm, naked front right up against her. To have his hands on her bare back...

To that she added her own hands gliding around him and coursing from just above his waistband to the widening V of his expansive shoulders. As she pressed her palms in a slow caress of smooth, satiny flesh over solid muscle, her mouth welcomed the kiss that thoroughly savored hers as if he, too, wanted the absolute most he could get out of tonight.

So for a while that's all they did, standing there, kissing profoundly as if there might not ever be other kisses, reveling in the glory of skin on skin.

Until desire and hunger took over. Then raw passion came into it, bringing too much drive to maintain anything sedate.

Liam's hands began a sumptuous massage of her back that made her ever more pliable as he kissed a path to the hollow of her throat and downward, until the kisses were on the upper curves of her breasts thrust above the half cups of her bra.

Dani wasn't sure what she wanted more, his hands or his mouth fully there, but for a moment the tiny nips he was taking of those swells stole her breath and made her bold enough to reach for the zipper in front of impressive proof that he really did want her, too.

Down that zipper went, leaving his pants bulging open but still in place, because just then he nuzzled one bra cup down to expose her breast completely and take it into his mouth. Dani was instantly lost in the black velvet warmth encasing her, in his tongue flicking at her nipple and tantalizing her as he bent her backward into strong arms that held her safe and secure.

Then he swept her up into those arms and took her to the bed, lying her on cool, crisp sheets before abandoning her to stand beside the mattress, where he took a condom from his pocket, setting it on the nightstand and dropping the remainder of his clothes.

She thought a little more light might have been nice at that point but since her eyes were adjusted to the dimness she still got to see what went with those incredible shoulders and biceps and pectorals and abs that had been first revealed to her at the pool. She still got to see what went with his long, thick muscular legs and that it was long and thick all on its own.

Then he crawled like a panther onto the bed with her, kissing her again as he stretched that magnificent body alongside hers.

She wasted no time letting her hands explore it. Every sinewy inch of his back and chest and tight derriere, sliding down those tree-trunk thighs and up again without quite reaching for that part of him that was difficult to ignore. But she wanted to choose her moment. She wanted to torment him just a little, the way his hand was tormenting her breasts with such a light touch that they were straining for more.

He made a sound that was somewhere between a laugh and a growl deep in his throat as he reached around and unhooked her bra with one hand. Casting it aside, he abandoned their kiss to again take her breast into his mouth, this time more greedily.

And while he was at it, he caught the front of her panties with one index finger and took those off, too, leaving her as bare as he was and sluicing a big hand down her stomach, between her legs and into her.

Her own hand went almost instinctively to him, closing around that long, hard staff to work him into the kind of frenzy he was working her into. Until neither of them could endure it much longer.

With another of those guttural sounds he pushed himself away and retrieved the condom, making quick work of sheathing himself so he could get back to her.

To her body, awakening and arousing everything before retracing his path between her legs to show her what he had in mind, bringing her to just a teaser of a climax that opened her thighs to him completely in obvious invitation.

He laughed and rose above her, sliding into her as if she were the very niche he was carved for.

And the fit was just perfect. Full and complete. And Dani couldn't help the part sigh, part moan that told him just how good it felt.

His mouth came to hers again to kiss her nearly into oblivion as he only pulsed inside her.

Until he drew out some and came back in.

Slowly at first. Gaining speed that Dani learned and kept pace with, drawing away when he did, returning home when he did, tightening around him with each thrust, filling her hands with the muscular mounds of his back.

Faster and faster it went, taking her to greater and greater heights, until she reached a peak that exploded through her and held her in a grip of ecstasy like nothing she'd ever known, a grip of brilliant white light flooding through her so intensely she wasn't sure where she was or what she was going to do when it let her loose, and could do nothing but let him take her there.

She felt him dive even more deeply into her in a climax of his own that embedded him to her core and rewarded her with yet another crest as his entire body stiffened and held them both frozen there for one mindless moment of devastating, awe-inspiring bliss.

Dani's heart was pounding in her chest when it passed, and she could feel Liam's pounding equally as hard in his as he carefully let his body relax atop hers, weighing her down in a way that was just right, as they both caught their breath, cooled and returned to sanity.

"Wow…" he murmured in a genuinely astonished tone.

"Yeah," she agreed, like him too thunderstruck to be coy.

A few more minutes passed as they stayed just like that, resting, recovering, basking in it all.

Then Liam said, "If you don't want to stay here with me and do this the whole night, you better run now while I'm too wasted to chase you."

"And miss knowing if that was only a fluke or if it could actually be reproduced?" she challenged.

He laughed. "Yeah, I'm kind of wondering the same thing," he said, letting her know that it had boggled his mind, too.

He slipped out of her and rolled off the bed, saying as he headed for the bathroom, "Now's your chance."

But even if Dani had had an ounce of strength to get out of there, there was no way she would have left that bed—or him—behind.

Instead she was waiting when he came out, threw himself flat on his back on the mattress and immediately cocooned her in his arms to bring her as close to his side as was humanly possible.

Then she felt him completely relax—all but his arms that tightened around her—and she let her body conform to his, her head cradled in the indentation between his chest and shoulder, her leg draped over his while her arm rested across his middle.

"Just a snooze and then we're gonna see if that was for real," he said, his voice already heavy.

Dani closed her eyes, for now content with the promise of more and needing that snooze, too.

And all she could think as she drifted off in the warmth of that amazing body was that there were definitely going to be no regrets for this one night, except maybe that it might be only this one night…

Chapter Nine

"Mr. Decker is finishing up with another client. It shouldn't be long. Can I get you coffee or tea?"

"No, thanks. I'm fine," Liam assured the attorney's receptionist.

"Then if you'd just take a seat. There are magazines and today's newspaper…"

Liam turned and went to a chair in the waiting area not far away. But he didn't check out the reading material. He had enough on his mind to occupy him.

He'd arranged for the DNA results to go directly to his lawyer in order to make sure that everything was kept at standards the court would accept.

Early this morning, after one more round of lovemaking with Dani—well, two because they'd showered together before dawn—someone from the attorney's office had called and left a message that the envelope with the DNA results had been delivered.

When he'd returned the call, the receptionist had given him an appointment that brought him here straight from the rehab center.

And now it was a matter of minutes until he would find out if he was Evie and Grady's father.

Over breakfast with Declan, when he'd told him about the appointment, Declan had commented on how soon it was that Liam's whole life might be changed.

Liam had made light of it, said Conor had said something similar about the game changing for him.

But the truth was that it felt as if the game, his life, already *had* changed.

It had hit him yesterday—that weird sensation he'd had when he'd initiated the conversation about the kids' future with Conor and Kinsey. He hadn't understood it at the time but as he sat there now, as he considered things to say to the attorney that he might want presented to the court, it began to sink in.

What had hit him wrong yesterday was the thought of anyone but him—or Dani—taking on anything to do with the kids.

Conor was right. He didn't want to only be the facilitator when it came to Grady and Evie's future. He *had* gotten wrapped up with the twins.

Maybe that was an indication that they *were* his, that his paternal instinct had kicked in. But regardless, he suddenly knew with calm, quiet certainty that there was no way he could just leave them with other people.

Thinking about it, he recognized when things had turned for him—the night in the mall parking lot when Dani's ex had approached them all. When Evie had taken his hand, when Grady had leaned against his leg. It had done something to him.

Why, he didn't know. But in that moment when the four-year-olds had been afraid of some guy being a jerk and had reached out to him, it had brought home just how damn small and helpless and vulnerable they were. It had brought home how much they needed to be protected so they could feel safe and secure and grow up the way he had—knowing his mother and Hugh were always right there for him.

But it still hadn't sunk in until yesterday that it wasn't

enough for him to tap other people to do that for them. That *he* needed to do that for them.

For whatever reason, by whatever design, those kids had become his kids. And he needed to be the one whose hand was there to hold or whose shoulder they could lean on. He needed to take care of them and raise them. He needed to be who saw them through.

The receptionist interrupted his thoughts. "I'm sure it will only be a few more minutes."

Liam glanced over at her and nodded but he had to fight the urge to just walk out. Not because he was tired of waiting, but because he kept thinking that he wanted to get out of there and get to Dani so he could tell her what he'd just realized. At that moment, that was a bigger deal to him than learning the DNA results.

He didn't budge but he did marvel at how strong his urge was to get a hold of her right that minute to tell her, to talk to her about what the decision meant for his future. To hash it all out with her. To know what she thought about it. To let her know that she didn't have anything to worry about when it came to the twins anymore.

She wasn't the reason he'd made the decision. But it was important to him that it would ease Dani's worries. And it was important to him to have contact with her at that moment, when his eyes had finally opened to what was going on with him.

Because *she* was important to him…

He wasn't altogether sure where that had come from, but once it snaked its way into his brain, he couldn't deny that it was true.

Dani was important to him, regardless of how things worked out with the kids. Yes, she was great with them and he knew that it would be great for them to go on having her in their lives, great for him to have more of her help with them.

But this was something separate from that. Completely and totally separate. Something that had only to do with what he felt when he was with her. What he felt about her...

Conor had made the comment that he was *more than just hot for* Dani. Now he had to admit that his brother had been right about that, too.

Although Conor had said it flippantly, the truth was the heat between them was no small thing—last night had proven that. Making love with her was like nothing he'd ever done before. Things were so hot between them that it was a wonder they hadn't burned down even that steel-and-glass house.

And yet as combustible as sex with her was, it wasn't just the heat between them that was causing what he felt.

There was something special about it. Something extraordinary in what he felt about her, about being with her, that he'd never felt before.

In his time as a marine he'd seen too many things he wished he hadn't. It had hardened something inside him and he carried that around. It sometimes colored his view, his thinking.

But the more he was with Dani, the more he seemed to be coming to a better place in the world and in his own head. A place where things were brighter and clearer, more hopeful. A place where some of the edges were softened.

She was caring and compassionate—things that had been trained out of him in large part. But being under her influence had helped bring back that side of him. It had changed him from the marine who had been looking in at this situation from the outside, to the man who now knew he had to act.

Thinking about her, he believed it was because of Dani that Evie and Grady were weathering their losses and grief and whatever fears and insecurities they had as well as they were. Dani made it seem as if everything would work out for the best.

She had the ability to take the worst of things—like what he'd found with Declan, like the missteps he'd taken at first with the kids—and not pass any judgments but patiently make suggestions, give instructions, guide to methods that might help.

And all with subtlety, without pushing. She just had a way about her that had somehow allowed him to let his guard down. To genuinely relax and loosen up. And it felt good.

It was no surprise that she was the first person to come to mind after making the biggest decision of his life. She was the first person he wanted to tell, the one he knew would understand it all, who would caringly point out to him where the difficulties might lie and how to wade through them the best way possible.

She was so much of what she'd described in her grandparents—affectionate, tender, generous. And she brought that into everything. Everything with the kids, with him.

And now that he'd had a taste of it, he knew he didn't want to let go of it.

He didn't want to let go of her.

Not for a day, a week, a month did he want to go without the sound of her voice, her laugh. Without being able to touch her, hold her, feel the silk of her skin or make love to her. He didn't want to go a minute without being able to share everything he thought or felt with her.

It had never before seemed as if any woman was the

sun and the moon and the earth to him. But that was what
Dani had somehow become.

And with or without kids, he wanted her. He wanted
a whole, full life with her...

The door to the lawyer's inner office opened and Mar-
vin Decker walked his other client to the outer door, saying goodbye and giving reassurances along the way.

Then he turned to Liam.

So the moment of truth had come.

But for Liam it had just become incidental to so many
bigger things.

Bigger things that he was suddenly desperate to say
to Dani...

"No? You said no?"

It sounded so harsh when Bryan said it. Or maybe it
was the way he said it—a little loud, with utter disbelief.
And maybe a little horror.

Dani was at their apartment when her friend and room-
mate got home from his office on Monday. It's where
she'd run after Liam had returned from the appointment
with his lawyer. The DNA results had proven what Audrey had contended—he was Evie and Grady's father.

Happy and relieved to hear that from him, Dani had
not been so happy to hear the rest of what he'd had to say.
And she definitely hadn't felt relieved by it. Instead it had
sent her into a tailspin that had resulted in her leaving him
to watch the twins while she fled here.

"Explain this to me, Dani," her friend said as he handed
her the cup of tea he'd made for her because he'd said she
looked like death warmed over.

Dani was huddled into a corner of the couch. She accepted the mug and took a sip before she said with a cutting edge to her voice, "In a nutshell? Marry the nanny

safety net and then you don't have to be on your own with kids you've just been surprised with. And I said no."

Bryan sat on the opposite end of the sofa and angled to face her. "So it was a panic proposal," he concluded sadly.

"No, there was no sign of panic," Dani said. "He had worked out everything—*everything*. He said it didn't matter what the DNA results were, he'd decided before he got them that he was going to resign from the marines so he could raise Grady and Evie himself. That there were other people who could do his job as a marine but it had to be him who stepped up for the twins. I guess he has some friend who retired a few years ago and formed a security company with an office here, and the guy has always let him know he has a job waiting if and when Liam leaves the service, too. He even called the guy on the way home from the lawyer and confirmed it. He already has a meeting to set it up."

Bryan backtracked from that. "He'd made the decision to take the kids even if they weren't his?"

"He talked about it with me the other night, about getting his brother and sister on board to become some kind of extended foster family for the kids if they weren't his. But he said that didn't feel right to him after he asked them, and today he figured out that it was because he wanted to do it himself."

"I think he gets gold stars for that," Bryan said tentatively, as if he was beginning to have trouble seeing the flaws that Dani's tone implied were there.

"Well, sure," she agreed, as if that wasn't the point. "But he came at me with this whole plan that made me think of Garrett—"

"Controlling and demanding?"

"Well, no, to be fair there wasn't anything controlling or demanding in any of it. But there was stuff about how he thought I'd be sorry if I sold the restaurant, that I should keep it and get my kid fix with Evie and Grady and however many other kids I'd want us to have—"

"So it was more of a suggestion? An observation that you might regret selling the restaurant?"

"I suppose. But that's *my* decision."

"A decision that you haven't been able to make because you aren't sure yourself if you'd regret it."

"But it's not up to him!"

"It doesn't sound like he thought it was. Just that he was giving an opinion."

"Whose side are you on?"

"Yours. Always yours," Bryan assured, sounding increasingly confused. "But it seems like he was thinking about you. Garrett would have pushed or ordered or demanded that you sell the restaurant, with himself in mind. And he wouldn't have cared that it might be hard for you—the same way he didn't care that Gramma needed your help sometimes."

Dani frowned. "All I know is, in the moment it made me think of Garrett—who I was engaged to until only three months ago, don't forget that. I'm not ready for a new relationship, let alone to make a commitment this huge," she contended so as not to lose her head of steam, piling on another of the reasons she'd said no.

Bryan didn't respond to that. "Was it more like a business deal than a proposal? Or like he was hiring you? I know he can be kind of stiff and formal."

Bryan was obviously trying to understand. And Dani was trying to make clear to him everything that had gone through her head when she'd been with Liam.

"No, he wasn't stiff or formal. He was…like he is with me—which he said, something about how I make him free to be himself—so he was actually kind of laid-back.

Happy. And he said a lot of nice things about how I was the first person he wanted to tell everything to, to share everything with. That I was the most important person to him. How great we are together," she said, her tone still finding fault somewhere in all of it.

"Get him over here so I can shoot him!" Bryan said theatrically, facetiously. Then he frowned at her as if she wasn't making sense and went back to his normal voice. "From what I've seen you *are* great together. And the four of you? It's like a perfect little family—Adam and I talked about that after you left Saturday night. You and Liam seem good for each other. You both seem so good for the kids…"

"Yeah, he said that, too."

"And that made you feel like he only wants you so he isn't on his own with Evie and Grady?"

"No, he only said he wanted us to raise Evie and Grady together after he said how great just the two of us are together…" She flashed back to all of Sunday night. To the very early hours of this morning before they'd had to go their separate ways. To hours of him making love to her until she was weak and spent and yet still craved more of him.

But that certainly didn't support her case so she said in an ominous tone, "He said that being a marine had hardened him but that I softened his edges and the way he saw things, his reaction to things. He said I had an effect on him that no one else ever had. He said stuff about how much he wanted and needed that now that he's had it…"

"And you thought of your dad," Bryan said as if a light had just dawned on him.

"That *is* what my mom tried to be for my dad. What she tried to do for my dad. I remember her telling him that she was his safe space."

"And that helped him but it wasn't always enough. And it terrifies you to think that Liam might have some of the issues your dad did."

"And some of the same issues Garrett had from his high-pressure job, too," she added. "Issues that just got bigger no matter how hard I tried to make them better," she said, feeling as if her friend was finally beginning to grasp it all.

"Drink your tea," Bryan said, as if he was buying time to think.

She did, certain that now he'd joined her point of view.

But then he said, "I think we need to separate your dad and Garrett. Because I never saw Garrett the way you did."

"I know the two of you didn't get to be friends. I hated that. He swore it wasn't because you're gay but—"

"He wasn't homophobic, Dani. And I'm gonna tell you what I never told you before—I don't think all his issues really came from his job or that he was as freaked out about your safety as he pretended to be."

Apparently Bryan could tell just by her expression she was going to refute that because before she'd gotten a word out, he said, "Yeah, sure, there was some of that. Of course he'd seen bad things and that caused him to worry about you more than someone else might have. The fact that there *was* some truth in it is how it got you sucked in. You connected the high pressure of being a cop with your dad's military stuff and were particularly accommodating when Garrett showed he was worried about you. You wanted to make it easier for him, to help him—"

"I didn't want him to get to the point Daddy got to."

"Right. But I think once he saw that you were willing to give a little to make him relax, he ran with it. By the end I think he mostly just used it as a way to keep you under his thumb. Every time he fed you the line? About how he could only really rest if you were with him and that was why he couldn't be comfortable, even if you were with me or Gramma or at the restaurant? I think he was working you more than looking out for you."

"You *really* didn't like him," Dani said, seeing the extent of it for the first time.

"I *really* didn't like that he wanted you all for himself. I didn't think it was healthy. And I *really* didn't like that he used your dad's problems to his own advantage—because that's what it looked like to me."

Dani thought about everything that had gone on with Garrett from Bryan's standpoint.

She could see where there was some merit to it. Especially when she recalled how much she'd come to feel manipulated by Garrett. About how, just when that was happening, he'd played up the things that reminded her of her father so she would ultimately indulge him.

"Okay," she allowed. "Maybe you're right. But what does that have to do with what's going on with Liam now?"

"You saw something in what Liam said to you this afternoon that reminded you of Garrett and I don't think you could be more wrong. I don't see in him what I saw in Garrett. Yes, Liam keeps himself under some tight control, but unless I've missed something, he hasn't tried to control anything else. I even asked Adam how he was with the kids at the park the other night and Adam said he kept a close eye on them, but he let them play just fine."

She was glad to hear that.

"So I don't think Liam saying that he thinks you should keep the restaurant and get your kid fix through Grady and Evie and other kids you might have should count against him."

Putting Liam and Garrett side by side in her mind, Dani thought what Bryan was saying had some validity. She had to admit Liam had merely presented her with his suggestions today; he hadn't been at all the way Garrett would have been about it.

And while he'd said he would hate to lose the restaurant and the warm, family-like feelings he'd encountered there himself, while he'd offered to do whatever he could to help her in whatever way she might need—like more maintenance and small repairs—he'd also still admitted that whether she sold out or not was up to her.

"Okay, maybe the whole restaurant thing *was* just him giving his opinion," she conceded. "He did say he knew selling the restaurant was my decision, just that he thought it was so much a part of my growing up, so much a part of my life with my grandparents, that I would feel as if I was cutting off my own arm if I sold it."

"A good point," Bryan said. "And just as a side note— I have always thought that when you have kids of your own they'd be enough kid contact to satisfy you, so I can see where he's coming from on that, too."

Dani sipped her tea but didn't comment.

"But that still leaves the other part of what got to you— Liam making you think he might have some of your dad's problems. *Have* you seen signs of PTSD in Liam?" Bryan asked reasonably.

Dani gave it serious consideration. "I thought that's what I was seeing the day he was withdrawn and quiet— that made me think about my dad because it was the way Daddy acted when he was getting into a slump."

"But you said that was about Liam's brother. The shock of seeing how injured he was for the first time."

"Right."

"And by that night Liam had talked it out with you and was okay again," Bryan reminded.

"Right."

"So that doesn't really count. It would bum anybody out to have someone they're close to injured, to see that for the first time. And he's been doing what he can to help his brother—like what your family did to help your dad. Your dad was too messed up to be of help to anybody else."

"He was."

"But Liam is still a marine. Like your dad was," Bryan said. "And he told you being with you makes him feel better."

"Right," she said apprehensively.

"But if he doesn't seem to have PTSD, couldn't it just be that he's a normal guy who's gotten to know you and like you and it feels good when he's with you? If he wasn't a marine and he'd said what he'd said about being with you, would you have heard it the way you heard it? Because Adam makes me feel everything Liam said you make him feel and I just see that as the reason our relationship works."

Dani stared into her tea.

Liam had said more even than she'd told Bryan, and when she remembered it all and forced herself to look at it without the shadow of her parents' problems cast over it, she could see where Bryan might have a point.

Why exactly *had* it scared her? That being with her made him feel so good, so right, so at home, that he wanted to be with her all the time? That he wanted to marry her and have a life and a future with her? That together he wanted them to give Grady and Evie the kind of loving upbringing that she'd had from her grandparents?

It had all just come at her so unexpectedly, and on top of so many other things in her own life that she was feeling pressure to sort out and make decisions about, maybe it *had* pushed her buttons.

"And you know," Bryan said after a minute, "that stuff about only being broken up with Garrett for three months? About not being ready for anything else yet? I don't get either of those things, Dani. Sure, you might not have been out of things with Garrett for long, but so what? Who says you can't meet the right person ten minutes after getting away from the wrong one?"

"I've only known Liam for about a total of ten minutes," she understated to make a point.

"Yeah, it's been quick." Bryan didn't dispute it. "But so what to that, too? From the minute you set eyes on that guy I've heard things out of you, seen things with you, seen the way you are when you're with him, that have made *me* envious. It's like from day one it just clicked. And call me silly, but I think that happened because you're right for each other. Good for each other. Meant for each other. So I just kind of think you're crazy for running from it."

"What if he does just want a nanny?" she said quietly, falling back on that initial concern.

"Well then, that would be lousy. I don't think that's what's going on, but if he gave you any indication that might be part of it, then yeah, I guess I'd say thank god he's Evie and Grady's biological dad and he wants them and they won't have to go into the system. Take heart in that and put this whole thing behind you. But do you really think he was just sweet-talking you to get your nanny services? That he's willing to *marry* you to get them?"

Hearing that from Bryan did make it seem a little farfetched. And everything Liam had said seemed genuine and heartfelt. So much so that it had triggered her fear he might need her as a crutch the way her father had needed her mother.

But she'd already discounted that idea and now she saw what he'd said in a much different light. A different light that allowed his words to actually reach her, to touch her, to make them mean so much more to her when they just came from the way he felt about her.

And he'd said he would want her, want a life and a future with her, even if the kids weren't in the picture.

When she thought about the way things had been between them when they were alone, she knew just how big it was. How intense.

He'd become important to her, too. He was the first person she wanted to talk through everything with, too, and she'd come to value what he had to say as much as she valued what Bryan said.

As she thought about it, she realized having Liam around had made her feel better about any number of things this last week, so there hadn't been any shortage of her needing him, too.

She had to admit to herself that he'd become her oasis. Something about that big, strong presence of his being there by her side made everything—even running the restaurant—seem less daunting.

And when it came to Evie and Grady…

She was so grateful that they wouldn't be left defenselessly in the hands of the court.

But to have the chance not to lose them herself?

She'd been with them through every stage so far, through illnesses, now through grief and loss—her own and theirs. She did love them. She didn't want to lose them at all. And while they couldn't be the reason she would say yes to Liam, getting to raise them, to continue seeing them grow, to go on caring for them and loving them was very appealing. Especially when the four of them together this last week really had come to seem like a family.

"Am I crazy if I do this?" she whispered to Bryan.

"It comes down to what you feel for him, Dani," Bryan said wisely. "Everything aside, is he who you want to go to bed with every night and who you want to wake up with every morning, no matter what?"

"He is," she said without hesitation because, stripped down to that, it was the plain and simple truth. Especially after going to bed with him last night and waking up with him this morning—she didn't want any day to end, any new day to begin that wasn't with him.

"Then go fix your face, run a brush through your hair, and I'll drive you back so I can wrangle kids while you tell him you just panicked."

"You think he'll let me in the door?" she said.

Bryan stood up and held out his hand to her. "If he won't I'll just beat it down to get you in," he said with a laugh.

But Dani was more worried about it than that.

She *had* said no—vehemently.

And then she'd run away.

What if it wasn't so easy now to just call a do-over...?

Chapter Ten

"Dani! Where'd you go?"

"We were s'posa go to the restaurant afer our movie was over but you were gone!"

"I know. I'm sorry," Dani apologized to Evie and Grady when they ran to her the minute she went in the Freelander front door.

"You din't even tell us you were goin' somewhere," Grady accused.

Under her breath, in a near whisper, Evie rolled her eyes toward Liam standing nearby and said, "Li'mum said we couldn't do nothin' wissout you."

Dani smiled slightly at the four-year-old's mispronunciations, especially Liam's name.

Before she could comment, Bryan came in behind her. Surprised to see him, they immediately forgot their peeves with Dani and went into their usual greeting of him—demanding to see his socks.

"You guys are gonna love them," he assured. "But let's go down to your playroom before I show you. I really need to do some puzzles today."

"We got a new one!" Evie announced as she and her brother took off like a shot, leaving Bryan a moment to greet Liam with nothing more than a raise of his chin in acknowledgment before he followed them.

And suddenly Dani was alone in the entryway with the big, broad-shouldered man standing like a sentry. He was expressionless but still looked fantastic in a short-sleeved, black T-shirt that stretched tight around the massive biceps that bulged from his arms crossed over his chest.

Just being near him—even when the tension between them was palpable—was enough to make her pulse race. And for a moment the power of the feelings she had for him seemed almost overwhelming.

But she didn't know what to say, where to start.

Liam took care of that by nodding in the direction Bryan had just gone and saying, "You needed backup? Is Bryan here to evict me or pack your bags?"

"Neither," she said. "I went to the apartment. I've been there talking to Bryan. He just came to occupy the kids so we could talk."

But she knew that Liam had said all he wanted to earlier today and, since her reaction hadn't been good, it was up to her to talk now as she faced the man who stood like a big wall of steel.

"I'm sorry for reacting the way I did and then disappearing," she said with a sincerity that hadn't been in her more casual apology to the kids.

"I just don't know what I said that scared you. Believe me, that wasn't what I was going for."

"It wasn't what you said," she assured. "What you said was…wonderful. And none of it should have affected me the way it did. It just got filtered through my own issues."

She went on to explain to him what Bryan had helped her realize.

When she'd finished Liam said, "I don't know anything about Garrett so I can't say if Bryan is right about him. But I think if you thought I'm anything like him, I'm insulted."

He didn't sound as if he'd suffered any injury from her misguided comparison, though, so that helped.

But then, in a very somber, serious tone, he added, "But I don't have PTSD, Dani."

"I don't think so either. Now," she said. "I guess maybe *I* have a little of it…after my dad."

"Ah… I could see that," he said as if that shined a light on things for him. "You saw some tough stuff as a little kid. That had to leave a mark. Then along comes another marine…" He shook his so-handsome head. "But we don't all have it just by virtue of being marines."

"I know. And if you don't want to get mixed up with someone who maybe has some fallout from being close to someone who did—"

"I didn't say that."

"But maybe you should think about it, because I can't promise that every time you get into a bad mood I won't worry that you're developing problems."

He smiled a small, soft smile. "You're giving us a future tense? That's something…" he mused to himself, as if it gave him some hope. Then he said, "I already told you that you're the first person I want to tell everything to— that means you'd be the first person I'd tell if I ever start feeling anything bothering me. So you can relax. A bad mood is just a bad mood unless I've told you otherwise."

There was only the hint of a lighter tone in his voice but, like his remark about being insulted to be compared to Garrett, it helped ease some more of Dani's stress.

Still, she needed a bit of reassurance. "Will you guarantee that you'll go for help before it can get out of hand?"

"I'll put it in writing if it makes you feel better," he offered. "But wanting you and everything I want us to have together, a future together, isn't about me using you for my own mental health. Is that how I made it sound?"

She shook her head. "I think it was more that it was

my takeaway when you said you feel good when you're with me, that you need that…"

"I *do* feel better when I'm with you but that doesn't mean I feel bad when I'm not. Being with you is just like… I don't know… Everything settles for me and just feels…right. It feels great. And yeah, I want that in my life. I need that now that I've found it. But only because it's so damn good. Not because without it I'm messed up."

"I know that now." And hearing him say the words again fueled her. Made her feel what she should have felt the first time.

"So we're okay on that part?" he asked cautiously.

"Better than okay," she confessed.

"And the part where you thought I only want you for your nanny abilities with the kids?"

"It isn't as if that's a reach," she defended herself.

"And it didn't occur to you that if that's all I wanted I could have just asked you to stay on the job?" he countered. "Do you really think that I'd make a commitment like I'm trying to make here for *any* reason except that it's you I want?"

She raised her eyebrows at him in question.

But apparently she'd lessened some of his stress, too, because he laughed.

"You've knocked me for a loop, lady," he claimed, uncrossing his arms and sliding his hands partway into his jeans pockets as he took a step closer to her in the entry. "I told you, if there hadn't been any kids, I'd have still been where I was this afternoon, wanting to be a part of your life, wanting us to make a life together. I know it's weird that it's happened so fast, but when it's right, it's right."

"That's what Bryan said."

"Then thank you, Bryan!" Liam said despite the fact that Bryan wouldn't hear it. "Sure, there's Evie and Grady, but I'm finding my way and I'll go on finding my way. And yes, this last week, no matter how you cut it, the four of us together has been like a really nice family. A family that I don't think should be broken up. But that isn't what's gotten me out of bed excited to face every day. It's been the thought that I get to spend that day with you. It's been the thought that after the twins go to sleep at night I get you all to myself. And then there was last night…"

There was amazement in the way he inclined his head, in the arch of his eyebrows. "Come on, after last night you can't for a minute ignore what we had—what we can have—together. You and I together is like nothing I've ever found before."

"I know," she whispered, certainly not trying to deny it. Any more than she tried to deny feeling the same way getting up every morning for another day with him. Looking forward to the end of every evening, just the two of them.

He closed the distance between them, lowered his voice and said what she'd cut him off from saying that afternoon. "I love you, Dani. That's the explanation for it all. Not anything else. I love you and I want to be with you. Kids. No kids. More kids. Restaurant. No restaurant. Good times. Bad times. No matter what. I love you from the inside out, and it isn't because my life has just gotten complicated, and of all the things I've been trained for, being a single parent isn't one of them. It's *only* because of what I feel for you."

"And you *would* be okay with me keeping the restaurant?"

"I'm hoping you will. I'm hoping that you'll keep ties with what's made you who you are. But—"

"I do think I'm going to keep it," she said before he finished, knowing he was going to tell her it was all right if she didn't. "There's something about it that's just in my bones, and I don't think I can let it go. I don't want to let it go. I want it to be a part of Grady's and Evie's lives, a part of the lives of any other kids. I want to feel like my grandparents are still going, just a little."

He smiled again. "Great, because that soup is the real reason I asked you to marry me."

"Oh, I forgot to worry about *that*," she joked, finally feeling as if she were standing on firm enough ground to venture it.

"How about you just stop worrying about everything and go with it," he advised.

It hadn't been easy for her to get there but as she looked up into those beautiful blue eyes, as her whole body ached for him to touch her, to take her into his arms, she suddenly knew without question that was exactly what she wanted to do—just go with it. Just go with what her heart was telling her to do, despite the arguments her head had mounted.

"I do love you, Liam," she whispered.

"That better not have a *but* coming after it," he warned.

"It doesn't. It's just an *I love you, Liam*. More than I can say."

"And you want to marry me and raise my kids with me and run your grandparents' restaurant and add more kids to the mix," he coached.

"I do," she answered simply. "I really do."

Then she got her wish and he took his hands out of his pockets to pull her into his arms, against that incredible body, just holding her for a long minute as if he needed the feel of her to bring home that this was actually happening.

He buried his face in the top of her head, and she could feel the heat of his breath in her hair just before he kissed her there.

Then he sighed and reared back enough to look into

her eyes, to let her see the vulnerability he felt when he admitted, "You scared the hell out of me."

She laughed. "I thought it was me who was scared."

"When you left you scared the hell out of me," he amended. "I was afraid you really meant all those noes you were shooting at me and that you wouldn't come back. Nothing has ever shaken me that much. I was thinking that my next mission was going to have to be to track you down and try to fix this somehow. Or take you captive and hold you prisoner. Who knew I'd get rescued by Bryan? Maybe we should enlist him in Special Forces."

"About that…"

"Bryan in Special Forces?"

"About you leaving the marines. Are you sure about that? It seems like that decision might have come out of the blue."

"A little, I guess," he admitted. "But I've never been absolutely sure that I'd be in the corps forever—it's why I have another job on the hook. And when I thought about leaving you or Evie and Grady behind, or dragging you to military bases to live while I'm gone on missions, I knew that wasn't what was best for any of us. And somehow it just followed that I needed to start a new chapter all the way around."

"You're okay with that?"

"I'm okay with anything that gets me into your bed every night and lets you be the first thing I see when I open my eyes every morning," he assured with a wicked one-sided smile on his supple lips. Until his expression altered to look slightly perplexed and he said, "But do we have to live in this house?"

Dani laughed. "I'd rather not," she confessed. "It belongs to the kids and once everything is finalized in court we can sell it and put the money away for them."

"And get our own place."

"Something cozier," she agreed, thinking of her grandparents' house and how she just might want to bring her own family to it. "In fact I have one we can look at…" she said.

"As long as I don't feel like I should be wearing a space suit to live in it."

She laughed again. "Definitely no space suits. But a great big garden in the backyard that my grandfather loved…"

He grinned, then something in his eyes softened and he said, "I do love you, Dani Cooper. Will you marry me?"

"I will," she said simply in answer to the question he'd asked hours ago that had set her off.

He smiled another warm smile and then kissed her, a deep, deep kiss that reclaimed her, reconnected them and reunited them for the future they'd already begun to plan together.

And in that moment, in that kiss, Dani suddenly knew this was the way things were meant to play out—for her and Liam, for the twins, even for the house she'd grown up in and the restaurant and the family she had there—because everything settled for her, too, and just felt right.

So right that even though her grandmother had encouraged her to leave the family business, every step had really only put her on track to returning to it.

With kids who would become her own.

With more kids she would have.

But most especially with Liam.

Who was, without a doubt, the one and only man she wanted to spend her life with.

* * * * *

MILLS & BOON

Coming next month

CINDERELLA'S NEW YORK CHRISTMAS
Scarlet Wilson

Leo finished the call. New York. He'd wanted to go back there for days. But somehow he knew when he got there, the chances of getting a flight back to Mont Coeur to spend Christmas with his new family would get slimmer and slimmer.

Here, he'd had the benefit of a little time. Everything in New York was generally about work, even down to the Christmas charity ball he was obligated to attend. As soon as he returned to the States...

His stomach clenched. The Christmas ball. The place he always took a date.

For the first time, the prospect of consulting his little black book suddenly didn't seem so appealing.

'Nearly done.' Anissa smiled as he approached.

'I have to go back to New York.'

Her face fell. 'What?'

She was upset. He hated that. He hated that fleeting look of hurt in her eyes.

'It's business. A particularly tricky deal.'

Anissa pressed her lips tight together and nodded automatically.

The seed of an idea that had partially formed outside burst into full bloom in his head. He hated that flicker of pain he'd seen in her eyes when she'd talked about being in Mont Coeur and being permanently reminded of what she'd lost.

Maybe, just maybe he could change things for her. Put a little sparkle and hope back into her eyes. Something that he ached to feel in his life too.

'Come with me.' The words flew out of his mouth.

Her eyes widened. 'What?'

He nodded, as it all started to make sense in his head. 'You said you've never really had a proper holiday. Come with me. Come and see New York. You'll love it in winter. I can take you sightseeing.'

Anissa's mouth was open. 'But…my job. I have lessons booked. I have chalets to clean.'

He moved closer to her. 'Leave them. See if someone can cover. I have a Christmas ball to attend and I'd love it if you could come with me.' His hands ached to reach for her, but he held himself back. 'I called you Ice Princess before, how do you feel about being Cinderella?'

He could see her hesitation. See her worries.

But her pale blue eyes met his. There was still a little sparkle there. Still a little hope for him.

Her lips turned upwards. 'Okay,' she whispered back as he bent to kiss her.

Continue reading
CINDERELLA'S NEW YORK CHRISTMAS
Scarlet Wilson

Available next month
www.millsandboon.co.uk

COMING SOON!

We really hope you enjoyed reading this book. If you're looking for more romance, be sure to head to the shops when new books are available on

Thursday
4th October

MILLS & BOON

LET'S TALK
Romance

For exclusive extracts, competitions
and special offers, find us online:

 f facebook.com/millsandboon

 ⊙ @millsandboonuk

 𝕏 @millsandboon

Or get in touch on 0844 844 1351*

For all the latest titles coming soon, visit
millsandboon.co.uk/nextmonth